VETERANS OF THE PSYCHIC WARS

WAYNE GERARD TROTMAN

Wayne Gerard Trotman
Happy 40th Birthday!

www.redmoon.co.uk

VETERANS OF THE PSYCHIC WARS

This First Edition published in 2011 by Red Moon Productions Ltd. PO Box 1519, Kingston upon Thames, KT1 9UW

ISBN 978-0-9567872-0-0

For Yvonne Teresa Trotman & Rita Enez Callender

Forever missed...

CONTENTS

Chapter 1

Roman Doyle activated his Bluetooth earpiece as he walked towards the cashpoint machine. The tall, twenty-five-year-old black man had a lean, athletic build and cast a long shadow from the amber street lamp a few metres away. Roman knew the wisdom of observing his shadow, especially when he walked the streets of North London late at night.

Seven years ago, observance of his shadow saved him from grievous bodily harm. Roman noticed his shadow swiftly approached by another, broader and shorter. Raised high, its thick arm bore a long thin object.

The stocky criminal, equipped with a metal pipe, did not know his potential victim was an accomplished martial artist. Had he known, he would have attacked the much larger businessman who barrelled past fifteen minutes before. At merely seventy kilograms, Roman seemed an easier target.

The astounded thug found himself the recipient of a shattered nose from a gyaku zuki reverse punch, and two broken ribs from a dwet chagi spinning sidekick. The mugger sailed through the air, and seconds later, slammed onto the kerb - unconscious.

A cool, relaxing summer breeze, starkly contrasted the urgently vibrating mobile phone in Roman's right jacket pocket.

It's very late.

This call was no surprise. He knew the caller; her striking Nubian features had suddenly flooded his thoughts seconds before the phone's mechanical response.

She's probably wondering where I am, he mused.

To an onlooker, Roman would seem schizophrenic as he spoke into the discreet receiver.

"Hello?"

The husky, playful tones of a familiar female voice reassured him that his intuition was yet again correct.

"Roman. Where are you Roman?"

It's Soraya.

Her mild Trinidadian accent immediately conjured up pleasant memories of his early childhood on the tropical island; vivid memories of swarms of brightly coloured butterflies surrounding him.

"I'm at a cash-point," said Roman, quickly scanning the secluded street.

He removed a leather wallet from his trouser pocket, slipped a debit card from it and guided the plastic into the slot of the silent cashpoint machine. The screen refreshed instantly:

ENTER PIN:

- - - -

"I've been thinking about you," Soraya said, and Roman recalled how similar her brown eyes were to those of his mother.

"Uh-huh?"

"I've been thinking about your name - Roman, such a strong, sexy name."

"Hmmm," he responded with a hint of sexual provocation.

"But I also like Moses," Soraya added unexpectedly.

A furrow suddenly appeared in his dark brow. He typed the last digit and the screen refreshed again, prompting him to enter the required cash amount.

"Soraya, we've had this conversation... I'd like to pass on my name," Roman divulged with more than just a tinge of irritation.

"But Moses so much better dan Junior," she claimed, not bothering to speak the Queen's English.

Roman typed 2 0 0, then pressed ENTER.

"So we'll call him Romeo. This is the fourth time we've had this discussion in as many days Soraya; it's late, and I'm not in the mood."

The debit card emerged from the slit in the machine with a low mechanical whirr and Roman returned it to his wallet.

"Romeo sound so - tragic," Soraya's playfulness now giving way to disappointment.

From his rooftop vantage point, with long black hair wildly billowing in the wind, a darkly clad man with Oriental features spied Roman through the viewfinder of an extremely sophisticated pair of binoculars. The ever-changing illuminated characters on the screen were thousands of years older than the Great Pyramid of Giza.

Even though Roman stood three hundred metres away, the display captured his every move with startling clarity. Betraying exceptional stealth, the man retracted the binoculars, tucked them within his black tunic, and silently leapt off the roof into the murkiness below.

"Honey," Roman said, grabbing the cash dispensed by the machine, "I thought we decided that we'd call him Roman? Moses will be his second name."

Soraya responded, "We'll talk about it when yuh get home. Doh forget meh peanut butter yuh know."

"Okay," a smile traced across Roman's face.

I almost forgot.

He quickly counted ten twenty-pound notes, placed them in the wallet, and returned the now bulging billfold to his trouser pocket. Roman proceeded across the seemingly deserted street, briskly heading towards his dark grey BMW E87 hatchback parked sixty metres away.

"An' de ice cream," Soraya added.

"Okay Sugar, I'll be home before you can say rum 'n' raisin."

"Bye," she purred.

"Bye."

He pressed a small button on his Bluetooth earpiece ending the call.

In an eerie snake-like fashion, five large men with Oriental features and shaven heads emerged from the darkness. They followed Roman, who remained oblivious to the menacing shadows, which gradually converged on his own.

With a wry grin, Roman anticipated the reward that awaited him if he found rum 'n' raisin ice cream and peanut butter after 1:00 AM.

Yes, Soraya would be most pleased.

Soraya, his wife of just eleven months, was two months pregnant. This was their secret. They had not told family or friends. During the past week, Roman developed the belief that profound changes in Soraya's hormone levels were the cause of these strange cravings.

Still smiling to himself, he suddenly experienced a sharp pain in his head.

What the hell?

Surprised, he winced and pulled the earpiece off his ear.

Maybe the earpiece is faulty.

Then, to his shock, Roman noticed a drop of blood at his feet and realised that he also had a nosebleed. Quickly tugging a neatly folded handkerchief from his back trouser pocket, he mopped the blood from his nose.

Ominous, whispered voices seemed to come out of nowhere, adding terror to Roman's unfolding nightmare - voices that grew louder within his mind, until they became a roar. Suddenly, he heard an inhuman cry, like a thunderbolt cleaving through the branch of a majestic oak tree.

Turning swiftly, he saw two of the five men charge. A gust of wind whisked the bloodstained handkerchief from his grasp as the pair approached with bewildering speed.

Before Roman could react, the men somersaulted over his head in unison. They landed three metres behind him. The other three stood their ground, glaring at him with undisguised malice.

Stunned and dizzy, Roman tasted blood as his nose continued to haemorrhage. His handkerchief sailed through the air unnoticed until someone shrouded in darkness snatched it from the wind.

For a painfully tense moment, Roman stood perfectly still. Two men blocked his retreat; three stemmed his advance. Characters, which seemed better placed in a graphic novel than on the streets of London, effectively surrounded him. Their outlandish weather-beaten clothing bore symbols that Roman could not decipher.

Suddenly feeling a surge of adrenaline, his experience with the mugger seven years ago flashed through his mind.

Roman reassured himself that at twenty-five years of age, he now weighed a healthier eighty kilograms, and through continued training, he attained third dan black belts in Shotokan Karate and Taekwondo. Roman felt certain he would achieve fourth dan grades in both forms before his twenty-sixth birthday. In the ancient arts of Karate and Taekwondo, the black belt not only signified maturity and proficiency, it also symbolised the wearer's imperviousness to darkness and fear.

Three years ago, not satisfied with the well-known Japanese and Korean arts, Roman commenced training in Muay Thai Boxing and Chinese Wing Chun – a fact, which many of his competition rivals were unaware of. This he felt gave him an additional edge. Confident in his abilities and proud of the many tournaments he had won, Roman held the opinion that few men could withstand a motivated assault incorporating all four styles.

Muggers beware.

However, *these are no ordinary muggers.*

Each man weighed over one hundred and fifteen kilograms, yet Roman had the impression they could sprint one hundred metres in under nine seconds. They moved with precision and perfect equilibrium. Their toned bodies, dark green tunics, leather utility belts and tall boots screamed military training.

Who are these guys?

The man at the centre appeared to be their leader. He stepped forward. In response, Roman took one stride back, quickly glancing over each shoulder at the men to his rear. The leader motioned with authority and his four henchmen stood frozen. In unison, threatening smiles appeared on the faces of all five antagonists.

Roman shot to full alert status and the leader's sinister grin transformed into a cold stare. Suddenly, metal rods slipped from under the leader's sleeves into his enthusiastic hands.

This could be serious, thought Roman.

The leader rolled one of the rods to Roman's feet and held the other firmly in his right hand. Then, with a flamboyant flourish, he stretched out his arm. His foot-long baton instantly extended three feet each side. The other men stood back in silent anticipation as their leader moved another step towards Roman.

One on one - how sporting.

Roman did not pick up the staff at his feet.

Instead, he shouted defiantly, "Listen, I've worked really hard for my money!"

Without further ado, the leader attacked, and Roman narrowly evaded his furious blows. In a fast-flowing movement, he picked up the shaft from the floor, activated it and counter attacked. But very soon, a relentless whirlwind of impossible force drove Roman into desperate defence. To his surprise, every parry threatened to crumble his wrists and elbows.

The sharp clamour of metal violently striking metal resonated across the surrounding streets of North London. Dizzy and distressed, Roman tried unsuccessfully to break the circle, but the four mountainous henchmen prevented any escape. They forced him to resume his battle for survival with a much stronger opponent.

This is no ordinary mugger.

Roman could not recognise the man's fighting style. It seemed a confusing mix of practically everything and nothing at all; at least nothing that Roman had encountered in his martial arts training.

Somehow the man anticipated Roman's every move. The blows Roman received, as a result, made his intolerable headache even worse. The throbbing flow of blood from his nose adversely affected his vision; and, for the first time in his life, it dawned on Roman that he would be clubbed to death.

During the fight, Roman failed to notice that his driving licence had fallen out of his coat pocket. Even if he had noticed, he could have done little about it. A devastating blow to the back of his head temporarily robbed him of his sight. Three blows followed in quick succession, forcing him to his knees, barely conscious and utterly defenceless.

The ease of his defeat seemed beyond comprehension. He tried to speak but his mouth failed to cooperate.

Take the car, take the phone, take my watch, and take the cash. Take it all; I just don't want my wife to be a widow...

The leader retracted his staff and smirked confidently. In unison, strange blades slid from the sleeves of the other four men into their eager hands. The four advanced collectively with a cry - arms raised, about to strike Roman.

The leader raised both arms, and his men stopped dead in their tracks. They froze momentarily then retreated with a sinister reluctance.

Roman's sight slowly returned. He used the long metal weapon in an attempt to stand, but an unseen force oppressed him. An invisible yoke prevented him from becoming upright.

Then, in an almost theatrical manner, the leader stretched out his right arm towards Roman and he instantly fell prostrate to the ground. Roman clutched his throat with his right hand; and to his astonishment, strangled himself.

Chapter 2

From his second-storey bedroom, William Norris, a fifty-six-year-old shopkeeper rubbed his sleepy eyes and peered through a gap in the thick drapes of a large Victorian window. Gangs of youths had tried to break into his shop on the ground floor several times before. The steel shutters, which covered the front of his mini-mart, did not deter young hooligans from crashing a stolen van into the store three weeks ago.

Four days later, the ram raiders were apprehended, but the incident left the shopkeeper enraged and paranoid. The current commotion suggested that more young offenders had arrived.

If it's trouble they want, it's trouble they'll get.

For a moment, the aging man could not understand why he had difficulty seeing.

Then, he remembered, *I'm not wearing my glasses.*

Cobwebs from a restless sleep clouded his mind, and he fumbled in the darkness.

Where are those bleedin' glasses?

He recalled leaving them on the wooden table adjacent to his bed. With varifocals firmly donned, he peered through the gap in the drapes once more.

Now I can see the brazen little bastards getting up to no good downstairs.

He consulted an alarm clock on the old bedside table.

It's 1:36 AM. The scallywag, who drove the Ford Transit into my shop three weeks ago, was only fourteen years old. What type of parents allowed their fourteen-year-old children to roam the streets at this hour? What has England come to? If I had a gun, I'd blast the little blighters to Hades, but then I'd be the one behind bars. Suppose I'll just have to call the Old Bill again. They have guns, at least their armed response team does.

So William phoned the police and added a bit of embroidery to his story. The type he thought would guarantee an immediate, aggressive response.

He lied, "There's a mindless mob of hooligans outside. They're all black, and one of them has a gun."

Seized by desperate panic and no longer in control of his body, Roman continued to strangle himself. Suddenly a dart-like object shot out of the surrounding shadows. Roman's unknown opponent moved with incredible speed to avoid being impaled. The object narrowly missed the startled man's shaven head; and instantly, Roman stopped suffocating himself. He immediately gasped for air. Dangerously close to fainting, he swooned with shock, unable to rationalise what just occurred.

What the hell is going on, did he use some kind of hypnosis on me?

Without the slightest trepidation, the silhouette of the mysterious dart-thrower strode confidently from the shadows. His black tunic, long dark hair and Fu Manchu moustache seemed to symbolise all that Roman's black belts did - *imperviousness to darkness and fear!*

The man in black stared with contempt at the feet of the five larger men who surrounded Roman. He considered their treacherous eyes unworthy of his piercing gaze. He tilted his head towards Roman, and in a fleeting moment, the twenty-five-year-old swore he heard a voice. It was faint, almost imperceptible.

The voice said, *"Rise Master."*

Then the man in black savagely attacked the four henchmen. Roman used the opportunity to sweep the leader off his feet, and the large man landed on his posterior, his face red with embarrassment. But he recovered in an instant and was upon Roman like a swarm of Africanised honey bees.

With the support of the darkly clad stranger, Roman regained much-needed strength.

Thank God he came when he did, but who the hell are these guys?

Steel rods and razor sharp blades clashed viciously, shooting silvery sparks into the summer air.

Roman observed that his attackers fought in an unfamiliar and unorthodox martial art - utterly unpredictable. Whatever it was, they all did it; and they did it exceptionally well. The henchmen fought with unnatural accord, engaging in a well-rehearsed dance of death, executed with fanatical accuracy.

Yet, the man in black seemed relentless. His form differed from that of his opponents. Far more refined, with a devastating elegance. Roman had no way of knowing that this martial art was called Hatari Ikou, the way of matchless power. Hatari Ikou had evolved into a supreme form of combat, millennia before an earthquake toppled the bronze Colossus of Rhodes; and the man in black was its consummate master. Exhibiting alarming agility and perfect balance, he hurled his body in a devastating arc, delivering brutal kicks to the heads of his four assailants. Propelling them an impossible distance before they hit the pavement like discarded rag dolls.

Gaining inspiration, Roman vengefully retaliated against their leader forcing the larger man to defend himself. Little by little a pattern emerged from the apparently random assaults, feints and deflections. There was a method to his opponent's madness.

The man-mountain was proficient in a fighting style based on deception. This secret art was older than the Sphinx. It was called Nyoka Sentou, the way of the serpent. But Roman, and the men who trained him, had no way of knowing this.

Every movement in Nyoka Sentou undermined, distracted, eluded and destroyed. An opponent encountered nonexistent openings, unstoppable strikes, and elusive targets.

The henchmen viciously retaliated. Faced with overwhelming aggression, Roman and his helper found themselves back to back with the five attackers enclosing them.

With an accent difficult to place, the man growled angrily, "Master Armon, have your custodians taught you absolutely nothing? Have they betrayed your father's trust? In light of your apparent lack of combat proficiency, wisdom dictates that I urge you to run."

Master Armon? Betrayed your father's trust?

Roman had just a second to ponder the stranger's odd statement, before the fight resumed - two against five.

Suddenly a silver BMW 5-Series Touring arrived at the scene. The armed response vehicle or ARV was crewed by three uniformed officers. Members of CO19, the name allocated to the Specialist Firearm Command branch of London's Metropolitan Police Service. With silently flashing blue lights, the estate swerved to an abrupt halt ten metres from the conflict and the officers within made an immediate assessment of the situation.

In the brawl, Roman was the only combatant distracted by this fortuitous development.

The long arm of the law has arrived. Perhaps I'll live to fight another day.

CO19 swiftly concluded that armed containment was necessary. Two of the crew, the officers designated as the 'driver' and the 'observer', deployed leaving the 'operator' in the vehicle to call for further reinforcements.

The driver barked, "Police! Drop your weapons!"

Both policemen drew their handguns. All three officers were equipped with standard-issue GLOCK 17 short recoil 9mm Luger semi-automatic pistols.

The armed response team had immediately responded to an urgent call. A black youth brandishing a pistol had threatened members of the public. The fact that Roman was the only person of African descent present suggested to the driver that the other members of the gang had wisely fled the scene.

He targeted Roman's chest with his GLOCK and his colleague set his sights on the leader of the Oriental gang. In retrospect, this action proved to be a serious mistake.

Displaying casual disregard, the Oriental warrior motioned with his hand; and like men possessed, both officers immediately raised their loaded pistols to their temples and fired. A terrifying eruption of blood brain skull and hair instantly followed.

"Shit!" the operator screamed into the police radio, as the twitching bodies of his colleagues crumpled to the pavement.

Horrified and frantic, Roman knocked one of his attackers off his feet with a reverse ankle sweep, then took the man in black's advice and ran like hell. As he fled, he narrowly avoided being hit by a second ARV. Looking over his shoulder, Roman saw the leader motion towards the swiftly approaching BMW. Instantly, the driver of this second vehicle veered and crashed into the first. The impact fatally pinned the officer within, instantly silencing his crazed requests for backup.

Roman looked around, but he could no longer see the man in black. Meanwhile, the five thugs painfully introduced the remaining CO19 officers to Nyoka Sentou. Roman ran a short distance before stumbling and falling to the pavement. He rose to his feet, dizzy and exhausted with blood still seeping from his nose.

You idiot, you're going the wrong way, he chided himself for foolishly running in the opposite direction of his BMW hatchback.

Roman hoped that, at any moment, he would wake from this terrible nightmare and prepare for another uneventful day as a primary schoolteacher. But the horror continued and a disturbing thought entered his mind.

Maybe this attack isn't just a random act of violence.

Wailing sirens approach from a distance and Roman's concern focused on his expectant wife, Soraya. He struggled to retrieve his mobile phone from his coat pocket and at that moment, the man in black appeared at his side.

"Thanks for helping me," Roman cried breathlessly.

The man said, "My duty is to serve you, Master Armon."

Bewildered by these words, teetering on the brink of unconsciousness, and unable to locate his mobile, Roman offered a weak plea.

"I need to call my wife."

"Forgive me Master," the man in black said.

He returned Roman's bloodstained handkerchief. Roman took it and gently dabbed a fresh stream of blood from his nose. Then, without warning, the helper jabbed a futuristic device into Roman's exposed neck. A hypodermic needle found Roman's internal carotid artery; and, paralysed by the unidentified substance forcibly injected into his bloodstream, Roman collapsed in a state of shock.

As he slipped into the darkness of oblivion, one question reverberated in his mind.

Why?

Chapter 3

Soraya Doyle nervously fingered the emerald-green pendant, which dangled from the elegant gold chain around her neck. With a furrowed brow, she peered out of a second-storey window to the empty parking space below. Her husband Roman had not returned.

Where is he?

A registered nurse at Barnet General Hospital, Soraya possessed a levelheaded maturity that transcended her mere twenty-three years. But now, an unusual sense of foreboding had her waiting anxiously at the couple's modest two bed-roomed flat in Friern Barnet, North London. On television, grim reports of conflicts in the Middle East, famines in Africa and monsoons in India, were less than reassuring.

Soraya poised the television's remote to switch channels, in search of something cheerful, when a news flash rolled across the screen:

'Four police officers have been killed and two reported as critical, following an incident near Victoria Park in Finchley, North London.'

Victoria Park is just fifteen minutes away, she thought; a sudden chill scuttled down her spine like an icy tarantula. Soraya now felt certain that Roman was in danger. She imagined him unconscious. In her mind's eye, she saw him lying on an old mattress in a dilapidated room. He was not alone; the silhouette of a man watched over him.

Once more Soraya clutched the pendant, a gift to her from Roman in celebration of their wedding engagement. Roman had informed her that the rare gem once belonged to his mother Miriam, and it had been Miriam's most treasured possession. Roman's parents died in a terrible accident when he was three years old, leaving no photographs and little in the way of memorabilia. As a result, he valued this emerald-green gemstone above everything else he owned. Now Soraya cherished the jewel as a symbol of love. She stared blankly at the television screen, unable to imagine life without Roman.

Where is he?

It was 2:35 AM. During the last forty-five minutes, Soraya made four calls to Roman's mobile phone. All were answered by a recorded voice.

The voice said, "The mobile phone you are calling is switched off."

The police helicopter, a giant marauding dragonfly patrolling in the distance, did nothing to ease Soraya's rising apprehension.

She tried to think happy thoughts and recalled the present Roman gave her a week ago: A Monsieur Peanut, Peanut Butter Maker. Described on the packaging as fun for ages five years and up, Roman joked that he had won it on an Internet auction listed under 'Emotionally Scarring Toys'. To make peanut butter, whole peanuts were put into Monsieur Peanut's oversized hat. Turning a crank ground the peanuts into a buttery mush, which would then ooze out of the side of the smiling, bespectacled Monsieur Peanut's head.

De peanut butter I made taste real, real bad, Soraya smiled.

But, when she thought of the errand she had sent Roman on, her smile slowly faded. She wondered if, like Monsieur Peanut, her peanut brain had oozed out of her ears.

I sent Roman out, to get peanut butter and ice cream, one o'clock in the morning. What was I thinking?

Soraya recalled her last conversation with her husband. They had easily agreed that a daughter would be called Arabella, but agreeing on a boy's name proved more difficult. Both believed that names were extremely important and spent hours delving into their origins and meanings. Soraya learnt that the name Roman had a Biblical origin and meant *'powerful'*, and the surname Doyle was Celtic meaning *'dark stranger'*. Then there was Soraya, a Persian name, which meant *'Princess'*.

If the twenty-week anomaly-screening scan confirmed their unborn child was in fact a boy, Soraya favoured the name Moses, the name of her grandfather, a decorated World War II veteran. A powerful, ancient name that she expected her husband to admire because of its links to Egypt. Roman thought highly of her grandfather and had an almost fanatical interest in Ancient Egypt. It was, therefore, difficult for Soraya to comprehend Roman's objection to this highly revered name, an Egyptian name, which meant *'drawn from the water'*.

Chapter 4

Seven miles away, on the outskirts of Haringay, the man in black boiled tealeaves on a portable gas stove. Hidden within a derelict flat and surrounded by shambles, the Master of Hatari Ikou experienced something unusual. He was faced with uncertainty.

The sub-dermal transponder functioned perfectly. The DNA test results are almost flawless. In fact, there is only a 0.000000000021213 probability of error; and yet, this is not at all what I expected. This individual is indeed Armon Sakara. But, had I not intervened, he would have fallen at the hands of the Asing. He is not prepared. How could this be possible?

As the shocking thoughts echoed in the warrior's mind, he turned his grim attention to Roman's body. Roman lay motionless on a foam mattress, situated on the floor, in the only part of the room not subdued by utter chaos. Next to Roman were several devices; all sophisticated in design, bearing symbols and markings written in an ancient language - a language, which predated Stonehenge by several thousand years. A few of these mechanisms appeared to have sustained minor damage. Some had the telltale signs of being scorched by extreme heat. One device, a cylinder about 90 centimetres long, emanated a fluorescent green glow. Together with the flames from the gas stove, it provided the room's meagre illumination.

The darkly clad warrior recalled the difficulty of bringing these objects to the squat undetected. The Kawasaki Ninja he first appropriated proved an ideal scout vehicle, but woefully ill suited for the transport of large equipment. As a result, he resorted to borrowing a Volvo Estate from Bounds Green Industrial Park. He used the automobile once before returning it to where he found it. The man in black had no intention of complicating his mission by involving local law enforcement officials, however unsophisticated.

The murders perpetrated by the Asing were regrettable. I have been in this city seven days - far too long. The elementary technology, primitive modes of transportation, archaic laws and barbaric customs were anticipated.

But it was the unexpected, which filled his heart with dread.

So many questions, so few answers. No responses have I received, to my coded transmissions. Where are the Master's custodians? I must locate them immediately, without their help all may be lost.

Roman found himself in a tropical garden surrounded by swarms of colourful butterflies. This was his favourite place, his parent's backyard. Gossamer wings brushed against his skin and the memory of his wife's smile intoxicated him.

Suddenly Roman remembered the man in black and was instantly gripped by fear. The lush garden became a desert, the butterflies vanished, and the cloudless, blue skies turned black.

Abruptly awake, Roman pretended to be asleep. For a brief moment, he wondered if the five muggers, the police suicides and the man in black were all figments of his imagination. Then Roman felt a sharp pain in his neck accompanied by an overwhelming headache and he plummeted back to reality, in abject terror.

Suddenly an eerie voice broke the silence. Roman heard the voice of the man in black, but at a slightly lower pitch.

He said, "Would you like some tea, Master Armon?"

A man who calls me Master has kidnapped me, Roman thought.

He opened his eyes, and the sight, which greeted him, did little to allay his fears. A thick, black plastic sheet completely covered the room's single window. There was rubbish everywhere. Amongst the trash lay objects, which seemed the product of some impossible technology. The flickering flames of a gas hob threw dancing shadows on the walls and ceiling, presenting the man in black as a menacing silhouette.

"Where am I?" Roman quizzed groggily, feeling the spot on his neck where he had been injected.

"Safe, Master Armon."

The man stepped towards Roman, and the green glow of the cylindrical device replaced the hob's shifting light. The light transformed the man in black, from a menacing silhouette, into an intimidating green hulk.

The hulk bowed with reverence and announced, "I am Chi-Ro Jin, your humble servant."

Roman immediately scanned the room for a way out. The front door provided the only exit from the small apartment. For a brief moment, Chi-Ro stood as a brooding sentinel blocking any chance of escape. Then the Oriental man switched off the gas hob, lifted the kettle and poured its liquid content into a Styrofoam cup.

He walked towards Roman and offered the cup of tea. Controlling his fear, Roman slowly rose to his feet and took the cup. But, he did not drink.

Probably spiked. Yet his confident posture, open body language and engaging gaze all suggest honesty.

Roman gently placed the Styrofoam container on a dilapidated book-shelf and observed the man who called himself Chi-Ro Jin.

"You drugged me. Why?"

"It is my sworn duty to protect you, Master Armon."

Protect me from what? Boredom?

"My name isn't Armon. You have the wrong guy."

"Master Armon it is you who are mistaken. My tests were both thor-ough and conclusive."

Chi-Ro reached into the folds of his black tunic. He bowed again and handed Roman the bloodstained handkerchief saying, "You are Armon."

Roman studied the handkerchief.

He wants me to believe he performed blood tests?

Roman relived recent events and his heart sank. This nosebleed was not his first. It happened once before, on a stormy morning, twenty-two years ago.

The name Armon sounds vaguely familiar. Could it be ancient Egyp-tian? Are these weirdoes part of a strange religious cult? Good Lord, I hope he's not a rapist.

"What do you want?" asked Roman, pretending to be calm.

"First I must speak with your custodians."

This guy must be a habitual drug user. What on Earth is he talking about?

"Custodians?"

"Tarom and Mina Rin, your protectors and guides."

He's delusional, possibly schizophrenic and, judging from the way he handled himself against those muggers, quite dangerous. I have to escape. I have to call Soraya.

"Oh yes, of course, I'll call them," Roman lied.

He nervously searched several jacket pockets for his mobile phone and unable to find it, Roman felt panic rising.

"I must've dropped my phone."

"Here is your Kian communication device. It is damaged," Chi-Ro re-plied with a hint of derision.

Kian?

Roman accepted the broken mobile phone with suspicion.

"What else did you take from me?"

Roman set the phone down, next to the cup of tea. He quickly retrieved his wallet from his trouser pocket and checked its contents.

Money, credit cards - all there.

Roman replaced the wallet and picked up the mobile. He flipped the clamshell phone open, and dark despair immediately rose from the pit of his stomach.

The LCD is damaged.

He speed-dialled his wife and placed the receiver to his ear.

Nothing.

Roman dialled again and again, doing his best to mask his growing frustration.

Chi-Ro said, "It would be most unwise to use your communication device, Master Armon. It would easily betray your present location, and you are in grave danger."

Roman smirked nervously.

"What are you planning to do?"

"Take me to Tarom and Mina Rin. The Asing will not rest until they find you. We must leave for Talis immediately."

"Look, thank you for helping me with those muggers but I'm sure the police..."

"What are muggers?"

"The men who attacked me..."

"The Asing are agents in the service of Seti Aljyk. Their mission is to kill you."

"What? I'm a schoolteacher," Roman laughed, "Most of my students love me, and those who don't aren't likely to have access to kung fu gangsters."

"Forgive me Master, but what is this kung fu?"

Houston, we have a problem.

Roman laughed nervously and moved slowly towards the closed front door of the flat.

"What planet are you from? You're Chinese, and you've never heard of kung fu?"

"I am not Chinese. I am Chi-Ro, son of Jin. Has Tarom Rin not spoken of me?"

"So, are you Vietnamese?"

"I was sent to this world by your father, Lord Sakara. He plans to return to Talis to claim his throne from Seti Aljyk. My mission is to escort you safely to your place at his side. I am your shamira, your guardian."

Chi-Ro bowed again.

He's a complete nutter!

Roman noticed one of the retractable rods on the ground amongst the clutter.

I'll have to get past the nutter, to pick it up.

"So Talis isn't in Asia?"

Chi-Ro could not mask his confusion.

"Like you, Master Armon, I was born on the planet Talis."

Roman backed away saying, "Now I understand. You should have explained that to me before. Erm, is there a phone box close by, so I can tell my wife... Erm, the custodians that you've found me, and I'm safe?"

Chi-Ro sensed deception.

Has life on this backward planet robbed Master Armon of his sanity?

Flames of sincerity glowed in his eyes when Chi-Ro announced, "You cannot leave this place."

"I promise to come right back," lied Roman, gradually moving closer to the exit.

Chi-Ro calmly positioned himself between Roman and the door, blocking any means of escape.

"I am the trusted sentinel of Lord Sakara Rey, a veteran of the Psychic Wars, and yet I sense that you do not trust me."

Chi-Ro's arms slowly dropped to his sides, his open palms signifying he was not armed.

"You are free to leave. Simply get past me."

Recognising the obvious challenge, Roman felt a sudden surge of adrenaline.

Fight, or flight?

With a deep breath, and another burst of adrenaline, Roman responded, "Remember just now when you asked about kung fu? Let me explain..."

Roman attacked Chi-Ro with a fierce combination of Karate punches, which all failed to connect. The elusive guardian stealthily avoided every blow.

Pathetic! What manner of folly is this? thought Chi-Ro, effortlessly anticipating Roman's technique.

Then, with a swift back step, Roman launched into a volley of perfectly executed kicks. They all missed.

How will I tell Lord Sakara that his heir is an imbecile?

Rising panic flooded Roman's thoughts.

Karate, Taekwondo, Wu Shu, Muay Thai, Boxing - all useless. Who is this guy?

What little confidence Roman clung to, evaporated when he heard an ominous rendition of Chi-Ro's voice.

"Your thoughts are transparent."

Oppressed by an unseen force, Roman stumbled and fell to his knees. He cried, "What do you want from me?"

From within the fabric of his tunic, Chi-Ro produced the futuristic hypodermic device. He injected Roman in the neck, and once more Roman drifted into the darkness of unconsciousness.

Chapter 5

In the interrogation room of Colindale Metropolitan Police Station on Grahame Park Way, Detective Chief Inspector Trevor Campbell slammed his fists into the wooden desk.

He bellowed, "You're lying!"

Known as Ranking Trevor by junior officers, the imposing plain-clothes detective of Jamaican descent glared intently at William Norris, and the fifty-six-year-old shopkeeper shuddered with fear. He nervously looked to the duty solicitor Danesh Hamid for support.

William had been brought to the Metropolitan Police Headquarters for the borough of Barnet, to be questioned regarding the deaths of four police officers. The men served in the Specialist Firearm Command Branch or CO19.

Two of the officers were shot in the head at point-blank range. All available evidence suggested that the men committed suicide with their standard-issue GLOCK 17 Luger semi-automatic pistols.

The third officer, designated as an operator, died when a second armed response vehicle crashed into his own, at high speed. Surgeons at Barnet Hospital's Accident and Emergency department pronounced the driver of this second ARV, dead on arrival.

Robert Marshall, Trevor's childhood friend, drove that second BMW Touring. News of his friend's unexpected death, made the already bitter detective even more intolerant and vengeful. William became the object of Trevor's wrath and William was obviously terrified. Fictional portrayals of police procedures did not prepare William for the thoroughly unsettling ordeal he experienced this morning. The atmosphere inside the police station seemed deliberately geared to creating a stressful environment.

William was not under arrest. He agreed to give his statement, only if afforded the support of the duty solicitor. The uniformed sergeant who brought him into the interrogation room seemed sympathetic. Unfortunately, at the behest of Trevor, this officer left the room to fetch tea and coffee.

William sat with his back to the only exit, with an old wooden desk keeping the intimidating Trevor at bay. Suddenly Trevor pushed this barrier out of the way.

He said in menacingly subdued tones, "Do you take me for a fool, Mr. Norris?"

"I swear that's what happened."

Trevor wondered why the old shopkeeper fabricated such an outrageous story. William claimed he lied in his call to the police, in order to get a quick response. He admitted there were no black youths with guns. He saw just one black man, fighting against five or six Asian men. William speculated that the men may have been Chinese and were armed with steel pipes and knives.

William said, "The fighting continued when the police arrived. Two policemen with guns, shouted at them to stop. Then the police put their guns to their heads and shot themselves. I couldn't believe it. Terrible, just terrible."

"What happened next?"

"The black fella and one of the Chinese ran off. Then the second police car came really, really fast and crashed into the parked one. The other Chinese men pulled two policemen from it and with steel pipes, gave them a real good hiding they did. Poor sods, they didn't have a hope in hell, those Chinese were big, strong lads - a bit bigger than you. By the time more police arrived, they'd already run off towards Victoria Park."

William's account suggested that seasoned officers committed suicide. William claimed that Trevor's friend Robert drove the 5-Series BMW with a criminal recklessness. This recklessness culminated in his death and the death of a fellow officer.

Trevor boomed as he stepped towards the cowering witness, "Perverting the course of justice is a serious crime, Mr. Norris; and you've already admitted to lying."

"How many times do you want me to apologise?"

"Four men are dead, and two are critical, because they responded to your call."

Hamid cried, "Chief Inspector Campbell I'm sure there is no need to remind you that Mr. Norris has not been arrested. Mr. Norris has volunteered to assist the police with their enquiries."

Trevor shot the solicitor a menacing stare. Sergeant Frank Brown entered the room with two cups of coffee and one tea.

Frank said, "Detective Chief Inspector Campbell is just reminding Mr. Norris of the gravity of the situation."

Turning to William, Hamid cried, "Mr. Norris you don't have to continue with this interview if you don't want to."

"There you go, Mr. Norris," said Frank handing the fearful shopkeeper the cup of tea.

Frank passed a cup of black coffee to Trevor and added, "There you go Gov'nor."

He kept the last cup of coffee for himself. As the men sipped their hot beverages, a tense silence descended on the small room.

Trevor broke the silence.

"I'll give you one last chance to come clean Mr. Norris. We have a second witness. If you want to avoid facing charges you'll need to tell the truth, the whole truth and nothing but the truth."

Then the police should know I'm not lying, thought William.

The second witness Trevor referred to, was the security camera at a cashpoint machine. A transaction receipt left on the machine recorded a cash withdrawal of two hundred pounds at 1:12 AM.

Trevor hoped the camera recorded vital evidence pertaining to the death of his colleagues. In the hours before its footage became available to police scrutiny, Trevor had only William's testimony and the illogical conclusions of the forensic team to help make sense out of nonsense.

"I'm sure you're very tired Mr. Norris. Tell us what really happened and Sergeant Brown will drive you home."

The shopkeeper tried to think of any detail he may have omitted from his previous accounts, but nothing came to mind. With a heavy sigh, William accepted that it would be a while before he returned to the comfort of his bed.

Chapter 6

Distant thunder woke Roman from his recurring dream. He had travelled through time, back to his parent's home in San Fernando, the Republic of Trinidad and Tobago's second largest town; and, once again, Roman experienced the velvet touch of butterflies.

In Trinidad and Tobago, there were over six hundred and twenty varieties of butterfly. One type remained most vivid in Roman's mind: Danaus plexippus, the Monarch. Roman's mother explained that monarchs were rulers and that one day he would also be a great ruler.

"Can you feel how happy they are to be alive?" she asked.

He nodded, "Yes," not understanding what his mother meant but finding happiness in the warmth and safety of her loving arms.

This happened before his third birthday. Before a tropical storm, in paradise, turned his world into a nightmare.

Now Roman's thoughts turned to his present predicament.

Is there a connection between my mother's words and this Chi-Ro's mad ranting?

Pretending to be asleep, Roman wondered how much the man in black's drug had affected him. The fact that he considered the possibility of being an alien from another planet implied that the drug had already compromised his intelligence.

Perhaps the drug also caused me to imagine the impossible. Hallucinations, diminished reflexes, and susceptibility to hypnotic suggestion, are all possible under the influence of certain drugs. But what about the policemen? How could they have been drugged? What caused them to commit suicide?

The familiar voice of his captor said, *"Rise Master."*

Roman heard Chi-Ro's voice, but Chi-Ro's lips did not move.

"There is no need for deception, Master Armon; I know you are awake, your thoughts betray you."

Roman asked, "How do you do that?"

"Have you not communicated with your custodians in this manner? If you are to survive the many perils ahead, you too must realise your full potential as a Psychic Warrior."

Chi-Ro stared into Roman's eyes, and Roman imagined his soul being probed. Then Chi-Ro stroked his Fu Manchu moustache and spoke normally.

"I see my task will be far more difficult than I first anticipated. You appear to know nothing of who you are."

"Why are you keeping me here? I'm not who you think I am. I'm just a schoolteacher; I don't have a lot of money. My parents died when I was very young. There is no one to pay you a ransom."

Upon hearing these words, Chi-Ro's demeanour became even more solemn.

"Your parents are dead?"

The warrior reached within his tunic and retrieved a palm-sized silver disc. He activated the device, and it produced a three-dimensional image of a man and woman in unfamiliar uniforms. Roman recognised them as Arthur and Miriam Doyle, his parents.

"Are these the ones you refer to as parents?" Chi-Ro asked.

"Where did you get that?" Roman responded hastily.

"You must take me to them immediately." Chi-Ro demanded.

"They're dead, you sick bastard."

"Impossible."

"Who are you?" Roman asked.

"Be still." came Chi-Ro's stern reply.

Within Roman's mind, the words echoed with a potency that suppressed all other thoughts.

"Who killed Lord Sakara's servants?"

"My parents died in a car crash."

Chi-Ro approached Roman slowly. His eyes searched with an intensity, which seemed to scorch Roman's mind. Roman felt dizzy, about to collapse. Chi-Ro reached out and gripped his head with both hands.

Chi-Ro demanded, "Show me."

Before Roman could resist, he experienced the sensation of falling through space. He hovered in the twilight zone between dream and reality.

Roman was airborne, dazzled by the first rays of sunlight that pierced the horizon. He could hear the sound of his steadily accelerating heartbeat. Roman burst through tropical storm clouds to see a familiar vehicle travelling on the rain-swept road below; a Gold 1983 Nissan 280C four-door sedan - his parents' car.

Flooded by waves of emotions, Roman battled memories he chose to forget. The year is 1984, and this is the worst day of his life.

Roman hurtled towards the fast-moving vehicle, which travelled north on the San Fernando Bypass. It was very early on a Sunday morning and most people wisely stayed indoors to avoid the bad weather. The San Fernando Bypass was almost deserted. Just one other vehicle braved the elements, a dark blue Holden Kingswood.

Roman had no recollection of this car, nor did he recall what happened next. With a sudden burst of acceleration the Holden deliberately shunted the Nissan 280C, and both cars swerved erratically.

Instantly Roman found himself inside the 280C, his parents' car. He sat on his mother's lap, securely held at the waist by her left arm. With her right hand, Miriam Doyle held a handkerchief to her son's nose. The three-year-old had a nosebleed. Mother and son cried hysterically. Arthur, Miriam's husband, drove the 280C. There were no tears in his eyes - only fear.

Lightning flashed, instantly accompanied by deafening thunder. Arthur Doyle struggled to maintain control of the Nissan, approaching the Cross Crossing interchange at high speed.

Roman's father focussed on the image of the Holden in his rear-view mirror and in an instant the large vehicle swerved out of control. The Holden slammed into the side of his Nissan before careening into the metal rails of the bridge. On impact, the bonnet crumpled upwards immediately pinning the male driver under his chin. The man's neck snapped instantly. Three seconds later, as he stared lifelessly through the shattered windscreen, the Holden burst into flames.

Instantaneously, Arthur Doyle lost control of his Nissan 280C at the Cross Crossing interchange. The Nissan crashed into the other side of the bridge. On impact, Arthur's sternum shattered on the vehicle's steering column and Miriam's head slammed into the windscreen. Miraculously, she did not crush Roman when her body violently lurched forward.

The doomed 280C tumbled over the metal barriers on the bridge. It balanced briefly, before plunging six metres into the Cipero River below. With both adults unconscious, the car landed upside down in the muddy, fast-flowing river. For thirty painful seconds, young Roman screamed in terror, before rising water engulfed him.

Arthur and Miriam Doyle drowned in the Cipero River, that stormy morning in 1984. The Holden had been stolen two days before the accident. The driver was never identified. A witness claimed that a vagrant known locally as Panman, pulled the three-year-old Roman to safety, but this was never confirmed.

Roman remembered being drawn from a river that stormy day in Trinidad. But, unlike the Biblical Moses, he remained deeply traumatised and developed a condition known as potamophobia, the fear of rivers. The mere mention of the name Moses reminded him of his secret phobia. A secret he shared with no one, not even his wife Soraya.

After the tragedy the Doyles' neighbours, an older couple with no children of their own, adopted Roman. Frank Thomas an Englishman employed in the island's thriving petroleum industry and his Trinidadian wife Nareesha became Roman's legal guardians. In 1988, the family moved to England, but sadly in 1991 Frank and Nareesha separated. Nareesha returned to Trinidad. In 2001, when Roman was twenty, Frank died of a heart attack.

Without warning, the sound of a thunderclap brought Roman back to the present.

Chi-Ro released him and said, "May the scribes record it."

The Oriental man's eyes could not hide his shock as he said solemnly, "I am sorry, Master."

"You were right, my parents were murdered," Roman responded in disbelief, and a single tear trickled down his cheek. "Tell me what you know."

"First, you should drink some tea."

Chi-Ro picked up the kettle and poured the liquid into a Styrofoam cup. He bowed as he handed Roman the warm drink.

"I am told it is a remedy for the ill effects of elidium. I trust you will find it most soothing, Master Armon."

Roman threw the cup and its contents against a wall, but Chi-Ro showed no emotion. The thunder and lightning raging outside matched the storm brewing within Roman's mind.

"Stop calling me Armon. It's an anagram of Roman isn't it? A-R-M-O-N. R-O-M-A-N. Just re-arrange the letters. What? Did you really think I wouldn't figure it out?"

"You must heed my counsel. The threat to your life is ever present. There are already at least five assassins on this world, charged with the sole purpose of killing you. Others will follow. Without training and regular doses of elidium, you will not be able to defend yourself."

"No tea, no needles and no attempts to hijack my mind."

"Forgive me Master, what does it mean to hijack?"

"No questions."

For the first time, Chi-Ro smiled.

"Good, you are beginning to behave like a prince."

"Not just any prince, an alien prince," said Roman sarcastically.

"Verily. You are human, but not of this world."

Chi-Ro once again activated the palm-sized alien disc. It produced another three-dimensional image. Roman saw a black man and woman dressed in royal finery, seated on regal thrones. The man's head was clean-shaven. He had a moustache and beard, which were well trimmed and followed the contours of a handsome face. His dark brown eyes had an unsettling depth.

The woman was beautiful. Her long dark hair had a tinge of red and gently caressed sharp cheekbones. There was kindness in her eyes.

Chi-Ro said, "You were born on the planet Talis. The only son of Sakara Rey, Lord of the Imperial Host, Emperor of the Cosmic Sea and the Empress Consort, The Noble Lady Akana-Benu."

Roman felt uneasy. He had to admit, at least to himself, that he strongly resembled the royal couple; and obviously, Chi-Ro seemed convinced they were his parents.

Chi-Ro replaced the holographic image of Sakara Rey and Akana-Benu with that of a man. The black man had piercing dark eyes, chiselled cheekbones, was bald, clean-shaven and presented in unfamiliar but impressive military regalia. A sheathed katana-like sword hung ominously from his side.

Chi-Ro said, "This is your uncle, Baron Seti Aljyk. He calls himself Emperor of Emperors and wears Najura, the lapys nerian Sword of Power. This sword and the Emperor's throne, belong to your father."

"Hmmm," was Roman's unconvinced response.

"Verily, you are His Imperial Highness, The Prince Armon, Lord Sakara's rightful heir," said Chi-Ro as he deactivated and placed the disc within his tunic.

Roman asked, "Doesn't this mean you have to follow my commands?"

"It most certainly does not," replied Chi-Ro, "My orders are from Lord Sakara Rey, and they are quite explicit. I must return you to his presence unharmed, using any means necessary. If I am to drag you across the Cosmic Sea, kicking and screaming, then so be it."

"OK then, I'm ready. Take me to your leader. Let's go hero."

"My name is Chi-Ro, son of Jin," he said, bowing reverently.

"I'm sorry, Chi-Ro. So, where's your ship Chi-Ro, in orbit? I'm ready now, beam me up and let's go."

"My starglider is not available."

"Starglider... Not available? Exactly what does that mean, Chi-Ro, son of Jin?"

"Master Armon, with regret I must inform you that my starglider has been destroyed."

Roman laughed, his head throbbed, and he felt a bit ill.

"The prototype drug I have given you is called elidium. It serves to neutralise the harmful effects of Ki's star. It is the star, which prevents you from attaining your true potential."

Chi-Ro poured another cup of tea and presented it to Roman.

Ki? That's an ancient Sumerian word meaning Earth. So Ki's star is an archaic way of saying Earth's sun. How poetic.

"This will stop the pains in your head."

If only that were possible, thought Roman.

He wondered whether this lunatic would ever let him go. With serious reservations, Roman drank the tea and to his surprise, he found that it had an instantly positive effect. He felt much better.

"So, what happened to your spaceship?"

"On my approach to Ki, I was intercepted by the five who attacked you, the Asing - the Brothers Zaar. Their vimana is heavily armed and, despite my best efforts, the Starbird Adara was disabled. Out of control, I hurtled towards Ki, and by the grace of the Great Spirit, a cloaked pod provided my escape, moments before the Adara exploded. I landed in a wooded area outside the city. It is unlikely my arrival was detected by Kian technology, nevertheless a mysterious dampening field exists on this planet and most of my equipment fails to function. It is highly unlikely that such a field is generated naturally..."

"What, no ray guns?" asked Roman relishing Chi-Ro's obvious embarrassment.

"This may be fortunate. I doubt the inhabitants of this planet have any effective defence against the particle beam weapons of our enemies."

Particle beam weapons huh? With his wacky imagination, I expected something a bit more exotic.

"It's obvious to me that you need help. I'm sure with the right counselling..."

"Counselling, is that a weapon?"

Roman replied, scratching his head, "Well, not really..."

"Then I have no need of it," said Chi-Ro.

I guess you're never alone with schizophrenia.

"Why did you pick me?"

"The Brothers Zaar are renegades from the Wu-Zan Mara Kai Temple on Talis. They have become the Asing, worshippers of the Winged Serpent - mercenaries employed by an enemy who possesses no honour. They are masters of Nyoka Sentou, and experts in the art of psionic warfare. Even so, in combat, they should have provided little challenge to any well-trained adult of the House of Enki. I followed them several days before I learnt something most disturbing."

"More disturbing than everything else that's happened tonight?"

"They possess a tracker with which they are able to find you."

"How do you know that?"

"I too have such a device. I believe these devices may be responsible for your nosebleeds."

Roman swallowed hard.

"How do they work?"

"They transmit a coded ENDAR signal which activates your personal transponder."

Roman asked cautiously, "And, where is this transponder?"

"The transponder is adjacent to the temporal bone on the right side of your skull."

"Why? Why not put it in an arm or a leg?"

"Personal transponders are used to establish the exact location of an individual and confirm whether that individual is alive or dead. By design, if the transponder is not in contact with living tissue containing your unique DNA, it would cease to function. Arms or legs can be lost without causing death."

"Nice. So soon we'll be having five guests?"

"Unlikely. The magnetic field produced by that device, with its shields removed, disrupts transponder frequency transmission," said Chi-Ro motioning to the cylinder with the green glow. "This is but a temporary solution as prolonged exposure, in excess of thirty hours, will lead to irreversible chromosomal aberrations."

Roman slowly stepped away from the alien device and asked, "What is it?"

"The Adara's hyperspatial initiator."

"Sounds like you have a severe case of TMS."

"Forgive my ignorance Master Armon, but what is TMS?"

"Too much Sci-Fi."

For a moment, Chi-Ro held Roman's gaze in silence, punctuated by the sound of distant thunder.

Then Chi-Ro said, "Your personal transponder must be removed."

Roman considered his years of training in the arts of Shotokan Karate and Taekwondo. Somehow, this martial training seemed inadequate preparation for the challenges that now lay ahead, with their disturbing promise of pain and suffering.

Chapter 7

A thunderstorm raged across North London. Within a derelict flat, on the outskirts of Haringay, an incredible story was being told. This was the revelation of Chi-Ro Jin, the Master of Hatari Ikou, a veteran of the Psychic Wars. As he spoke, Chi-Ro continued to work on a small piece of equipment, which like many of the objects in the room, had a futuristic design.

Roman thought: *If I didn't know better, I'd believe this truly was an example of alien technology, but I do know better and it's probably made in Japan.*

Chi-Ro said, "I suspect there is much you do not know regarding this planet's history. Before his death, my father revealed to me a terrible secret. Thousands of years ago, in the infancy of the United Empires of Talis, long before Mark Six Jinzou Ningen and their Great Ningen Wars brought human life to the brink of extinction, and eons before the establishment of the Democratic Talisian Commonwealth, six Talisian scientists became marooned on Ki, this planet you call Earth. And, in violation of the United Empires most sacred laws, they conducted genetic experiments on the indigenous lifeforms."

Here we go, Ancient Astronaut Theory. Pseudoarchaeology at its deluded best, Ki is a term used in ancient Sumerian mythology with reference to Earth.

"The scientists created hybrids - a combination of Talisian and Kian genes. These hybrids were great leaders, giants and heroes, who in time grew more and more ambitious and prone to extremes of violence. They waged terrible wars against the native humans and finally against each other, in repeated bids to completely subjugate the planet."

Just as I thought: tales of the Anunnaki. He's obviously read Sumerian mythology.

"Why didn't the scientists stop them?" asked Roman.

Chi-Ro said, "Exposure to Ki's sun, which was referred to as Shamash, reduced the lifespan of the Talisians and eventually robbed them of their psionic abilities."

"So, you're saying that aliens have roamed the Earth for thousands of years."

"No. A United Empires battlecarrier located the surviving Talisians on Ki, and they were exiled to a world in the outer rim called Karella, together with the hybrids they created. To destroy evidence of their existence on this world, the United Empires fleet synchronised the explosion of four extremely powerful particle bombs, above the planet surface. The explosion caused a chain reaction, which eventually led to the destruction of almost all human life on the planet."

I wonder what asylum this guy escaped from?

Chi-Ro activated the device he had been working on, and it silently pulsed with an ominous red glow. Wary of it, Roman slowly inched away. He nervously glanced his watch, and through the cracked face, spied the time frozen at 1:47 AM.

"Yeah right... Men from Atlantis built the Great Pyramid of Egypt," Roman mumbled sarcastically, before asking, "What's that you're working on?"

"The sensor module from my starglider. We will need it to find the craft used by the Brothers Zaar."

"You want to find them? I thought we were hiding from them."

"We will need their vimana to return to Talis."

This man knows his myths. Vimana is a Sanskrit word referring to a mythical flying machine. Descriptions of these technologically advanced war machines can be found in ancient Indian literature. So, for a nutter, he's pretty well read. I wonder what drove him over the edge?

"Lord Sakara's heir cannot hide forever. Burying your head in the sand does not make you invisible it only leads to suffocation."

Upon hearing those words, Roman experienced a profound déjà vu.

I've heard this man say these words before, I'm sure of it. What is happening here?

"Listen and learn," continued Chi-Ro, "The Supreme Emperor of the United Empires and his many advisors underestimated the resourcefulness of the rogue scientists and their genetically enhanced progeny. On Karella, in the course of thousands of years and despite an extremely violent history, the Karellans gradually developed their natural psionic abilities. Eventually, thirty-nine years ago, after repeated covert attempts at impairing Karellan psionic advancement through genetic manipulation failed, the High Council of the Talisian Commonwealth concluded that the Karellans had become too great a threat to Talisian security. And, in their twisted wisdom, the ruling Chancellors proposed the Great Cleansing, the systematic murder of all Karellans."

One way or another, I have to get out of here, thought Roman, *Maybe if I play along, he'll drop his guard.*

"In human history, inhumanity is a recurring theme," said Roman, clumsily attempting to appear sympathetic.

I can't believe I said that, he cringed.

Dismissing the interruption, Chi-Ro continued, "So it was, that the First Psychic War began. Many Talisian warriors of strong ethical conviction disagreed with the Talisian High Council's sinister objective and joined forces with Karella's military leader, Supreme Commander Rey Enki. Your grandfather had two sons: Seti Aljyk with his concubine Amisi Aljyk, daughter of Aljyk Jabari; and Sakara Rey with his consort, The Illustrious Lady Parvana of Tye, daughter of Grand Duke Anu Kishar. Rey Enki rightfully chose his second son, Sakara, the son of his consort, to be his successor and heir. So the scribes recorded that when the Karellan Senate and the Cabinet of the Talisian Commonwealth proclaimed Rey Enki First Consul, your father, Sakara Rey and his half-brother, Seti Aljyk, led the war against the tyranny of the Talisian High Council."

"I thought you told me that Seti Aljyk was the one who hired assassins to kill me?"

"Verily, and perhaps if I'm allowed to complete my account, you will understand why."

Somehow I very much doubt that.

"After a further nine years of bloody war, and another eight billion deaths, First Consul Rey Enki finally succeeded in defeating the superior forces of the Democratic Talisian Commonwealth, in the battle of Rak No-Var. And, with the overwhelming support of both Talis and Karella, he seized power from what remained of the corrupt Talisian Commonwealth's High Council, crowning himself Lord of the Imperial Host and Emperor of the Cosmic Sea."

Yep, definitely TMS.

"Lord Rey bestowed the noble title of Baron to Seti Aljyk and appointed him governor of Karella, establishing the Baron's government in the new capital city of Daneka. The Emperor bestowed the title of Prince of the Blood to Sakara, his rightful heir, and appointed him the title of Commander of the Imperial Host. But, in the third year of his reign, Lord Rey was mortally wounded during a hunting expedition and Lord Sakara became the second Emperor of the Cosmic Sea. The scribes recorded thirteen years of peace. But your uncle wanted more than governorship of Karella. In the capital of Talis, the Imperial City of Avaris, he staged a military coup. The Siege of Avaris led to Lord Sakara's exile and the murder of my father, Space Commodore Jin Lan."

Space Commodore, it's like something from an old arcade game. Maybe his father died in the Korean War or maybe even Vietnam. He could be Vietnamese... I'm clutching at straws. Even so, I know all too well what it's like to lose parents.

"I'm sorry. I'm sorry to hear of the death of your father," Roman said with genuine sympathy.

Chi-Ro responded with a low bow and resumed his revelation.

"The Cosmic Sea was told that you perished at the hands of Seti Aljyk's assassins. Only Lord Sakara's most trusted servants knew that you were still alive. General Tarom Rin and his consort Mina volunteered to be your Imperial Custodians and, by the grace of the Great Spirit, you were secretly brought to Ki for your protection. Recently a traitor within the ranks of Lord Sakara's sentinels alerted Seti Aljyk of your existence. Your uncle has ordered your death."

"Do you know who the traitor is?"

"Verily, I know him quite well. He was my mentor, long before he became known as the Butcher of Cyclo."

"Have you considered writing a novel? The Butcher of Cyclo would make a great title."

Chi-Ro suddenly assumed full alert status. He stood motionless, calling on all his senses.

Roman was about to speak, but an eerie rendition of Chi-Ro's voice barked a stern order.

"Be silent!"

"How did you do that? Your lips didn't move..."

Suddenly a vein throbbed painfully in Roman's temple. He felt nauseous and leaned against a wall for support, vaguely aware that he again had a nosebleed.

With a crash, the wooden door of the flat, blown off its hinges, hurtled towards Roman but Chi-Ro intercepted it, shattering it with a swift kick, smashing the bulk of its splintered remains harmlessly against the nearest wall. In the bright, silvery-blue illumination of a flash of lightning, Roman saw that Chi-Ro stood before a large silhouette of a man blocking the doorway.

Terrible thunder rolled as Roman focused on adjusting his vision to the outside storm's constantly shifting illumination. With considerable effort, he observed that the grim intruder, a large Caucasian with long blond hair and piercing blue eyes, wore a deep-purple tunic and trousers similar to Chi-Ro's unusual black garb. Striding into the room's meagre light, the intruder's strength of purpose and precision of movement betrayed fearsome physical aptitude.

Great, just what I need, another nutter, bigger than the ones before, thought Roman.

Very slowly, Chi-Ro back-pedalled; moving closer to Roman, standing defiantly before the intruder.

Chi-Ro growled, "Brakis Tarn," and his voice carried both awe and malice.

Roman thought: *What the hell is a Brakis Tarn?*

Soon, he would learn that Brakis Tarn was a Master of Kon Jou, the way of the spirit warrior. An art of combat based on philosophies developed by the martial monks of the Holy Order of the Brotherhood of Mysteries. Kon Jou strove to achieve astral projection through physical, mental and spiritual discipline.

On Earth, the concept of astral projection or astral travel is thousands of years old, dating back to ancient Chinese mysticism. But Kon Jou was developed thousands of years before the unification of China in 221 BC. In fact, Kon Jou predated all the civilizations on Earth.

In his mind, Roman heard Chi-Ro say, *"Compose yourself, Master Armon. Prepare to escape, for this is my old mentor, the Butcher of Cyclo, and his skill is matchless."*

Brakis Tarn entered the gloom, immediately focussing his malicious attention on Roman.

Chi-Ro hurled himself forward protectively and projected, *"Prepare yourself, Master!"*

In the moment of Chi-Ro's hesitation, Brakis Tarn drew a combat knife similar to a Japanese tantō dagger and hurled it directly towards Roman. Dazed, nauseous and gripped by shock, Roman found himself incapable of avoiding the deadly weapon.

But, once again, Chi-Ro moved with unbelievable speed, clasping the middle of the hurled blade between his palms. For an agonisingly brief moment he stood, eyes closed, statuesque, with the double-edged knife held in his clasped hands as if immersed in profound prayer.

Roman noted that the tip of the dagger's blade stopped mere millimetres from Chi-Ro's exposed neck and marvelled at the skill required to catch a thrown knife in this manner.

Suddenly opening his eyes, with a sharp exhale; Chi-Ro threw the combat knife to the floor, embedding the razor tip deeply into the old floorboards.

Brakis Tarn's eyes smiled then narrowed. He assumed a Kon Jou ready stance, while Chi-Ro slowly shifted to that of Hatari Ikou.

Roman's wide-eyed attention darted from the belligerent warriors, to the doorway, to the retractable rod on the floor, then to the hot kettle filled with Chi-Ro's herbal concoction. His head throbbed painfully to the rhythm of his racing heartbeat as adrenaline flooded his beleaguered system.

Roman's frantic mind hatched a simple plan, to hurl the boiling contents of the kettle at the intimidating intruder. But, before he could execute this plan, the memory of a vaguely familiar nightmare unfurled before his mind's eye.

Roman recalled a vision of a man, amongst the vivid fragments of extraordinary experiences gained in dreams within dreams.

Brakis... son of Tarn Hayek... No, Brakis, son of Tarn Havek. But how could I possibly know that?

And, from the dark and the deep of restless sleep, Roman remembered slowly looking down, to discover that an extended rod had impaled his stomach, a rod very similar to the one lying on the floor of the derelict flat, a rod held by the man Chi-Ro described as the Butcher of Cyclo.

I remember it... I remember the future. Or is this just a possible future? Should I pick up the rod lying on the floor, instead of the kettle? Will that prevent Brakis Tarn from using it? Or will he overpower me and use it against me? Is this rod the same one from my dream?

Mentally returning to the present, Roman caught a fleeting glimpse of Brakis Tarn's vengeful gaze moments before experiencing sudden, tight, excruciating pain in his chest that crept relentlessly up his neck to his jaw, spreading to his limp arms. A feeling of dread, unlike any he had ever felt, accompanied the pain, and Roman slowly slumped to the floor, gasping for breath.

My God, am I having a heart attack?

"Do you not know basic self defence? Protect yourself from his psionic attack!" came Chi-Ro's voice reverberating in Roman's mind.

In a lethal blur of precise physical movement, the warriors clashed in unarmed combat, and the whipping sound of clad limbs parrying each other saturated the room. Brakis Tarn rained twelve-blow-per-second assaults on the defensive Chi-Ro who defiantly impeded the larger man's progress towards the fallen Roman.

Is my body reacting adversely to Chi-Ro's drugs, or am I actually experiencing some kind of mental assault? Maybe I'm stoned...

Then, to Roman's surprise, Chi-Ro countered with a savage kick, which knocked Brakis Tarn backward into the wall near the doorway. As Brakis Tarn appeared to fumble for the light switch, in a state of disorientation, Roman felt a glimmer of hope.

But, to Roman's horror, it immediately became obvious that Brakis Tarn's apparent disorientation was deception. He had absorbed ambient energy from the electrical storm and now amplified and channelled that energy through the room's old wiring.

In desperation, Chi-Ro used his body as a shield, absorbing a bolt of electricity arced from the empty light socket dangling above - a bolt of deadly plasma directed towards Roman.

Stumbling to his knees, Chi-Ro managed a mental whisper, *"Master, you must run."*

Brakis Tarn stood upright and with victorious disdain he announced, "The great Chi-Ro Jin, my most gifted student - my greatest failure."

His mocking laughter filled the room with darkness.

Seizing this opportunity, filled with rage, Roman swiftly grabbed Brakis Tarn's dagger from the floor and hurled the weapon at the blond warrior who instantly stopped laughing, caught the dagger by its hilt and with a flourish, returned it to its ornate scabbard.

I should've thrown the kettle.

Then, the impossible occurred; Brakis Tarn's astral twin manifested itself, a grim silhouette of the man, like a black hole in space-time, absorbing the meagre light emanated by Chi-Ro's futuristic mechanisms.

Darkness descended on the room, and Roman feared that death and despair were at hand. The evil twin lunged forward and its black hand reached into Roman's chest gripping his heart. Roman stared into nothingness, a complete absence of light. Unimaginable pain and terror gripped his very soul.

Then, something even more inconceivable occurred. Roman's fear became ferocity. The white-hot rage shot from his lower abdomen into his spine and became dark energy. For the briefest moment, he experienced a sublime state of absolute clarity. He was no longer Roman Doyle; he was Armon Sakara, and his spectral form broke free of its mortal shell. Free from the confines of his physical body, this entity grabbed the dark consciousness of Brakis Tarn by its neck.

Roman's physical body slumped to the ground as Brakis Tarn's spectral twin released his heart and engaged in a terrifying struggle with his shadowy consciousness.

Chi-Ro stared in disbelief for a moment, before he rose slowly to unsteady feet and charged the bewildered Brakis Tarn.

Brakis Tarn reacted instantly, parrying the impossibly swift attacks delivered by Chi-Ro. Distracted by this relentless assault, the intruder's astral twin could no longer be sustained and it retreated to his physical form with a rush of dark energy.

Moments later, Roman's spectral essence also returned to his physical form and his body, which had lain motionless on the floor, inhaled sharply as if returning to life.

But, to Roman's dismay, he found that he was experiencing sleep paralysis. It was not the first time. Roman had experienced hypnagogic hallucinations in the past. They were usually frighteningly vivid, dream-like experiences he endured in the twilight before waking or falling asleep. Roman's unsettling ordeals of being mentally alert but having partial or complete skeletal muscle paralysis always accompanied involuntary episodes of sleep paralysis.

This is not a good time to be paralysed, he thought.

As the masters of Hatari Ikou and Kon Jou battled in the dilapidated room, Roman wondered whether he was still dreaming or hallucinating, quickly concluding that his senses could no longer be trusted.

Perhaps it's a side effect of elidium, he thought.

Locked in a fierce struggle with the relentless Brakis Tarn, Chi-Ro reeled in disbelief. The Emperor's trusted servant could not do what Armon Sakara just did. He could not astrally project.

In recent Talisian history, Brakis Tarn was the only individual known to be capable of such a feat and the only being Chi-Ro feared.

The electric shock had drained Chi-Ro of vital strength, and so it was, that the son of Jin Lan waged a battle he knew would soon end in his defeat. And, under present circumstances, defeat most certainly meant agonising death.

But Chi-Ro's resignation was premature. To his utter astonishment, Roman rose from his temporary immobility.

Clearly I'm under the influence of a potent psychotropic substance, Roman thought: *I need to see a doctor and a psychiatrist, and I'm not the only one. Chi-Ro is clearly insane and badly injured.*

Dismissing fears of a possible future, Roman retrieved the retractable staff from the floor and snapped it to full length. Then, with a desperate growl, he attacked Brakis Tarn, the Master of Kon Jou.

Chapter 8

Brakis Tarn felt exhilaration reminiscent of his first kill on the southern plains of Navora Karavak. He was the youngest cadet in a notorious guerrilla group known as Piros Kreegan. His grandfather, Havek Izom, a Shudyar smallholder from the Mevaal valley, had formed this rebellious group in opposition of the crippling taxation levied on Karellan agricultural trade by the Commonwealth's Chancellery, which had no Karellan representatives. And now, Brakis Tarn's father, Tarn Havek, an adept of the forbidden art of Kon Jou, led the fearsome Kreegan warriors against the invading tyranny of the so-called Democratic Talisian Commonwealth.

At an early age, Brakis Tarn had impressed his father with uncanny intuition and an enviable aptitude for psychic combat. Finally, the sixteen-year-old embarked on his first mission, elated that his father had reluctantly agreed to allow his participation in the dangerous raid of a Talisian weapons depot.

Intelligence reports had suggested that the Talisian Invasion Force, engaged in fierce battles, in the Northern Territories, left the weapons depot vulnerable to attack. But, Commonwealth stormbringers had telepathically suggested this misinformation to Piros Kreegan spies, and Tarn Havek led his men into a trap.

The scribes recorded that a battalion of one thousand Talisian assault troops led by Supreme Chancellor Rameses Gor surrounded the three hundred Kreegans.

The battle raged for three long hours, until the opposing wills of rival stormbringers created unmanageable psychic anomalies and widespread mental chaos. In the confusion that ensued, Brakis Tarn became separated from the protection of his father, and found himself alone, pinned down behind a rocky outcrop, amongst a sea of wild ryzagrass.

For two desperate hours, with precision blasts from his Koroba A2L Ultra assault phase rifle, Brakis Tarn managed to keep his pursuers from advancing on his position. He felt a heady rush of pride, finally managing to wound a fleeing soldier in the right buttock. Later, he would claim that he had shot an officer in the right shoulder.

Brakis Tarn managed to keep the Supreme Chancellor's troops at bay for another hour, before depleting his assault rifle. For a moment, all seemed lost, but fortune favoured the boy. Retreating Piros Kreegan guerrillas, blasted the position of the soldiers who had hindered his escape, and Brakis Tarn used this opportunity to run.

He had sprinted just over one hundred metres before his intuition compelled him to dive for cover. As he dove, an energy bolt sliced through the atmosphere vaporising every particle in its wake.

Brakis Tarn rolled to his feet and hurled his dagger, aiming for his opponent's throat but only succeeding in wounding him in the right shoulder. With the desperation that only a boy facing certain death knows, he leapt forward in a spin kick, bringing his right heel down on the Daxia H1-09 Compact pistol held by the Talisian veteran. The blow knocked the man to the ground and the plasma weapon out of his reach.

Recovering quickly, the assault trooper pulled the blade from his shoulder with his left hand and attempted to drive it into Brakis Tarn's solar plexus.

The boy used his knee to shove the trooper's knife hand upwards. Then, clasping the man's wrist securely with both hands, he twisted him off balance, fluidly wrenching the knife from his grasp and throwing him to the ground with a right-heel sweep.

But, taking advantage of the youth's distracting sense of achievement, the fallen Talisian locked Brakis Tarn's ankles with his legs and brought the boy to the ground with a painful thud. The opponents rolled apart instantly and stood facing each other.

In desperation, the young Karellan hurled the dagger again, but this time the older Talisian caught it by its hilt and with a menacing smirk, casually threw the weapon away.

Brakis Tarn rolled to the ground and retrieved his Koroba A2L Ultra, but the trooper immediately probed the boy's mind and learnt that the assault rifle was depleted.

"I will enjoy killing you," were the sinister thoughts Brakis Tarn discerned from his opponent.

The Talisian pulled a standard-issue retractable sok-bou power rod from his belt and assuming the ready stance of an Arashi Paksa fighter, extended the sok-bou, relishing the idea of giving this peasant boy a first and last lesson in the way of the storm.

Brakis Tarn cleared his mind. He knew Arashi Paksa's strength lay in its speed, but the art of Kon Jou his father had secretly taught him, employed psionic mastery as its ally. The sixteen-year-old doubted that this well-fed older man could match his youthful stamina. Nor would he expect a lowly Shudyar to employ the art of Kon Jou, reserved for the scholarly Brahmyars and regal Khatras by the strict kurai system of social ranking, imposed on Karellan society by the Talisian High Council.

"May the scribes record it," said Brakis Tarn defiantly.

The Talisian launched a swift attack and Brakis Tarn used his depleted phase rifle to parry the deadly blows of the sok-bou, painfully aware that the angrily buzzing plasma elements on either end of the power rod could easily vaporise flesh and bone. Wilfully shielding his thoughts from the trooper's probes, Brakis Tarn defended against relentlessly speedy attacks, waiting for the Talisian to make an error.

Then it occurred. The trooper's concentration lapsed for just a second, a second that Brakis Tarn exploited by projecting anxiety into the man's mind. As the suggestion of fear grew into debilitating terror, the boy mentally attacked the trooper's cardiovascular system. His heartbeat became wildly irregular and his breathing inadequately shallow. The storm of the assault trooper's Arashi Paksa slowly became nothing more than the flatulence of a dying old man.

Delivering a single blow with the butt of his Koroba A2L Ultra, Brakis Tarn ruptured the Talisian's spleen. The man fell to his knees in agony, with his autonomic nervous system in shambles. His heart rate approached critical levels, his blood pressure plummeted and an unbearable pain emanated from his left shoulder. Finally, waves of dizziness clouded his vision as darkness encroached.

The victorious Brakis Tarn enquired, "What is your name?"

"*Enu Omari,*" projected the trooper.

Verily, a name befitting an arrogant Vyshar landowner, thought Brakis Tarn contemptuously.

"Enu Omari, when you meet with the Great Spirit, be sure to mention that a lowly Shudyar named Brakis Tarn broke your neck."

With that, Brakis Tarn clasped the head of his fallen foe and wrenched it with all his might. The sickening sound of Enu Omari's neck being broken followed by the even worse sound of him struggling for his last breath brought a wide-eyed smile to Brakis Tarn's sinister face.

As Enu Omari's lifeless body slumped to the ground, Brakis Tarn noticed the ornate hilt of the Talisian's dagger, secured to his waist in an equally flamboyant scabbard. He pulled the dagger from its scabbard and saw, that unlike his common Karellan militia combat knife, Enu Omari's dagger was no mere melee tool but a superior weapon crafted by an artist of old.

Discarding his standard-issue scabbard and replacing it with Enu Omari's, Brakis Tarn growled, "You will not need your dagger during your audience with the Great Spirit, Vyshar."

Then, overwhelmed by a psychotic sense of gratification, he fled the battlefield to be re-united with his father, Tarn Havek and forty-eight Piros Kreegan survivors, proudly displaying his prize, the dagger of Enu Omari, which would never leave his side.

Since that day, Brakis Tarn had become a consummate killer. In time, he would be responsible for the deaths of millions of men, women and children across the Cosmic Sea. But, memories of his first kill never failed to bring warmth to his cold heart.

Now, the Master of Kon Jou wondered if that pleasure would be surpassed by the execution of his treacherous student, Chi-Ro Jin, and the termination of Sakara Rey's bastard, Armon.

Chapter 9

Brakis Tarn had hoped to find a worthy opponent in The Prince Armon. Ne-Ro Jos, Grandmaster of The Order of Mysteries, described Armon Sakara as the dark star destined to attain the unattainable. Ne-Ro declared that Armon would utterly transcend physical limitation, and he advised Seti Aljyk that Armon was the soter prophesied in the Biblicara Mysterium books of Kasgar, Leemar and Mithnos. Ne-Ro foresaw Armon developing the ability to transform his physical body into an indestructible astral entity at will. So Seti Aljyk feared Armon Sakara, almost as much as he feared Sakara Rey. But Brakis Tarn knew better.

I see Seti Aljyk for the pathetic abomination that he truly is. Fool! Misplacing his faith in crude drugs and insidious hypnosis to bend the wills of weak millions! He underestimates me because of my humble heritage, and that will be his undoing. Against Seti Aljyk's decree, Ne-Ro Jos instructs me to capture. But, for the death of my father, I have sworn vengeance on the House of Enki. I will learn all of worth from the Khatras. Then I shall kill, until all the descendants of Enki are no more. Soon, a lowly peasant shall rule the Cosmic Sea.

The sok-bou Roman wielded lacked the benefit of deadly plasma energy. For reasons unknown, energy weapons did not function on this planet the inhabitants referred to as Earth.

Regarding Roman with arrogant disdain, Brakis Tarn thought: *Surprisingly, the runt achieved astral projection; but without control and I sensed great fear and confusion in him. It is obvious he has not been trained in the rudiments of psionic warfare. Death whispers his name to me.*

Roman began with a shoulder-neck bō-staff attack manoeuvre, swiftly rotating the sok-bou once under his right arm, around his shoulder, then around his neck to the grip of his right hand. But, raising a bemused eyebrow, Brakis Tarn easily anticipated this technique.

What is this kak, some Kian dance?

Brakis Tarn effortlessly avoided Roman's blows and retaliated with a perfectly executed palm strike, sending Roman hurtling through the open door of the flat, to crash in the dark, dilapidated hallway.

This is obviously the soter! Brakis Tarn thought mockingly.

Dragging himself upright, Chi-Ro launched a mental assault on Brakis Tarn's central nervous system, prompting the Karellan warrior to counter with the projection of incapacitating despair. Once again Hatari Ikou clashed with Kon Jou, and impossible blows met unimaginable parries, until Brakis Tarn's well-placed palm strike sent Chi-Ro crashing into a wall on the opposite side of the room. He slumped to the floor and moved no more.

Brakis Tarn turned his attention to where Roman had fallen, only to find that he had vanished.

Have I underestimated the son of Sakara?

"No you have underestimated the son of Jin," came Chi-Ro's stern projection.

Placing both hands firmly on the wall, Chi-Ro employed his formidable psionic ability. He used the old wiring of the dilapidated room to channel a bolt of amplified electricity, which hit Brakis Tarn squarely in his chest and propelled him backward into the large window, shrouded by a black plastic sheet. A deafening thunderclap masked the cacophony of Brakis Tarn's body violently smashing through the thick glass.

The fall from the third-storey window would have killed most human beings, but Brakis Tarn was not an ordinary human being. He was the product of thousands of years of genetic manipulation and the strongest man on Earth.

A young, intoxicated couple, driving home from a party, witnessed Brakis Tarn's painful plunge.

"Oh my God, oh my God, somebody threw a body out of that window," exclaimed the terrified woman as her stunned boyfriend brought the Rover 25 to an abrupt halt.

"Call an ambulance," the man shouted to the woman, as he leapt out of the car and into the pouring rain to investigate.

He vaguely heard the woman's muffled voice shouting, "Flippin' heck, where are you goin'?"

The sight of Brakis Tarn's prone body, partially wrapped in torn black plastic and covered in jagged shards of broken glass, caused the man to hold his breath. Lightning flashes illuminated deep-red streams, washed into the gutter by the stinging downpour and the shock of seeing so much blood, made the man light-headed. For a brief moment, he stood mesmerised by the horror of human injury before him.

"What're you doin'?" the suddenly sober woman shrieked through the rolled down window of the Rover's passenger seat.

"Did you call an ambulance?" he shouted above distant thunder, cautiously moving closer to Brakis Tarn's motionless body.

Brakis Tarn focussed on the approaching man. In his injured state, the blond warrior needed every iota of energy at his disposal to achieve his next incredible feat.

The woman pleaded, "Chris, let's go!"

Chris turned towards her, and his face seemed strangely vacant as he announced, "We must assist this man. He requires immediate medical attention."

"What? Are you havin' a laugh?"

"We must not let this man die," Chris added.

To which the hysterical woman responded, "He's dead already, genius!"

Rolling her eyes, she rolled up the window, shivered and wiped the rain from her forehead with the back of her hand.

Chris grabbed the badly injured Brakis Tarn under his armpits, and proceeded to heave him in the direction of the parked hatchback.

"Assist me," he barked at the woman.

She screamed, "Who the hell do you think you're shouting at? I don't wanna be dealin' with the flippin' police, stinkin' of booze in a car stinkin' of weed. Just leave him and take me home. We'll be damn lucky if whoever threw that sod out the window, doesn't come lookin' for us."

Chris approached the car, opened the passenger door and knocked the woman out with a single punch.

He threw her unconscious body onto the drenched pavement and proceeded to load the large Karellan into the seat she previously occupied.

Chris calmly walked around the front of the car to the driver's seat, where, for a long moment, he sat and stared at the illuminated dashboard, before the ignition key finally caught his attention. He started the engine and crunched the car into first gear. Then, like a man possessed Chris drove off, leaving his senseless girlfriend sprawled on a secluded pavement in Haringay during a thunderstorm.

Chapter 10

In the murky darkness, punctuated by dramatic flashes of silvery blue lightning, Roman dragged his body down the concrete stairway of the derelict block of flats. The blow to his chest had left him in excruciating pain and with every agonising step he prayed that he would wake from his nightmare. Roman imagined that the lunatic called Brakis Tarn would kill Chi-Ro Jin.

Then he'll come looking for me, he thought.

Clutching the retracted sok-bou close to his chest, Roman awkwardly made his way down to the small, dilapidated lobby of the block of flats. The wild wind rushed through gaps in boards where a front door once stood, scattering debris and creating an eerie wail.

Dashing into the elements, the heavy rain stung his face and dulled his senses. Roman stumbled on the slick pavement, with no idea where he was. Then, he spied a phone box in the distance and jogged towards the grey metal and glass beacon of hope, ignoring the waves of pain that racked his body. Roman anticipated experiencing the relief of speaking to his wife Soraya and knowing she was safe.

Light-headed, breathless and exhausted, he hauled open the metal-framed door of the public phone box, trying to quell a din of voices in his troubled mind. His attempts failed. He felt certain that the drug, which Chi-Ro referred to as elidium, had created his sensory disorder.

The alarming thought, that Brakis Tarn would appear at any moment, remained foremost in Roman's mind as he hastily entered the booth, and rummaged through his trouser pockets for coins with which to make a call. Nervous tension gripped his soul as he dialled his home telephone number.

"Hello," answered Soraya with unmasked urgency.

Realising he had been holding his breath, Roman exhaled with relief and cried, "Soraya, it's me."

"Where are you? I've been worried sick."

"No time to explain. Soraya, you have to go to your mother's right now!"

"What? Birmingham? Now? Roman you have the car, you're scaring me, what's happened?"

Quickly running out of credit, Roman scrambled to put more coins into the phone, but could find no more change in his pockets.

"Just pack a few things and leave now. I'll meet you there..."

The LCD of the public telephone suddenly began to flash ominously:

INSERT COIN

In desperation, Roman checked the coin return and to his elation, fingered a pound coin within the metal receptacle. But in his haste, he dropped it; and, as he bent to pick up the money, a projectile hit the phone, narrowly missing his head. Roman turned in horror to see three of the Brothers Zaar approaching ominously. The leader hurled another dart and Roman needed no further incentive to run for his life. The three large men gave chase.

In the master bedroom of the Doyles' apartment in Friern Barnet, Soraya paced in a state of frenzy.

She called desperately into the phone, "Roman? Roman?"

Soraya's friend Eve Taylor rushed into the room, awash with concern. The pleasantly plump brunette's hazel eyes, betrayed an unwaveringly jolly sincerity. This morning, Soraya needed Eve's sense of humour and positive outlook more than ever.

The twenty-two-year-old international law student had been up till the early hours studying for exams, and around 3:00 AM she received an unexpected text message from her good friend.

It simply asked, *R U AWAKE?*

After a brief exchange of text messages, Eve called Soraya and offered to come over. After all, she only lived two streets away. Now as her best mate repeatedly uttered the name *Roman*, Eve feared that something terrible had occurred.

"Soraya, what's going on?" she asked cautiously.

Soraya seemed oblivious of Eve's enquiry and continued to call into the phone, "Roman?"

"Soraya, what's going on? Eve repeated, with growing unease.

Soraya hung up, and placed trembling hands to her head, attempting to clear muddled thoughts.

"I don't know," came her delayed response, "he didn't explain."

"Well at least he's alright," Eve chirped, ever viewing the bright side.

With glistening brown eyes, Soraya intently looked at her friend before adding, "Roman wants me to go to my mum's."

"In Birmingham? Is there something you're not telling me?" Eve asked tentatively.

Soraya picked up the phone again and quickly dialled.

"Who are you calling?"

"His friend Zach, I bet he knows what's going on..."

Unexpectedly, the doorbell rang startling the anxious women.

"Who's that?" asked Soraya, in a concerned whisper.

"You call Zach, I'll check the door," volunteered Eve.

As she briskly walked through the lounge to the front door, Eve listened to Soraya speaking to Dr. Zachary Silverman.

"Zach, it's Soraya again. I'm sorry, but Roman called. I'm still worried sick... I don't know... He's not coming home. He wants me to meet him in Birmingham... I was about to ask you the same thing..."

Eve peered through the peephole of the door, and to her surprise, saw two large Oriental men standing on the other side. But, to her dismay, one of them seemed to be preparing to kick the door in!

Eve screamed as the wooden door burst open, knocking her sprawling to the floor. Fearing for her life, she immediately leapt to her feet and grabbed a martial arts trophy from the mantelpiece.

Like synchronised predators, the two brothers invaded the apartment, quickly assessing it for possible threats. In desperation, Eve hurled the trophy at one of the assassins. Pencha Zaar, the youngest and most impetuous of the five brothers, effortlessly caught the trophy in his left hand while he hurled a dagger with his right.

With singular precision, the blade impaled Eve's forehead, and her hazel eyes faithfully expressed immeasurable trauma as she fell backwards and hit the floor with a loud thud.

Soraya rushed into the lounge, greeted by Eve's corpse and the implied promise of a swift death.

"Oh my God," she screamed.

The Brothers Zaar: Pencha and Kirato, showed no emotion when they noticed the pendant dangling from the thin gold chain around Soraya's neck. But they immediately recognised the exotic gemstone. It was not an emerald as Roman had presumed; it was in fact a rare, naturally occurring crystal called *lapys viridian* - a priceless green stone from the distant moon of Spiro Majur.

A few miles away, in an isolated alleyway somewhere in Haringay, Pencha and Kirato's brothers had cornered Roman. Tonn, Mika and Felani smiled threateningly at Roman whose nose bled profusely.

Believing the prophesies of Ne-Ro Jos, they had trained long and hard for their encounter with Prince Armon Sakara. The Karellan soothsayer Ne-Ro Jos had claimed that the son of Sakara Rey had the potential to become an indestructible astral warrior, a feat well beyond the realms of psychic warfare.

But the brothers found amusement and relief, in their discovery that Armon Sakara showed no signs of an aptitude for astral combat, and apparently had no psionic skills whatsoever.

To them, the Prince seemed utterly retarded. In fact, never before had they encountered a Talisian of such poor intellect.

This imbecile would serve no purpose in the court of our benefactor, Lord Seti. It would be an act of incredible kindness to swiftly terminate this freak of nature, a compassionate act, carrying the promise of political prestige and great wealth. May the scribes record it, Felani Zaar thought as he stepped forward.

Felani, the eldest of the Brothers Zaar and the current leader of the Cult of the Asing, decided to bring about Armon Sakara's end by causing the Prince's puny brain to explode!

Suddenly Roman heard a sinister voice, but the lips of the Nyoka Sentou master did not move.

"Armon Sakara, you have been charged with high treason and sentenced to death by order of the Emperor of Emperors, Lord Seti Aljyk. I am Felani Zaar, your executioner. When you are face to face with the Winged Serpent, tell him I showed you mercy by ending your miserable life swiftly."

Felani Zaar launched his psionic attack, and an almost imperceptible ringing began in Roman's ears, rising to an unbearable, unimaginable crescendo. But the elidium, Chi-Ro had injected into Roman's bloodstream, had silently begun its work. Dormant genes had been activated and once more Roman's fear transformed into seething rage.

No, he thought.

The simplicity of the thought surprised Roman, as did what happened next. The Brothers Zaar were instantly hurled backwards by a wall of psionic energy, and tumbled across the alleyway, like paper dolls in a hurricane.

Felani, who bore the brunt of the attack, found his eyebrows had been singed. Never before had he experienced anything like this.

We have been deceived, he thought.

"So, you are not as helpless as you led us to believe. Good. During your afterlife audience with the Winged Serpent, you can profess that I granted you the honourable death of a worthy adversary," Felani projected to Roman.

With a deep growl Felani retaliated, and it was Roman's turn to be hurled backward by concentrated psionic energy. Felani leapt and grabbed Roman by his head; and, with incredible strength, he pressed his thumbs firmly into Roman's temples. Feeling his life draining away, Roman screamed in pain and grabbed Felani's groin in desperation.

Roman discovered: *This man has no balls.*

Reacting quickly, he called upon his rage and threw Felani Zaar four metres into space. But the master of Nyoka Sentou twisted into a somersault and landed firmly on both feet.

Growing frustrated, Felani projected for the assistance of his brothers, *"Tonn! Mika!"*

Once more a sense of clarity overwhelmed Roman, and a tingling sensation rose from his spine, saturating his very being, knocking the Brothers Zaar to the ground. Rising swiftly, no longer capable of reading his thoughts, they briefly found themselves unable to counter the primitive Kian fighting styles Roman employed. To make matters worse, he randomly assaulted their organs, their muscles, their central nervous systems and even their thoughts.

The only advantages the Asing possessed were discipline and years of experience in the art of psionic warfare. Unfocussed and unable to fully understand the power he possessed, the Brothers Zaar began to gradually turn Roman's psionic abilities against him.

Then Felani discovered a dark secret and flooded Roman's mind with images of water. Rising water. Fast-flowing water. Deadly water.

Roman collapsed to his knees, suddenly overwhelmed by crippling fear and in devastating unison, Felani, Tonn and Mika extended their sok-bou and proceeded to beat him to the ground. But, with a desperate burst of mental energy, Roman caused their optic nerves to cease functioning. With his opponents temporarily blinded and disorientated, Roman limped away, bruised and battered, into the windy darkness of the thunderstorm.

When their sight finally returned, the Asing found that ghost images of their deepest fears clouded their judgement and prevented them from resuming their chase.

The snake worshippers had completely underestimated their quarry, but as long as the transponder lay hidden within his skull they would find Armon Sakara again.

Chapter 11

When Detective Chief Inspector Trevor Campbell left Colindale Metropolitan Police Station an hour ago, he had no idea that an urgent call would bring him back to Grahame Park Way so soon. Trevor became more and more infuriated. For several crucial hours, the forensics team mislaid an important piece of evidence - a vital clue that could identify the young black man William Norris saw fighting on the street. The UK driving licence, found at the scene, belonged to a twenty-five-year-old man named Roman Doyle, and on the licence was *Flat 16, St Benedict's Court, Friern Barnet Lane, Friern Barnet, London N11.* It was a twenty-four-minute journey from Colindale that Ranking Trevor and his team of officers would make in just ten minutes.

For a brief moment, Roman stood before the entrance to his flat, immobilised by a crushing feeling of dread. He stared in dismay at the wooden door. Smashed and left ajar, it allowed the lounge light and the indistinct sound of the television to seep into the hallway.

Mustering the courage required, Roman gently pushed the door open with trembling hands and cautiously entered the home he shared with his wife Soraya. The shock of what he saw made him unsteady on his feet. The supine corpse of a woman lay on the wooden floor of the lounge, in a pool of blood. Roman could feel his heartbeat's pounding rhythm in his temples as he stared into Eve Taylor's lifeless eyes. Realising that all the blood had streamed from a single, open wound in Eve's forehead, Roman became nauseous. He felt pangs of guilt, for selfishly feeling a sense of relief upon realising that Eve, not Soraya, lay dead on the floor.

Next to the dead body, a shiny object suddenly grabbed his attention, the thin gold chain he had given Soraya as an engagement present. He picked up the broken necklace and studied it.

Where is the pendant? Where is Soraya?

Roman placed the chain into his coat pocket, and gently closing her eyes with his fingertips, silently shed tears of sorrow for Eve and tears of terror at the prospect of finding Soraya dead, in another room within the flat.

Then he thought: *The killer may still be here.*

Instinctively, Roman reached within his coat and removed the alien power rod he had been carrying and activated it. The sok-bou immediately extended to full length and Roman assumed a kobu-do ready stance, holding the rod in the manner of a Japanese bō staff.

Unlike karate, kobu-do had always been shrouded in mystery. Roman considered himself very fortunate to have been taught this covert form of stick fighting, especially since it had been developed in utter secrecy, so many years ago. Before his recent battles, he had considered himself quite competent in bō-jitsu, the art of using the bō. Now, he doubted his martial arts abilities but remained certain of his determination to lay down his life in the protection of his beloved Soraya.

Alert, muscles taut like coiled springs, Roman crossed the lounge silently, taking care not to step into Eve's coagulating blood. He approached the master bedroom and immediately noticed light emanating from within.

Who's in there?

Roman used the end of his sok-bou to gently push the door open, and adrenaline coursed through his bloodstream as he peered into the bedchamber through dilated pupils. He immediately noticed the telephone receiver, left dangling off the edge of the bedside table. It remained silent - silent because the phone's connecting cable had been cut.

The slightly ajar door of the wardrobe caught Roman's attention, and his heart skipped a beat.

It's big enough to hide an alien. Someone could be in there.

The thought brought a sudden chill. Armed with the sok-bou, he gingerly moved towards the large built-in wardrobe, only to be taken aback when he saw the image of himself in its full-length mirror. Roman studied the reflection of an exhausted and dishevelled man, whose tired eyes had mysteriously changed colour, from a very dark brown to light chestnut.

Shrugging this anomaly aside for the moment, Roman focussed on the possible peril that lurked within the confines of the wardrobe. He took a deep breath before slowly aligning the end of the power rod with the gap in the door.

Suddenly, hearing a sharp hiss from behind, Roman spun on his heels. He saw a blur leave the room. His heart raced, and he took a fleeting second to suck air down his tight, dry throat. Then, armed with the sok-bou, he lurched through the bedroom doorway and saw a beautiful Abyssinian cat run across the lounge towards the front door of the flat. Thousands of years ago, these cats had been worshipped as *Children of the Gods* on the banks of the Nile in ancient Egypt.

Whose cat is that?

Avoiding Eve's spilt blood, the golden-brown shorthaired cat stopped at the open front door. The cat turned its arched neck, gazed at Roman with large almond-shaped green eyes, before uttering a defiant meow and escaping through the doorway.

Roman suppressed the urge to laugh hysterically. His lack of sleep, the elidium in his bloodstream and the stress and violence of the last few hours threatened to push him over the edge.

I'm losing my mind.

Roman closed the front door, tried to ignore the scent of blood and quickly searched the rest of the flat for clues.

Who killed Eve? Was it Brakis Tarn, the Asing or someone else? What the hell really happened here? Did Soraya escape, or was she abducted? The telephone cord... It had to be cut for a reason.

Roman checked the LCD of the telephone in the master bedroom. The phone recorded the last number dialled, and he instantly recognised it as the number of his good friend.

Zach... Soraya called Zach... Maybe he knows where Soraya is; that's if they haven't killed him too.

Roman grabbed a black sports bag, hastily shoved the retracted sok-bou and a few items of clothing into it. Then, in an afterthought, he turned to the wardrobe, retrieved a nunchaku and also stuffed this martial arts weapon into the bag.

Sticks against Brakis Tarn or the Asing, he thought. *Who knows? I might be able to hit the bastards while they're busy laughing at me.*

Roman quickly took a few items of food from the kitchen, before leaving the flat, deeply preoccupied with worry about Soraya and immersed in thoughts of what he should or should not tell the police regarding recent events. Filled with a sense of foreboding and distracted by morbid fears, he failed to notice the inquisitive Abyssinian cat, which observed him intently as he left St Benedict's Court.

Roman did not get very far before a silver Vauxhall Vectra in police livery, and an unmarked metallic grey Rover 75 hastily arrived with blue flashing lights. The police vehicles came to an abrupt halt in the parking area of St Benedict's Court.

DCI Trevor Campbell exited his Rover and scanned the block of flats as if trying to activate x-ray vision. Sergeant Frank Brown left the Vauxhall Vectra manned by a young police constable and joined Trevor on the pavement.

Two minutes later, another police vehicle arrived - a Vauxhall Zafira from the Dog Support Unit. The specially adapted response vehicle, fitted with kennel compartments, soundproofing and air conditioning, had blacked-out rear windows. Max, a longhaired German Shepherd, travelled in such relative luxury. His handler, PC Graeme Lock, drove the vehicle accompanied by PC Amanda Powley.

En-route to St Benedict's Court, Inspector Campbell had been informed of a 999 call received from Dr. Zachary Silverman. Dr. Silverman became very alarmed when he overheard loud screams of terror during a conversation with Soraya Doyle. When Soraya failed to return to the phone, Zach alerted the police using his mobile.

Glancing over his shoulder, Roman saw police officers enter his block of flats. He paused, slowly coming to his senses.

Soraya is missing and Eve's been murdered in our flat. I have to go to the police.

His mind made up; Roman headed back towards St Benedict's Court with conviction. But, as he walked, his head began to throb, and he noticed a trickle of blood from his nose. Suddenly someone grabbed Roman into a secluded alleyway. Pale and haggard, Chi-Ro struggled to remain steady on his feet.

He said, "Master Armon, I'm glad you are alive."

"My wife is missing. An innocent woman is dead in my flat! I'm taking you to the police."

"Wife?" exclaimed Chi-Ro, "If by wife you mean consort, there can be no wife. You are to be bonded to Princess Rhia Kan."

"Did you hear what I said?" snapped Roman.

Suddenly Chi-Ro stumbled. Roman caught him and added, "The police can take you to a hospital."

"No. I will recover. We must leave this planet as soon as possible," came Chi-Ro's weak response.

"Leave the planet? What is your major malfunction? Didn't you hear what I just said? A woman is dead in my flat, and my wife is missing."

Gradually, the sound of sirens approaching from the distance added to the tension of the moment.

Chi-Ro replied, "I know where your wife is. We must go now if we are to save her."

"No, you're lying. We have to go to the police."

"You saw how easily the Brothers Zaar dealt with your law enforcement agents. Are you willing to put your faith in these ill-equipped Kians?"

"You've drugged me. I don't know what to believe anymore."

"Believe this, Roman Doyle is a character created by your custodians, Tarom and Mina Rin. He never existed. You are, and always have been, Armon Sakara, heir to the Imperial Throne. Come with me now, it is the only way to save your wife."

The sirens got louder. Roman hesitated, for what seemed like a painful eternity.

Then he exclaimed, "OK, take me to my wife."

"May the scribes record it," responded Chi-Ro.

Chapter 12

Dawn slowly brought light to a gloomy north London street, as an Abyssinian cat stealthily followed two very desperate men. With green eyes, the creature intently watched Roman Doyle and Chi-Ro Jin approach a black Ford Mondeo Estate.

Despite his life-threatening injuries, Chi-Ro had managed to load the alien devices from his derelict home into the stolen vehicle. But now, he could no longer ignore the debilitating agony.

Chi-Ro cried, "I fear I no longer possess the strength to effectively pilot this craft, Master Armon. You must take us to my escape pod outside the city."

Chi-Ro gave Roman the car keys.

"No-no-no. I don't want to hear about space pods. We are going to find my wife," said Roman sternly.

"Despite your astral abilities, you are not yet prepared to do battle with the Brothers Zaar, and I am currently unfit to assist you. To be of use to you, I must first be healed. It is, therefore, imperative that I return to the escape pod."

"Meanwhile, there is no telling what those psychopaths would do to my wife."

Chi-Ro attempted to search Roman's mind. He sensed that Roman held a secret regarding the Kian woman. Unfortunately, the elidium, which enhanced the Prince's natural abilities, made it difficult to read his thoughts.

"The Asing have no interest in pleasures of the flesh. As part of their twisted faith, they have chosen to become eunuchs."

"I feel much better knowing that. Thanks for the update. This is a very nice car, where did you get it?"

"I persuaded the owner to part with it. I have found the Kian mind to be remarkably pliable."

"You bought it?"

"I borrowed it."

"I see," was Roman's sarcastic reply.

He stole it.

The Abyssinian stalker observed silently, as Roman climbed into the driver's seat of the Ford and started the engine. Chi-Ro painfully occupied the front passenger seat. An ambulance and more police vehicles converged on St Benedict's Court, as the Prince and his guardian made their brisk escape.

Moments later, the four-stroke Boxer engine of a BMW R1200GS growled, as the black and silver 'adventure' motorcycle came to a halt next to the shorthaired Abyssinian cat.

The darkly clad rider opened the well-ventilated rear door of a grey Pet Kennel Carrier, secured to the rear of the bike. Arching its beautiful neck, the golden brown feline uttered a meow and leapt into the welcoming hands of the rider.

The dark rider gently placed the pedigree cat into the reinforced heavy-duty plastic carrier, then aggressively powered and turned the BMW motorcycle in pursuit of the Ford Mondeo Estate.

Chi-Ro mentally directed Roman onto the North Circular Road towards Enfield. The schoolteacher wondered how long it would take the police to capture them in the stolen car.

Roman imagined explaining to Scotland Yard detectives that he was actually the heir to the throne of a galactic empire and that aliens from outer space had come to Earth to assassinate him.

These alien assassins were following the orders of his uncle who usurped the Imperial Throne, naming himself Emperor of Emperors. The invaders from outer space had kidnapped his wife Soraya and were responsible for the brutal murders of Eve Taylor, and several police officers.

He, therefore, had no choice but to drive his guardian Chi-Ro Jin, a veteran of the Psychic Wars, to the escape pod from his spaceship using a stolen car. This was so that Chi-Ro could be regenerated, and would be fit to assist him as he fought to rescue his wife, using a combination of psychic and astral techniques. After rescuing his wife, they planned to return to Talis, the planet of his birth.

Roman realised the gravity of his situation; and the manic urge to laugh hysterically, returned with a vengeance. At best, he could look forward to spending the rest of his life in a secure mental institution. At worst, he would spend the rest of his days in prison. Either way, he was doomed.

Roman glanced at his alien passenger; pale, breathing laboriously and slipping into unconsciousness. Fearing that Chi-Ro would die before they reached their destination, Roman broke the silence.

"Tell me more about my father."

Chi-Ro responded weakly, "Have you finally accepted that Tarom Rin was not your real father?"

Roman smiled, "Let's say I have an open mind."

"Your father, Lord Sakara Rey, is a great man and a great leader. He is perhaps the best military tactician in the Cosmic Sea, and he brought us peace. But he loved a half-brother who lusted for his death and this misplaced affection cost him his throne and returned the Cosmic Sea to the horror of bitter war."

"Why does my uncle hate my father?"

"Greed, jealousy and envy. He felt robbed of his birthright. Seti Aljyk is Rey Enki's firstborn but the son of a concubine."

"So?"

"The offspring of a consort are considered rightful heirs."

So a consort is the equivalent of a wife, whereas a concubine holds a lesser station. Technologically more advanced civilisations adhering to traditions considered archaic on Earth?

"Tell me about the traitor, Brakis Tarn."

"Our fathers were close friends. A friendship, which I believe created jealousy in the heart of one of your father's sentinels - Brakis Tarn."

"You were his student?"

"Indeed. Brakis Tarn was the finest warrior in the Cosmic Sea. I was proud to be his disciple."

Brakis Tarn is a psychopath, Roman thought.

Chi-Ro smiled weakly and added, "My former teacher proved to be unworthy of my continued admiration."

"And this amuses you?"

Chi-Ro could barely keep his eyes open as he replied, "Your thoughts are transparent, Master Armon. If you desire your actions to be righteous, you must learn to avoid all malice, even towards your mortal enemy. I oppose Brakis Tarn because it is ethical to do so."

"So now he serves my uncle?"

"For the moment, but I suspect he has ambitions beyond being a servant. Brakis Tarn was one of Lord Sakara's most trusted sentinels. His father, Tarn Havek died in the battle of Rak No-Var. And, at first, Brakis Tarn blamed my father under whose command Tarn Havek served. But in time, Seti Aljyk convinced him that Lord Sakara had deliberately eliminated all potential threats to his dominance. Brakis Tarn believed that your father murdered Tarn Havek by sending him to the battlefront. My former teacher betrayed your father. It was Brakis Tarn who gave Seti Aljyk details of your escape to Ki."

"How could my uncle mislead someone capable of reading thoughts?"

"By employing psychic deception," Chi-Ro responded.

"You lie mentally?"

"Verily."

"I was hoping with advanced technology you'd have superior ethics."

"On Talis we have a saying, *Lovers and warriors are not bound by the rules of fair play.* And, Seti Aljyk is a consummate warrior."

"So, an uncle I never met, wants me dead," declared Roman with a sinking heart.

Chi-Ro's eyes rolled back, and he slumped into unconsciousness.

Roman panicked, "Whoa. Chi-Ro! Shit!"

"My name is Chi-Ro Jin," came the weak reply from the veteran of the Psychic Wars.

"For a moment there I thought I lost you."

"How would you lose a person in a vehicle as small as this?"

The guy's a comedian.

As the black Ford Mondeo Estate turned left at traffic lights onto the A1010 towards Waltham Cross, its occupants remained unaware that a dark rider, accompanied by an Abyssinian cat, followed them on a BMW motorcycle.

The motorcyclist's black helmet had been modified. An array of ever-changing, illuminated characters scrolled across the bottom of the visor – characters, which predated the Great Wall of China by thousands of years.

Chapter 13

DCI Trevor Campbell's Rover 75 barrelled along Great North Way towards Mill Hill. The vehicle took the irritated policeman back to Colindale Metropolitan Police Station, to interview Dr. Zachary Silverman.

With the discovery of a corpse at Flat 16, St Benedict's Court, less than an hour ago, Trevor's case became a full-fledged murder investigation. Roman Doyle and his wife Soraya were chief suspects.

Warrants for their arrest had been hastily issued. Soon their images would be circulated across the United Kingdom and throughout Europe.

But Trevor remained baffled. His confusion not only gave him a monumental headache, it made him angry. He could see no obvious link between this murder and the incident near Victoria Park, which resulted in the bizarre deaths of four police officers. Nevertheless, his instincts told him a connection existed.

The police knew Roman Doyle withdrew two hundred pounds from a cashpoint machine at the scene of the incident. Moments before all CCTV cameras in the vicinity simultaneously ceased to function, the security camera at the cashpoint recorded the schoolteacher being followed by five Oriental men - possibly Chinese triads. Trevor speculated that Roman had been involved in a drug-related street fight with these men.

But first, the forensics team would have to meticulously gather evidence from the scene of the murder. Once their job was complete, Max, the German Shepherd, would be employed in the search for narcotics.

Sensing that Chi-Ro approached death's door, Roman increased the speed of the stolen Ford Mondeo Estate to 110 mph. In the fast lane of London's M25 motorway, Roman kept a vigilant eye on his mirrors. A BMW motorcycle caught his attention when it increased speed and overtook several cars, but not being a police vehicle, he quickly dismissed it. Roman continued to show concern for his injured passenger.

I have to keep him talking... Keep him awake.

"The wooded area, outside the city where you landed in your space pod, is called Epping Forest," Roman advised.

"Do these creatures pose a threat?"

"What creatures?"

"Eppings."

"There are no eppings, it's just a name."
"What does this name mean?"
"I have no idea."
"A place without meaning is no place to be."

Lying to the north east of London, and spanning almost six thousand acres, the ancient woodland of Epping Forest is unique on Earth for being the largest open space near a capital city. It has never been enclosed or cultivated.

In Norman and Medieval times, the forest served as a royal hunting ground. Now, the home of the mythical white stag played host to an alien vehicle - the escape pod from Chi-Ro's starglider.

As directed by Chi-Ro, Roman brought the Mondeo to a halt in a clearing on the edge of the forest, far away from public car parks or sightseeing trails. An early morning fog shrouded the woodland, making it highly improbable that tourists or the general public would observe them. Nevertheless, driving a stolen car had made Roman acutely paranoid.

As they left the car and set off on foot into the misty woodland, Chi-Ro asked, "What troubles you, Master Armon?"

"The police. Brakis Tarn. The Asing. You're certain the Asing won't harm my wife?"

"It's unlikely."

"Unlikely? Where exactly is she?"

"I suspect she is being held in orbit."

"Chi-Ro, listen to me very carefully. All I care about is my wife."

"That is regrettable. Billions of lives hang in the balance. The war does not go very well. Your father needs you. He believes you have the potential to bring this war to an end."

"I didn't ask to be a part of your mission or his war."

"The enemy knows you are here, Master Armon. Seti Aljyk will stop at nothing to destroy you, and he is quite willing to sacrifice every life on this planet to fulfil that task."

"Can he do that? Can he destroy Earth?"

"Yes."

Roman shook his head and rubbed his forehead in frustration.

"You cannot make me responsible for the entire planet!"

"I wish not to oppress the heart, which is already laden. I merely state the facts."

I am willing to sacrifice my life for the lives of my wife and my unborn child.

Approximately four hundred metres away, a darkly clad motorcyclist released an Abyssinian cat into the forest. The figure observed the Prince and his guardian through an extremely sophisticated visor, before activating a wrist device. Suddenly the dark rider became virtually invisible.

They had walked slowly for half an hour. Chi-Ro grew weaker with each step. Finally, Chi-Ro collapsed and could not walk any further.

Roman linked the shoulder strap from his sports bag and Chi-Ro's weapons belt together to form a sling. With Chi-Ro lying flat on his back, he placed the sling under Chi-Ro's thighs and lower back, allowing a loop to extend from both sides. Lying face up between Chi-Ro's outstretched legs, Roman shoved his arms through the loops and grabbed Chi-Ro's left hand and trouser leg. He rolled to the right, hauling Chi-Ro unto his back. Ensuring that the sling held Chi-Ro securely in place, Roman slowly rose to a kneeling position and picked up his bag of clothes and food. Then, exhaling sharply, he stood upright, supporting Chi-Ro on his shoulders.

Exhausted, Roman set off with his great burden, grateful for the television documentaries that had taught him how to perform a pistol-belt carry.

The recent rainstorm had made the terrain muddy and treacherous. Thick fog considerably reduced visibility; and at times, Roman could not see beyond arm's length.

On a clear day, under different circumstances, he would be in awe of the stunning beauty, which now surrounded them - English Oak, Silver Birch, European Beech, Hornbeam and Holly. The centuries old pollarded trees with their thick, trunk-like branches and vast crowns of dense foliage were an unusual sight. These trees made Epping Forest unique in appearance, and unlike any other forest on Earth. To Roman, the outlandish surroundings seemed an ideal setting for a visitor from another world.

The fog rose momentarily, to reveal ponds and bogs in the distance and even further away a herd of English Longhorn cattle grazed the forest floor. When Chi-Ro asked if they were eppings, Roman dismissed the question as the product of delirium.

The curious cat stealthily followed. Almond-shaped green eyes studied the two men as they slowly approached a small clearing. On the left, a great Oak tree cleaved in two by a lightning strike, to the right, a large pond.

"Where is it?" Roman asked, gently placing Chi-Ro on the grass.

He quickly opened his bag, reached into it, produced a bottle of still mineral water, and offered Chi-Ro a drink. Chi-Ro drank slowly before returning the bottle to Roman. Swallowing the water in large gulps, Roman watched Chi-Ro retrieve a small rectangular object from the folds of his dark tunic.

Chi-Ro said weakly, "Behold."

He activated the device, and suddenly an extraterrestrial craft became visible in all its splendour.

Roman stood frozen in a state of shock, with his mouth open, oblivious that the mineral water spilled onto his clothes. He observed the manifestation of an impossible dream - proof of advanced civilisations on other planets, and overwhelming evidence in support of Chi-Ro's fantastic story.

The shimmering grey space vehicle, a conical metacrystal shape-memory alloy disc, approximately twelve metres in diameter, had no rivets or seams of any kind. The craft appeared much larger than the term *escape pod* had suggested to Roman.

Now, as the implications of this alien revelation took his breath away, Roman half expected to be greeted by a giant robot accompanied by the eerie wails of a theremin.

Instead, he found himself no longer able to stand. With the weight of seeing the alien vehicle too heavy to bear, Roman sat next to Chi-Ro, and stared at the technological marvel.

"Master, perhaps now is not the time to sit and admire Talisian engineering," said Chi-Ro weakly.

"I don't believe it."

"Verily. Your thoughts are transparent."

Chi-Ro attempted to rise. Roman snapped out of his state of shock, suddenly remembering that Chi-Ro's injuries required immediate medical attention.

He quickly stood and assisted Chi-Ro to his feet. Chi-Ro again activated the rectangular object in his hand, and Roman saw the faint outline of a door become etched on the vehicle's shimmering hull. The door slid open silently.

With a twinkle in his eyes, Chi-Ro said, "Come, there is nothing to fear. This would not be the first time you have entered a spacecraft, and it will not be the last."

Roman gazed at Chi-Ro's Oriental features, his outlandish clothes and Fu Manchu moustache.

I'm about to enter a space ship, with an alien from another planet, he thought.

And, somehow, this thought did not seem so strange after all.

Chapter 14

Following Chi-Ro out of the small airlock, and into the main chamber, Roman felt relieved to find that no robots lurked within the alien craft.

At the centre of the ship, a cylindrical pillar, with four pods attached to it in perfect symmetry, dominated the biomorphic interior. Each pod, an elongated tube with a transparent canopy, housed a reclined chair. Almost everything within the ship seemed to have a grey metallic finish. Roman saw no screens of any kind. He could not recognise or understand any of the illuminated markings within the ship, nor could he discern any controls.

Chi-Ro placed the small rectangular object he had been carrying, into a socket on the large pillar. He activated the device with a wave of his hand, and a green glow appeared in two of the four pods.

Chi-Ro announced, "We must regenerate, but first my injuries must be treated and your transponder removed." "Are you talking about the device, which you say is in my head?"

"Verily."

"No-no-no. There is absolutely no way I'm going to let you operate on me."

"Since I am not a surgeon, I am quite relieved to hear you say that, Master Armon."

"So who's going to remove the transponder?"

Chi-Ro raised his left eyebrow, nodding in the direction beyond where Roman stood. Roman turned immediately, alarmed to find that a tall, dark, slim man stood a metre behind him. The man wore a white tunic, had expressionless purple eyes and an oval face.

With an unfamiliar accent, the man said, "Commander Chi-Ro, you are injured and in need of urgent medical attention."

"Where the hell did he come from?" blurted Roman.

"Hell is not a world I am familiar with. I downloaded Teev Meg from the ship's memory core. He is my Jinzou Ningen assistant."

"You downloaded him from the ship's memory core?"

He repeats all I say like an imbecile. Perhaps my tests have been flawed, Chi-Ro thought. *This cannot be the heir to the Imperial Throne.*

Roman exclaimed, "Too damned right, only an imbecile would entertain your delusions!"

Chi-Ro felt well-hidden surprise that Roman heard his private thoughts. "What do you mean you downloaded him?" continued Roman.

Chi-Ro sighed, "I lack both the time and the inclination required to explain the teleportation processes that permit inanimate energy patterns to be converted into living matter."

"Should I explain the processes to your guest, while I treat your injuries, Commander Chi-Ro?"

"No Teev Meg that will not be necessary."

"Teev Meg is your Jinzou Ningen assistant? Didn't you say they brought humanity to the brink of extinction?"

Teev Meg replied, "The slave revolts known as the Great Ningen Wars, ended eighteen thousand years ago. All Ningen guilty of crimes against humanity, were terminated in a series of genocides, during the Age of Darkness that followed. In the Cosmic Sea, all men are free. All forms of slavery have been abolished for over fifteen thousand years.

Unconvinced, Roman stared at Teev Meg for an uncomfortable moment, then turned to Chi-Ro and said, "OK Chi-Ro, you get treated, regenerate yourself then take me to the Asing. I don't want any part of your war or your mission. I just want my wife back."

"As you wish, Master Armon, but I am saddened by your decision. I thought I had made progress in making you aware of your imperial duties. I lack the strength required to argue."

Chi-Ro slumped into one of the illuminated pods with a heavy sigh. Teev Meg immediately retrieved a cylindrical device from his tunic and scanned Chi-Ro's body.

"I hope you can help him," said Roman, to Teev Meg, with genuine concern.

Teev Meg replied, "May the scribes record it."

Roman walked towards the airlock leaving Teev Meg to treat Chi-Ro's injuries. Dark anxiety gnawed at his soul. He wondered what horrors Soraya faced in captivity by the Brothers Zaar.

Thirty-six thousand kilometres above the Earth's surface, Soraya prayed that she would see her husband's face again. Held within a secure chamber in the Asing starship, her body seemed to tremble constantly. Her captors had casually murdered her friend Eve Taylor, and now, Soraya feared for the life of her unborn child.

These men were psychopaths, capable of anything. They referred to her husband as Armon Sakara and claimed he was guilty of treason. They even suggested that Roman came from another planet, and the emerald pendant, which he gave her as an engagement present, originated from a distant moon, called Spiro Majur.

Soraya had fainted at the flat and awoke in this strange, dark room. Had she known, that this prison lay in the bowels of an alien starship, orbiting the planet Earth, she would be hysterical.

Soraya felt drugged, and voices inside her head relentlessly asked questions upon questions upon questions. They mentioned names she did not know, such as Chi-Ro Jin and Sakara Rey, and spoke of a distant war. If Soraya failed to cooperate, the voices threatened she would be sacrificed to someone called Shon-Ghūl.

On the bridge of the vimana Su-Neku, Felani Zaar remained deeply puzzled. This Kian woman could somehow resist their mind probes. Not even their psychic storm generator yielded positive results. Felani had hoped, that by now she would have divulged the location of Armon Sakara and his protector Chi-Ro Jin. But something made her impervious to psychic interrogation. Nevertheless, this female appeared to have bonded with the Prince.

Such good fortune! She may yet prove valuable as bait.

Roman sat in silence on a tree stump, ten metres away from Chi-Ro's cloaked, invisible spacecraft. The snacks he ate had done little to alleviate his hunger or restore his strength. Increasingly paranoid, Roman feared that if he took Chi-Ro's advice and regenerated, he could be subjected to brain surgery without his consent. He could awake on an alien planet wracked by war.

Anyway, what exactly does regeneration entail? Chi-Ro and his purple-eyed friend are aliens. It's hard enough trusting people from this planet, let alone men from somewhere light years away. What if humans are just an exotic delicacy to them?

Chi-Ro had twice injected Roman with the mysterious drug elidium, without sanction. He seemed driven by his mission, and more than capable of allowing the strange Jinzou Ningen, to perform a dubious surgical procedure on Roman whether or not Roman granted permission.

Jinzou Ningen - why does that name sound so familiar? How can Chi-Ro download a human being? Are these aliens even classed as human? How long will this regeneration take anyway? I've been sitting here for almost an hour. I need to find Soraya.

As a child, Roman entertained dreams of being an astronaut. Now the thought of actually going to space filled his heart with dread.

For Soraya's sake, Roman decided he needed to trust Chi-Ro. After all, Chi-Ro had sustained grievous injuries in Roman's protection. Physically and emotionally drained, Roman grabbed his bag, rose unsteadily from the tree stump and admitted to himself that he had felt invigorated after receiving Chi-Ro's unsolicited doses of elidium.

According to Chi-Ro, the Asing are holding Soraya. With a tracking device in my skull, what hope do I have of mounting an effective rescue? Even if I managed to find Soraya, the Asing or others like them would track me to the ends of the Earth. Chi-Ro's right; the transponder has to be removed. Instead of wasting my time sitting on this tree stump, I should have regenerated.

Roman walked towards the cloaked spacecraft. The vessel recognised him and responded by making only the open doorway visible.

Suddenly Roman felt an inexplicably overwhelming urge to dive for cover. As he threw himself to the ground, an energy bolt seared through the air above him. Roman heard a high pitch shriek and quickly turned to face the source of the noise. He saw that Teev Meg had been shot in the chest.

For a confused instant, Teev Meg swayed wide-eyed, his mouth opened in a silent scream, the seared fabric of his white tunic revealing a gaping wound. Teev Meg's dark flesh had been vaporized, and Roman saw that this flesh had covered not bone but metal.

Horrified, Roman remembered, *Jinzou Ningen is Japanese for artificial human.*

Teev Meg held an unknown device in his right hand, but before he could use whatever it was, another energy bolt shot through his right eye. Teev Meg's head exploded, showering Roman with organic and synthetic material.

Roman turned towards the source of the attack; and there, to his utter disbelief, sat an Abyssinian cat - the same cat he had seen in his flat.

As Roman scrambled backwards, pondering the implications of a world where cats carried ray guns, a figure appeared out of thin air. Directly behind the pedigree feline, dressed in black and wearing a helmet, the unknown assailant stood armed with a futuristic pistol - a pistol, ominously aimed at Roman.

I should have taken Chi-Ro's advice, he thought - possibly for the last time.

Chapter 15

9:45 AM and Colindale Metropolitan Police Station buzzed with the solemnly attentive task of a fresh murder investigation. Within the small interrogation room, an exhausted Sergeant Frank Brown sat silently near the exit. He listened intently as his irritated Gov'nor - DCI Trevor Campbell painstakingly quizzed Dr. Zachary Silverman. A digital recorder on the desk in front of the academic captured every well-spoken word. The witness - Roman Doyle's thirty-year-old friend had dark hair, deep blue eyes and an athletic build, developed from sharing Roman's passion for martial arts.

Zachary's grandparents, Aharon and Hudes Silbermann, were German Ashkenazi Jews who fled Nazi Germany in November 1941 with their two children, three-year-old Zacharia and six-month-old Devorah. The Silbermann family had been very fortunate to escape Adolf Eichmann's implementation of the *Endlösung der Judenfrage* (Final Solution of the Jewish Question), which was introduced to the *Fatherland* in January of the following year.

In 1943, two years after their arrival to Great Britain, having endured racism, anti-Semitism and accusations of being a German spy, Aharon Silbermann changed his name to Aaron Silverman by a Deed of Change of Name. Similarly, Hudes became Judith, Zacharia became Zachary, and Devorah became Deborah.

In 1945, the family mourned the death of Zachary from tuberculosis. And in 1976, Deborah, a strong-willed and independent single mother, named her newborn son Zachary in memory of her beloved brother. Deborah never spoke of the boy's father. He remains a mystery to this day.

Dr. Zachary Silverman had a greater distrust of those in authority than most Britons of his generation. But in spite of his almost debilitating cynicism and unremitting suspicion, he willingly answered all of the Senior Investigating Officer's questions. Zachary had a soft spot for West Indians and felt certain that Trevor's crusty personality was just a front, annoying only if taken seriously.

With every answered question, Trevor's frustration inched towards critical levels. Roman Doyle seemed to be the only link that connected the deaths of the four police officers to Eve Taylor's brutal murder. But based on Zachary's testimony and evidence independently compiled by the police, Roman and Soraya Doyle looked more and more like the victims, not the perpetrators of crime.

A vivid picture of a loving couple devoid of even commonplace vices, such as smoking or drinking, emerged from hours of police investigation.

Soraya's newfound love of peanut butter hardly counted as an indictment of suspicious behaviour. Drug abuse or any involvement in the traffic of drugs seemed out of the question.

This apparently loving couple made the recently divorced Detective Chief Inspector sick to his stomach.

A man going out in search of peanut butter, at 1:00 AM, for his wife? Bombaclaat! Peanut butter must be the new code on the street for crack. Yeah, they look like the perfect couple, but I've been a police officer long enough to know that looks could be deceiving.

So, with eyes bloodshot from lack of sleep, DCI Trevor Campbell stared intently into Dr. Zachary Silverman's deep blue eyes and repeated his question, "Did Mrs. Doyle say why her husband wanted to meet her in Birmingham?"

"No", came Zachary's unemotional response.

That crusty personality was beginning to get annoying, despite Zachary's efforts not to take it seriously. He glanced at his Rolex watch impatiently.

Trevor added, "Mrs. Doyle's mother, Christina Williams claims that the last time she spoke to her daughter two weeks ago, there was no mention of visiting her in Birmingham."

"As I explained before, Soraya told me she had no idea why Roman wanted to meet her in Birmingham and neither do I."

Trevor stared intently at Zachary trying to find any glimmer of deception in those deep blue eyes. He could detect none.

"Dr. Silverman, as a professional and someone who knows Roman Doyle quite well, what would you say could drive him to act in the manner he did last night?"

"I wouldn't like to speculate."

"Indulge me. What about a professional opinion, a psychological evaluation?"

"You mean from the perspective of a psychiatrist?"

"Yes," Trevor responded coldly. He interpreted Zachary's hesitation as a prelude to deception.

"Since I'm a physicist and not a psychiatrist that would be ultimately useless."

Trevor's dark skin could not hide the blush, which coloured his embarrassed face.

"A physicist? I have to complement you on your impeccable taste Dr. Silverman. Nice suit. And I like the Rolex. A career in research must be very rewarding these days."

"I'm no longer involved in research. I have a Ph.D. in theoretical quantum mechanics, but I work for a financial institution in the city. I'm the senior manager of the Risk Management and Technology department."

Trevor echoed, "The senior manager of the Risk Management and Technology department."

The uncomfortable senior policeman glanced over at Sergeant Frank Brown who sat silently near the exit.

Frank said, "I didn't know physicists worked in banking."

Zachary answered, "It's not that uncommon. There are quite a few people with physics, mathematics or engineering degrees employed in the financial sector. Personally, I view trading within the money markets as fundamentally a scientific exercise. Quantifying financial risk requires strong mathematical and problem solving skills."

I need to get some sleep, thought Trevor.

Parking the Rover 25 and making his way to Colindale Metropolitan Police Station, Brakis Tarn cursed the frail body his consciousness now inhabited. It was the body of Christopher Pratt.

Most people called him Chris, including his ex-girlfriend. Several hours ago, during a raging thunderstorm, Chris knocked his ex-girlfriend senseless with a single punch and dumped her oblivious body on a pavement in Haringay. But it was not Chris's fault; Brakis Tarn made him do it.

The alien Brakis Tarn now possessed Chris's anatomy. A fall from a third floor window had left the alien's body incapacitated. Chris drove Brakis Tarn's injured physical form to his shuttlecraft, which remained effectively cloaked in Epping Forest a mere three kilometres from Chi-Ro's escape pod. There, in the seclusion of the ancient woodland, Brakis Tarn's Jinzou Ningen could repair the psychic warrior's broken body.

Brakis Tarn's former student Chi-Ro Jin had chosen an excellent location for his crash landing.

Only the Great Chi-Ro Jin would dare attack a vimana in a Talisian glider, he mused.

Chi-Ro's starglider the Starbird Adara was one of the fastest starships in the Known Universe; and on his desperate mission to locate and protect Armon Sakara, he was able to overtake Brakis Tarn's Karellan raider. But Chi-Ro's triumph was short-lived. In the vicinity of Saturn, 1.2 billion kilometres from Earth, he engaged the formidable vimana Su-Neku of the Asing.

Brakis Tarn witnessed the final conflict of the Starbird Adara from his cloaked vessel. After sustaining extensive damage to her energy shields and sensor array, the vimana finally vaporized Chi-Ro's starglider with a volley of phase torpedoes.

Chi-Ro used the massive explosion to mask his escape in a cloaked pod. But his former teacher knew his tactics well. Undetected, Brakis Tarn tracked Chi-Ro's escape pod to the shelter of Epping Forest.

There would be no escape for Chi-Ro Jin this time. Despite their best efforts, the Talisians have been unable to find an effective antidote to the psychosis virus I uploaded into his pod's memory core. I have badly injured my former disciple and to survive he would have to regenerate. How ironic to be murdered by one's Jinzou Ningen.

Having possessed the body of Christopher Pratt, Brakis Tarn entered Colindale Metropolitan Police Station on Grahame Park Way. He confidently approached the desk officer.

"Greetings, I am here to escort my sibling Dr. Zachary Silverman to his dwelling. Where is he?"

The baffled policeman asked, "Excuse me?"

Taken aback by this response, Brakis Tarn felt certain his language had been well executed. The coded transmissions he intercepted from the local law enforcement agencies clearly stated that Dr. Zachary Silverman, a close friend of Roman Doyle, was currently at this location.

At that moment, two men emerged from an adjacent room. They were DCI Trevor Campbell and Dr. Zachary Silverman.

"Thank you for your cooperation Dr. Silverman. Please be sure to notify me if you intend to leave London," came Trevor's assertion.

Before Zachary could respond, a very enraged male voice sliced through the lobby like a sonic cleaver.

"You tosser!"

Controlled by Brakis Tarn, Chris turned his head swiftly to find a hulk with a large baldhead looming inches from his face. Before Brakis Tarn could force Chris to react, a savage head-butt knocked him painfully to the floor.

Why could I not read this intention?

Focusing on the mind of his attacker, Brakis Tarn reached a startling conclusion, *there appears to be no mind to read.*

"Restrain that man, ordered Trevor.

"Chris you pillock," screamed a familiar female voice.

Wearing dark glasses to hide an unattractive black eye, Chris's ex-girlfriend Mandy Spooner had come to the police station to report last night's assault. Her brother Gary accompanied her. Three policemen, including the desk officer, rushed to control the lumbering thug.

Gary received the shock of his life when Chris leapt to his feet and delivered a barrage of expertly executed punches, swiftly followed by a devastating sidekick. As he sailed through the air, Gary's limited intellect had great difficulty fathoming how the eight-stone weakling could inflict such an impossibly powerful blow. A second later, his baldhead slammed into the front door of the police station, and he was unconscious.

Palpable silence immediately replaced the buzz of activity in the police station. For a startled moment, everything and everyone seemed frozen.

Then, as she hastily whipped off her sunglasses, Mandy screamed to everyone, "Look at my eye, that wanker did this to me!"

All eyes followed an invisible line from the tip of Mandy's pointed forefinger to a vacant-looking Chris.

Not willing to take any chances, the officer closest to the possessed Englishman reached for his extending baton.

This proved to be a catastrophic error. Chris swiftly disarmed the officer, dislocating the larger man's shoulder in the process. The officer howled in agony.

Armed with the extending baton of the policeman, and under Brakis Tarn's expert direction, Chris broke the forearm of the desk officer with a single blow. The third policeman attempted to use CS spray. But, using his right leg, Chris kicked the canister out of the policeman's hand and with his left he delivered a devastating blow to the policeman's head, knocking him unconscious.

The remaining officers, including DCI Campbell and Sergeant Frank Brown rapidly converged on Chris. Brakis Tarn had seconds to execute his plan. He focused on subduing and possessing the mind of Dr. Zachary Silverman, but to his surprise, his attempt failed.

Once more Brakis Tarn focussed his considerable psychic arsenal. This time Zachary swooned and slumped slowly to the floor.

Then an astounding revelation seared through Brakis Tarn's consciousness, *Silverman is not Kian; he is Talisian.*

The Master of Kon Jou had no time to ponder the implications of this unexpected development. The situation demanded immediate action. Chris's demeanour instantly transformed, and he stood in a relaxed manner with a bemused expression etched on his face.

He asked blankly, "What's goin' on?"

Trevor immediately silenced him with a nose crushing Kon Jou palm strike. Chris's unconscious body slammed into a wall and crumpled onto the floor of the station lobby.

The buzz returned. Shocked members of the public and journalists, who had been awaiting an official statement from Trevor, launched a wave of questions, comments and photographs.

Dr. Silverman slowly rose from the floor and brushed his fine Armani suit. Sergeant Brown offered his assistance.

"Are you alright Sir?"

"Yes, I just need some air I think," came Zachary's embarrassed response.

"Get Dr. Silverman a glass of water will you," Frank said to a young constable.

Just then, Trevor's gaze caught Zachary's. The policeman's eyes had an intensity that sent a chill down the doctor's spine. An overwhelming headache quickly followed the chill. Frank Brown grabbed Zachary's arm and prevented him from falling down.

"Easy now. The medics are on the way, maybe they ought to have a look at you."

"No, I'll be quite alright, I don't do well in crowds," Zachary lied.

"What a mess," Sergeant Brown whispered as Dr. Silverman hastily left the station.

Trevor ignored all the questions being fired at him and followed the physicist.

Zachary stumbled past a Vauxhall Zafira from the Metropolitan Police Dog Support Unit, as he staggered to his red Alfa Romeo Spider. A quick glance over his shoulder reinforced Zachary's fears. Trevor was following him. Illogical and unscientific instinct, as real as his love for life, told Zachary he had to get away from Trevor.

Something very odd had occurred in the lobby of the police station, and Trevor was at the core of it. In a fleeting moment, Zachary saw images of a terrible war, unspeakable loss of life, brutality and savagery.

"I know who you are Dr. Silverman," came the ominous voice of Trevor.

The north London scenery began to spin around him. Zachary felt his knees buckle. He slumped onto the well-polished bonnet of his Italian convertible.

A burning question now filled his mind, *where is Armon Sakara?*

It was a question he could not understand.

The excruciating pain increased. His headache became utterly unbearable. Suddenly, another voice emanated through the streets. Unlike Trevor's, this voice was frantic.

PC Graeme Lock shouted, "No Max, no!"

Max, the longhaired German Shepherd, leapt upon Trevor, knocking the large man onto the dirty pavement. At that moment, Zachary felt as if an immeasurable pressure had been lifted from his mind.

He recovered quickly, scrambled into the Spider and started the convertible's two hundred and forty brake-horsepower engine. As he made his getaway, Zachary observed that the German Shepherd had effectively kept Trevor at bay.

What the hell is going on?

Zachary could not explain how he knew it, but it was clear that his friends Roman and Soraya were in mortal peril. And perhaps, so too was he.

Chapter 16

For sixty seconds, Roman Doyle anticipated being shot. An eternity punctuated by memories of his past. Once more, in his mind's eye, Roman travelled to his favourite place - the home of the only parents he knew - Arthur and Miriam Doyle also known as Tarom and Mina Rin.

Swarms of butterflies greeted him when he opened the backdoor. Scarlet Anartia Amatheas, bright orange Gulf Fritillaries, Viceroys and Monarchs were everywhere.

Roman reverted to being a toddler again. He inhabited that carefree magical world that only children understood. A land of make-believe where only joy existed.

He looked up towards the sky. It provided a deep blue canopy, which he missed terribly as an adult living in England. Then a single Monarch landed on his cheek. It tickled. A moment passed, and it took flight again, becoming lost amongst the vibrant multitude of colourful butterflies, which surrounded him. Roman giggled.

Suddenly a strong gust of wind forced the toddler backwards onto the lawn. Horrified, he watched helplessly as the butterflies were all swept away. High above, even the clouds rolled back with tremendous speed. The blue sky became ominous grey.

Terror replaced joy. The sobs of a frightened, helpless child replaced laughter. Roman called for his mother. He saw her at the opened backdoor.

She smiled warmly and said, "Rise Armon Sakara, the ground is no place for a Talisian Prince."

Roman's jaw slackened. The motorcyclist who stood before him armed with a futuristic pistol was a woman. He could not see the individual's face hidden behind the dark visor, but the voice he heard was unmistakably female.

Chi-Ro Jin warned Roman that assassins would come, and Roman assumed they would be male. Images of mercenaries such as the Asing or fearsome warriors like Brakis Tarn flashed through his mind. He never considered a woman. Especially a woman who possessed a voice as gentle as the one he just heard.

Roman stood slowly. Anger soon replaced fear, and he resolved not to die without a fight.

The rage began. A tingling sensation crept up his spinal column to the base of his neck, and he prepared to unleash his astral entity.

The woman announced, "Your Highness, do not be alarmed. It is my mission to protect you. Please stay here."

She lowered her small pistol and gazed toward the Abyssinian cat. The animal immediately ran into the opened airlock of the space pod and the woman then turned her attention to the fallen Jinzou Ningen.

Suddenly Roman's body collapsed to the ground, releasing his spectral form.

During the second it took for the woman to consider firing, it was too late. The icy cold hands of Roman's dark entity disarmed her. His touch completely drained her strength, and she slumped to the ground next to his paralysed body. Armed with the woman's pistol, Roman's astral double swiftly followed the cat into the ship's airlock.

As Roman entered the main chamber of the spacecraft, the Abyssinian cat hissed and quickly escaped. Roman's astral form witnessed a nightmarish scene.

An alien countdown progressed. He could not understand the alien language spoken by the mechanical voice, nor the luminous orange characters that appeared on the ship's central pillar. But Roman felt certain he had to remove Chi-Ro Jin from the craft immediately.

To Roman's surprise, another Jinzou Ningen lay motionless on the floor of the pod. His head faced the wrong way. It had been twisted completely around. The artificial human's dark visage remained frozen with eyes and mouth agape as if issuing a silent scream.

In the regeneration pod, closest to where the twisted body had fallen, was Chi-Ro Jin. The veteran of the Psychic Wars had suffered a grim physical attack. His torn tunic and bruises on his neck suggested he had been strangled.

My God, is he dead?

Roman lost his concentration, and the pistol fell from his hand. A dire situation became worse. He found he could no longer maintain his astral form.

Roman battled waves of panic. He had just seconds to disable the self-destruct mechanism, before the involuntary return of his astral essence to his incapacitated body.

There were no discernible controls, and he had absolutely no idea how to prevent the ship's self-destruction. Abandoning any attempt to decipher the alien hieroglyphics, Roman tried to lift Chi-Ro hoping to haul him to safety before the ship exploded. He could not. His astral entity had begun to fade.

With rising desperation, Roman studied the large cylindrical pillar at the very centre of the ship.

Something's not right, he thought. *The gadget that Chi-Ro used - it's missing. That must be the control. Where the hell is it?*
Then he recalled the Jinzou Ningen outside the craft. *There was something in his hand.*
Struggling to maintain his astral form, Roman exited the pod.

Outside the pod, Roman immediately noticed that the woman had crawled towards the ship. As he approached, she slowly rolled on her back and removed her helmet with both hands. Roman gazed into the lime-coloured eyes of a woman in her mid-twenties. She had Mediterranean features, short dark hair and dark, tanned skin. She was strikingly beautiful.
Beauty can be a deadly weapon, he thought.
Almost imperceptibly, she said, "The self-destruct has been activated. The control device is attached to the memory core. The correct code must be spoken into it."
With a burst of astral energy, Roman gave his form more substance and retrieved the device from the grasp of the headless Jinzou Ningen.
He turned to the woman and demanded, "What is the code?"
The eerily deep voice of his astral body sent a chill down her spine.
"The code is known only to the ship's commander. The core will respond only to the commander's voice. Only Chi-Ro Jin can disarm the self-destruct."
Roman cried, "I think Chi-Ro is dead."
"Then so are we. In exactly 90 seconds, the ship and everything within one kilometre will be vaporised."

Roman experienced an all too familiar sensation. It featured many times in his recurring nightmares - a desperate need to run, in a body that failed to respond. Roman's disembodied essence had legs that were made of lead. At least, that's the way they felt as he re-entered the airlock of Chi-Ro Jin's spacepod.
The metallic grey regeneration unit reminded Roman of a sarcophagus. Within it, lay the unmoving form of the Master of Hatari Ikou.
When Chi-Ro read my mind, he held my temples with both hands. I can't risk touching him in this form. It seems I drain energy from those I touch. If he's still alive, touching him may kill him.
Roman knew he had to read the Talisian's mind whilst maintaining his astral manifestation. It would take too long for his physical body to recover from temporary paralysis. Unsure how he should proceed, Roman listened to the relentless progress of the alien countdown.

I'll just have to trust my intuition, he thought.

Thirty seconds elapsed when suddenly an almost inaudible gasp escaped Chi-Ro's lips. First Roman saw very quick flashes of light in his mind's eye. Then alien voices echoed unintelligible phrases.

Finally, he could see and hear Chi-Ro's thoughts. Roman had a depressing realisation.

He thinks in Talisian. I have no idea what he's thinking.

Roman concentrated on making sense out of what he saw and felt, not what he heard.

Roman swiftly relived Chi-Ro's experiences of the last half hour. He learnt that the first Jinzou Ningen, Teev Meg, had successfully performed the procedure required to treat Chi-Ro's life-threatening injuries. Teev Meg activated the pod's regeneration process, and this triggered a second Jinzou Ningen called Teev Yergoo. Teev Yergoo appeared out of nowhere.

Whilst Chi-Ro lay helplessly sedated, Teev Yergoo brutally attacked Teev Meg. He savagely wrenched Teev Meg's neck. A lifeless Teev Meg fell to the floor with his head facing his back.

Chi-Ro barked unintelligible orders in Talisian. Teev Yergoo delivered a devastating punch to the powerless warrior. The dark features and purple eyes of the android became a mask of pure hatred. Infected by the Karellan psychosis virus, Teev Yergoo strangled Chi-Ro Jin.

Systems within the ship suddenly came to life. Characters appeared on the metallic interior of the craft and the ship's computer voice spoke, but Roman could not understand what it said.

Teev Yergoo's purple eyes widened with surprise when a holographic image of the Abyssinian cat appeared. He observed the approach of the golden brown pedigree to the cloaked spacecraft and became hysterical. He hastily aborted Chi-Ro's suffocation, quickly grabbing a hypodermic needle from the small operating table. He callously ripped open Chi-Ro's tunic and plunged the needle into his exposed chest.

Ignoring Chi-Ro's convulsions, Teev Yergoo removed the rectangular control device from the ship's central pillar and barked a command into it.

The robot activated the self-destruct, not Chi-Ro. Only the robot can de-activate it. And the robot had his sick head blown to bits. There is no way he will ever speak again. This is hopeless.

As Roman focussed on the alien words extracted from Chi-Ro's mind, he had an idea.

Wait a minute; Teev Yergoo and Teev Meg seem identical. Maybe Teev Meg can be re-activated somehow. Or maybe, I can find a way to speak with his voice.

Roman activated the alien ship's control unit and placed it on the floor next to Teev Meg's mouth. He used all his remaining willpower and mental energy to force his dark entity into the lifeless body of Teev Meg. Roman suddenly experienced shocking cold. The android immediately vomited and its body continued to twitch.

The cold burns... I can feel myself fading. I'm fading fast. Teev Yergoo activated the self-destruct. Ten seconds to oblivion. Think... What did Teev Yergoo say?

Roman did not see the woman enter the ship, and he did not see her pick up the gun; but he saw her take aim and knew he could not stop her from doing what she was about to do.

Out of energy and almost out of time, Roman cried with the voice of the artificial human, "Jinzou Ningen, mavala ti nava seti."

The countdown did not stop.

Five seconds. I have to get it right this time.

"Jinzou Ningen. Marala ti nara seti," came another outburst from Roman in the body of Teev Meg.

The woman stood silently above the fallen android and fired, her deadly aim perfect. The energy bolt from the alien pistol seared through Teev Meg's skull. His purple eyes became flame red, seconds before his head exploded. The countdown stopped on the final character, plunging the ship into cold silence. The self-destruct sequence had been deactivated.

Chapter 17

Inside the escape pod, the mysterious woman quickly holstered her pistol within her black leather jacket. At her feet lay the lifeless body of the Jinzou Ningen called Teev Meg. His head had been blown to bits.

The woman immediately focused her attention on the unconscious Chi-Ro Jin. She turned the warrior's left hand palm-side up, and then placed the first two fingers of her right hand along the outer edge of his left wrist, just below where his wrist and thumb met. There she found Chi-Ro's almost undetectable pulse. Symbols on his regeneration unit confirmed that the Master of Hatari Ikou was dying. The woman picked up a device equipped with a hypodermic needle - the same device Teev Yergoo used to inject Chi-Ro.

She removed a small glass vial from the device and observed that most of the pale yellow liquid it contained had been spent. As she studied the alien symbols etched in the tube, her beautiful features registered deep concern. A dark reflection slowly appeared in the glass.

With incredible speed, she turned, throwing the vial towards Roman who had silently entered the ship. With his right hand, Roman caught the transparent receptacle centimetres from his face. When he lowered his hand, he saw that the woman had already drawn her pistol and taken deadly aim.

"Get away from him," Roman ordered.

"Who are you?" the woman asked.

"Apparently, I'm your Highness."

"Prince Armon, had I not witnessed it with my very eyes, I would not have believed it. You possess the power of darkness. Just as Ne-Ro Jos has foretold."

Roman laughed briefly then said, "I'm no demon. I'm only a schoolteacher."

"Then it would seem that schoolteachers have great power," the woman responded.

"Give me the gun."

"Your Highness, I am Nuri Nemsys and right now, you must trust me."

Nuri holstered her pistol and turned her attention to Chi-Ro.

Roman asked, "Is that your name, or a title? What are you doing?"

"Saving his life."

She placed another vial into the hypodermic device, intent on injecting Chi-Ro with it.

Roman barked, "Stop."

"He will die," protested Nuri.

Roman gently placed his fingertips on Chi-Ro's temples and said, "There's another way."

"What are you doing?"

"Saving his life."

"But..."

"Be quiet."

Roman focussed his thoughts. That now familiar sensation appeared at the bottom of his spine - the tingling of intense psychic energy. Roman's hands began to shake. He closed his eyes and grimaced as his entire being experienced the strain of profound exertion.

A single tear trickled down Roman's left cheek, and suddenly a deep gasp escaped Chi-Ro's pale lips.

Roman took his hands away from Chi-Ro's head and swooned. Nuri grabbed him, preventing his fall.

"I'm OK."

Nuri looked down upon the face of Chi-Ro. He had begun to regain consciousness.

"Commander Chi-Ro, can you hear me?"

Chi-Ro Jin replied weakly, "I wish to speak with the Prince."

"I'm right here," Roman declared.

"Master Armon, you must promise never to risk your life in this manner again. I am expendable, you are not."

"You're welcome. Just hang in there."

"How and why do you propose I hang in such a confined space?"

Roman shook his head, about to walk away, when Chi-Ro grabbed his forearm, pulled him close and whispered in his ear, "Thank you for saving my life, Master Armon."

"You'd do the same for me."

"Now tell me, who is that woman?"

I can't get these strange thoughts out of my mind, Dr. Zachary Silverman realised.

He sped his red Alfa Romeo Spider towards Waltham Cross, nervously checking his mirrors to ensure he had not been followed. The cigarette he smoked did little to calm his nerves.

Somehow when DCI Campbell said he knew who I was, I had the feeling he wasn't talking about my Ph.D. or my Jewish heritage. He's after someone called Armon Sakara and when I think of that name all I see is Roman's face.

Zachary remained completely unaware that two unmarked police cars followed him. Trevor drove alone in his metallic grey Rover 75, closely accompanied by PC Amanda Powley driving a dark blue Ford Mondeo 24v. Sergeant Frank Brown occupied the passenger seat.

Amanda said to Frank, "Pardon me for asking Sir, but what was that all about back at the station?"

"You mean the lass with the black eye?"

"No I mean the Shakespeare."

"Sorry Amanda, I don't think I quite follow you."

Impersonating Trevor's booming voice, she said, "Let the scribes record it." Then speaking normally, she added, "You'd swear he was reading from stone tablets."

"I'm sorry PC Powley, I wasn't aware Shakespeare carved his work in stone."

"Make haste, we must pursue Dr. Zachary Silverman, he may lead us to the fugitive Roman Doyle. Police Sergeant Frank Brown, Police Constable Amanda Powley, you must assist me at once. It is imperative that we remain undetected. A vehicle without law enforcement insignia is required."

"Now that's enough young lady, and that's not exactly what DCI Campbell said."

"He's been hitting the wacky tobaccy if you ask me."

"There'll be no more of that talk," said Frank sternly, "The Gov'nor just needs a good night's sleep. By the way, just for your education, it was Moses who had stone tablets, not Shakespeare."

"Must've been a helluva headache," said Amanda with a smile.

"You see, that's the problem with youngsters your age, no respect. No knowledge or appreciation of anything that took place before 1980. I bet you couldn't tell me who Winston Churchill was."

"Of course I know who Winston Churchill was."

"Go on then."

"He's the bloke who invented car insurance."

Frank stared silently at Amanda and shook his head with dismay. Amanda kept her eyes fixed on the road. After a moment of thick silence, the sergeant sighed deeply.

Amanda laughed and impersonating Winston Churchill, she said, "We will fight on beaches, on landing grounds, in fields, and in streets. We will fight in the hills and in the Mondeo. We will never ever surrender!" Then speaking normally, she added, "Some of us youngsters have grandparents and some of them are even older than you, Sir."

"Watch it," Frank warned.

The instrumental ringtone of Zachary's mobile phone interrupted the reassuring growl of the Alfa Romeo's 240bhp 3.2-litre engine. The phone was tucked in his inside jacket pocket.

He said to himself, "Shit," and fumbled to reach within the pocket with his right hand.

Zachary's seatbelt made the manoeuvre difficult, and he struggled to steer with his left hand.

Zachary managed to retrieve the phone, seconds before swerving to avoid a collision with a white transit van coming in the opposite direction.

He could faintly hear obscenities shouted by the white van man as he answered the phone, "Hello?"

"Zach?" came a familiar voice through the earpiece.

"Roman! Where the hell are you? England is looking for you."

"Zach, there's no time to explain, you have to meet me in Epping Forest."

"It's your lucky day, I happen to be headed that way. Roman, Eve is dead."

"I know."

"Is Soraya with you?"

"No, that's why I need your help."

"Epping's a bit bigger than a cricket pitch. Any chance of more precise directions?"

"Follow the beep."

"The beep? What beep?"

"And Zach, this is important, make sure no one follows you. Trust no one. I'll explain everything when I see you."

"What beep?"

The call disconnected abruptly. Zachary placed the mobile in a hands-free cradle on the dashboard.

What beep? Is it me, or is the whole world going mad?

Suddenly, the ringtone played again.

Zachary pressed the phone's call button and answered, "Hello?"

A very loud beep broke the silence.

What the hell is this?

The beeps from the mobile phone slowly increased in regularity, as Zachary approached Epping Forest.

It's a homing device. How is Roman doing this?

Outside the cloaked escape pod, Roman returned the futuristic communications device to Nuri.

"Thank you, that's a very funky phone you've got there."

His dry humour seemed lost on the tanned woman who declared, "Your friend cannot accompany us to Talis."

"He's my friend, I know him. I don't know you. Talis can wait. First, I have to find my wife."

A sudden gust of wind gave Roman a chill. He instinctively looked up to the sky. Strange, dark clouds materialised out of thin air, darkening the sun.

"Prince Armon, we must leave at once."

"Looks like we have company. Did you use your funky phone to call your friends?"

Drawing her pistol, Nuri said, "The artificial human must have activated the pod's homing beacon."

"Put the gun away. You won't need it. I surrender."

"Your Highness, what you see above you is a cloaked vimana. It is the war vessel used by the Asing."

"Yeah, I've met those guys before."

"Then you know that they intend to kill you."

"Well, they'll certainly try."

"You must trust me. It is my sworn duty to protect you."

"Trust you? You shot me."

"I had no way of knowing you had possessed the artificial human."

"Do you often shoot first and ask questions later?

"The ship's systems, including the artificial humans, had been compromised. I've had several negative experiences with artificial humans in the past. I do not trust them. When you took my viridian pistol, I felt that perhaps you had been compromised as well."

"Do I look like an android?"

"Your behaviour seemed irrational. You attacked me."

"Before you even introduced yourself, you pointed a gun at me. This is England. You can get hung, drawn and quartered for pointing a gun at a prince. Count yourself lucky all I did was take your ray gun away."

"With all due respect Prince Armon, again I am baffled by your illogical behaviour. The Asing will be here at any moment. Perhaps you are experiencing shock."

"I haven't been myself lately."

"If you have not been Armon Sakara, then who have you been?" asked Chi-Ro, exiting the cloaked escape pod.

"Nice to see you up and about, Chi-Ro. Nuri, are the Asing able to blast us from the air?"

"No, their weapons will not function."

"So they'll have to get down here, face to face."

"Yes Your Highness."

Chi-Ro added, "Master Armon, the Asing will not rest until you are dead."

"Then I'll be dead. Nuri, is there a stun setting on your gun?"

"No Prince Armon, we are at war and you will find that, in my hands, the viridian pistol is a most lethal weapon."

"Yes, the two headless robots would testify to that. Good, I'll just sit here then."

Roman sat on the ground. Nuri could not mask her utter astonishment. Chi-Ro asked her, "Where did you get this weapon?"

"Commander Chi-Ro, surely you have heard of me."

"Yes, Nuri Nemsys, your exploits are legendary. Few have seen your face and lived to talk of it. You are a mercenary, reputed to be an efficient spy and deadly assassin. It surprises me that my Lord, the True Emperor, would recruit one such as you to protect his only son."

"Desperate times call for desperate measures."

Without warning, Roman slumped to the floor.

Nuri immediately put on her futuristic helmet and reached within her black leather jacket.

Chi-Ro cried, "Master Armon."

"Don't move," said the woman with her gun aimed at Chi-Ro's chest, "I poisoned the Prince. He is dead, and you are now my prisoner."

In a clearing at the edge of the forest, Dr. Zachary Silverman parked his red Alfa Romeo next to the Ford Mondeo Estate stolen by Chi-Ro Jin. This is where the increasing beeps from the mobile phone had led him.

Zachary got out of the convertible and quickly took in his secluded surroundings.

With the mobile phone in his outstretched right hand, he listened for subtle changes in the intensity of the beeps and followed the trail created by Chi-Ro and Roman hours before.

Gradually, an ominous darkness covered the forest. Zachary looked towards the shrouded sun and marvelled at the strange clouds that formed overhead. He wondered what surprises awaited him in the ancient forest, which once served as Dick Turpin's hideout.

Moments later, DCI Trevor Campbell parked his grey Rover 75 next to Zachary's Alfa Romeo. Trevor came out of the car and stared intently at the fresh tracks Roman's friend had made.

A minute later, PC Amanda Powley brought the dark blue Ford Mondeo to a halt in the clearing beside the Rover.

As they left the Mondeo and walked to where Trevor stood, Amanda told Sergeant Frank Brown, "I think it's going to rain again, Sir."

Before Frank could respond, Trevor turned quickly to the officers and declared, "Dr. Zachary Silverman intends to meet with Roman Doyle not far from here."

"Sir?" said Frank in bewilderment.

"Sergeant Frank Brown, Police Constable Amanda Powley, you are to follow this trail. I am certain it will lead you to the fugitives."

Then, Trevor turned and started walking off to the left.

"Excuse me Gov'nor, but where are you going?"

"Do you believe details of my destination will assist you in carrying out your orders, Sergeant Frank Brown?"

Frank looked into Trevor's eyes and felt a chill run down his spine.

He swallowed and answered meekly, "No Sir."

"Then proceed."

"Yes Sir."

Frank and Amanda set off into the forest in pursuit of Zachary.

Amanda whispered, "May the scribes record it."

"Shut it," whispered Frank.

Amanda chuckled.

For a moment, Trevor observed their progress before walking off to the left. He followed a different trail - one that had been created by Brakis Tarn.

Chapter 18

Chi-Ro Jin peered down the barrel of the viridian pistol aimed at his chest. He tried to probe the mind of the woman holding the deadly weapon but found that he could not. Instead, he glared at Nuri Nemsys defiantly.

On the ground, next to the treacherous assassin, lay Roman Doyle also known as Prince Armon Sakara. Blood seeped from the Prince's nostrils.

I have failed. The Prince is dead, and all is lost, Chi-Ro thought.

"You will regret this act of treachery," he growled venomously.

Nuri calmly responded, "Perhaps one day you will find it in your heart to forgive me, Chi-Ro Jin."

Chi-Ro remained silent.

Suddenly, a sound like distant thunder reverberated from the dark sky and three bolts of blue light shot from grey clouds to the forest below.

DCI Trevor Campbell opened his eyes and saw a dark, cloudy sky obscured by a thick canopy of dense foliage. Trevor had awoken from what he thought was a disturbing dream, to find himself lying on his back below a pollarded Beech tree.

Trevor sat upright and looked around the misty forest.

Am I still dreaming? Where am I?

Trevor noticed movement to his right. To his surprise, a large blond man dressed in a purple tunic, stepped out of an invisible doorway. The blond strode towards Trevor, prompting him to slowly rise to his feet. Trevor felt weak and disorientated.

Staring into piercing blue eyes, Trevor asked, "Where am I?"

The man replied, "You are where I brought you."

"Who are you?"

"I am Brakis Tarn."

"What am I doing here?"

"Dying."

Trevor fell to the floor and convulsed. His lungs no longer functioned. The level of carbon dioxide in his bloodstream rose steadily until finally, starved of oxygen, his brain ceased to function. Under a Beech tree, in the heart of Epping Forest, DCI Trevor Campbell died.

Following the trail left by Dr. Zachary Silverman, Sergeant Frank Brown and PC Amanda Powley could hear a repetitive beep in the distance.

Amanda asked Frank, "What do you think it is?"

Frank whispered, "Shhh... Just keep your wits about you."

The pair continued their trek until suddenly the beeping sound stopped.

Frank announced, "Come on, he can't be far," and his brisk walk quickly became a trot.

Jogging to keep up, Amanda said, "Maybe Ranking Trevor caught up with him."

Frank said, "That's Detective Chief Inspector to you, Missy."

Before Amanda could respond, Frank screamed in agony and fell to the ground holding his ankle.

"Did you twist it?" asked Amanda rushing to his side.

"No, I've been bitten."

"Bitten by what?"

"I think it was a snake. A bleedin' adder!"

Amanda drew her extending baton instinctively.

"What are you planning on doing with that? Call a bleedin' ambulance," Frank ordered.

Amanda turned to Frank. Her face had a blank expression.

Frank asked, "What are you waiting for?"

With a swift movement, Amanda delivered a devastating blow to the side of Frank's neck.

The police sergeant immediately crumpled to the ground. His struggle to breathe abruptly ended when Amanda struck him again, this time at the back of his head.

Amanda ignored Frank's dying breath. With a vacant expression still etched on her face, her police baton slipped from her hand, falling at her feet. Then, Amanda's staring eyes suddenly rolled back, and she collapsed.

PC Amanda Powley died of a massive ruptured cerebral aneurysm - several arteries within her brain had spontaneously haemorrhaged.

Slowly walking past the dead bodies, Pencha Zaar smiled callously. He thoroughly enjoyed terminating Kian law enforcement agents. They seemed remarkably predisposed to following orders, even if the orders directed them to self-destruct.

His older brothers, Kirato and Tonn, treated murder with indifference. To them, the police officers were simply in the wrong place at the wrong time.

They would only serve to complicate our mission to retrieve Armon Sakara, they thought.

Instinct kept Zachary alive. He had heard movement within the forest and thought it wise to switch off his mobile phone and hide below a dense shrub.

From his hiding place, he saw two police officers approach - a young woman and an older man. Suddenly the man screamed and fell to the ground. Then to Zachary's horror, the policewoman battered the male officer to death with her baton.

He resolved to intervene when he noticed three Oriental men approximately ten metres behind the police.

Wondering why he had not noticed these men before, an overwhelming feeling of dread cautioned Zachary. The same feeling he experienced during his encounter with DCI Trevor Campbell.

Zachary had been trained to defend himself. Like his close friend Roman, Zachary had third dan black belts in both Shotokan Karate and Taekwondo. But somehow he knew martial arts would not be enough to deal with these three men.

The female officer collapsed, confirming Zachary's fears. He knew the woman had died, and the three men had somehow caused her death.

Waves of panic threatened to overcome Zachary as the Brothers Zaar walked towards his hiding place. He hoped that Roman was nearby.

Perhaps together we could deal with these three, he thought.

Intent on making his escape, Zachary turned only to find himself face to face with the golden brown Abyssinian cat. The cat's almond-shaped green eyes were centimetres from his own deep blue eyes.

Suddenly the cat's pupils dilated, and Zachary heard an ominous female voice, *"If you wish to live, do not speak, do not breathe and do not think."*

What? thought Zachary.

The female voice in his head said, *"I see you wish to die, which is why you have proceeded to ignore my instructions."*

Zachary asked mentally, *"Who are you?"*

"Death whispers your name to me."

Zachary held his breath and focussed on clearing his mind. He visualised an extremely bright light. The light became a sun, the sun a flame, and the flame - nothing.

The three brothers walked past Zachary and the Abyssinian cat, completely unaware of their presence.

Chapter 19

Within the small, secure chamber on the Asing starship, Soraya Doyle felt nauseous. She experienced a sensation very similar to the feeling she had, while riding a high-speed elevator to the eighty-sixth floor observation deck, of New York's Empire State Building. However, this experience felt far more sudden.

It took just over a second for the vimana Su-Neku to descend from its geostationary orbit thirty-six thousand kilometres above the Earth's surface, to hover above London's Epping Forest. Thick, dark, artificially produced rain clouds shrouded the pulsating orange glow of the electromagnetic flux produced by the alien craft.

Soraya remained unaware that the Asing held her captive, in what the news would later describe as an unidentified flying object, high above Epping Forest.

"It's okay Moses," she whispered to her unborn child, feeling a single tear trickle down her dark cheek, "Everything will be alright Darling, Daddy will find us."

The door to her cell slid open, causing Soraya to shriek. The threatening figure of Mika Zaar entered the chamber. Soraya backed defensively into a corner shaking with fear.

Mika projected telepathically, *"Soon you will be re-united with your bond. We have located the traitor, Armon Sakara. May the Winged Serpent, Lord of the power of the air, find your sacrifice pleasing."*

"You think you could scare me with your Obeah tricks? God protects me."

"I know not this God, of which you speak; but rest assured, soon you will..."

Mika experienced a sharp pain in his head. He stared deeply into Soraya's brown eyes, attempting to extract answers from her resistant mind. Despite Soraya's best efforts, a vivid mental flash revealed the Doyle secret to her sinister captor.

Life stirs within the womb of this Kian female. Armon Sakara has an heir.

Zachary opened his eyes and saw a strange sight. Directly above, were the darkest, most ominous rain clouds, he had ever seen. It took him a moment to remember that he was in Epping Forest intent on finding his friend Roman Doyle.

Why am I lying on the ground, did I faint?

With the sun effectively masked, the forest became quite dark, and the mournful wail of the wind rushing towards the peculiar phenomenon in the sky, had become the only discernible sound.

Disturbing images of recent events flooded Zachary's mind. Shocked, he began to doubt his faculties; it was not the first time and unlikely to be the last.

For several years, Zachary remained adamant he had been abducted and examined by extraterrestrials. Only his mother and the psychiatrist, who counselled him, knew this potentially embarrassing secret.

But eventually, with the help of these women, he became convinced that his experiences were elaborate fantasies, hallucinations and dreams brought on by electromagnetic pollution, a vivid imagination and an almost overwhelming desire to be special.

Growing up without a father and with a sense of profound rejection had created a young man who desperately yearned to be special. Zachary imagined, or perhaps hoped; that the father he never knew was from a distant more advanced world.

In time, his alien abduction fantasies had become dim memories. That is, until his meeting with DCI Trevor Campbell this morning. Zachary felt that he had been the victim of a violent psychic assault by the policeman; and then, there was that business with the cat.

Zachary rose slowly and looked around but could not see any sign of the Abyssinian cat.

Perhaps the homing beacon received by my mobile phone, created an unusually powerful electromagnetic field, a field powerful enough to cause hallucination. Either that or I've finally lost my mind. I just had a telepathic conversation with a pedigree cat. I suppose it's true what Roman says, "You're never alone with schizophrenia."

His urge to laugh faded, when Zachary noticed the dead bodies of the two police officers. Fresh footprints created a trail that led to a very large Oak tree in the distance. The tree had been split in two as if broken asunder by a giant axe.

Jogging towards the great Oak were the three strange men. From Zachary's point of view, they now seemed to have bladed weapons in each hand. Without warning, one veered right, the other left and the last kept his bearing towards the damaged tree.

Roman. They're going to kill Roman, Zachary thought.

Giving chase, Zachary immediately felt the exhilarating effects of adrenaline. Like a predator, he focussed on the remaining man who kept to the track. Zachary hoped the howling wind masked his approach and granted him the element of surprise. However, these were not ordinary men. On the path, Pencha Zaar slowed down to walking pace and suddenly stopped. He casually looked over his right shoulder and smiled at Zachary, running as fast as he could towards him.

Zachary immediately began having difficulty breathing, and fell to the ground gasping for breath.

He rolled onto his back struggling for life. Above him, almost completely hidden by the dark clouds, he saw an object he believed only existed in his dreams - a flying saucer with an amber glow. It was the last thing Zachary saw, before slipping into oblivion with a bemused smile etched on his face.

With snake-like stealth, the two brothers silently emerged from the shadows of the forest. Tonn Zaar stood before Nuri Nemsys whose viridian pistol remained aimed at Chi-Ro Jin's chest. A few metres behind the woman stood Kirato Zaar. The two Asing were baffled.

"Where is Pencha?"

"I am here," came his psychic response.

Pencha revealed himself. He stood to the left of Nuri, closest to Roman's fallen body. His face visibly scarred.

"Did you run into a tree, young one?" projected Kirato.

"I encountered a strange, indigenous creature. I believe it is called a miw."

"Ah, the ancient enemy of the serpent: the cat," projected Tonn.

"Drop your weapons," barked Nuri, moving to the right, switching her aim from Chi-Ro to the brothers and back again.

Pencha laughed, *"Should we tell this fool that phase weapons do not function here?"*

"This is not a phase weapon. Drop your weapons, if you wish to live."

"We have come to claim Armon Sakara, dead or alive. Give him up or face the consequences," declared Pencha, sporting an annoying grin.

"The name is Roman Doyle," said Nuri through gritted teeth. Intent on firing a warning shot, she aimed above Pencha's head and squeezed the trigger of the pistol. Nothing happened. She tried again but to no avail.

"Shit."

Nuri threw the gun to the ground, engaged her personal cloaking device and vanished.

"Ha," came Pencha's defiant response.

Chi-Ro took advantage of the unexpected diversion. Reaching into his dark tunic, he spun on his heel, unleashing several shuriken-like bladed objects at the Brothers Zaar. All three evaded the deadly darts by throwing themselves to the ground, but they sprang upright in an instant and assumed Nyoka Sentou ready stances. Their formidable blades shimmered in the subdued light.

The arrogant Pencha fell first, swept by an unseen leg. He went berserk with rage. Rising quickly, he sliced through thin air with surprising speed, and to an uninformed onlooker, Pencha appeared immersed in the elaborate kata of an obscure martial art.

Pencha fought a futile battle against the forest mist, leaving Kirato and Tonn to engage Chi-Ro Jin.

Hatari Ikou, the Way of Matchless Power executed by its consummate Master, proved too much for the snake worshippers.

Chi-Ro became a deadly tornado of whirlwind punches, somersault kicks and devastating close-quarter strikes, which employed his elbows and knees. Tonn fell to the ground grasping a fractured sternum. Then, from the horizon of his subconscious mind, came a relentless riptide of fear - a fear of death, callously suggested by Chi-Ro's intrusive imagination.

Chi-Ro savagely disarmed Kirato, subjecting him to a blistering eighteen-strike assault. The eighteenth blow: a palm strike to Kirato's forehead, so powerful that Kirato flipped upside down, violently smashing his head into the ground. The hulking snake-worshipper's powerful neck saved him from certain death as the full weight of his body descended onto it.

Wasting no time, and intent on terminating his unconscious foe, Chi-Ro picked up one of the large Asing blades; but an invisible kick sent him reeling backwards onto the ground.

Pencha immediately propelled himself with razor-sharp blades poised to deliver a deathblow to Chi-Ro. But, an unexpected kick from Nuri flipped the Mara Kai renegade in midair. He crashed to the ground, fortunate not to have impaled himself.

Chi-Ro leapt to his feet and assumed the Hatari Ikou ready stance.

"You, Zaar, offspring of a most disreputable female, I have reserved your education for last," he promised Pencha.

Nuri said, "Yeah, he's a son of a bitch, but I need him alive."

Pencha employed years of mental discipline to counter the images and suggestions of defeat projected by Chi-Ro. Despite the howling wind, the Asing could discern almost imperceptible sound and movement. He spoke as his eyes settled on the position of his cloaked target. Nuri stood close to Roman's body.

Pencha shouted, "Insults are easily spoken when hidden behind a veil of invisibility."

He hurled his blade at the woman with malice, but Roman, already in motion before Pencha, caught the lethal weapon centimetres from Nuri's exposed neck. A moment later, Nuri deactivated her stealth shroud as the cloak of invisibility was called.

Looking into Roman's chestnut eyes, she could not mask her disappointment.

Nuri said, "You violated me."

Roman wiped away the trickle of blood that seeped from his nose and said, "Yes... That was a mistake; I should have trusted you."

"Master you are alive," exclaimed Chi-Ro, "My suspicions have been confirmed, you took possession of this woman's body."

"Sorry I didn't let you both in on my little ruse."

"So the bastard of Sakara Rey lives," Pencha spat, "Your consort Soraya has provided me with hours of..."

Before the Asing could finish his sentence or project imagery of the most deranged sexual violation, Roman had already launched his attack. Pencha narrowly avoided Roman's blade as the intensity of the assault drove him backwards into the hull of the cloaked spaceship.

What sorcery is this? thought Chi-Ro, *The Prince has gained knowledge of Hatari Ikou.*

At that point, Tonn attempted to rise and assist his youngest brother. Chi-Ro casually thwarted that plan with a well-placed sidekick to Tonn's head. The man's brain twisted on its stem, disrupting the vital flow of oxygenated blood. He was unconscious before his body hit the ground.

Nuri picked up her pistol from the ground and declared, "I will put a stop to this madness."

Chi-Ro calmly said, "There are things which must be done if a man is to consider himself a man. Protecting the honour of his consort is such a thing. Let us grant the Prince an opportunity to teach this impertinent mongrel a lesson."

"By your judgement, I will allow it."

The Way of Matchless Power chastised, harassed and humiliated the serpent warrior until Pencha Zaar began to accept defeat at the hands of his royal rival.

A lapse in concentration and an error in judgement allowed Pencha to be disarmed by Roman. Armed with both Asing blades, Roman now had an overwhelming advantage but chose to discard it. To the astonishment of his opponent, Roman threw the lethal weapons to the ground and wiped away the blood from his nosebleed with the back of his hand.

Pencha smiled, *"You foolish..."*

Once again Roman stopped Pencha in mid-sentence. This time, with a devastating slap to his right cheek; then another and another, swiftly followed by a back-fist from Roman's right hand smashing his nose.

Pencha raised his arms in defence only to have two fingers on his right hand broken by a swift Muay Thai kick. The Asing howled in agony and retaliated with a swift Jai Zou kick. Roman evaded the blow and in a fluid movement delivered a sweep, which sent Pencha crashing to the ground on his back.

The mercenary rose quickly to receive blows so swift that only the sound of fists, elbows and knees savagely impacting against his face, ribcage, solar plexus and groin gave any indication that he had been struck.

The agony of broken ribs brought the former Mara Kai monk to his knees, whereupon Roman launched himself into the air and delivered a devastating elbow strike on Pencha's forehead. The powerful blow savagely drove the man's fractured skull violently into the ground. Miraculously, Pencha was unconscious but alive.

"Excellent," said Chi-Ro.

Suddenly surprised and somewhat embarrassed by the savagery of his attack, Roman wondered if he truly intended to kill his opponent.

To draw the focus of all present away from his loss of temper, Roman turned his attention to Nuri, holding her viridian pistol at her side.

"Nuri your ray gun does not work."

"No your Highness, the weapon functions perfectly."

To prove her point, like an American Wild West gunfighter, Nuri quickly shot both Pencha and Tonn.

She coldly added, "I simply removed the lapys viridian crystal."

Then casually, Nuri took deadly aim at Kirato who remained unconscious.

Roman screamed, "Stop! What are you doing?"

"My duty, Your Highness."

"What is wrong with you? You killed them."

"Precisely; I vaporised both their hearts."

"I can't believe you murdered those men."

"Master Armon," said Chi-Ro, "We are at war. Furthermore, the Asing in the craft above will no doubt scan for life forms. They expect to detect three brothers and you as their prize. Four individuals."

"You agree with Calamity Jane?"

Motioning to the unconscious Kirato, Chi-Ro asked, "Did you not prevent me from beheading this one?"

"Insane; you are both insane."

"Your attitude surprises me Master Armon. Audio-visual transmissions from Ki are rife with all manner of murder and acts of violence. It suggests a cultural preoccupation with death and killing."

"I don't look at TV," Roman lied.

"That is unfortunate. If you did, I suspect you would be better prepared for what lies ahead."

Suddenly, Nuri turned her upper body swiftly and took aim with her technologically advanced handgun.

Zachary stood transfixed with his arms held high.

"Do not shoot," Roman ordered.

Nuri lowered her weapon.

"It's okay Zach."

"Are you sure? I had the feeling I came at a bad time. Are you wearing contact lenses?"

"No; it's a long story. Listen, Soraya is in danger."

"Okay; so, where is Soraya?"

Roman said, "She was in orbit." Then Roman pointed to the mysterious clouds above and added, "Now she's in there."

"Typical; tell a woman to meet you in Birmingham, and she ends up in outer-space."

"I have to get her back, and I could use your help."

"I'm happy to help, but getting her down from up there may be a tad tricky. There's a flying saucer in those clouds, and I get the feeling it's not British."

"Zach, maybe you ought to sit down."

"I'm a big boy, I can take it."

"Let me introduce you to Chi-Ro Jin. Chi-Ro this is my good friend Dr. Zachary Silverman."

Zachary offered his hand to shake, but Chi-Ro ignored it and simply bowed.

"And this is Nuri Nemsys."

Nuri did not remove her dark helmet. Zachary tried unsuccessfully to see the face behind the visor. She silently offered her hand to shake, and the quantum physicist gripped it firmly.

"Pleased to meet you, Mr. Nemesis."

"It's a woman," Roman whispered before adding loudly, "Nuri and Chi-Ro have insisted on protecting me from the individuals lying on the ground."

Zachary turned to the aliens and said, "You've done a fine job. Now I need to speak to my friend in private, is that okay?"

Nuri declared, "We are here to protect and serve His Highness."

Chi-Ro bowed, maintained eye contact and said, "You can have privacy within my escape pod."

He removed the control device from his tunic and deactivated the ship's cloaking device, immediately revealing the Talisian spacecraft. The shock almost caused Zachary to pass out a second time.

Roman grabbed his friend by the arm and said, "Come with me Zach, let's talk."

"I can't go in there," whispered Zachary.

"It's okay, trust me."

"No Roman, I'm telling you I can't go in there, let's just go behind the ship."

"Whatever you say."

As the two men walked to the side of the craft, the Abyssinian cat emerged from the trail leading to the great Oak tree. It scampered towards Nuri.

Zach said, "I had a conversation with that cat a little while ago."

"Did you?"

"Yes Roman, I did."

"Odd, it hasn't spoken to me."

Chapter 20

On the bridge of the vimana Su-Neku, Felani Zaar's mental faculties directly connected to the ship's systems by means of the command helmet. This impressive device, integrated into a life supporting regeneration pod, amplified the wearer's will, allowing that individual limitless control over all of the vessel's key systems.

With his thoughts amplified, in this manner, Felani had brought the battleship out of orbit and transported his brothers to the ancient forest below. Now, his insidious intellect greeted the surprising news of Soraya's pregnancy with glee.

Felani projected to his brother Mika, *"A most valuable secret. Perhaps Armon's offspring can be groomed and manipulated to serve our cause. His seed may well be the key to our control of the Cosmic Sea."*

"I fear this child is an abomination, Felani. Such psychic ability prior to birth is unprecedented."

"Once our brothers return with the son of Sakara, we shall seek the wise counsel of Lord Shon-Ghūl."

"We will need to secure another offering."

"Verily. The city below is teeming with well-fed Kian females. Once the fugitive Prince is secured we shall abduct one of the dim-witted creatures."

Roman allowed himself just five minutes to explain to Zachary what had transpired in the last fourteen hours. Not enough time - time had become too valuable to squander.

"And you actually believe this?" Zachary asked.

"Based on my recent experiences, I have to consider that most of it is true. Both Chi-Ro and Nuri have hidden agendas. Keep an eye on Nuri, I'm fairly sure she's not who she claims to be."

"These extraterrestrials are obviously far more advanced than we are - technologically; chances are they're much better liars, as well. They seem completely human. They could be anyone anywhere. I think I was interviewed by one of them today, a police detective called Trevor. Funny, before today, I thought aliens were all grey."

"Why would they be grey?"

"Roman, there is something I never told you. You can't share this information with anyone, not even Soraya. Four times, since the age of fifteen, vicious little grey bastards have abducted me. They did things to me that..."

"Zachary, Soraya's been up in that Asing ship for hours. Now is not the time for jokes."

"Exactly what is funny about a fifteen-year-old boy having a metal probe shoved up his rectum?"

Roman cried, "What? Are you serious?"

"My mother, my psychiatrist and an assortment of sedatives eventually convinced me I was delusional. But the appearance of these ships and details of your bizarre story, has me thinking that what I experienced all those years ago was actually real."

"You have a psychiatrist? Zach, if you're not up for it just say so, I won't hold it against you."

With a heavy sigh, Zachary responded, "I do have a lot of scientific curiosity. Who knows, maybe I'll find the answers to a multitude of questions; and quite frankly, I'd love to wring the necks of those grey paedophiles. I suppose that means I'll be going up to that flying saucer with you."

Roman smiled. The friends walked towards where Chi-Ro and Nuri held Kirato Zaar captive.

"If it's any consolation, the Talisians haven't mentioned any grey aliens."

"You haven't asked. So, is this Noreen Nemsys hideous?"

"No Nuri isn't hideous, she's just a bit pissed off with me at the moment. I think her helmet protects her from psychic attack."

"Right. At least she isn't hideous."

"Be careful what you think, when you're around them. Talisians are psychic."

Yeah right... A telepathic race would almost certainly lose the ability to speak.

"I'm serious Zach, I didn't accept it until I experienced it myself. A telepathic race wouldn't necessarily lose the ability to speak. Just because you can run, doesn't mean you forget how to walk, and it certainly doesn't mean you'd run instead of walk. Projection is more efficient than speech, but it soon leads to mental fatigue."

Realising that his friend had read his thoughts, Zach responded, "That is just wrong."

Roman immediately noticed that the dead bodies had been removed. Nuri held Kirato at gunpoint.

Gagged and cuffed at the wrists and ankles, the defeated Asing sat near a tree stump, his eyes aflame with sadness and rage over the death of his brothers.

Roman asked Chi-Ro, "Did you put the bodies in the ship?"

"Yes Master Armon," came the veteran's reply.

"Okay, let's do this. Nuri I'll need the gun."

"I'm sorry, Your Highness, I cannot comply with that request. The weapon will be scanned by the Asing if it is not shrouded by my stealth cloak."

"Well, remain cloaked until we get up to their ship."

"Only scanned matter can be transported."

"Brilliant."

"My ship is cloaked not far from here. I will join you in orbit. Here, you will need this," she said, placing a metal bracelet on Zachary's right wrist.

"What is it?" he asked.

"A unique transponder. As far as the ship above is concerned, you are now Pencha Zaar and Commander Chi-Ro is Tonn Zaar."

"What's a Zaar? Do any of these devices release electromagnetic fields of about fifty to sixty hertz?"

"You are an amusing man."

"Why does everyone think I'm joking when I'm serious?"

"Won't I need a bracelet?" asked Roman.

Chi-Ro replied, "The transponder in your skull will serve to identify you."

Zachary asked Roman, "You have an alien device in your skull?"

"Take the cuffs off the Asing and put them on me," Roman told Chi-Ro, "Don't lock them."

Referring to Kirato, Chi-Ro asked Roman, "Master Armon, are you certain you can control him?"

"Trust me. And guys, please don't drop my body."

"What are you going to do?" asked Zachary.

"Hopefully I'm going to perform a brilliant impersonation of this charming gentleman."

"To be fully equipped for the task at hand you must take another dose of elidium, Master Armon."

Roman searched Chi-Ro's eyes and quickly found the sincerity he looked for.

"Do it."

Chi-Ro injected the drug into Roman's carotid artery, and the effects were instantaneous. Roman felt light-headed, but his increased physical strength and mental abilities prevented a total blackout.

Taking only a moment to compose himself, he turned his attention to the Asing prisoner.

Kirato struggled in vain as Roman systematically tore down all his mental defences and entered his consciousness.

Chi-Ro and Zachary prevented Roman's body from falling to the ground whilst Nuri holstered her weapon and removed the gag from the Asing.

"He's strong, and I'm exhausted. We'll have to be quick," said Roman in the body of Kirato Zaar.

Nuri swiftly removed the cuffs and a possessed Kirato rose to his feet.

"Roman." said Zachary.

"Yes Zach."

"You're freaking me out."

"Get yourself ready, we're not sure how many of them are in that ship. They could have androids, and there is a strong possibility their weapons will work. You've seen what big holes they make."

"I'm ready," Zachary lied.

Using Kirato's body, Roman turned his attention to Nuri and said, "So we'll see you soon."

"Yes Your Highness, may the scribes record it. Commander Chi-Ro, Dr. Zachary Silverman, may good fortune follow you."

As Nuri walked away, the Abyssinian cat joined her. They both vanished under stealth cloaks simultaneously.

Nice arse, thought Zachary.

He suddenly remembered Roman's warning when he turned around and caught Chi-Ro's disapproving glare.

"I told you," said Roman.

The United Kingdom has a substantial array of Early Warning assets to defend against air attack. These operate on the premise that air attacks will originate from locations on Earth, and are designed to neutralise the threat long before it ventures within British territorial borders. The unprecedented, sudden appearance of a possible threat within British airspace is treated with the highest priority.

For the third time since its arrival seven days ago, the Asing vimana had been detected. A mysterious dampening field, within the Earth's atmosphere, not only neutralised the warship's phase and plasma armament, it also made the alien craft visible to radar.

London Military Air Traffic Control immediately contacted two US Air Force F-15 Eagles on routine manoeuvres from RAF Lakenheath in Suffolk. The Boeing air superiority fighters were directed to intercept the unknown target that appeared on radar hovering at three thousand feet.

Commercial aircraft were directed well away from the flight path of the two tactical fighters that raced towards Epping. Within fifteen minutes, the American Eagles established radar-lock with the Asing starship.

Felani Zaar found the primitive Kian war machines, deeply amusing.

They advance like suicidal insects, drawn to a deadly flame.

Although an inexplicable force rendered the ship's phase and plasma arsenals inoperable, within the Kian atmosphere, the vimana was far from defenceless.

Felani would wait for his brothers to return with the son of Sakara before swatting the impertinent insects.

Possessed by Roman's consciousness, Kirato removed a communication device from his utility belt and signalled the spacecraft hovering far above.

He turned to Chi-Ro and asked, "Do you think they'll beam us up?"

Zachary interrupted, "The power required for matter transfer would be inconceivable, and it's highly unlikely that living tissue could ever be transported using this method."

Suddenly Zachary, Chi-Ro, Roman and Kirato were each engulfed by what appeared to be four separate lightning bolts.

The four men materialised in the matter transfer room of the Asing vessel. Unable to believe his senses, Zachary stood frozen in wonder.

"Inconceivable," said Roman impersonating his incorrect friend.

"Clearly these Talisians have read a couple more science journals than I have," admitted Zachary.

On the bridge, both Felani and Mika immediately sensed that something was amiss. There had been no telepathic greeting from their brothers. Using his command helmet, Felani willed the download of a Jinzou Ningen into the matter transfer room.

Anticipating this tactical move, Chi-Ro, the veteran of the Psychic Wars, had warned Roman who immediately transferred his consciousness from Kirato into the Jinzou Ningen and disabled it. Before Kirato recovered, Chi-Ro had quickly removed the cuffs from Roman and locked them on the wrists and ankles of the snake worshipper.

Meanwhile, at the speed of thought, Roman's intellect countermanded all of the vimana's security measures. Like a virus, his consciousness spread throughout the ship's systems in search of his wife. However, instead of his beloved Soraya, Roman found Felani Zaar.

The pilots of the F-15's made visual contact with the unidentified object, shrouded at the centre of apparent storm clouds. They described it as black and saucer-shaped with a bright orange glow, not a balloon and unlike any aircraft they had ever seen.

Suddenly, in a flash of blinding light, the U.F.O. shot upwards at impossible speed and vanished. All that remained was a round hole in the dark clouds where the object previously hovered.

One pilot asked the other, "Did you see that?"

The other replied, "Yeah and hopefully I'll never see it again."

The vimana Su-Neku spun out of control towards the sun with Roman and Felani battling telepathically for its control.

Cloaked in her formidable starship, Nuri gave chase and feared the worse. The illuminated display on the visor of her command helmet, informed her that the Su-Neku would impact with Shamash - the sun, in thirteen minutes. Nuri focussed on generating a magnetic beam, powerful enough to slingshot the Su-Neku away from the star at the centre of the Solar System. This was not a manoeuvre she had attempted before, and she had substantial doubt it would succeed.

Chi-Ro tossed the Jinzou Ningen's Blastron P-19 phase pistol to a bewildered Zachary and ordered, "Dr. Zachary Silverman, protect the Prince," before hastily exiting the room.

"Wait, where are you going?" Zachary cried, but received no response. The sudden acceleration of the ship left Zachary disorientated and feeling sick to his stomach. With the room's temperature steadily rising to an unbearable level, he wondered if they were still within the Earth's atmosphere.

Zachary began to deeply regret his decision to accompany Roman onto the flying saucer. That regret turned into panic when another Jinzou Ningen suddenly materialised.

Zachary asked fearfully, "Roman, is that you?"

The purple-eyed android quickly drew his phase pistol and Zachary instinctively fired. Shot in the stomach, the Jinzou Ningen discharged his weapon in a spasm. The energy bolt missed its intended target. It mortally wounded Kirato Zaar, who sat slumped against a wall in a semi-conscious state.

Gripped by fear, Zachary pulled the trigger once more and did not release it. The resultant stream of sustained energy from the Blastron P-19 completely vaporised the android. Lowering the weapon to his side, Zachary breathed a sigh of relief and in a strange coincidence Kirato Zaar breathed his last breath.

For what seemed an eternity to them, Roman Doyle and Felani Zaar had been engaged in a psychic battle of wills. Finally, Roman called on his astral twin. He had been reluctant to resort to this dark entity, fearing its power and recognising his inability to control it.

Thought manifested the propulsion and navigation of the Su-Neku. Like all interstellar craft in the Cosmic Sea, the ship could travel great distances via hyperspatial leap. Thoughts received by the command helmet were amplified millions of times and channelled through the vessel's powerful electromagnetic drives.

When Roman attempted astral projection within the ship's systems that thought was also amplified millions of times.

Nuri engaged the magnetic beam and observed to her horror the transformation of the Su-Neku into dark energy. Now a shadow of its original form, the vimana hurtled inexorably towards the sun.

The Asing vessel's incomprehensible astral field pulled Nuri's starship in its wake. Then, in an instant, the Su-Neku and Nuri's starship no longer existed in normal space and time.

Chapter 21

Roman awoke to find himself seated on a bench in a park in San Fernando, Trinidad. The man he called father, had often taken him to this familiar place as a child. Roman felt good to be home, relieved that his nightmare had ended.

His body and everything around him seemed strangely luminous. Even the deep blue sky had an optimistic glow, and all this seemed perfectly normal. The only thing that puzzled him was the fact that the park and the surrounding streets were utterly deserted. Not a soul could be seen anywhere. Just as he started to wonder how long he had been asleep, someone sat beside him.

"I've missed you," Roman said gently.

"I know son," replied the woman he called mother, "but it's time for you to let go."

"Have I died?"

"You've been given a choice."

"Why?"

The woman smiled and said, "It is what your heart requested."

"And what is my choice?"

"You can stay here with me and find the answer to every question you have ever asked."

"Or?"

"Or, you can wake from this dream and save the ones you love."

"But if this is a dream, it isn't real."

"Your dream is my reality and my dream is you."

"I am afraid."

"I know, and the more you care the more afraid you become. You are torturing yourself, son."

"If I leave this place will I ever see you again?"

"Only time will tell."

"Is it true?"

"Yes, it is true. My name is Mina Rin, the consort of Tarom Rin; and you, Prince Armon, are the son I always wished for."

"So..."

"No more questions, I have to leave now," said Mina as she stood gently smiling, "Embrace the truth or fail to fulfil your destiny."

With Mina's words reverberating within his mind, Roman looked down to the ground, afraid that his emotions would get the better of him.

Finally, his choice made, he looked up to find Mina no longer there. Instead, he noticed a Monarch butterfly on the armrest of the bench.

Roman sighed, and the beautiful creature took flight. Gossamer wings soared towards a dazzling tropical sun and vanished in the brilliant light.

Chapter 22

Within the matter transfer room of the stricken Asing warship, Roman Doyle woke to a pitch-black, bitterly cold reality.

Struggling for breath in the thin air, he could hear the laboured breathing of someone close by. His eyes slowly adjusted to the scant light that emanated from control panels within the room and Roman recognised his friend Zachary. In a deep sleep, Zachary lay next to the dead body of Kirato Zaar. Roman recalled the events, which had brought him to this moment in time.

"Zachary, wake up," he said.

Zachary flinched and opened his eyes.

"Where am I?"

"We're on the Asing spaceship."

"Shit. I can barely breathe. What's that smell?"

"I don't know."

Rising slowly, Zachary picked up the Blastron P-19 phase pistol from the floor and said, "I think you'll need one of these."

With no other pistols at hand, Roman retrieved Kirato's sok-bou. He tested it by extending the staff and activating the plasma elements before deactivating it and tucking it within his coat.

Referring to the alien weapon, Zachary said, "I take it you've used one of those before."

Roman nodded, "Yes."

The men cautiously left the matter transfer room and proceeded along a very dark corridor.

From his mental venture into the ship's systems, Roman knew that there were two secure compartments on the ship's lower level. He believed that Soraya was imprisoned in the smaller of the two.

The closer they got to the brig, the greater the stench.

"What is that smell?" Zachary whispered, "It's like sewage and rotting meat."

"Shhh," responded Roman who wondered what unspeakable horrors awaited them in the darkness.

On the dimly lit command deck, Mika Zaar woke to the reek of burnt flesh. Fear gripped his soul when he realised he could not perceive the minds of his brothers. Feeling sick to his stomach, Mika hauled himself out of the regeneration pod and immediately discovered the source of the stench. It was his eldest brother Felani, or at least, what remained of him. Felani's smouldering corpse lay reclined in the vimana's command pod, with bulging eyes completely black, ears, nostrils and opened mouth grotesquely scorched. Upon closer inspection, Mika realised that Felani's skull had been fused to the vimana's command helmet by some inexplicable discharge of energy.

The electric sound of a sok-bou being activated sliced through the bitter silence. Consumed by well-hidden rage, Mika turned slowly, to see the silhouette of Chi-Ro Jin in Hatari Ikou ready stance. In the darkness, the neon blue plasma elements of the staff shone like twin beacons of death. Mika said nothing. He simply moved away from his brother's pod and without flourish, activated his own sok-bou.

For a tense moment, the grim warriors stood frozen, silently experiencing the staff battle in their minds. Finally, thought became movement and both men lunged forward in swirling, silvery-blue vortices of electricity. Their metal rods clashed repeatedly in quick succession, at times sending bolts of plasma energy into the floor and ceiling.

Rage and lust for revenge drove Mika relentlessly forward, until an unanticipated low strike from Chi-Ro grazed his right knee. Mika immediately lost balance, stumbled and fell onto the waiting element of Chi-Ro's dispassionately poised sok-bou, melting his flesh like butter. Leaving him to stand on legs he no longer felt, Chi-Ro swiftly withdrew the deadly plasma element from what used to be Mika's heart. And, spinning on his heels, he confidently turned his back, retracted the weapon and walked purposefully, towards the ship's secondary command pod, ignoring Mika's pathetic attempts to utter obscenities. Chi-Ro had already donned the secondary command helmet, when Mika exhaled sharply, crashed to the floor, released his spirit, and joined his brothers in death.

On the lower deck, of the battleship, Roman Doyle and Dr. Zachary Silverman cautiously approached Soraya's prison chamber. The darkness seemed almost palpable. A foul stench permeated the thin air and had the friends resisting the urge to vomit.

Suddenly, a familiar but completely out of place sound broke the tense silence. It was the sound of a large animal: a cow.

"I guess these aliens love fresh milk," said Zachary.

Roman immediately activated his sok-bou.

Zachary asked him, "What are you doing? Do you think it's a man-eating cow?"

From the strobe light emanated by the sok-bou's plasma elements, Roman could see the cow on the other side of the deck adjacent to Soraya's cell. The animal's eyes had the unmistakable look of blind terror.

Without warning, Zachary threw up, forcing Roman to fight the urge to do the same.

Roman declared, "Just wait here. I'll get Soraya."

He walked briskly towards the cell, eager to be re-united with his wife.

Suddenly the head of an impossibly large snake lunged out of the adjacent chamber and caught the cow in its massive jaws.

Roman and Zachary froze in terror, watching the unfolding horror of the cow struggling in the reptile's gargantuan maw. Gripped by the fearsome creature, the large mammal seemed as helpless as a doomed rodent in the mouth of a boa constrictor.

Scrambling away from the monster, Roman shouted to his stunned friend, "Shoot it! Shoot it!"

Zachary fired but missed, and the giant snake quickly dragged the cow out of sight into the large compartment.

This monster, which the Asing called Shon-Ghūl, was a large serpent from the Beli-Al System, a very intelligent creature with the gift of hypnosis and an unmatched capacity for evil. It considered humanoid females an unrivalled delicacy and was deeply disappointed that it had not received its human sacrifice.

Driven by panic, Roman attempted to get as much distance between himself and the snake as possible. Unfortunately, he slipped on Zachary's vomit and crashed into him. Winded, Zachary lost his grip on the handgun, which clattered onto the metal deck just beyond his reach.

Roman turned in time to see Shon-Ghūl re-emerge from the filthy compartment, having completely swallowed the cow. The creature's piercing stare held him immobilised.

Seized by dread, Zachary rolled away from his friend and attempted to grab the gun. Nevertheless, as he glanced at the insidious reptile, he also became a victim of Shon-Ghūl's hypnotic gaze.

The loud scream of a woman broke the serpent's mesmerising spell. From her cell, Soraya Doyle saw the creature prepare to sink its venomous fangs into her husband, and she screamed again in terror.

Zachary acted quickly. He immediately retrieved the phase weapon, turned and took careful aim. But, like a giant cobra, Shon-Ghūl flared its hood using elongated ribs and with the muscular contraction of its venom glands spayed an incapacitating mist into Zachary's eyes. Crying out in pain, Zachary fired blindly, missing the serpent once more.

Soraya continued to scream; and the colossal serpent, insane with anger, prepared to strike at the closest target - Roman. Roman rolled on the floor, desperately trying to untangle the deactivated staff, snagged under his coat.

Shon-Ghūl lunged at the very instant that Roman retrieved and activated the sok-bou. The serpent's jaws locked on the plasma weapon. With its mouth held open by the trapped staff, the reptile launched into a wild and terrifying spasm. In its throes, the snake's gigantic head crashed into Roman, sending him sprawling ten metres across the cold metal floor.

Blasted by its foul, hot breath, Zachary fired a sustained burst of energy, at point-blank range, into the mouth of the raging beast, vaporising its large head. Its long body writhed uncontrollably for a sickening moment until finally it accepted the inevitability of death.

Zachary tried to rise to his feet, but he found himself being sick once more.

Roman got up, walked over to his friend, and gave him a reassuring pat on the shoulder.

Zachary announced, "I can't see."

"It sprayed venom into your eyes," said Roman, "there's a small infirmary on the upper deck. Maybe Chi-Ro can treat you there."

"Is he a physician?"

"Let's just get the hell out of here Zach," Roman declared, taking Zachary's Blastron P-19 and firing into the control panel on Soraya's cell.

"At least Soraya's had some medical training," Zachary mumbled to himself.

Roman slid the heavy metal door aside; and, in the darkness of the cell, he spied Soraya huddled in a foetal position, whimpering and trembling with fear.

Too afraid to watch Roman's confrontation with Shon-Ghūl, Soraya had withdrawn to the chamber's darkest corner and descended into a deep state of shock, convinced that the serpent had surely devoured her husband.

When Roman appeared at the open door offering her his hand, she instinctively slapped it away, shrieked and scrambled into a corner of her cold, dark prison.

"Soraya, it's me," he said warmly.

Staring blankly, she whispered, "You were gone for hours. At first I thought you were dead. I thought they killed you, just like they killed Eve. Then, for the sake of the baby, I convinced myself you were still alive. Is it really you, or is my husband in the belly of a giant snake?"

Roman said reassuringly, "Zach shot the snake, it's dead. We can go home now."

Sobbing with love, joy and mental exhaustion, Soraya leapt into the waiting arms of her husband.

She crushed him with the weight of release, fearful that separation would once again transform her fragile optimism into an unbearable nightmare.

Chapter 23

On the illuminated bridge of the vimana Su-Neku, Chi-Ro Jin assumed the role of ship's commander, relinquished by the macabre death of Felani Zaar. Reclined in the command pod, he wore the vimana's secondary command helmet. Chi-Ro had successfully restored life-support and brought the vessel's navigational array online, but now his deeply furrowed brow and clenched jaw, betrayed the heavy burden of an unwelcome realisation.

Chi-Ro's search for the planet Ki proved fruitless. By inexplicable means, the vimana Su-Neku had left the confines of space-time and entered a place, which defied all reason - a void of absolute nothingness. Furthermore, the ship was rapidly losing power.

Chi-Ro tried to dismiss thoughts of the ancient legends, which had enthralled him as a young boy: Tales of a mythical dimension called the Fields of Eternal Oblivion and of a young Prince who would emerge from the darkness and bring peace to the Cosmic Sea.

Prince Armon is not the Soter, he mused.

Chi-Ro's features softened. He recalled how his initial disappointment with Armon had been transformed into growing respect.

Spending his formative years amongst simple Kians, has afforded Armon Sakara a level of humility seldom present in Talisian royalty.

By means of the secondary command helmet, Chi-Ro mentally activated the ship's intercom. His thoughts were converted into words, spoken by the ship's processors, in a convincing reproduction of his voice.

"Master Armon, this is Chi-Ro Jin. The remaining Asing have been neutralized, and I have assumed command of the vimana. The ship's records suggest the presence of an extremely dangerous creature on the lower deck. I am unable to locate it using internal sensors, so I insist you remain in the matter transfer room until I have completely secured the vessel."

From the intercom came Roman's response, "Chi-Ro, the snake is dead. I need your help in the infirmary right away."

"Have you been injured?

"No, I'm fine. Zachary had venom sprayed in his eyes, and I think my wife is in shock."

"I will be there presently. Are you quite sure the serpent is dead, Master Armon?"

"Yes, Zachary killed it."

Surprisingly impressive, thought Chi-Ro.

"I sense you played a part in slaying the beast, Master Armon. I urge you to refrain from such mindless heroics in the future."

Chi-Ro removed his helmet, rose out of the command pod and made his way across the bridge and into the lift.

"Upper," he barked; and the lift automatically took him down to the upper deck, and slid open its metal door.

Walking towards the infirmary, Chi-Ro thought: *Most impressive - modesty, resourcefulness and courage. Unfortunately, the Prince's obsession with the Kian female compromises his suitability as a monarch. The proposed bonding between Prince Armon and Princess Rhia Kan would secure the continued allegiance of her father, Archduke Kan Junai Parentiis, to Lord Sakara Rey. The logic is clear and the benefit to the Empire obvious. Such an alliance would tip the balance of power sufficiently in Lord Sakara Rey's favour, to elicit the eventual defeat of Seti Aljyk. But convincing Prince Armon to enter into such an arrangement may not be easy. I fear he may abdicate for love of the Kian woman. And his impetuous cousin, Margrave Rin Mur-Rain, would most likely inherit the task of restoring Lord Sakara's empire.*

Chi-Ro laughed and shook his head.

I am but a warrior. The eternal sea of politics is best left to politicians. Yet here I am, in an enemy vessel, marooned in what may be the dreaded Fields of Eternal Oblivion, entertaining thoughts regarding matters of state. Have faith, son of Jin. The Great Spirit may yet perform a miracle, which speeds us to Lord Sakara's court. After all, Prince Armon may still be the Soter.

Chapter 24

At the centre of the vimana's infirmary, were four empty regeneration pods arranged in symmetry, around a large pillar.

Presented with Soraya Doyle, Chi-Ro Jin bowed respectfully.

He said, "I am Chi-Ro, son of Jin. I am most pleased to finally meet the Prince's consort. I trust you have not been harmed by the Asing, Milady?"

Confused by Chi-Ro's obscure titles, still experiencing the after-effects of trauma and unable to fully grasp the implications of being on an extraterrestrial spacecraft, Soraya did her best to be gracious.

"I'm okay, just a bit shaken. Forgive me Mr. Chi-Ro, but all of this is a bit of a shock."

"Verily. I have restored full life support in the upper deck and bridge. All the regeneration pods in the infirmary are fully operational, would you care to regenerate now?"

Soraya turned to Roman hoping for a translation into plain English.

Roman said, "Thank you Chi-Ro, how soon will we return to Earth?"

"Master Armon, I regret I have grave news."

"No-no-no," said Zachary shaking his head in dismay, "Let me guess, we're lost in space."

Chi-Ro replied, "It appears we are no longer in space."

Zachary was about to speak, but with a gesture of his hand and a look that implied, *Now is not a good time for insults, sarcasm or dry humour,* Roman motioned his friend to remain silent.

Roman asked, "Where are we Chi-Ro?"

"We are in a void which defies description, outside the space-time continuum."

Zachary began to laugh mockingly.

Chi-Ro responded, "Dr. Zachary Silverman take heed; three decades of warfare, robbed me of patience when faced with the foolish."

"As a scientist, I can say with complete confidence that what you just said, regarding us being outside the space-time continuum, is absolute bollocks!"

"Dr. Zachary Silverman, it may interest you to learn that, on the planet Kyto Ril, no one is blind. The primitives believe that loss of sight creates an incurable infection of the brain. Those unfortunate enough to lose their vision are tortured and killed to prevent the spread of pathogens."

"What have you been up to while we were sleeping, Fu Manchu?"

"Zachary, be quiet," interrupted Roman, "Chi-Ro can you restore his sight?"

Chi-Ro replied, "By your judgement, Master Armon." Then he turned his attention to Zachary and said, "Dr. Zachary Silverman please enter this pod, so that I may attempt to restore your vision."

"Roman, you don't seriously expect me to trust this psycho. Am I the only one who interpreted the fable of Kyto Ril as a threat?"

"Zachary, don't you think it's a bit stupid to aggravate the only person on the ship who can treat you?"

"You're buying into this void nonsense, aren't you?"

"I think I know how we got here."

"What? This I have got to hear."

"I tried astral projection while in the ship's systems."

"Astral what? What the hell are you talking about? You really believe all this rubbish about being the alien Prince of the Galaxy?"

Soraya asked, "Roman, what is he talking about?"

Before Roman could respond, Zachary continued, "Yesterday you were a schoolteacher, today you think you're a superhero..."

With a threatening smile, Chi-Ro cried, "Master, permit me to silence this impertinent imbecile."

Zachary retorted, "Who the hell are you calling an imbecile? Roman buys into your tall tales, but I don't. As it happens, I'm a scientist, but you don't need to be a scientist to question the wisdom of an emperor sending one middle-aged man to rescue the Prince of the Universe."

Chi-Ro growled in a low, ominous voice, "Your tongue digs you an early grave, Dr. Zachary Silverman. The prototype stealthship, with twenty Imperial Guards, initially sent to retrieve Master Armon exploded on the rim of the T'Harian Gate, an act of cowardly sabotage."

Roman said sternly, "Calm down, both of you. This bickering is not going to get us out of the mess we're in. Zachary, the choice is yours, permit Chi-Ro to treat your eyes or get used to being blind."

Zachary responded with unmasked anger, "As you wish, Your Highness, but remember I agreed to help you find Soraya, not sign up to some diabolical alien war."

Soraya searched Roman's eyes for answers and said, "Roman?"

He replied softly, "I'll explain everything." Then turning to Zachary he added, "Thanks for helping me find Soraya, you are a true friend Zachary. If you let him, Chi-Ro will treat you; and I'll do my best to get us back to where we should be. Just trust me."

Zachary said to Roman, "I'm sorry, I don't know what came over me." Then Zachary turned to Chi-Ro and added, "I'm sorry Chi-Ro."

"Perhaps this dark place is also affecting our minds," Chi-Ro suggested.
Roman asked, "Why do you say that?"

"It appears to be draining the ship's power."

"Is it safe to treat Zachary now?"

"Yes Master Armon, I suggest that we all regenerate. It may clear our minds and assist us in finding a solution to our present predicament."

"Treat Zachary first, I'll enter the ship's systems again and try to reverse the course that brought us here."

"And what of your transponder? The enemy can still track you."

"I brought us here, and I may be the only one who can take us out. You can remove the transponder once we return to normal space."

"May the scribes record it," said Chi-Ro, beginning to attend to Zachary. "To access the ship's systems, you will need to use the secondary command helmet situated on the bridge. I will instruct you in its use, once I have restored Dr. Zachary Silverman's vision."

"Okay, I'll wait. Chi-Ro, what is the T'Harian Gate?"

"It is the mouth to a space-time umbilicus that connects the Cosmic Sea to the Anu Sea."

"The Anu Sea?"

"I suspect he's talking about a traversable wormhole that connects their Cosmic Sea Galaxy to the Milky Way Galaxy," said Zachary, "Since the late eighties, our science has been able to demonstrate the possibility of traversable wormholes in general relativity."

"The location of the T'Harian Gate and the existence of Ki are well-guarded secrets," added Chi-Ro.

"Are you going to tell me what's going on?" whispered Soraya to Roman.

"In private," said Roman softly.

"Excuse us a moment," said Soraya to Zachary and Chi-Ro, "the Prince and I have much to discuss."

She grabbed Roman's hand and led him out of the infirmary.

From the corridor, Roman said to Zachary and Chi-Ro, "Meet us on the bridge."

Chi-Ro replied, "We will be there presently."

The door closed. Soraya was about to speak, but Roman placed a finger on his lips signalling her to remain silent. He grabbed her hand and led her to the lift.

Once on the bridge, Soraya whispered, "Can we talk now?"

"I think so. Chi-Ro is psychic..."

"I don't trust him. I think the aliens want our baby," said Soraya.

Roman replied in a whisper, "I don't think Chi-Ro knows about the baby. It's best he doesn't for the time being."

"Roman, wha' goin' on?"

Roman related to Soraya all that transpired, since he first encountered the Asing warriors.

"Chi-Ro saved my life."

"But will he protect the life of our child? What you said suggests that these aliens have big plans for you. Your human wife and child are not a part of these plans."

"Soraya, you have to be careful what you think."

"Yuh askin' meh to do the impossible. The other aliens found out. Ah think they read meh mind. I think maybe this Chi-Ro Jin knows already, he just foolin' you."

"Still, for the time being, do your best to control your thoughts."

"Can't you see, Zachary is right? You've changed already."

"Soraya, if we're going to survive this, we all have to change."

"That's not what I mean, you enjoy the idea of people bowing and calling you Master. You can't take our child to war Roman; I won't let you."

"You don't understand. I don't think we'll ever be safe on Earth again."

"Earth is home. God alone knows where this Chi-Ro Jin will take us. If something in your head allows them to track you, then take it out and lets go home. I've been so worried. Ah pray just to feel the baby kick, just tuh know he still alive."

Suddenly Roman felt a sharp, excruciating pain in his head.

With deep concern, Soraya asked, "Are you okay? Wha' wrong?"

"The baby," he said holding his head, "the baby is psychic." Roman took a moment to recover then added, "I felt a mind reaching out... Abstract thoughts... Very powerful..."

Tears welled in Soraya's eyes, "Yuh scaring me. What does that mean? What we going to do?"

"I'll find a way to take you home."

"Take me home? Yuh not coming?"

"According to Chi-Ro, they're quite able to wipe out all life on Earth."

"What yuh saying?"

"If I go with him, maybe I could prevent that from ever happening."

"Listen tuh yourself, Zachary was right, you really think you're a super-hero. You're not a superhero, Roman."

"I'm not who I thought I was."

Soraya slapped him on the face.

With fire in her brown eyes, she said, "Don't you dare."

"I will die, before I allow anything to happen to you or the baby."

"And, if you die, where will we be without you?"

Chapter 25

Chi-Ro attached a small memory disc to the central pillar of the infirmary; and, within moments, a backup copy of his faithful servant, Teev Meg materialised.

"Greetings Commander, how may I serve?" asked the tall, dark, artificial human.

Startled by the unfamiliar voice, Zachary asked, "Who's there?"

"Dr. Zachary Silverman, this is Jinzou Ningen Teev Meg, he will treat your eyes," responded Chi-Ro.

"There's a Japanese doctor onboard?"

"Forgive me but what is Japanese?"

"Never mind, for a minute, I forgot I was in the Twilight Zone."

Teev Meg's purple eyes scanned his unfamiliar surroundings and he said, "Commander Chi-Ro, I sense discontinuity in my memory files. A corruption has been removed, prior to restoration. We are no longer aboard the Starbird Adara?"

"No old friend, Adara was destroyed by the Asing vessel we are currently aboard."

"Are we prisoners of war?"

"No, with the aid of Dr. Zachary Silverman, Master Armon and I were able to capture this vessel."

"Splendid. Commander Chi-Ro, please state the nature of Dr. Zachary Silverman's ailment."

"His eyes were sprayed with Shon-Ghūl venom."

"May the scribes record it," said Teev Meg, scanning Zachary's eyes with an alien hand-held device.

I'll never see again, thought Zachary.

Leaving Zachary to recover from the medical procedure performed by Teev Meg, Chi-Ro made his way from the infirmary to the bridge.

He dismissed his growing unease.

An ill effect of being in the Fields of Eternal Oblivion, he thought.

Suddenly, barely audible above the low drone of the ship's formidable electromagnetic drive, Chi-Ro heard the whisper of a familiar voice - the voice of his former Master - the voice of Brakis Tarn.

The voice said, "Death whispers your name to me, Chi-Ro, son of Jin."

Perhaps we are not alone in the darkness, Chi-Ro mused.

On the bridge, Chi-Ro explained the workings of the secondary command helmet to Roman who reclined in the ship's command pod.

Soraya asked, "Is this perfectly safe?"

"It is quite safe," responded Chi-Ro.

Masking any visible traces of self-doubt, Roman donned the command device and cleared his mind. Within a few moments, he could feel the presence of several of the vessel's systems as if they were extensions of his physical body.

He immediately ascertained that the ship's long-range communications array was inoperative - an unwanted souvenir from the previous engagement with Chi-Ro Jin's Starbird Adara.

All around the vimana, Roman sensed nothing.

Chi-Ro's description was accurate, he thought.

They no longer existed in normal space, and without difficulty, Roman sensed the drain on the vimana's power in the stifling darkness.

He needed to take the vimana out of the all-consuming dark, into the light of normal space, or they would all perish.

A flutter started in his stomach, soon followed by a familiar, warm tingle at the base of his spine. But on the threshold of astral projection, Roman felt something unexpected, a surge of phenomenal power. He could hear his own heartbeat thumping in his temples and instinctively knew he had to stop.

"Master Armon, the ship's drive came close to critical, and yet it appears we have not moved."

Suddenly exhausted, Roman feared he lacked the ability to control the astral forces required for a safe return to Earth. He needed to regenerate before attempting astral navigation again.

"I can't do it. I need to rest first," he told the concerned Chi-Ro.

"How long can we stay here?" asked Soraya.

"Six days give or take a couple hours," replied Roman.

Soraya's eyes widened, betraying unspoken concern.

"Faith Milady, we will yet escape the Fields of Eternal Oblivion," said Chi-Ro as he ushered husband and wife towards the lift. "Once regenerated, a solution to our predicament will present itself."

Soraya put on a brave face and said, "Yes, I'm sure you're right, Mr. Chi-Ro."

Suddenly a loud klaxon sounded, and several panels around the bridge sprang to life.

"Proximity alert," revealed a grim-faced Chi-Ro who briskly entered the command pod and placed the helmet on his head.

"Brakis Tarn?" asked Roman.

"Sensors cannot confirm... Raising shields... Weapons charged. The vimana is now on full alert status."

"What's happening?" asked Soraya.

Roman looked into her searching eyes and replied, "I think the Psychic War just found us."

Chapter 26

Standing in expectant silence on the bridge of the alien spacecraft, Roman wondered what twists of fate could bring a lowly schoolteacher face-to-face with such fantastic possibilities. If he died - right here, right now - who on Earth would imagine the strange turn of events that led him to this place and time?

Death in The Fields of Eternal Oblivion, he mused.

Roman suddenly transported back in time to the sandy beach of Tobago's Store Bay. It was their honeymoon, and Soraya sat silently at his side, watching the setting sun. They were alone, in that moment, the only souls in a tropical paradise.

Soraya turned to him, tilted her head, closed her eyes and said, "A kiss for the dying," and kissed him passionately.

However, the voice he heard was not the voice of his wife. Breaking the kiss, Roman realised that the woman in his arms was Nuri Nemsys.

"Nuri?" asked Roman, hurtling back to reality.

"What?" asked Soraya.

Chi-Ro activated the vimana's holographic viewfinder and announced, "ENDAR contact, coming into visual range."

An image of the approaching spacecraft, shrouded in darkness, appeared on a metallic grey wall.

"A vessel of Talisian configuration," advised Chi-Ro, "Glider class – but sensors detect an unusual power reading. For your safety, you must both enter life support pods," he told Roman and Soraya.

"It's Nuri," said Roman to Chi-Ro as he led Soraya by the hand to an adjacent life support pod.

"Who's Nuri?" asked Soraya.

"A Talisian soldier sent to protect us."

Soraya reclined in the alien device.

"A woman? Hmm, I can't wait to see the woman sent to protect you," she said.

"Interstellar communications are no longer functional on this vessel. I cannot establish the intent of the approaching craft."

"What are you going to do?"

"What I must - the craft approaches in an attack vector with shields set to maximum."

"It's Nuri Nemsys, you have to trust me," Roman said, "we're no longer in space, we have no idea what will happen if weapons are fired."

"That vessel is heavily armed; if they fire first, we will be destroyed."

"Chi-Ro, don't do it."

"Target established. Weapons locked."

"Don't," shouted Roman seconds before the violent impact of an energy blast rocked the Su-Neku.

"We are under attack by a second vessel, of unfamiliar configuration... Invisible to ENDAR... Shields holding at thirty percent," declared Chi-Ro, "Returning fire."

"Wait," said Roman, scrambling into an adjacent pod.

Suddenly on the holographic screen, Roman, Soraya and Chi-Ro witnessed a bright glow envelop the attacking craft. The glow dissipated, swiftly followed by static electrical discharges.

"What happened?" asked Soraya.

"It appears the vessel's weapons malfunctioned," said Chi-Ro.

Roman turned to Chi-Ro and said, "The normal laws of physics don't apply here. If you'd fired weapons, we'd probably be dead."

"The unidentified starglider has assumed a position between us and the alien vessel."

"They're all alien vessels," mumbled Soraya to herself.

"The alien ship," said Roman to Chi-Ro, "could it be Brakis Tarn?"

"I cannot sense my old master," replied Chi-Ro."

Without warning, Teev Meg materialised on the bridge, causing Soraya to shriek.

Teev Meg said, "You need not be alarmed Madam, the unfortunate events of the Great Ningen Wars are ancient history. Artificial humans have evolved considerably since those dark times. I am incapable of causing you harm."

Soraya gave Roman a look that asked, *who the hell is the man with the purple eyes?*

"Milady, this is Teev Meg," said Chi-Ro, "he has been my loyal friend for almost twenty of your Kian years."

"You summoned me, Commander?" said Teev Meg.

"The Asing archives are unsurprisingly limited. Can you identify these vessels?"

"Alien vessel - no exact match in my memory. I cannot confirm identification."

Roman asked, "Do you have records of anything similar?"

"Accessing."

Soraya whispered to Roman, "Is that man real? Or is he a hologram?"

"He's real. He's an android."

"I have no recollection of a similar vessel," said Teev Meg, "Curious... The Talisian starglider is unregistered."

Chi-Ro announced, "I am taking weapons and shields offline."

"Why?" asked Roman.

"Power reserves are rapidly draining - now at forty-five percent," said Chi-Ro with unmasked concern.

"But doesn't that mean..."

"Yes Master, we will be completely defenceless."

Suddenly a blinding light absorbed the belligerent vessel; and, in stunned silence Roman, Soraya and Chi-Ro watched the vessel vaporise.

From the Su-Neku's intercom, the slightly garbled, familiar voice of Nuri Nemsys broke the silence.

"Commander... Asing vessel... Please respond."

"Greetings Nuri Nemsys," Chi-Ro responded mentally, "what is your status?"

"Minor damage entering this void. Was your mission a success?"

"Verily. Can you identify alien attacker?"

"The vessel has been neutralized and poses no further threat. There is much I must discuss. Permission to transport aboard."

"Denied. Matter transport may yield unwelcome results."

"Agreed. Permission to dock."

"Granted."

Roman asked, "What happened to the ship?"

"I do not know," responded Chi-Ro, "it was as if the vessel just ceased to exist."

"A doorway out of the Fields of Eternal Oblivion?"

"Perhaps Nuri Nemsys can provide some answers."

Nuri manoeuvred her starglider to the port side of the larger Asing vessel. She extended and locked docking clamps. From an adjacent pod, the Abyssinian cat silently observed the procedure via the main holographic viewer screen.

"Only the Prince need know of the Neph Alim," the cat projected telepathically.

Nuri removed her command helmet and responded, *"Yes Mistress."*

The cat and the woman left their pods and made their way to the lift, which would take them to the airlock on the lower deck.

"Your thoughts are transparent," the cat communicated to Nuri, *"I sense your happiness that the son of Sakara is unharmed."*

"He is somewhat attractive," Nuri responded with a teasing smile. They entered the lift, and she said, "Lower."

"For a man," projected the cat, *"I have always harboured an indifference towards men, I find the fairer sex far more appealing."*

The pair left the lift and headed towards the airlock on the far side of the deck.

"With regards to his appearance, I believe you refer to his strong family resemblance. Do not allow sentiment to cloud your vision, the mistakes made with Rin Mur-Rain cannot be repeated. It is imperative that you successfully complete this mission, Kiya."

"I will not fail, Mistress."

"Allowing the son of Sakara to overcome you, was well executed; and I sense the seeds of trust have been effectively sown, but do not underestimate him, he is far more dangerous than Seti Aljyk suspects."

"I am confident he can be convinced to safeguard the colony."

"Do you place your faith in reason, or your genetically enhanced pheromones?"

"He is after all, only a man."

"Is that a trace of blue I see in your green eyes Kiya?"

"I assure you, I have no feelings for this Talisian."

Nuri performed a quick check on the power reserves of her viridian pistol and holstered it within her black leather jacket.

Without hesitation, she pulled her communicator from her belt and spoke into it, "Commander Chi-Ro, permission to board."

"Granted," came Chi-Ro's immediate response.

"Chi-Ro Jin does not trust me," she projected, *"He could create complications."*

"This master of Hatari Ikou is no match for you, my young apprentice. Time is short, go now and complete your duty."

"May it be written."

"May it be done."

Chapter 27

Nuri Nemsys entered the Su-Neku through the airlock, and was greeted by Chi-Ro Jin with a formal bow.

"Commander Chi-Ro, the Great Spirit has been merciful," Nuri declared.

"Verily, Master Armon has survived thus far, despite several attempts on his life."

They walked along the dimly lit corridor, Chi-Ro's grim features doing little to mask his obvious distrust.

"Where is His Highness?" asked Nuri.

Without looking at her, Chi-Ro replied, "Prince Armon became fatigued and has retired."

"I see."

"So tell me, what do you know of the vessel which attacked us?"

"I thought I was alone in the darkness until the vessel appeared on my long-range sensors. After a brief pursuit, it became obvious that the ship was on an intercept course with the vimana. Why did you not respond to my hails?"

"The communications array of this vessel is inoperative. The alien ship was cloaked, how did you track it?"

"My sensors detected the ship's energy field."

"Interesting, you appear to have access to a technology beyond anything I've encountered," said Chi-Ro, thoughtfully stroking his Fu Manchu moustache.

"Such access should not be surprising, I am an intelligence agent in His Majesty's service," declared Nuri.

"Verily, and I am shamira to the Prince. You assumed an attack vector..."

"Prompting you to raise the vimana's defensive shields."

Chi-Ro chuckled, "The Great Spirit has shown exceptional mercy. I could have destroyed your vessel."

"It was a risk I was prepared to take."

"May the scribes record it. Again I ask what do you know of the vessel which attacked us?"

"I was unable to identify the vessel. I could find no match in the Talisian database. Its origin and intent are unknown."

They entered the lift, and Chi-Ro barked, "Bridge," he turned to Nuri and seemed to peer into her very soul. He said, "These Fields of Eternal Oblivion harbour many mysteries."

"So it would seem," responded Nuri, breaking eye contact.

Chi-Ro and Nuri entered the bridge to find Zachary reclined in the ship's command pod.

"Ah Noreen, such a delight to see you again, you wouldn't happen to have a cigarette would you?"

"Dr. Zachary Silverman, it would be wise for you to remove yourself from the command pod immediately," said Chi-Ro sternly.

"Whoa Chi-Ro, I didn't know this was your special chair," said Zachary, rising to his feet, "The seat's all yours."

Chi-Ro glared at Zachary for the briefest moment before reclining in the ship's command pod and donning the secondary command helmet.

Nuri looked deeply into Zachary's bloodshot eyes and said, "Your eyes are red and swollen, have you been crying?"

"I thought I'd never see you again," came his sarcastic response.

"You are an amusing man."

Nuri sat in a pod adjacent to the command pod and activated the small console within the enclosure.

"Thanks for sorting out my eyes Chi-Ro. Thank Teev Meg as well."

Chi-Ro simply nodded in response.

"So what are you two planning on doing?"

"We need to ascertain how to return to normal space," replied Nuri.

"Perhaps I could help, I'm a quantum physicist; I'm sure if we work together we could find a solution."

Nuri raised a cynical eyebrow and said, "Your planet has only the most rudimentary understanding of quantum mechanics."

Zachary reclined in a pod and responded, "I learn quickly and I'm an optimist."

"Optimists are usually inexperienced," added Chi-Ro, the ship's central processing unit transforming his thoughts into spoken words.

"Okay then, have it your way," said Zachary, rising from his seat. He walked towards the lift and added without looking back, "At least I confirmed Einstein's theory regarding infinites."

"What is this theory?" asked Nuri.

"Einstein believed that only two things are infinite - the universe and the human capacity for stupidity."

Zachary entered the lift, and the doors closed behind him.

Chi-Ro asked Nuri, "Who is Einstein?"
"I don't know, but he seems to have great insight regarding Kians."
"Without doubt."

Zachary returned to the empty infirmary and gazed at his reflection in the shiny metallic wall panels. He looked as he felt - exhausted. Sweeping his right hand through his black hair and staring deeply into the silvery image of his deep blue eyes, Zachary thought he saw a strange glow in his pupils. To get a better look, he moved closer to the panel and instantly, his face morphed into that of the giant serpent - Shon-Ghūl. Lurching backward in shock, Zachary stumbled and fell into a regeneration pod. Then, rising cautiously, his anxious gaze returned to his tired reflection on the wall. Relieved to see he had not become a snake, he lowered himself back into the regeneration pod and exhaled laboriously.

I just need some sleep.

He removed the lethal phase pistol from within his jacket and held it firmly in his lap.

Better safe than sorry.

The heat of brilliant sunshine, stung Roman's exposed face. He opened his eyes squinting in the white light, and realised he stood in an endless sea of sand dunes. In the distance, unmoving and foreboding, stood a silhouette of a man.

How did I get here? he thought.

"I have brought you here," came a reply from a familiar voice, the voice of Chi-Ro Jin.

A strong gust of wind forced Roman to turn away, lifting his hands to shield his eyes from the burning sand. Looking back towards where he had previously seen Chi-Ro, Roman discovered he had vanished. Instinct compelled Roman to turn around and there, standing ten paces behind him, was Chi-Ro Jin.

"I have brought you here to commence your training," said Chi-Ro, the Master of Hatari Ikou.

"Where am I?" asked Roman.

"You are in the desert of your mind."

"Am I dreaming?"

"Precisely."

"What is this training?"

"The Great Spirit has bestowed upon you very impressive gifts, but you lack the knowledge and discipline required to adequately use them. Before you, there are many trials - many battles - such is your lot in this time of war. You must either overcome them or perish."

"Aren't we still trapped in the Fields of Eternal Oblivion?" asked Roman.

Chi-Ro replied, "For the moment."

"Shouldn't we be concentrating all our efforts to get out of the Fields of Eternal Oblivion?"

"Nuri Nemsys and I have discovered the means of our escape."

"So what are we waiting for?" asked Roman, barely able to contain himself.

"You," Chi-Ro said calmly.

"Huh?"

"We are waiting for you to develop the skill required to use your abilities to transport us from this astral plane back into normal space."

"I did it once, I could do it again," said Roman confidently.

"We must avoid a repeat of the power surge which developed in your last attempt. With only thirty-two percent available power, the effect on the Asing vessel would be catastrophic."

"Do we have enough time?"

"Asleep you can experience many hours whilst only a few waking moments have passed. This is why dreams are an ideal platform for training."

"Okay, I'll try."

"To try is to invite uncertainty. Where confidence goes, success usually follows."

Chi-Ro the philosopher, Roman mused.

"Let the exercises begin," Chi-Ro shouted, sharply clapping his hands.

It sounded like thunder. Roman struggled to maintain his balance. The ground shook terribly beneath his feet, shifting the sand and creating new dunes for many kilometres.

Suddenly, two metres away, a massive black monolith rose from the sand, blocking the sun and casting a threatening shadow that totally engulfed Roman and Chi-Ro.

The dark monolith, approximately three metres tall, two metres wide and one and one-half metres deep, absorbed the light that shone on it.

"The object of the first exercise is quite simple, said Chi-Ro, "You must shatter the monolith with a single blow."

"That's it?" asked Roman, poking and nudging the large block, attempting to ascertain its strength and composition, "What is it made of?"

"The monolith is composed of the hardest substance in the Cosmic Sea, lapys nerian."

"It's cold - unaffected by the heat," said Roman

"Precisely."

"You expect me to break solid rock - four feet thick - with my bare hands?"

Chi-Ro inhaled very slowly with a low growl then delivered a single lightning-fast palm strike into the centre of the monolith. It shattered into a thousand pieces.

"A true master will not deceive an able disciple. You are hampered by the limits you set and no limit can be set on skill," said Chi-Ro, calmly.

"Whose dream is this?" asked Roman, staring in awe.

"This dream is a shared experience but all that exists within it, are yours to command through force of will."

Chi-Ro clapped his hands once more, and the sandy ground quaked violently. Another monolith, identical to the first, erupted out of the sand and cast an equally formidable shadow.

Roman turned to the imposing slab, clearing his mind. He filled his lungs with air and with a sharp exhale launched a strenuous reverse palm strike. However, the giant block did not budge. Roman crouched to the sand, distracted by the physical agony of his failure.

This is stupid, he thought, *what does smashing this rock have to do with anything anyway?*

"You crave winning and fear losing instead of just doing. To succeed you must remove your self-imposed limitations. Breaking the monolith is far simpler than leading an army, ruling a nation or facing Brakis Tarn in single combat. In many ways, a triumph over lapys nerian is symbolic of having freed your consciousness and attained perfect self-awareness."

"I still don't understand how you expect me to smash the hardest substance in the universe."

"Listen to your conviction, even if it sounds absurd to your reason. Follow the instructions of your heart, letting nothing perturb you."

"You're saying the strength of the monolith is irrelevant?"

"The monolith is as hard as you make it. You will free your consciousness when you learn to be neutral."

Without hesitation, Roman spun on his heel, retracted his fist with a sharp inhale and launched it with a swift, smooth exhale. He felt a tingling through his stomach and at the base of his spine. A split second before impact with the monolith he extended his fingers into an open palm strike.

In the dream, Roman's flesh colliding with lapys nerian sounded like muffled thunder. The monolith reverberated and to Roman's satisfaction, a crack appeared on the slab's black surface. The joy of this minor victory soothed the pain he felt in his hand.

"Conviction is required, not impulse," said Chi-Ro, "Focus on cause, not effect."

"I've only just started," exclaimed Roman with pride.

Without warning the monolith ignited, engulfed in a raging inferno. The ground trembled once more; and the shifting sand poured into fissures and cracks, that extended from the root of the burning slab.

"What's happening?" asked Roman, cautiously backing away from the searing heat.

The monolith began to melt, becoming less like rock and more like tar, as it sank into an ever-widening fissure. Darkness descended on the desert shrouding the sun but to Roman's surprise, the ambient heat increased substantially.

Desert sands became molten lava, and Roman's sense of accomplishment became unadulterated dread.

"Chi-Ro?" he asked.

"Curious," said Chi-Ro, shaking his head with dismay, "Your misguided creativity has managed to transform the dream into a nightmare. You are the first of my students to achieve such a feat."

"So I'm unique. Isn't that good?"

"Only if you enjoy the comforts of fire and brimstone," said Chi-Ro grimly.

As more and more of the ground transformed into super-heated lava, Roman's panic increased exponentially. Looking to his right, he noticed a path of raised rocks through the rivers of molten lava, leading to a relatively safe plateau about forty metres away.

Shockingly, with a thunderous explosion of illumination and sound, a crack of lightning streaked from the sky and crashed into the centre of the plateau. At the point of impact, a small eruption of gas and lava heralded the dramatic rise of another monolith.

"Hurry Chi-Ro," shouted Roman, "this way!"

"Follow you? I think not," replied Chi-Ro.

Roman began to jog towards the monolith, which had become his beacon of hope in the rising tide of deadly lava.

"Run Chi-Ro," he cried as molten rock engulfed more and more of the land bridge.

Roman stumbled and was forced to hurl himself onto the plateau seconds before a stream of lava buried what remained of the path.

Desperately, Roman looked over his shoulder, shocked to find Chi-Ro had not taken his advice. Instead of running to the safety of the plateau, Chi-Ro walked at a steady pace, apparently unconcerned by the encroaching danger.

Roman rubbed disbelieving eyes, *he's walking on molten rock!*

As Chi-Ro neared the plateau Roman asked, "How did you do that?"

"I am a master of Hatari Ikou and this, as real as it may seem to you, is but a dream. In such a reality, my will is boundless."

The left sleeve of Chi-Ro's black tunic abruptly ignited, and he casually rubbed the flame out with his right hand.

"Now," he said, motioning to the monolith, "complete your unfinished task."

Roman tried unsuccessfully to block out the distraction caused by the surrounding heat, gas and lava.

His mind strayed to his thoughts just before the scenery became hellish.

It's hot, but things could be worse, we could be near a volcano.

And then, what would be an innocuous thought under different circumstances, popped into his mind.

Thank God we were in a desert. If the lava flow came into contact with a body of water...

A steadily increasing rumble interrupted Roman's thought.

"Is that what I think it is?" he asked.

Without emotion, Chi-Ro replied, "I prefer more pleasant surroundings - lush green meadows with fragrant flowers - peace and serenity. I leave you now, to ponder the cause of your failure; but I expect your mind will focus on its effects that, due to your lack of discipline, will be upon you shortly."

"Wait. You're leaving?" asked Roman in disbelief.

"Rest assured that I would continue your training during your next sleep cycle. I hope you achieve a few significant advancements by then."

"But you brought me here," Roman declared.

"The venue has always been of your choosing," responded Chi-Ro, "Remember, growth of consciousness does not depend on the might of the intellect but on the conviction of the heart. May the scribes record it."

Chi-Ro vanished, leaving Roman alone on the plateau. Roman slowly turned to face the source of the rumble that had become a deafening roar. As he feared, a wall of water three hundred metres high surged towards him.

A tsunami.

Roman closed his eyes, clinging to the only thought that offered any comfort - *This is only a dream.*

Chapter 28

Brakis Tarn had been alone in the void two standard Karellan days - two days to contemplate the unanticipated developments in his mission to locate Armon Sakara.

A dampening field, engulfing the planet Ki, rendered Karellan weapons and long-range communications useless. While on the planet, Brakis Tarn could not relay confirmation to his master Seti Aljyk, that Prince Armon Sakara was alive.

The foolish Asing were overpowered before he could intervene. Now he feared his former student Chi-Ro Jin commanded their vimana.

Brakis Tarn also sensed that Armon Sakara's friend, the one called Dr. Zachary Silverman, was not Kian. Like the son of Sakara, this individual appeared not to have realised his full potential. He wondered how many Talisians had found refuge on Ki and how many of these were unaware of their true heritage.

The primitive world offers mineral resources, and an abundance of slave labour, the Karellan thought; *with an Avenger class vessel, and a garrison of Karellan Shock Marines, I could seize Ki for myself, despite its mysterious dampening field.*

In the forest, Brakis Tarn observed another individual – a Talisian, apparently loyal to Sakara Rey. This individual had come to the aid of Chi-Ro Jin and seemed to employ an unknown, highly advanced technology. The vessel Brakis Tarn followed into the void was no ordinary starglider. It used an unidentified power source and had weapons of an unknown configuration.

Is this alien craft responsible for opening a doorway into the darkness? Is Sakara Rey amassing a formidable attack force somewhere within this void with a new generation of starglider? If so, would such a development tip the scales of victory in his favour?

Two days of deep contemplation provided no answers to his questions and no solution to his present predicament. After following the vessels into the rift, Brakis Tarn found himself utterly alone. The Asing vimana and the Talisian starglider had vanished without a trace.

His raider's sensors indicated an absolute absence of matter within its range. Brakis Tarn had somehow ventured into a state beyond the space-time continuum. With power reserves rapidly draining, he hovered on the verge of abandoning all hope; when suddenly, long-range sensors detected a surge of unidentified power within the endless darkness.

Cloaked, having engaged sub-light propulsion, Brakis Tarn mentally adjusted his raider's trajectory to an intercept course with the mysterious energy source.

Unknown forces are at work in this place, which he now believed to be the Fields of Eternal Oblivion of ancient myth.

His power reserves, in free-fall, past the twenty-two percent mark; Brakis Tarn established ENDAR contact with the vimana and starglider.

To reduce any chance of detection, he cut engines and deactivated all systems except the cloak and close-range sensors. The only active life support remained within his command pod. Maintaining the cloak meant he had just over a standard day before his raider would run out of power - just over one standard day to return to normal space with the captured son of Sakara Rey.

Roman Doyle awoke in a dimly lit room relieved to be alive; and, as his racing heartbeat gradually returned to normal, he realised that he had been asleep in the crew compartment aboard the Asing vimana, Su-Neku.

He looked at Soraya asleep in the regeneration pod adjacent to his own, and relief turned to despair. For a fleeting moment, Roman had hoped that, like the tsunami, Soraya's abduction by aliens was part of a dreadful nightmare.

This is all my fault, he thought; *I brought us into this darkness, and I'll have to find the way out of it. I have to get Soraya and Zach back to Earth.*

For a while, Roman studied the contours of Soraya's face as she slept peacefully.

So beautiful, he thought.

Soon the reassuring sound of her rhythmic breathing would put him to sleep. But before he drifted into that alternate reality, Roman wondered how he would complete the task set by Chi-Ro Jin.

How will I break the monolith with my bare hands?

On a snow-capped glacier in the landscape of his dream, Roman focussed on the lapys nerian monolith before him. He was not alone. His shamira, Chi-Ro Jin, observed him with a furrowed brow.

"Are you hoping to shatter the monolith by employing the evil eye?" projected Chi-Ro, *"Scream like a Miruvian Grey-tailed Raptor, perhaps the lapys nerian will shatter from fear."*

With a heavy sigh, Roman admitted, "I can't do it. I can't do what you do. There is no way I can break this."

"And so it will be. Your wish will be your reality."

"Oh, come on, are you implying that the only reason I can't smash the rock is because I don't believe I can?"

"That and your masochistic morbidity. Look at our surroundings."

Roman turned around and felt the warmth of brilliant sunshine sting his cheeks.

"At least it isn't freezing cold..."

Immediately, darkness shrouded the sun. A strong gust of wind, whipped up clouds of snow, and swiftly became a blinding blizzard.

Chi-Ro closed his eyes. Shaking his head with dismay, he said, "Have you not learnt anything? Thought is the basis of the relative state we call reality. There is nothing more dangerous than thought."

Shocked and embarrassed Roman simply laughed.

Suddenly, Chi-Ro opened fiery eyes. With astounding speed, he reached into the folds of his tunic and hurled shuriken-like objects at Roman. Roman flung himself backwards as the metal blades whizzed past his head.

Falling into the soft snow, he heard a loud growl. Roman looked over his shoulder, in time to see the silhouette of a large man emerge from the monolith. The unmistakable astral form was that of Brakis Tarn.

Chapter 29

Black, ghostly hands grabbed Roman Doyle by the neck, lifting him out of the rising snow. With darkness and cold boring into his very soul, he tried to reassure himself.

It's only a dream.

Though Roman could no longer see him, he sensed that Chi-Ro Jin approached as fast as he could. Roman wanted to cry out but couldn't.

He even considered saying something clever such as, *Brakis Tarn; I've been expecting you. Welcome to my nightmare.*

Unable to breathe, and despite attempts to reassure himself, Roman feared his life was being drained away.

Chi-Ro exerted his will, instantly banishing the blizzard. Within seconds, he would be upon Brakis Tarn, giving his life to save the Prince; but Chi-Ro was too late. Brakis Tarn's astral form dragged the helpless Prince into the black monolith and was gone.

For a long time, Roman fell in complete darkness; and as he fell, he grappled with Brakis Tarn's spectral twin.

He heard a loud, piercing noise; similar to a sound he had heard many times on television dramas - the sound produced by a flatline, on an electrocardiograph machine.

Am I dying?

Soraya awoke suddenly. She felt her unborn child move, and at first she was very surprised.

It's unusual to feel movement this early. I read that women don't usually feel anything before sixteen weeks.

Then Soraya felt elated.

My baby is alive.

With a smile on her face, Soraya turned to look at her husband Roman, asleep in the regeneration pod beside her. She wanted to share this special moment with him.

Roman's eyes and mouth were wide open, as if frozen in a silent scream. Soraya screamed, and it was not silent.

Above the flatline sound, Roman heard Soraya's scream. He could not understand what was happening. The deafening high-pitched noise increased as he continued to fall, locked in a desperate struggle with Brakis Tarn's sinister phantom.

Roman's fear and confusion transformed into ferocity. The rage became a burning sensation that shot from his lower abdomen into his spine. Once again, he was about to unleash dark energy. Then he stopped, recalling Chi-Ro Jin's advice.

You will free your consciousness when you learn to be neutral.

Roman's objective became crystal clear. He had to rid himself of the anger and fear. He had to conquer his emotions and purge his feelings - a difficult objective.

Sensing Roman's determination to seize control of his untapped potential, Brakis Tarn spoke.

"Surrender willingly and I will spare your life. Continue the struggle and you will surely die."

Roman smirked, "Today is a great day to die."

"Your death will not be swift and painless young Prince," said Brakis Tarn, "You mask your fear well. But, in this astral plane, I am like a God; and I know what you fear most. Look down. Observe where your end lies."

Roman looked down and saw nothing but the complete absence of light - unending darkness.

"Let me guess, we're going to your basement flat in Hell."

"Behold, young Prince," said Brakis Tarn.

It took a moment for the high-pitched sound to be replaced by a rumble, like rolling thunder, and another moment for Roman to notice something grey far below. Then he felt moisture on his face.

At first, he thought it was rain; but he soon realised that the water on his face was not rain, and the sound he heard was not thunder.

"No, son of Sakara," boomed Brakis Tarn, "your senses do not deceive you. It is a river."

The river flowed into a waterfall.

"It's not real," Roman told himself.

"What is all too real," said Brakis Tarn, "is your fear of rivers. It is this all-consuming fear, which will kill you. Even now your heart nears the point of failure. Oh no, young Prince there will be no escape for you, no waking from your nightmare. You will hit the water like a meteor, and your body will be broken on the rocks below. You will drown alone in the cold darkness. After you die I will enjoy many pleasures with your consort, then I shall cut your offspring from her living body and feed it to my Ramani sabura."

Brakis Tarn realised his error, but it was too late. The words were spoken. The fear which threatened to end Roman's life was instantly replaced by something beyond rage - something, which defied definition.

This volcanic emotion could not be expressed in words. Roman growled like a savage beast. Darkness erupted from his lower abdomen spreading relentlessly until he was no longer a man but a shadow of a man. Roman had become a wraith.

The release of astral energy forced Brakis Tarn to lose his grip. Roman immediately grabbed the Karellan's head, and the men plunged into a steadily accelerating dive towards the river below. Suddenly in a blinding burst of light, everything changed.

Brakis Tarn crashed through the thick canopy of a rainforest, snagged on a branch and tangled in wild vines fifty metres above the ground. Fresh blood stained his purple tunic, from a gash he received in his left arm as he fell. No longer a spectre, he had resumed his flesh and blood form.

Where am I? he thought.

A voice like thunder reverberated all around him.

It said, *"You are in a dream within a dream. And here, I am the master."*

A man dressed in a black tunic swung from under the branch, delivering a devastating double kick into Brakis Tarn's mid section. Brakis Tarn broke free of the vines, falling several metres before grabbing a branch and propelling himself to another tree.

The son of Jin is more formidable than I thought.

But the man in the black tunic was not Chi-Ro Jin. Already on the tree, Roman stood behind Brakis Tarn in a Hatari Ikou ready stance. Brakis Tarn spun around and activated the sok-bou he had hidden in the sleeve of his tunic.

Roman back flipped to avoid being struck. He reached into the folds of his black tunic and produced nunchaku in each hand.

Brakis Tarn said, "Young Prince, you dare do battle with tye-sok-bou? This weapon is a relic from an age long..."

Roman attacked Brakis Tarn with bewildering speed and ferocity, forcing the master of Kon Jou to engage all his years of experience in order to maintain his balance and parry the relentless strikes of the two-piece rods.

Nevertheless, despite his youthful bravado, Roman was no match for Brakis Tarn. Brakis Tarn launched a devastating counter attack that forced

Roman to relinquish his precarious footing on the branch. With Brakis Tarn close behind, Roman swung from one vine to another until low enough to leap to the ground. Brakis Tarn's sok-bou, a deadly plasma whirlwind, forced Roman relentlessly backwards.

Suddenly, the ground gave way beneath Brakis Tarn's feet; and he realised that the son of Sakara had lured him into a primitive trap. However, lightning reflexes prevented Brakis Tarn's fall into the pit and Herculean strength propelled him to safety.

Short-lived safety. A wall of fire suddenly surrounded Brakis Tarn as Roman launched a psychic attack against his central nervous system.

Brakis Tarn counter attacked, and Roman fought to prevent images of drowning from flashing through his mind.

Soon he could hear Soraya screaming, "Help me Roman. Help me!"

The wall of flame that kept Brakis Tarn at bay vanished; and he launched a savage attack that cost Roman the nunchaku in his left hand.

"Surrender or I will kill everyone on the vimana," said Brakis Tarn.

"You're forgetting something."

"And what would that be, young Prince?"

"This is my dream."

Roman rolled to the ground avoiding Brakis Tarn's deadly sok-bou, striking the Karellan's right ankle with his remaining nunchaku. Brakis Tarn fell hard onto his back.

The two men rose swiftly, and Brakis Tarn immediately observed that Roman no longer held a tye-sok-bou. Instead, he had an entirely different weapon. A weapon called an FN P90 submachine gun, but there was no way the Karellan could have known that. It took Roman just over three seconds to empty the gun's fifty-round magazine into Brakis Tarn's body.

Roman threw the weapon to the ground, walked towards where Brakis Tarn had fallen, only to turn away, sickened by the sight of the Karellan's bullet-riddled body.

"What have I become?" he asked himself.

Suddenly he felt a sharp pain and a devastating numbness. Looking down, Roman saw the tip of Brakis Tarn's sok-bou protruding from just below his solar plexus. With everything slowly turning pale yellow, Roman looked over his shoulder.

Brakis Tarn gasped, "It is a great day to die."

Mortally wounded, Roman fell to his knees. He felt relieved that Brakis Tarn would not be able to harm his wife and unborn child. Then Roman entertained uncertainty that filled his heart with dread.

Isn't this only a dream?

Chapter 30

One dream ended - another resumed. Something was clearly wrong. Roman was still dreaming. In normal dreams, an incident such as being impaled by an alien plasma weapon would have awoken him immediately.

Roman plummeted to the raging river, wondering if there truly was life after death. He considered the fact that he could not swim, struck by the absurdity of the thought.

The fall alone will kill me.

It suddenly occurred to Roman that, in astral form, he might be able to cheat death. He might even be able to take control of the nightmare.

I need to overcome my fear, he thought.

Two voices now echoed in his mind.

His voice said, *"This is only a dream."*

Chi-Ro's voice said, *"You will free your consciousness when you learn to be neutral."*

As he fell, Roman closed his eyes and shut out the images of drowning, which flowed through his mind. Instead, he focussed on changing as he did before, during his aerial struggle with Brakis Tarn. Roman focussed on becoming a wraith.

Seconds before he plunged into the murky depths of the fast-flowing river, Roman achieved his goal. He was no longer a man, he was a shadow.

Roman did not recall hitting the water. He could not remember feeling an impact but confusing sensations filled his consciousness - swirling, tumbling sensations. Then he crashed against smooth rocks and briefly opened his eyes to see red in the greyish brown water.

Roman realised what happened. Moments after plunging into the river he reverted to his human form. He became flesh and blood again, a drowning human being.

Panic ensued. He gulped for breath, but water filled his lungs. He reached out, clutching at shadows but felt only swirling, muddy water.

Roman heard a familiar female voice with a Trinidadian accent scream, "Oh Gawd he dead! Roman dead!"

No, not yet, he thought.

Roman wanted to swim, but he had never learnt how to. He thrashed his legs in a frantic attempt to propel himself to the surface, but his legs cramped. In the churning, dragging current, he didn't even know which way was up. Then, as he began to lose consciousness, he thought he felt the embrace of something, or someone.

Is this how it feels to die?

Chi-Ro Jin struggled to remove the command helmet as the ship's systems fluctuated wildly. One moment, sensors indicated that the Asing vessel remained trapped in an indefinable darkness, the next they reported the warship was in normal space.

Mentally linked to the ship's main computer, Chi-Ro's mind and body were also adversely affected. Irregular heartbeats, muscle spasms, headache, nausea, confusion and hysteria combined forces and threatened to overwhelm the Master of Hatari Ikou.

Chi-Ro dropped the helmet on the metallic floor of the bridge and hauled himself out of the command pod. He had blurred vision and could barely stand. All around, panels and consoles flashed erratically.

Chi-Ro tried to wake Nuri Nemsys, reclined in an adjacent pod; but found, to his dismay, he couldn't. She appeared to be in deep sleep - dreaming.

Before Chi-Ro could fully consider the cause of her condition, Zachary's desperate voice blurted out of the intercom.

"Chino, can you hear me? It's Roman, he's had some sort of fit. Chino, are you there? Bloody alien technology, how am I supposed to work this out?"

In the background, Chi-Ro heard Soraya sobbing, "Oh Gawd, oh Gawd he dead!"

Chi-Ro barked into a communication panel, "Teev Meg, report to the infirmary immediately," and bolted into the lift.

Unaware he had suffered cardiac arrest and only vaguely aware he was no longer submerged in water, Roman tried to open his eyes but could not.

Gradually, his senses returned. He felt the hardness of the ground on which he lay in his soaked clothing. He felt sand and mud with his fingertips. And curiously, he felt a mouth pressed against his own.

Roman said weakly, "Soraya, a kiss for the dying?"

A female voice responded, "Your Highness?"

Roman stared into eyes of deep green.

This isn't Soraya; it's Nuri Nemsys.

Roman felt embarrassed and guilty of cheating. He had enjoyed Nuri's life saving mouth-to-mouth resuscitation far too much.

He asked her, "Am I dead?"

She replied, "You are no longer dead, Your Highness."

Roman tried to make sense of her words, but they sounded like gibberish. His head felt filled with cobwebs.

Did she say I was no longer dead?

Roman mumbled, "I don't understand."

"You suffered cardiac arrest; and, for nine Kian minutes, you were clinically dead."

Did she say I was dead for nine minutes?

"I thought this was only a dream."

"Yes Your Highness, this is a dream. Unfortunately, it is a dream you are experiencing whilst in a coma."

A coma? I can't tell what's real and what isn't anymore.

Roman felt something warm trickle down the side of his face. He touched it, then looked at his fingertips. They were covered in blood.

"Are you a figment of this dream?" he asked, suddenly aware of his own slightly slurred speech.

"No Your Highness, once I became aware of Brakis Tarn's presence, I entered this dream in an attempt to assist you. Now, like you, I find myself unable to wake."

"Where is Chi-Ro Jin?"

"When I entered the dream, Commander Chi-Ro was in the midst of a psychic storm - the creation of Brakis Tarn."

"Brakis Tarn threatened to kill everyone on the ship, we have to wake up."

"I sense that, Commander Chi-Ro's android is successfully reversing the ischemic injury you have endured."

"Huh?"

"I think the popular term in English is brain damage."

Outside the infirmary, Soraya, Zachary and Chi-Ro waited anxiously as Teev Meg performed the medical procedure required to save Roman's life.

Chi-Ro silently thanked the Great Spirit that the ship's systems had stopped malfunctioning. Zachary comforted Soraya who felt, that due to her nursing qualifications and close relationship to Roman, she belonged in the infirmary.

"The android knows what he's doing. Look at my eyes. I think I can actually see better now that he's operated on them. Roman will be just fine."

Unable to wait any longer, Chi-Ro spoke into a communication panel, "Progress report, Teev Meg."

"Commander, the patient is still in a coma. Disturbances in brain metabolism have occurred including water and electrolyte shifts. Areas of the

Prince's cerebral cortex have experienced failed perfusion. Sudden depolarisation of the neurons has occurred, with loss of intracellular potassium..."

"Confound your medical babble, Teev Meg. Can you fully restore Master Armon's health?"

"Yes Commander, I was about to say that I expect His Highness to fully recover."

Chi-Ro responded with relief, "Thank you, old friend."

Roman could see clearly now, and marvelled at his surroundings. The scenery reminded him of photographs he once saw of a waterfall, which acted as a natural border between Argentina and Brazil.

He thanked God that he had plunged into the river, at a point that was quite deep, about three hundred metres from the bottom of the waterfall.

The river's spray could easily have been mistaken for a steady drizzle of rain and Roman and Nuri were soaked to the bone but the brilliant sunshine kept them warm.

"Thanks for pulling me out of the water," said Roman.

"My duty is to serve, Your Highness."

"I'd prefer if you just call me Roman, I can't get used to the whole royalty thing."

"Curious that you would prefer the alias given to you by your guardians to the name given to you by your parents."

"I never knew my real parents, and Roman is the name I've known all my life."

"It is an anagram of Armon."

"Apparently. And what is your name - your real name?"

Nuri said with a flash of anger in her green eyes, "Did you not learn all my secrets when you violated me?"

"I'm sorry about that. It was a mistake. I didn't trust you."

"And now, do you trust me?"

Roman glanced at Nuri's lips, then into her deep green eyes and said, "If you tell me the truth, I'll trust you."

"May it be written," she said.

Roman knew that the correct response should be, *May it be done,* but he chose to remain silent.

Nuri said, "I am an intelligence agent in the Osirian Guard. My name is Kiya Mankuria, and I was born on Earth."

Chapter 31

Kiya's last words thoroughly shocked Roman. He searched her lime-green eyes for evidence of deception, but found none.

She was born on Earth? Were alien races actually living on Earth?

"How much has Commander Chi-Ro told you regarding the Talisian influence on Earth history?" asked Kiya.

"He told me that thousands of years ago, rogue Talisian scientists marooned on Earth, conducted genetic experiments on prehistoric humans. Eventually, the Talisian military arrested the scientists and bombarded the Earth, destroying evidence of their presence on the planet. He told me about my father, my uncle and the Psychic Wars."

"Commander Chi-Ro did not tell you everything."

"I've known Chi-Ro Jin just a short time, but I'm pretty sure he's not prone to deception."

"Commander Chi-Ro told you all he knew, but there is much he does not know. To all but a select few, in the Cosmic Sea's Ruling House, knowledge of Ki - of Earth, is strictly forbidden. The Talisians feared the super-sensed hybrids, created from genetic manipulation on Earth. The race they call Karellan... A race we call the Hyskoth... Your race."

"Brakis Tarn is Karellan, but Chi-Ro said I was Talisian."

"You are Talisian by birth. But your father and his father before him were born on a planet in the outer rim, a planet called Hyskoth. Talisians call this planet Karella. Sakara Rey sought to bring peace by removing any official distinction between those born on Talis and those born on Karella. He intended to banish racism and social prejudice by banning the kurai, the Talisian-imposed social caste system. In the Cosmic Sea, the old ethnic distinctions would be removed; replaced by a human race comprised of Talisians and Karellans, both natural and artificial."

"Chi-Ro told me he brought peace."

"Yes, he did, until his brother Seti Aljyk, gained the support of a small but powerful group of Karellan nationalists and usurped his throne."

"Yes, yes, I've already heard this from Chi-Ro."

"What the Talisians and Karellans do not know is that two of the scientists escaped with a small group of hybrids and remained on Earth. The bodies of the scientists' cloned doubles were discovered by androids - Jinzou Ningen sent to exterminate the hybrids they had developed. The Talisians assumed that the two brothers committed suicide rather than face their punishment. They were wrong."

"Who were these brothers?"

"Sons of Geb Rey, the greatest scientific mind ever known. The brothers were called Osiris and Seti."

"Seti is a variation of Seth. Geb, Osiris and Seth are important figures in ancient Egyptian myth."

"Yes, many historical facts are often dismissed as myth."

"So you're saying that aliens have been on Earth for thousands of years."

"Forgive me Your Highness but all the members of the Osirian Colonies and all the Followers of Seti were born on Earth. Earth history is our history. You were born on a planet, many light years from Earth. You may not want to accept it but, from my perspective, you are the alien."

"So that mysterious dampening field, which prevents phase and plasma weapons from functioning..."

"One of several security measures established by Osirian Colonists."

"This is unbelievable. Your technology is superior to that of the Talisians and Karellans, despite the age of their cultures?"

"Earth never experienced interstellar wars or the devastating Age of Darkness that ushered the fall of the United Empires of Talis. We retained the secrets they lost. And we continue to hide in plain sight among them. I am one of many operatives ensuring that Talisian and Hyskoth technological knowledge is shared with Osirians."

"You're a spy."

"I am dedicated to protecting the Earth. Do not forget, the Talisians once sought to rid the Earth of all sentient life, and there are much greater threats in the universe."

"Why are you telling me this? Why are you trusting me with this information?"

"Because it directly concerns you."

"But why are you telling me this now?"

"It is possible I will not survive this dream."

"What are you talking about? How can a dream kill you?"

"Like you, I am in a life support pod connected to the ship's systems. Systems linked to the infirmary are quite stable. Systems on the bridge are not."

"Can't Teev Meg save you?"

"That is uncertain, and the information I must pass to you is too important."

"You risked your life to save me?"

"As I hope you will live to save us all. Our intelligence reports have led us to believe that Sakara Rey is dying. The great pretender, Seti Aljyk, must not be allowed to continue his tyrannical rule."

Chapter 32

Soraya Doyle prayed silently that her husband would wake. She prayed that nine minutes of clinical death did not damage Roman's brain. She prayed that everything could return to how it was before she sent him out to find rum 'n' raisin ice cream and peanut butter - before the revelation of his royal status - before she became a hostage.

Soraya was exhausted, but found it difficult to relax on the spaceship. Three hours of restless sleep, the grey interior, recycled air and artificial gravity, inspired the most morbid of thoughts. She feared an invisible passenger aboard the alien warship - watching and waiting. She feared the angel of death.

Within his cloaked raider, Brakis Tarn watched the holographic image of the Su-Neku docked with Kiya's extraordinary starglider. His attempt to subdue the son of Sakara during the dreaming had failed; and, in less than a day, life support on his fighter would also fail.

I will not wait for a slow humiliating demise, cowering in the shadow of my enemy. My death will be the death of a warrior. I will attack, he thought.

But his weapons could not be brought online. He discovered that the mysterious starglider had created a dampening field, which disabled the phase and plasma weapons on his raider.

A dampening field identical to the one encountered on Ki.

The Japanese word *kamikaze*, which literally meant God-wind, was not in Brakis Tarn's vocabulary. Nonetheless, what he planned to do was similar to the acts of war committed by military aviators from the Empire of Japan on Earth in the 1940s.

The only effective weapon left at his disposal was the ship itself. He would activate the vessel's self-destruct mechanism. He would ram the vimana with his raider and kill them all.

On the bridge of Kiya's starglider, a proximity alert klaxon blared its grim warning. Consoles embedded in the metallic walls displayed ever changing illuminated characters, characters from a language thousands of years older than the city of Jericho.

The Abyssinian cat approached the ship's empty command pod, sat and stared silently. Suddenly the animal underwent an incredible transformation. It became a luminous humanoid that briefly glowed with a muted inner light; iridescently shimmering, before finally emerging a beautiful woman.

The nude woman remained prostrate for a moment then used her slender arms to push herself into a sitting position. She looked in her late forties with Mediterranean features; dark, tanned skin and long thoroughly white hair.

She stared at the main holographic view-screen with almond-shaped lime-green eyes that widened in terror. She had just seconds to prevent a catastrophic collision.

The white-haired woman swiftly entered the command pod, donned the command helmet, and targeted the Karellan raider with a repulsor ray - but it was too late.

Diverted by the repulsor ray, Brakis Tarn's raider missed the vimana but slammed into the aft section of the starglider. To his disappointment, the ships did not explode. The starglider's dampening field had affected the raider's self-destruct mechanism.

With its protective cloak lost, and its internal systems swiftly approaching overload, Brakis Tarn's raider hurtled uncontrollably away from its intended target. Both Brakis Tarn and the woman knew that, in their unfamiliar surroundings, the resultant explosion could still destroy or irreparably damage the vimana and the starglider.

Violent shock waves rocked the docked vessels. The starglider's aft shields failed completely; and the woman immediately activated sub-light engines, attempting to put as much distance as possible between Brakis Tarn's crippled raider.

The raider would explode at any moment, and the woman feverishly worked to re-route power to the starglider's aft shields. Unfortunately, there was no power available. The sub-light engines and the darkness, which enveloped them, had drained the starglider's energy reserves. If she remained docked to the Su-Neku, she would endanger the lives of all aboard.

The woman deactivated shields, released docking clamps, applied maximum thrust and simultaneously used the repulsor ray to nudge the Su-Neku away from the starglider.

Suddenly, a bright orange glow enveloped Brakis Tarn's Karellan raider. The electromagnetic drives had reached critical, and the ship exploded.

Chapter 33

Roman stared at Kiya with disbelief as they walked, along the bank of the river, away from the waterfall.

"Why didn't Chi-Ro tell me my father was dying?"

"The Commander does not know."

But you know?

"How did you get this information?"

"From someone very close to your father."

"An Osirian?"

"Precisely."

"Who?"

A sudden blast of wind and water threw Roman and Kiya to the ground. Surprised, they quickly leapt to their feet and looked around for the source of the disturbance. They could see nothing in the river or the surrounding landscape, which explained what just occurred.

Roman asked, "Kiya, what just happened?"

"Your Highness, please do not call me Kiya. It is of vital importance that my true identity is never divulged..."

"OK-OK! Nuri, what the hell just happened?"

"This is your dream."

In the distance, they heard a sound, which did not belong - the sound of a klaxon.

Nice.

Their surroundings slowly became darker, and the sound became louder.

"That sounds like..."

"Red alert," Kiya interrupted.

"Brakis Tarn is trying to make good on his promise. We have to wake up. We have to wake up now."

On the bridge of the vimana, the red alert klaxon blared. Chi-Ro fought mentally to regain control of the ship's trajectory while at the pod next to him, the Jinzou Ningen known as Teev Meg, battled to save Kiya's life. The explosion of Brakis Tarn's ship had made a bad situation much worse.

Drained by the unusual surroundings, the Su-Neku's shields absorbed the resultant shock wave then failed completely. The warship spiralled uncontrollably in the darkness.

Teev Meg said, "All attempts to rouse the patient have failed. I detect indications of lucid dreaming. Disturbances in brain metabolism are identical to those observed in Prince Armon Sakara. Identical areas of this patient's cerebral cortex have experienced failed perfusion..."

"Will she live?" barked Chi-Ro, impatiently.

Teev Meg responded, "I am sorry Commander. The patient is dying."

"The Prince shares her dream. End the dreaming. Sever the link."

"There is a sixty-five percent probability that both patients will die if either is disconnected from the ship's systems."

"The ship's systems are failing."

"Then it is imperative that I wake them before complete failure occurs."

"The Prince must not die. Use whatever resources you deem necessary."

In the ranks of the Karellan Marines, Chi-Ro Jin learnt many things as Brakis Tarn's apprentice. Brakis Tarn's greatest lessons were in the fine art of deception. During the battle of Sandovahl, Brakis Tarn with Chi-Ro as his co-pilot launched a foolhardy attack against a Talisian starcruiser.

A Karellan raider attacking a Talisian starcruiser is like a wasp attacking a fighter jet. But this particular wasp did not use its sting. Seconds after its pilot and co-pilot ejected, this wasp self-destructed. The explosion masked their escape and caused minor damage to the starcruiser.

The arrogant commander of the starcruiser believed that the damage to his vessel's fourth field generator was inconsequential. He was wrong. Minute traces of magnetically charged particles created a unique trail that Karellan vessels could detect. Brakis Tarn's plan had succeeded. The damaged starcruiser would reveal the exact location of the Talisian 6th fleet.

Several hours later, a Karellan marauder rescued the two members of the elite Shock Marines. A day later, the marauder detected the Talisian's magnetic trail. Supported by two other cruiser class vessels, it engaged and destroyed the Talisian warship before it could rendezvous with the 6th fleet at Thot Narev.

The Talisian hero, Marshal Archos Axum, commanded the destroyed warship. Malik Rameses son of Chancellor Rameses Gor was its first officer. The death of these prominent men and their shipmates was a turning point in the war against Talis, the war to liberate Karella led by First Consul Rey Enki.

The 3rd Karellan Armada, under the command of Baron Seti Aljyk, ambushed the Talisian 6th fleet at Thot Narev. The previously undefeated 6th, led by Viceroy Mol Kadar, surrendered without firing a single shot. Karellans celebrated a decisive victory. Brakis Tarn received the Star of Ra for heroism and outstanding bravery. Several years later he would lead a mission to capture Margrave Rin Mur-Rain, a mission, which led to genocide. Three million innocent colonists on Cyclo were killed.

    Brakis Tarn, hero of Sandovahl, Butcher of Cyclo, Chi-Ro thought.

    "Are you dead, my old teacher?"

    "Pardon me, Commander?" responded Teev Meg.

    "We are not alone, old friend. My old master, Brakis Tarn, is among us."

Chi-Ro stabilised the Su-Neku but allowed it to drift in a parallel course with the stricken starglider.

    He removed the secondary command helmet and climbed out of the command pod.

    Turning to the android, he said, "Teev Meg, protect the Prince at all cost. Everyone else is expendable. I'm going aboard the starglider. If I do not return in thirty minutes, this ship has two remaining quantum missiles. Use them."

    "But..."

    "That's an order, old friend."

    "I will proceed with orders received."

    "Good fellow."

    "Commander, may I ask, what do you hope to find on the starglider?"

    "Her pilot."

    "May the scribes record it."

Chapter 34

Within the dream, Roman stood silently near the riverbank. Kiya watched intently as he focussed on waking from their shared experience. Sounds and images flashed through Roman's mind, distractions he sought to banish.

In his mind's eye, he saw Soraya as she said "Please wake up."

He saw Chi-Ro wearing a black environmental suit and helmet, walking with stealth and purpose, through the corridor of an unfamiliar ship. Then Roman had a fleeting glimpse of Brakis Tarn dressed in a purple environmental suit. The blond warrior stood over the body of a naked woman, a woman whose face Roman could not recognise, a woman with long white hair.

He's near.

Roman brought all his willpower to bear.

He must be stopped.

On the bridge of Kiya's starglider, Brakis Tarn stood above the naked body of his vanquished foe. The woman had fought bravely using an unusual combination of Hatari Ikou and another style, which Brakis Tarn could not identify.

She had been well trained - physically and mentally. However, only Sakara Rey's shamira, the great Mara Kai Grandmaster Kai-Ita Wah, matched Brakis Tarn in single combat. This was before Brakis Tarn discovered the secret of astral warfare, before he became the embodiment of darkness.

The blond warrior smiled as behind him his former disciple silently entered the bridge.

"Ah, Chi-Ro Jin, I have been expecting you," he projected.

"Am I to add defiler of women to your list of crimes, my old master?" responded Chi-Ro.

Brakis Tarn laughed, and the bridge of the starglider became a darker place.

He turned to face his enemy and said, *"We will end this here and now, my young disciple."*

Chi-Ro Jin activated his sok-bou and said, "May the scribes record it."

In his mind's eye, Roman witnessed the battle between the man sworn to kill him and the man sworn to protect him. He would not allow Chi-Ro Jin to commit suicide.

The feeling began in the pit of Roman's stomach - a mild burning. He focussed and was rewarded with a warm tingling sensation at the base of his spine. His body felt electrified - more alive than before; and finally he became infused with clarity. The vimana Su-Neku became Roman's body and his astral vision perceived the light beyond the Fields of Eternal Oblivion.

Everything made perfect sense; and, for a fleeting moment, Roman admired the sheer simplicity of it all. Then his concentrated will, applied tractor beams to Kiya's stricken starglider and set his Su-Neku body in motion, bending the darkness and setting them all free. The starglider and the Su-Neku returned to normal space.

Roman awoke with a gasp, in a regeneration pod, in the infirmary aboard the Su-Neku. To his horror, Soraya and Zachary lay unconscious on the floor.

He hauled himself out of the pod and rushed to Soraya. She appeared unhurt. He placed his hand gently on her forehead and knew that she was unhurt, but Soraya was emotionally and physically exhausted.

"I'm sorry for what I put you through," he whispered, "you and the..."

Baby.

Roman placed his hand on Soraya's abdomen in an attempt to confirm that his unborn child was unharmed. Suddenly he experienced a sharp pain behind his eyes as if someone had pierced them with white-hot needles. He lurched backwards feeling the warmth of blood that accumulated in his nostrils.

Terror. The child is terrified. There are ships approaching - hundreds of ships. Ships commanded by Seti Aljyk.

Roman cautiously approached Soraya, lightly resting his hand on her abdomen once more.

Sleep, he thought.

He picked up Soraya, placed her gently in an adjacent regeneration pod, then stooped over Zachary and said, "Zachary wake up."

Zachary mumbled, "Roman, it's Saturday; I never work on Saturday."

"Get up," barked Roman.

Zachary instantly sat upright and said, "I'm up."

"Good."

Zachary brushed away the cobwebs of sleep and said, "Roman, thank God you're OK. Soraya and I were worried sick. Even Chino began to fret..."

Roman pulled his friend to his feet. The pair left the infirmary and jogged towards the bridge.

Roman asked, "Since when did you start believing in God?"

"I think it must've been after my molecules got scrambled by the matter transporter. Are we out of the great blackness?"

"Yes, but you'd better start praying because a couple hundred battle-ships are heading our way."

"And these wouldn't be friendly battleships would they?"

"Do you actually feel that lucky?"

"Why oh why does the toast fall on the buttered side each and every time?"

"At least try to think happy thoughts."

Who's the naked woman with the white hair? thought Zachary.

"How did you do that?" asked Roman.

"Do what?"

"Read my thoughts."

"You've been thinking about naked, white-haired women?"

"You know what? Later."

Roman and Zachary entered the bridge of the Su-Neku and found Kiya Manku-ria alone. She remained reclined in the secondary command pod, her eyes closed. They could not immediately ascertain whether she was simply asleep or still comatose. Roman approached her cautiously, placing his hand on her forehead.

"Is she still in a coma?" asked Zachary, furrows of worry appearing on his forehead.

"Is that your idea of a happy thought?"

"A simple 'no' would suffice."

"No."

"So where's our artificial friend?"

Roman grabbed the secondary command helmet from an adjacent pod and said, "No idea. We have to get out of Dodge right now."

"Put down the helmet," barked a familiar voice.

Roman turned to see Teev Meg on the other side of the bridge. The Jin-zou Ningen looked very ill. Wiping rivulets of sweat from his pale face, he stared with wild, blood-shot purple eyes, shakily aiming a Blastron P-19 phase pistol at Roman's head. Roman gently placed the secondary command helmet back into the command pod.

"What the hell are you doing?" Zachary asked Teev Meg.

"Do not move," replied Teev Meg now aiming the pistol at Zachary.

"Whoa, whoa. Easy," said Zachary, accepting the gravity of the situa-tion.

"Do not move."

"Hey, don't shoot."

Roman said calmly, "You're not going to shoot my friend are you Teev Meg?"

"His lips are constantly moving, and he fails to follow commands," came Teev Meg's unstable response.

Roman said softly, "Zach, whatever you do, just shut up."

Zachary's terrified eyes had become like saucers.

"The Prince must be contained and all other personnel neutralised," said Teev Meg, on the verge of hysteria.

"Did Chi-Ro Jin give you that order?" asked Roman, with pretended composure.

"Chi-Ro Jin is an enemy of The Cosmic Sea. I received my mission brief from my lord and master Brakis..."

Suddenly Teev Meg's head exploded in a halo of synthetic matter. His lifeless arm fell to his side before dropping the Blastron P-19. Then his headless body crashed to the ground.

Roman said, "I thought you were asleep."

"I was," replied Kiya, holstering her viridian pistol.

"Thanks for saving my life," added Zachary.

"It was not my intention to save your life."

"Right."

She has a sense of humour and an amazing arse...

"For your sake, I hope arse is the Kian word for intellect," said Kiya, with well-acted grimness.

"C'mon, you know I love you," said Zachary, his blue eyes twinkling.

Kiya raised an unimpressed eyebrow.

"Am I the only one worried about the Imperial fleet heading this way?" asked Roman, "Chi-Ro is on your ship Nuri. He went there to face Brakis Tarn. I think the monster's already killed your co-pilot."

"Co-pilot, what co-pilot?" asked Kiya.

"The woman with white hair."

Panic overcame Kiya. She slumped back into the pod trying to catch her breath.

"Who is she?"

Kiya pulled her communicator from her belt and spoke into it, "Nisa t'kul tilu."

"Who is she? repeated Roman.

"She's my mother," she said to Roman, and then to Zachary, "My mother..."

Chapter 35

It is fifteen minutes before Roman Doyle summons the willpower necessary to propel the Asing vimana Su-Neku, dragging Kiya's starglider, clear of the expanse of darkness known as the Fields of Eternal Oblivion. Fifteen minutes before both ships violently return to normal space. On the bridge of the starglider, a battle rages - beautiful, terrible, sublime. In such a battle, fifteen minutes is an eternity.

Both warriors dismiss the restrictions of their environmental suits. They are veterans of The Psychic Wars and have engaged in the dance of death countless times. Costumes are irrelevant - not permitted to hinder their steps. They know each other well. Once they were master and apprentice - closer than father and son. Now they are mortal enemies - Talisian against Karellan.

Chi-Ro Jin sensed no weakness in his old master. If anything, Brakis Tarn had grown even stronger. Every physical attack effortlessly parried. Every mental assault casually dismissed.

Brakis Tarn had several advantages: greater experience, superior strength and most importantly, the psychological advantage a master has over his pupil.

However, Chi-Ro Jin had a formidable ally: speed. He also believed that his was the righteous path. This faith, more than anything else, banished fear that would grip the soul of any other man.

Brakis Tarn parried Chi-Ro's sok-bou strike with his own. Twisting his upper body, he brought his Herculean strength to bear. Chi-Ro felt the strain in his wrists and bent like a taya reed deflecting Brakis Tarn's kinetic energy - forcing him to shift his balance.

Chi-Ro swiftly sought to exploit this shift but Brakis Tarn had danced the dance of death too many times. He recovered with a blow directed at Chi-Ro's grip on his weapon, simultaneously launching a psychic assault on Chi-Ro's optic nerves.

For a split second, 2.4 million nerve fibres registered only blinding pain, a familiar sensation to Chi-Ro. In fact, he almost laughed. He sucked in air and exhaled using his abdomen, releasing endorphins that banished the pain and strengthened his body. His mind's grim resolve could not be so easily shaken.

Chi-Ro Jin does not need eyes when the enemy's thoughts are so transparent.

Chi-Ro's sok-bou became a tornado, which threatened to impale the Karellan with lethal plasma electrodes. Very soon Brakis Tarn had enough.

My astral twin will end this once and for all, he thought.

Brakis Tarn suddenly spun his body low, threatening to sweep Chi-Ro's left ankle with his right leg. Anticipating the move, Chi-Ro leapt high, his crackling sok-bou poised for the kill. Continuing his movement, Brakis Tarn rose in a spinning kick, smashing his heel into the side of Chi-Ro's head. Simultaneously, Chi-Ro swung his upper body violently bringing the tip of his sok-bou into contact with Brakis Tarn's gloved left hand.

Brakis Tarn howled, losing his weapon; and Chi-Ro's aching body tumbled over the starglider's command pod. Sensing what Brakis Tarn intended to do, Chi-Ro retracted his sok-bou and quickly sprang to his feet.

Infernal guns, Chi-Ro thought.

Reaching for his own standard-issue sidearm, Chi-Ro leapt out of the way as a phase bolt hit the command pod. Brakis Tarn adjusted his aim, but Chi-Ro was blindingly quick. He rolled on the metal floor then sprang to his feet turning. Before he could fire again, Chi-Ro shot the Melcor HG-13 pistol out of Brakis Tarn's gloved hand and cursed his poor aim - he had missed Brakis Tarn's heart.

Brakis Tarn somersaulted backwards. Falling low to the ground as if about to perform push-ups, he propelled himself into a roll sideways, avoiding Chi-Ro's repeated shots of phase energy.

Preoccupied with his moving target, Chi-Ro did not discern the astral form, which lurked behind - until too late. His Daxia H3-16 pistol violently slapped out of his hand, he endured a devastating barrage of body blows too swift for any human to counter. Finally, a palm strike to the sternum sent Chi-Ro Jin airborne.

He crashed into a wall, then to the floor. He rose immediately in a Hatari Ikou ready stance having retrieved his sok-bou from his belt. However, before he could activate it, the grim spectre of Brakis Tarn motioned with his right hand. Chi-Ro's sok-bou immediately wrenched from his grasp. It flew across the room at terrific speed into the waiting hand of the black wraith. The wraith tossed the sok-bou away casually.

Brakis Tarn spoke, his voice low and ominous, "You thought you could defeat me, my young apprentice? What mindless folly. So, how does one punish a treacherous student?"

The wraith motioned again. A powerful telekinetic force threw Chi-Ro Jin into another wall.

"What a disappointment you have been my young disciple."

Chi-Ro flew into the ceiling like a rag doll discarded by a spiteful child. The impact consigned him to the periphery of consciousness, and he barely perceived his own body slamming into the cold metal floor.

Verily, there is no dishonour in death at the hands of a far superior enemy, he thought, *and mine is the path of righteousness.*

Like predators, Brakis Tarn and his astral twin converged on the fallen warrior.

"The path of righteousness? You are but the pathetic lackey of Sakara Rey. So much like your father. His path of righteousness, led to his death at my hands - so too will yours, my foolish pupil."

Chi-Ro's mind commanded his body to stand. His will urged his being to avenge the death of his beloved father; but his body could not stand, and his being could not comply with the wishes of his will. A psychic storm raged through Chi-Ro's consciousness, and concussion relieved him of vital faculties.

Holding his hands high like a conjuror, Brakis Tarn's astral form absorbed Chi-Ro's physical strength.

He said, with a voice that shook the bridge, "Only now at the end will you truly see the strength of my spirit."

"You place your faith in the spirit when it should be invested in the body," said the naked woman to Brakis Tarn.

She stood behind the Kon Jou master and his astral twin, armed with a viridian pistol.

Brakis Tarn laughed mockingly, "I thought you were dead."

"Foolish man."

She shot him. He lurched backward with pain and shock etched on his face. His dark entity immediately turned to mist and was gone. The woman fired again.

Suddenly, the ship attained unthinkable velocity. The phase bolt seared through the tip of Brakis Tarn's left ear. Brakis Tarn, the woman and Chi-Ro Jin were thrown from the deck of the vessel. They tumbled along the metal floor stunned and disorientated. They tumbled for seconds, which seemed like minutes. They tumbled until finally the starglider escaped the Fields of Eternal Oblivion and returned to normal space.

Mortally wounded, Brakis Tarn pulled an object from his utility belt. He exhaled slowly and laboriously as if reluctantly releasing his very soul. He activated the thermal grenade. Soon the excruciating pain in his chest would be no more. He stared at the fallen Chi-Ro Jin, and a sinister smile appeared on Brakis Tarn's pale face.

Yes, soon it will all end.

Chapter 36

On the bridge of the Asing vimana Su-Neku, Roman Doyle felt a chill scuttle down his spine. He had a disturbing vision of an explosion. Roman saw Chi-Ro Jin, the woman Kiya called mother and Brakis Tarn, blown to bits by Brakis Tarn's thermal grenade.

Roman saw the imminent future. He stood seconds away from immeasurable loss. He did not meditate, he did not focus he just acted. Instinct turned his physical body into an astral entity. Instinct propelled him through the metal wall of the bridge, through the outer hull and into outer space.

Faster than the speed of thought, Roman entered the bridge of Kiya's starglider. The noble Chi-Ro Jin, master of Hatari Ikou, was already in motion. He hoped to perform his last selfless act. He leaped towards Brakis Tarn in a desperate attempt to absorb the grenade's thermal discharge. Chi-Ro hoped to preserve the life of the brave woman who had just saved him from certain death.

"Flesh and bone are not an effective shield," projected Roman.

His astral body knocked Chi-Ro Jin away from Brakis Tarn and landed on the Karellan.

Roman stared deep into Brakis Tarn's stunned blue eyes with the gaze of grim darkness. With astral vision, he saw the red hues of Brakis Tarn's aura and understood the fundamental weakness inherent in the man. For an instant, Roman felt pity; but the feeling passed quickly.

Roman said, "Death whispers your name to me, Brakis Tarn."

Brakis Tarn's wraith leaped out of his mortal body and passed through the astral form of Roman Doyle.

From her viridian pistol, the white haired woman fired several times at Brakis Tarn's hovering wraith, but his darkness absorbed each bolt of energy and remained unharmed. He turned to her with contempt - contempt, which manifested itself in a massive telekinetic discharge. The woman soared like a leaf in a blizzard. She slammed into the ceiling and then crashed to the floor unconscious.

The evil spectre turned to Roman.

His voice shook the bridge as he calmly said, "You have learnt much son of Sakara but you have yet to master the dark ways."

Faster than the speed of thought, Brakis Tarn's astral twin phased though the starglider hull and merged into the darkness of outer space.

Chi-Ro's voice, thick with emotion, shouted, "Master Armon."

The thermal grenade exploded instantly, vaporising Brakis Tarn's physical body and immediately sending massive shockwaves through the starglider. The concentrated energy discharge broke Roman's resolve. Having absorbed the brunt of the explosion, Roman's astral form phased through the floor. He fell uncontrollably, regaining human form seconds before his body crashed onto the lower deck.

On the bridge of the Su-Neku, Zachary and Kiya stared at each other in disbelief.

"What the hell just happened?" mumbled Zachary.

He tried to sit on a low console but instead slipped and fell hard on his buttocks.

"It appears His Highness has many hidden talents."

Zachary rose to his feet clearly embarrassed and said, "I need a bloody cigarette."

The Su-Neku's red alert klaxon suddenly blared its stern warning, and Kiya immediately snapped out of her daze. She entered the command pod and donned the secondary command helmet.

"There has been a thermal discharge on the starglider."

"Roman?"

"More likely a grenade."

"No you robot, is Roman alive?"

"I'm detecting three humanoid life forms."

"And one of them is Roman?"

"We are being scanned."

"Why would he scan us?"

"We are being scanned by the flagship of the Imperial fleet, you silly man."

"Why didn't you just say so in the first place?"

Kiya immediately drew her viridian pistol and aimed it at Zachary.

"Be useful or be dead."

"Do you really think now is the right time to flirt?"

"Get the Prince's consort and proceed to the armoury. Retrieve three phase rifles, two phase pistols and as many thermal grenades as you can both carry."

"I hope they're labelled."

Kiya shook her head with dismay. Zachary left the bridge to perform his important task.

The proximity alert on the bridge of Kiya's starglider blared unmistakably. Several automated systems came to life. Chi-Ro peered through the hole in the deck made by the thermal explosion and saw Roman lying on the deck below. He telepathically scanned Roman for life.

Alive. Thank The Great Spirit; Master Armon is alive.

Chi-Ro moved into the starglider's command pod and put on the command helmet.

The white-haired woman regained consciousness. Naked and bruised, she stood slowly and placed her hand above a wall panel, which slid back silently. From the hidden compartment, she retrieved a black stealth suit identical to Kiya's.

The mysterious woman casually dressed, then turned to Chi-Ro.

She said, "Chi-Ro Jin I respectfully request that you tend to His Highness. I am Anah Sadaka. This is the Starbird Sanura, and I am her commander."

Chi-Ro stepped out of the command pod. He removed the command helmet, bowed and offered the helmet to Anah.

"Anah Sadaka, I owe you my life."

"Consider that debt repaid."

Chi-Ro looked deeply into her lime-green eyes.

"You have many questions, and many will be answered; but our time now grows short, shorter with each and every heartbeat."

"Verily. Time has not stood still. While we were marooned in the Fields of Eternal Oblivion, time in normal space has moved forward almost three years."

"And now, here in the outer rim, Seti Aljyk himself bears down upon us like a Currian fire raptor. But all is far from lost Commander Chi-Ro, Sanura my kitten is no ordinary vessel."

"May the scribes record it."

Chi-Ro left the bridge deeply puzzled by the fact he could not read Anah Sadaka in any way - no thoughts, no emotions, no clues.

Aboard the Asing starship, Zachary and Soraya made their way to the armoury. Soraya's thoughts and emotions were a whirlpool of worry, shock, fear and regret.

"So now we're gonna play soldier Zachary, is that it? What is Roman doing on the other ship?"

"That's a good question. It's probably best he explains it all when he sees you."

"What sort ah nonsense yuh feeding me Zach? Just tell me the truth."

"Well Roman, your husband, my friend, turned into what looked like a black ghost and flew through the hull of the ship and out into space. I haven't seen him since."

"You'll have to run that by me one more time Zachary, I'm only a country girl from Cedros. Roman woke from his coma, mentally brought both ships out of the empty darkness, then he turned into a black jumbie and flew, that was the word you used wasn't it? Roman flew through the walls of the ship. The technical word is hull isn't it? Roman flew through the hull into outer space."

"If a jumbie is a ghost then yes. That's exactly what happened."

"Let me ask you just one more question. Does any of this have anything at all to do with that green-eyed woman?"

"I think maybe her mother was on the other ship - the starglider. Roman thought she was the co-pilot..."

"Zachary don't say anything else. Now I'm glad you're taking me to the armoury. I'll need a gun or two."

"Soraya you're making me nervous."

Chi-Ro stooped over Roman, reassured to find him conscious and alert, with no serious injuries.

"Master Armon, I am glad you are alive, but saddened that once more you put your life in jeopardy for my sake. I am expendable, you are not."

Chi-Ro helped Roman to his feet.

"I couldn't just let you die Chi-Ro."

"You would abandon your wife and unborn child to save your shamira?" he asked telepathically.

"All this time, you knew?"

"Verily I say unto you, secrets are hard to keep in the presence of a veteran of the Psychic Wars."

"Is Nuri's mother alright?"

"Mother?"

"I thought secrets were hard to keep in the presence of a veteran of the Psychic Wars?"

"Perhaps this mother is also a veteran. Come Master Armon, the enemy is upon us. At this time, the bridge is the correct place for Lord Sakara's heir."

"My father is dying Chi-Ro. In fact, he may already be dead."

"How did you learn this?"

"Nuri Nemsys."

"I do not fully trust Nuri Nemsys or Anah Sadaka."

"I don't think we'll make it out of this predicament without their help."

Chi-Ro sighed, *"May the scribes record it."*

Chapter 37

The Royal Host of the Karellan Imperium, an armada of two hundred and twelve vessels, traversed the region of space known as the Fields of Aaru. This area, on the frontier of The Cosmic Sea, was also called the Fields of Offerings.

Here, the Karellans believed, the ailing Sakara Rey would regroup his forces. Here, they believed he planned to launch a final, desperate attempt to regain his throne.

Aboard the Imperial flagship Anhur, a squat grey-haired Karellan clad in ostentatious purple robes, sat at a large desk in his ready room. This is Archduke Herkol Proxis Teh-Chin, reviewing the results of multiple vessel scans on a holographic display.

"Sub-commander Zu Ree, you are certain this Talisian glider class vessel is the Starbird Adara, last commanded by Chi-Ro Jin?"

The thin sub-commander's lips trembled nervously when he spoke into the communication console.

"Yes, Your Grace, Imperial records confirm transponder and pulse beacon registry of the Starbird Adara. Long-range sensors detect an unusual energy signature. It is likely the vessel has been modified in the three years since it was last subjected to Imperial scans."

"And the vimana?"

"Positive identification of the vimana Su-Neku, last commanded by Felani Zaar of the Asing. This vessel has also been missing approximately three years."

"Curious."

The trembling of Zu Ree's lips spread to his voice.

"The vessel's communications array has sustained substantial damage. At this range, we received only weak audio transmissions."

"Continue."

"The Su-Neku's new commander claims to have taken Chi-Ro Jin into custody."

Archduke Herkol chuckled with disbelief.

"Who is this new commander?"

Zu Ree stuttered his response, "He c-claims to be B-B-Brakis Tarn and demands an audience with the Emperor."

Brakis Tarn? Is there truth in this? He has been presumed dead these last three years.

"Has he used the correct security codes and protocols?"

"Yes Your Grace, he provided the codes last assigned to him."

"Anything else sub-commander?"

"Yes Your Grace, sensors detected an unidentified transponder signal emanating from a humanoid within the vimana."

"What frequency?"

"Six-two-six point six-one, Your Grace."

The Archduke's pale face got even paler.

Six-two-six is an old royal signature. This frequency has not been used for the last thirty years, he thought.

The Archduke did not betray his concern when he said, "His Majesty the Emperor is asleep. I will speak with Brakis Tarn."

"The son of Tarn claims his words are for the Emperor's ears only."

"What impertinence!"

"Begging your forgiveness Your Grace, he cites Imperial order Tan-Kyu."

The Archduke's heart skipped a beat, his hands shook, and sweat appeared on his brow.

"Scan this area of space thoroughly, sub-commander and await further instructions. Inform me as soon as we are within matter transport range of the Su-Neku."

At the heart of the citadel, Seti Aljyk sat on his high, dark throne and scowled down at the diminutive form of Archduke Herkol Proxis Teh-Chin.

The False Emperor, an imposing black man with piercing dark eyes, wore a lavish black robe and a dark flowing cape emblazoned with the red, white and black symbol of the House of Seti: the long-snouted, jackal-bodied beast of Typhon. This regal garment did not fully conceal his athletic build. His head and face were clean-shaven; and evidence of an old battle scar ran from the left edge of his mouth, down to his dimpled chin.

At his right hand, dressed in crimson finery, stood Ne-Ro Jos, Grandmaster of The Holy Order of the Brotherhood of Mysteries. To his left, dressed in a shimmering black tunic, stood the False Emperor's shamira, Shan Kur-Karnah, the matchless Kon Jou master and wielder of the ancient ree-sok-bou or three section plasma staff. He gazed threateningly at the small Archduke and stroked his impressively long white Fu Manchu moustache.

During the last four months, Seti Aljyk suffered the irritating ill effects of insomnia. He was exceedingly displeased to be awoken, but he suppressed his desire to have the Archduke executed.

It would not do to be Lord of a universe inhabited solely by serfs.

"So pray tell Herkol, what news would prompt you to disturb the slumber of your Emperor?"

The Archduke's knees trembled as he knelt before the most feared man in the Cosmic Sea.

"My deepest apologies, Your Majesty. Your servant Brakis Tarn claims to have captured the traitor Chi-Ro Jin and humbly requests your audience."

"Remarkably bold for the son of a Shudyar peasant."

"He cites Your Majesty's order Tan-Kyu."

Seti Aljyk raised his left eyebrow.

He projected to Ne-Ro Jos, *"Ne-Ro seek the truth of it."*

"Your will is my command, my Emperor."

The evil monk's eyes rolled back, and he muttered words in an ancient, long forgotten tongue.

"The son of Tarn's thoughts are strangely elusive. I clearly sense the mind of Chi-Ro Jin and the presence of the one foretold. Your nephew is aboard the snake worshipers' vessel. I feel his power. Tread carefully My Master, this may be a trap."

So, Sakara's brat lives.

Archduke Herkol began to rise from his kneeling position, but Shan Kur-Karnah slowly shook his head disapprovingly. The Archduke resumed his submissive pose.

Seti Aljyk spoke to his terrified subject.

"Brakis Tarn is to be brought before me. Shan Kur-Karnah will personally lead the mission to retrieve the son of Tarn and his prisoner. My trusted sage, Ne-Ro Jos will accompany him. He will attend to the Tan-Kyu. And Herkol, see to it that my loyal servants have access to only your finest shock marines. Be sure you can trust these marines with your life Herkol, as your life is forfeit."

The Archduke swallowed audibly.

"By your will, Your Majesty."

Kiya, Zachary and Soraya, were now aboard Kiya's starglider. They all wore black stealth suits and reclined in life supporting pods. Kiya wore the vessel's command helmet.

Kiya said, "The first stage of our plan appears to have been successful. The Karellans have uploaded our falsified logs, and the virus I planted within them appears to have been undetected."

"Is this virus similar to the virus Brakis Tarn infected Chi-Ro's android with?" asked Zachary.

"This virus specifically targets Karellan weapon systems."

"Let's hope they haven't found a cure during the three years we were in the Dark Fields of Eternal Oblivion."

"Indeed."

Kiya remained calm and focussed. Soraya and Zachary did not. Soraya replayed the last words she uttered to Roman in her mind.

"I hope you're satisfied now," she told him with undisguised rage, "we'll be fighting your war, God help us all."

She regretted what she said.

I should have told him I loved him, she thought.

Something else troubled Soraya. She feared her unborn child was somehow abnormal - alien, not human. At first she thought her increasing paranoia was the product of being trapped in the Dark Fields. Now Soraya feared that the child was responsible for her premonitions and nightmares. She feared the child was evil.

Soraya noticed Kiya's intense gaze and recalled the telepathic ability the aliens possessed.

Soraya said to Kiya, "Roman once told me that the Fields of Offerings was the ancient Egyptian version of heaven."

Kiya replied, "I believe it was known as the realm of the deity Osiris."

"I can't say I'm experiencing bliss right now," interrupted Zachary.

The women ignored him.

Soraya said to Kiya, "You are very different to Chi-Ro Jin, you and Anah Sadaka. You know a lot about Earth."

"We are covert operatives; and, as such, we are exposed to secret information."

"Hmm," said Soraya.

Kiya thought: *She is not easily deceived. This woman has extraordinary insight and hidden talent.*

Suddenly Kiya felt a sharp pain behind her eyes. It was a pain unlike any she had felt before. Mercifully it came and went quickly. Kiya wondered if Brakis Tarn's consciousness had possessed Prince Armon's consort, but swiftly discarded the notion.

"Are you certain these evil aliens can't scan us?" asked Zachary.

"No Doctor, nothing is certain, particularly since three years have elapsed while we were trapped in the Dark Fields."

"You'd think I'd be used to all this after three years, but to me it feels like I was living a normal life on Earth just a week ago. Oh wait a moment, I was living a normal life on Earth just a week ago."

"You made a choice to assist your friend in his time of need. You played your part in rescuing his consort. Do you regret this?"

Zachary shot an embarrassed glance at Soraya, then said protestingly, "No, of course not."

"Then I suggest you follow the advice given by His Highness and think happy thoughts."

On the bridge of the Su-Neku, Anah Sadaka, who had assumed the large, blond Karellan form of Brakis Tarn, stood behind Chi-Ro Jin and Prince Armon Sakara. She held a Melcor C-51 phase rifle and her prisoners wore cuffs. The bridge had the telltale signs of a firefight, with several walls and consoles riddled by phase blasts.

Chi-Ro said, "Soon the Karellan fleet will be within transport range."

"Indeed," replied Anah Sadaka, with Brakis Tarn's gravelly voice.

"Before this day, I thought changelings were the stuff of fantasy."

"There is often truth at the core of fantasy, Commander Chi-Ro."

"Yes it is a day worthy of song."

"They are here," announced Anah Sadaka.

At that moment, the Su-Neku's damaged communications array received a boosted transmission and the holographic display came to life, revealing the distorted image of Shan Kur-Karnah. In the shadows behind him, lurked Ne-Ro Jos.

Shan Kur-Karnah said, "Brakis Tarn, it has been a while since we fought side by side in the battle of Minas Jeem."

"Age has made your memory unreliable, old man. It was my father Tarn Havek who harassed Muhd Golash's pitiful sentinels at Minas Jeem."

"I had to be sure it was truly you, young pup. Where are the brothers Zaar?"

"Killed by my old disciple, with the help of this abomination he was charged to protect."

"Let me speak with the son of Sakara," interrupted Ne-Ro Jos.

Ne-Ro Jos moved out of the shadows. The light caught his eyes; and, for a fleeting moment, his pale pupils appeared to illuminate from within.

"Ah yes, I can feel your power, Armon Sakara. Undisciplined. Driven by deep emotions and mental confusion. But you will be trained, and you will serve the Emperor of Emperors well."

Ne-Ro Jos attempted to probe Roman's mind. He was blocked.

Perhaps I have underestimated the son of Sakara.

He bowed to Roman and shrank back into the shadows, recalling chapter 25, verse 11 of the Biblicara Mysterium book of Leemar:

'In the Fields of Reeds, the faithful shall find him, riding the back of a magnificent bird; and his word will cause rampant chaos, yea even the false

king shall bow and cower by his word.' This is the prophecy revealed. The original scrolls speak of the Fields of Aaru. Aaru is the Ancient Talisian word for reed and vimana literally means raptor. A bird of prey. A magnificent bird. There is a storm coming, for which the Emperor may not be prepared.

Away from the communications console, Ne-Ro spoke into the comlink on his wrist.

"Archduke Herkol, have the Tan-Kyu transported to the inner sanctum immediately. Only brothers of The Mysterium can control this abomination."

"Forgive me soothsayer, but I do not believe in magic. I will, however, indulge you to provide psychic storm cover," said the Archduke with royal disdain.

"Consider the deed done," said Ne-Ro with a smile that looked like a grimace.

"I will immediately despatch six of my finest shock marines to your sanctuary," said the Archduke.

"Surely you refer to the Emperor's shock marines; nevertheless my answer is no. Warriors' ways cannot restrain the darkness that dwells within Armon Sakara.

"Your Eminence, did you say Armon Sakara?"

"Yes Your Grace, the son of Sakara has returned from the wilderness."

Shan Kur-Karnah said to Anah Sadaka disguised as Brakis Tarn, "Perhaps it is fitting that you have re-appeared here in the Fields of Aaru. Prepare for transport."

The transmission ended and the holographic display deactivated.

Chapter 38

In the gloom of his ready room, Archduke Herkol knelt in silent prayer to The Great Spirit. He slowly rose to his feet, with grim determination etched into his round, aged face. A wave of his right hand activated a previously indiscernible panel door in the wall above his desk. The door silently slid back, and the Archduke gazed at a sophisticated communications device. Terror and excitement threatened to overwhelm the Karellan nobleman.

Several alien characters briefly flashed on the holographic display - characters, which already existed when woolly mammoths roamed the Earth.

Finally, a logo appeared on the screen. The logo represented the Arosian Ten-Shi - the symbol of The House of Enki - the symbol of Sakara Rey. On Earth, the orange, black and white creature was easily recognisable. A king of Argos, from Greek Mythology, inspired the creature's scientific name - *Danaus plexippus*. But many people on Earth knew the creature by a simpler name - Monarch butterfly.

A robotic voice from the device said, "Imperial security protocols over-ridden. Perimeter secure. Channel secure. Awaiting instructions."

The Archduke took a deep breath and ushered in what courage his small body could muster.

He said, "Proceed with operation Moto Benu."

"May the scribes record it," said the robotic voice.

The Archduke motioned with his right hand and the panel door silently hid the secret communications device. He picked up a silver orb from his desk and activated it. A hologram of a young woman appeared. The Archduke stared lovingly at the static portrait, and a single tear ran down his cheek.

Here in The Fields of Aaru we will be reunited, my beloved.

Six Karellan shock marines materialised on the bridge of the Starbird Sanura. They appeared in battle-ready formation with Blastron M-24 rifles trained on the life support and command pods.

The battlesuit of a shock marine is designed to strike terror in the heart of the enemy. The life-supporting uniform was made of a dark grey metallic material that reacted to light and augmented its camouflage properties. The battlesuit also incorporated an exoskeleton, which enhanced the physical strength of the wearer.

A shock marine's helmet had the visual attributes of a sinister metallic skull. His sophisticated visor gave the appearance of evil yellow eyes and voice synthesisers made the Imperial soldier sound like a demon from hell.

Osirian stealth suit technology rendered Kiya, Zachary and Soraya invisible to the elite warriors; but fear overcame Soraya, and she sucked in her breath.

A normal human being would not have noticed this sound, but sensors on a shock marine's helmet could be adjusted to detect a heartbeat four feet away.

The six marines immediately trained their weapons on Soraya's position. She stopped herself from breathing but could not stop her heart from beating.

In the throne room of the Imperial flagship Anhur, Archduke Herkol once again knelt and trembled before the False Emperor, Seti Aljyk. Two sentinels, wearing blood red battlesuits, flanked the sinister tyrant. The sentinels were unarmed.

No weapons of any kind were permitted in the presence of the False Emperor. He alone bore arms. As always, at his side, Seti Aljyk wore Najura, the katana-like lapys nerian Sword of Power. The sword had been presented to his younger brother Sakara Rey, but Seti Aljyk believed the sword to be his birthright.

His voice reverberated, "Herkol, again you interrupt my slumber and are presented at my feet. Has Ne-Ro Jos secured my nephew?"

"The son of Sakara is to be transported to the inner sanctum this very moment, by order of Ne-Ro Jos."

On his dark throne, the False Emperor leaned forward and raised his left eyebrow.

He lowered his voice and said, "So Archduke, why have you requested another audience?"

Herkol felt Seti Aljyk's restraint. He sensed the calm before the storm.

"Your Majesty, I believe the son of Sakara's presence here in The Fields of Aaru is part of an elaborate trap. He must not be permitted aboard this vessel."

"You base your premise on telepathy?"

"No Your Majesty, we have just deciphered a coded message from Sakara Rey."

"Oh. A message to his son?"

"No Your Majesty, a message to you."

"Speak the words of it."

No longer afraid, Archduke Herkol looked deeply into the eyes of the
False Emperor.

The Archduke said, "Death whispers your name to me."

Then suddenly, the Archduke exploded.

In the main matter transfer room of the Imperial flagship Anhur, the operator
locked onto the bio-signatures of Brakis Tarn, Chi-Ro Jin, and Armon Sakara.

Brakis Tarn and Chi-Ro Jin were to be teleported directly to the main
matter transfer room. Armon Sakara would be redirected to the inner sanctum.

Six marines armed with Melcor C-51 phase rifles anticipated the arrival
of Brakis Tarn and his prisoner.

The operator activated the matter transfer process, but Brakis Tarn and
Chi-Ro Jin did not appear. Instead, the bodies of Kirato and Mika Zaar materialised.

"They are dead," muttered the shocked operator.

"So are you," said the most senior of the six marines.

He shot the operator. His marines quickly removed the bodies from the
matter transfer pads. Each man placed two thermal grenades at strategic points
on the consoles within the room. The leader then activated the matter transfer
sequence and the six soldiers dematerialised.

Chi-Ro accompanied by Anah, in the form of Brakis Tarn, materialised in the
matter transfer room of Kiya's starglider. They immediately realised that all had
not gone to plan.

"Master Armon is not with us," barked Chi-Ro.

"I fear he intends to face his uncle alone," said Anah with Brakis Tarn's
voice.

"Then all is lost," said Chi-Ro.

Roman materialised within a containment field, in the centre of the dim hexagonal room called the inner sanctum. The mysterious energy of lapys nerian
powered the field. Shimmering black and purple rays surrounded him.

At each of the room's six walls stood a dark monk. Shrouded in gloom, the faces of these hooded figures remained obscured. The long crimson cloaks they wore covered their entire bodies including their hands and feet. The sight of them chilled Roman's very soul.

Voices within voices whispered ancient incantations as their sinister wills generated a psychic storm - a barrage of mental confusion used to completely overwhelm an enemy.

Roman wrestled with images of dark, flowing rivers. Thoughts of drowning flooded his consciousness. The psychic attack forced him to relive the horrible death of his foster parents.

Like an evil spirit, Ne-Ro Jos slowly approached the containment field. He stared at Roman with eyes that betrayed contempt and envy. Roman tried to transform himself into his astral form but could not.

Ne-Ro Jos said, "I regret superpowers are not allowed at this engagement, young Prince."

On the bridge, of the Starbird Sanura, Kiya wanted to use her viridian pistol but the psychic storm generated by the monks aboard the Anhur had incapacitated her.

A vivid daydream gripped Zachary. He had no recollection of how he became a prisoner in a German Prisoner of War Camp during World War Two. Over and over grim officers of the Luftwaffe demanded his name, rank and serial number.

Zachary could not remember his name. He did not know his rank and had no serial number. All Zachary knew was that his commanding officer ordered him to think happy thoughts, but he had no idea what a happy thought was.

The Karellan shock marine levelled his Blastron M-24 rifle barrel at an invisible Soraya. Though unaffected by the raging psychic storm, Soraya was consumed by terror. The shock marine clearly heard the sound of her racing heartbeat.

He slowly applied pressure on the trigger of his phase rifle. But the marine's commanding officer had other plans. He shot the marine in the base of his skull at point-blank range. Soraya filled her lungs with much needed air and screamed.

Two large explosions in quick succession wracked the Imperial flagship Anhur. The first devastated the throne room. A second, much larger, explosion utterly destroyed the main matter transfer room and breached the outer hull.

Seconds later, energy feedback developed in the tractor beam holding the Starbird Sanura captive. The Anhur's tractor beam operators fought to re-establish the lock. Their efforts were brief. Six shock marines materialised unexpectedly and quickly terminated them.

The marines on the bridge of the Starbird Sanura lowered their weapons. The sergeant quickly removed a device from his belt and activated it. Soraya, Kiya and Zachary, became instantly visible.

"I am Sergeant Kordo Vanne," declared the marine to Soraya, "My men and I are loyal to the True Emperor, Sakara Rey."

The sergeant deactivated Kiya's command console and removed her command helmet. Kiya remained entranced.

"Where is Roman?" Soraya asked Kordo Vanne.

"Roman?"

"Where is Prince Armon?"

The sergeant nodded at a corporal. That marine pulled a device from his belt and scanned it. He shook his head as if to say, "I don't know."

Soraya said, "You have to find him."

"Listen to me very carefully; we have to leave now, or we will all die. You must pilot the ship."

"I can't do it. You have to do it," protested Soraya.

"To do that I would have to remove my helmet. If I remove my helmet, I will become a victim of the psychic storm just like your companions."

"You must pilot this ship."

"I don't know how."

"The ship will follow your will. Think about leaving this place quickly using the safest route and the ship will do so."

"Where is Chi-Ro Jin? Maybe he can..."

"He is aboard this ship in a catatonic state."

"You have just ten seconds to get this starglider away."

Soraya put on the command helmet.

"Will the ship to full power," said Kordo Vanne.

The starglider's electromagnetic drives rumbled to life.

"Go. Go now," he added.

Soraya focussed. The vessel shot away many times faster than a speed-ing bullet, rocking the much larger vimana. The Starbird Sanura left the Su-Neku and the Anhur far behind in its wake.

Suddenly the Su-Neku exploded, utterly destroying the forward shield-array of the Imperial flagship Anhur. With its navigation and communication arrays badly damaged, the huge avenger-class battlecarrier was effectively crippled, and revolt raged within.

Chapter 39

Aboard the Karellan flagship Anhur, in the inner sanctum of the monks of the Order of Mysteries, Roman Doyle remained trapped within a lapys nerian containment field.

The field prevented Roman from transforming into an astral entity. But it could not suppress his extra-sensory perception. Above the din of the psychic storm, Roman intercepted powerful notions from Grandmaster Ne-Ro Jos.

It has begun, thought Ne-Ro.

A tremor resonated throughout the sanctuary. Within the citadel, in the presence of Seti Aljyk, Archduke Herkol Proxis Teh-Chin committed suicide.

Unperturbed, Ne-Ro Jos stared intently at Roman.

Oh, how the mighty have fallen.

Moments later, the floor shook violently. A second more massive explosion destroyed the main matter transfer room two decks below. Mutiny swept through the battlecarrier. Rogue marines executed their commanders and committed acts of sabotage.

Ne-Ro Jos said, "Chi-Ro Jin believes you are the Soter. Do not be deluded, young Armon. You are not. The real threat to the Karellan Imperium comes not from you, but from your son."

Roman swooned. His eyes widened with shock.

He knows Soraya is pregnant?

"Oh yes, young Prince. All has been foretold. All has been foreseen. For decades, I anticipated the events which are currently unfolding. Soon, the Karellan Imperium will acquire its greatest weapon and a new order will rule the Cosmic Sea."

Roman stared deeply into the evil soothsayer's grey eyes.

Despite Ne-Ro's efforts, Roman found answers to several questions.

"It's been you all along. You manipulated Seti Aljyk. You're the traitor. You're behind the Psychic Wars."

Unexpectedly, six Karellan shock marines materialised in the room. They appeared behind Ne-Ro Jos in battle-ready formation. Six Blastron M-24 phase rifles trained on Roman, still trapped within the lapys nerian containment field.

At each wall of the hexagonal chamber, the crimson-cowled monks continued their relentless psychic assault. They were not distracted by the sudden appearance of the elite warriors. But their Grandmaster, Ne-Ro Jos, could not mask the blind fury that erupted within his twisted being.

The son of Sakara is more powerful than I foresaw. He has clouded my vision. I did not anticipate the appearance of these troops.

Facing the squad, Ne-Ro Jos told their corporal, "How dare you violate the inner sanctum of The Mysterium? I told the Archduke your presence here was not required."

"Our orders are from the Emperor, Your Eminence."

"The Emperor?"

Ne-Ro Jos twitched as if stung by a wasp. The look of anger on his face quickly transformed into one of deep concern.

"There has been an explosion in the throne room. You must protect the Emperor at once."

The corporal cried, "Our orders are from the True Emperor, Lord Sakara Rey."

The six marines opened fire.

In the throne room, at the heart of the citadel, twelve unarmed sentinels converged on the position of Seti Aljyk and assumed a defensive stance. Behind a protective energy field, the False Emperor sat on his throne shaking his head with dismay.

Shan Kur-Karnah materialised before the False Emperor. He knelt on one knee, his head bowed in humble submission.

"Your Majesty."

"Rise, Lord Shan. Once more, your instincts were proven correct. The Archduke was indeed a traitor."

Rising to his feet, the warrior said, "I vow to crush His Majesty's enemies."

"Indeed, Lord Shan, indeed."

Sub-commander Zu Ree entered the throne room. He led another squad of unarmed sentinels.

"Your Majesty, the revolt is being contained."

The False Emperor deactivated his security field and rose before the trembling officer.

"Excellent, sub-commander."

Seti Aljyk approached the thin Karellan.

He stared into his eyes and said, "So tell me sub-commander, how could the Archduke bring such an insidious weapon into the presence of your Emperor?"

"The technology employed in this explosion is alien and beyond our s-science. The Archduke himself was the explosive. His entire body was a bbiomolecular device. Our scanners can only detect the release of the triggering enzymes several seconds before detonation."

"I see," chimed the False Emperor, "Archduke Herkol was a relative of yours, was he not?"

"He w-was my w-wife's paternal grandfather," replied Zu Ree.

"Unfortunate."

Seti Aljyk drew the katana-like Najura in a flash. Then, with shocking speed and grace, he flicked Zu Ree's blood from the lapys nerian blade, before returning the deadly sword to its sheath.

Zu Ree tried to speak. Instead, his head toppled from his shoulders onto the floor. Zu Ree's decapitated body fell backwards and convulsed.

Seti Aljyk casually turned to Shan Kur-Karnah and said, "Lord Shan, ensure that all relatives of Archduke Herkol Proxis Teh-Chin are publicly executed. Obviously he did not work alone. This treachery originated from a more intelligent mind. Extract the truth of it. This revolt ends now."

"Yes, Your Majesty."

"So, my shamira, where is my brother's son?"

"He is in the inner sanctum."

"Ah yes. Have Ne-Ro Jos bring my nephew before me at once. Somehow my soothsayer failed to foresee this attempt on my life. Let us hope he does not explode."

Lord Shan said, "By your will," and bowed reverently.

Seti Aljyk returned to his throne.

As an afterthought, he asked, "Lord Shan, is the Adara underway?"

"Yes Your Majesty, seven raiders are in pursuit."

"I trust our agent is safely aboard."

"Yes, Your Majesty."

"Excellent."

In the inner sanctum, Ne-Ro Jos and his six monks were unharmed. The enraged Grandmaster raised his hands in the manner of a wizard. The shock marines struggled against psychic suggestion too powerful for their helmets to block. Like automatons, they turned to each other and took deadly aim.

"You fools, did you really think your pathetic weapons could harm me?" said Ne-Ro Jos.

"They weren't targeting you – you moron," said Roman.

Ne-Ro Jos quickly spun on his heels. Wide-eyed, he saw the field generator had been blasted, the containment field deactivated. The black wraith of Roman Doyle stood before him, unrestrained.

"This cannot be," Ne-Ro mumbled.

Roman grabbed the Grandmaster by his head. Ne-Ro Jos howled in agony and the marines swiftly targeted Roman.

Roman brought his formidable will to bear. Suddenly, the marines spun in unison and levelled their sights on Ne-Ro's unarmed monks. The Grandmaster grimaced with effort.

"Now I'll know what you know," said Roman.

"No," screamed the soothsayer.

Roman saw images of Soraya asleep in the bedroom of their Friern Barnet flat. In horror, he watched helplessly as a man materialised in the darkness. The intruder injected his wife's neck with a device identical to the one used by Chi-Ro Jin.

Was that elidium?

Roman could not tell, nor could he see the administrant's face.

Roman tightened his grip on Ne-Ro Jos's skull. He peered into eyes that fought to avoid his piercing gaze. He saw secrets within secrets. Fantasy and deception obscured the truth. Ne-Ro Jos was an accomplished psychic liar.

Then indelible images of genocide tortured Roman's soul. He saw himself as a wraith, seated on a dark throne. All around him was evil and death.

Is this what I'll become?

His instincts convinced him that this was deception – a desperate attempt by Ne-Ro Jos to hide the real truth.

Roman said, "You evil bastard," and lost control.

The shock marines opened fire. The six monks fell to the ground - they were dead.

Roman felt sick to his stomach.

I killed them, he thought.

"You cannot escape your evil destiny," cried Ne-Ro Jos.

"Neither can you," said Roman.

He released Ne-Ro Jos. The cleric immediately threw himself to the ground screaming. He rolled about as if demon-possessed. The Grandmaster wrestled with his deepest fears. In his mind, he had fallen into a pit of Elosian vipers. The aggressive snakes bit him repeatedly.

Roman quickly realised he could not sustain his astral form much longer. His struggle against Ne-Ro Jos and his evil followers left him drained. But he vowed to complete the task he had set himself.

I will learn the whole truth, he thought.

Abandoning the convulsing soothsayer, Roman phased through a wall of the inner sanctum. He emerged into a deserted corridor and quickly accessed a system panel. He reached out with his astral consciousness.

Where is Seti Aljyk?

Released from psychic control, the shock marines turned their attention and weapons to Ne-Ro Jos. But before they could execute the crazed cleric, twelve infantrymen loyal to Seti Aljyk appeared in the inner sanctum. In the gunfight that ensued, nine infantrymen and all six rebels were killed.

Shan Kur-Karnah retrieved his ree-sok-bou from the giant sentry on duty outside the throne room. He strode with purpose towards the inner sanctum of the Mysterium.

Suddenly Roman emerged through a wall. He stood, having resumed human form, ten metres away from Shan Kur-Karnah, silently evaluating his predicament.

"Remarkable," said Shan Kur-Karnah, "You possess an incredible talent."

The sentry immediately moved to take aim with his formidable Gonda PC-64D phase cannon.

Shan Kur-Karnah calmly told him, "At ease soldier."

The giant lowered his weapon.

"His Majesty has been expecting you Prince Armon," said Shan Kur-Karnah.

Of course, entering the citadel was far too easy. The security arrangements for one pretending to be the Emperor of Emperors seem suspiciously inadequate, especially in light of the recent mutiny. No, they've planned this. They want me to enter the throne room. It's a trap. Ne-Ro Jos certainly believes he's pulling all the strings, but I suspect he's just a victim of his own arrogance.

Roman walked slowly towards Shan Kur-Karnah and the giant sentry. Without warning, twelve sentinels armed with Blastron M-24 phase rifles materialised around Roman.

"Lower your weapons," barked Shan Kur-Karnah.

The soldiers immediately complied.

Roman moved only his eyes. He committed the position of each sentinel to memory. He was careful but confident.

Roman acquired several skills from the unique individuals he encountered during his adventure. From Chi-Ro Jin, Roman absorbed knowledge of Hatari Ikou. From Brakis Tarn, he learnt Kon Jou, the way of the spirit warrior. And, from Kiya Mankuria, Roman drew the secrets of an obscure Osirian art called Ma Isha, an art unfamiliar to both Karellans and Talisians.

Roman resolved to conserve his astral energy. If necessary, he would fight using only his mind and physical body. He needed his astral energy to escape once he completed his task.

"Your men are making me nervous," he told Shan Kur-Karnah.

"Curious. I sensed no discomfort. I shall have them removed at once." Shan Kur-Karnah nodded to the sentinel leader.

Immediately, the soldier spoke into his wrist communicator, "This is lance corporal Burr Kaych requesting retrieval from sector zero-zero-one."

A voice from the comlink replied, "Standby for transport to level four. Prepare to engage rebel marine squadron. Execute with extreme prejudice."

"Proceeding with orders received."

The red-armoured sentinels raised their weapons and assumed a battle-ready stance. A moment later they dematerialised.

Roman continued to walk towards the large double doors of the throne room. Shan Kur-Karnah removed his ree-sok-bou and returned it to the sentry. The giant took the ancient weapon then stepped aside.

Shan Kur-Karnah turned to Roman and respectfully bowed low. The massive doors slowly swung open to reveal Seti Aljyk seated on his throne.

A sense of apprehension rose from the pit of Roman's stomach and settled in his throat.

I'm willingly walking into a trap, he thought.

Roman stepped inside, and Shan Kur-Karnah followed. Behind them, the immense double doors slowly swung shut.

Chapter 40

The Starbird Sanura, piloted by Soraya Doyle, hurtled at sub-light speed towards the Aaruan Nebula. The interstellar cloud of plasma, dust and hydrogen gas marked the end of the Fields of Aaru and the frontier of the Cosmic Sea. The scribes recorded that no Talisian or Karellan vessel had ever returned from the Aaruan Nebula. It was believed that nothing could survive the plasma storms that raged within.

Seven Karellan raiders pursued the Starbird Sanura. Three years ago, this Osirian prototype could easily outrun any fighter vessel in the Cosmic Sea, but the Sanura had remained in the Fields of Eternal Oblivion three years. Karellan technology improved a great deal during that time. Soraya sensed the Karellan raiders would overtake the Sanura before it could enter the Aaruan Nebula. But this did not bother her. She had no intention of entering the nebula.

Soraya willed the Sanura into an impossibly small arc and the seven raiders shot past, their pilots bewildered by the illogical course change and the astounding manoeuvrability of the much larger starglider.

"What are you doing?" asked Kordo Vanne.

"My husband needs me," replied Soraya.

"Milady, you are being affected by the psychic storm."

Kiya and Zachary stirred in their life supporting pods.

"No sergeant, the storm has passed."

Suddenly an unseen force wrenched the marines' phase rifles from their grasps. For a brief moment, the weapons remained suspended in midair. Then the barrel of each hovering rifle swiftly targeted each of the five marines' chest.

Soraya willed the Sanura on an intercept course with the Karellan armada. The seven raiders recovered, regrouped and resumed their pursuit.

Soraya said to Kordo Vanne, "Just take it easy man, we only goin' for a short ride."

"With all due respect, Milady, you are gripped by madness," said Kordo Vanne.

Soraya sucked her teeth loudly, and the Blastron M-24 aimed at Kordo Vanne's chest suddenly targeted his head. He wisely decided not to speak another word.

Zachary opened his eyes and saw the five marines held at gunpoint. He closed his eyes in disbelief.

I must be dreaming, he thought.

"Zach, could you do me a big favour?" said Soraya, "Grab Nuri's gun. Take these men below and lock them up. They messin' with meh concentration."

"Soraya, what's going on? Who are these guys and why are you flying the ship towards certain doom?"

"I'll explain later."

"You're flying the ship. Why are you flying the ship? And what's with the rifles, are you doing this?"

"You'll have to trust me Zach. Please, just get these soldiers to the brig."

Zachary said to himself, "I take a nap and mild-mannered Soraya develops telekinesis and an attitude. Am I the only normal human being in this galaxy?"

Zachary climbed out of his pod and approached Kiya. As he reached for Kiya's viridian pistol, she drew the weapon with lightning speed. Just as quickly, Zachary gripped the barrel of the weapon and with a swift twist disarmed her.

Zachary aimed at Kiya's chest and said, "Lovely Nuri, as much as I'd love to flirt with you, now really isn't the time."

Kiya resorted to her secret weapon - pheromones. The effect on Zachary was instant. He immediately noticed the protrusion of her nipples under her skin-tight stealth suit. He tried to fight the distraction but felt light-headed.

Stop thinking with your genes, Zach. She's an alien with no sense of humour.

At first Zachary only wanted to kiss her. Just one kiss. He imagined holding her close, and tasting her full lips. And, in an instant, he wanted more. His breath became shallow; and between his legs, an obvious and embarrassing reaction occurred.

Zachary's carnal yearning abruptly ended when Kiya's knee crashed into his groin. He doubled over and fell to the floor howling in agony. Immediately, Kiya flew out of the pod and slammed into the ceiling like a leaf in a gust of wind. She remained pressed against the cold, grey metal in a spread-eagle position. An incredible telekinetic force made it difficult for her to speak.

"Lady Soraya, what you plan to do is suicide... The choices you make now will affect the entire universe... What you possess is more valuable to the Karellans than Prince Armon. The source, of your power, is the child you carry in your womb... They must not get your son..."

Soraya gasped in shock. Kiya and the five Blastron M-24 rifles suddenly crashed to the deck. The shock marines swiftly retrieved their weapons. They brought them to bear on Soraya, Kiya and Zachary who levelled the barrel of Kiya's viridian piston on Kordo Vanne's chest.

"Let's try to remain calm," said Zachary threateningly.

"Milady, in the interest of safety, I am assuming command of this vessel," said Kordo Vanne.

"You will do no such thing," came the voice of Anah Sadaka, "I am charged with the command of Sanura and my will alone shall decide her fate."

Anah and Chi-Ro were on the bridge. Armed with viridian rifles, they targeted the marines.

"Stop! All of you," shouted Soraya.

Suddenly Anah, Chi-Ro and the marines had their rifles wrenched from their grasps. Before they could even try to retrieve their hovering weapons, Soraya activated the ship's matter transporter and initiated a site-to-site transport.

Anah, Kiya, Chi-Ro and the marines materialised in the ship's brig. The marines looked to their commander for direction. Sergeant Kordo Vanne had none. Kiya sat in a corner of the room, stared at Anah and shook her head with dismay. Anah's gaze lowered to the deck, burdened by disappointment.

"Confound it," Chi-Ro shouted in frustration, slamming both fists into the metal wall.

"It appears recent events have adversely affected Soraya's mind," came Anah's telepathic projection, *"This was not anticipated."*

"Not anticipated? So, has the spider rejected the web of your design?"

Anah stared at Chi-Ro and raised a quizzical eyebrow.

Chi-Ro continued mentally, *"Madam, it is clear to me that neither you nor this woman, who claims to be Nuri Nemsys, are Talisian. What is not clear to me is the purpose to which you are directing your efforts."*

"I assure you Chi-Ro Jin, our actions and intentions are in the interest of peace and stability in the Cosmic Sea. There is far more at stake than the life of your beloved Prince Armon. Forces more malevolent than those of Karella are poised to destroy everything we value."

"Who are you?"

"A friend."

Anah gazed deeply into Chi-Ro's eyes and clasped his hands in her own.

On the bridge of the Starbird Sanura, Soraya Doyle mentally coaxed as much sub-light speed as possible from the Osirian craft.

"I'm glad you didn't make me disappear," said Zachary.

He held his stomach and grimaced as he returned to his life-supporting pod.

"You're the only one on this ship I trust."

"You didn't do anything rash like materialise them in space, did you?"

"No Zach, they're safe in the brig."

"Just checking."

Soraya managed a smile. She understood Zachary's need to diffuse a crisis situation with humour.

"Sorry about my outburst earlier, I just remembered that business on the M25 a couple years ago."

"That was not my fault. In no way was that accident a reflection on my driving."

"No-no-no, I agree... But it was a damn shame, what happened to that horse. Besides, driving a car and piloting a spaceship are two completely different things. You clearly have the piloting under control, maybe I can help with weapons."

"That won't be necessary."

"Huh?"

"I've convinced the pilots of the ships chasing us that they are our armed escorts."

"What? You can do that? How on Earth can you do that?"

Soraya did not answer. Staring into her eyes, Zachary noted that they had changed colour. Her eyes were now a much lighter shade of brown.

Just like Roman's, he thought. *Is Soraya an alien too?*

"Soraya, what's happened to you?"

"You'll have to ask Nuri and that Ligahoo she calls her mother."

"A Ligahoo is a shape-shifter from Trinidadian folklore, right?"

"Yep, but I assure you, they ain't Trinidadian."

"No, Trinidadians have a sense of humour, unlike that alien dyke who crushed my nuts..."

"So many voices whispering in my head... I just want them to stop."

Soraya clenched her fists. The bridge became more illuminated, and Zachary noticed a tremor under his feet. He suddenly felt on edge, and a chill ran down his spine.

"Is it true, what Nuri said? Are you expecting?"

"Yes."

"Brilliant. That's great news, congratulations. You guys kept that quiet..."

Instinctively, Soraya gently rubbed her pelvis. Then, her eyes filled with tears.

"Hey, I'm looking forward to being a godfather," said Zachary.

"I'm scared Zach. I'm afraid of what I'm capable of doing, what Moses and Roman are capable of doing. Even if we all get out of this mess alive, how could we return to Earth? We've become freaks."

"Don't be silly, you've just developed some new talents. Who knows? This may be the next step in human evolution. I see it as a positive development, especially in light of our present predicament. Let's rescue our best friend and get the hell out of this bloody nightmare."

"Lord, forgive me for what I'm about to do."

Zachary swallowed hard. Soraya's last comment echoed in his mind. Zachary was unsure what Soraya intended to do, and he was too afraid to ask. He focussed his attention on the steadily growing holographic image of the Imperial flagship Anhur. The avenger class battlecarrier represented the very things Zachary's martial arts training aimed to conquer - darkness and fear.

I need a cigarette, he thought.

Chapter 41

In the citadel, of the Karellan flagship Anhur, Prince Armon Sakara, also known as Roman Doyle, stood before the False Emperor, Seti Aljyk. Roman held the sharp gaze of his uncle who sat silently on his dark throne, flanked on each side by six unarmed sentinels.

Roman realised that his newfound abilities had made him overconfident. Chi-Ro's holographic images of Seti Aljyk did not prepare Roman for the dread he experienced standing in Seti Aljyk's presence. The formidable monarch seemed to draw energy from everything in the room. He exuded darkness and instilled fear.

Shan Kur-Karnah fell on his knee before Seti Aljyk and said, "Your Highness, I present Prince Armon, son of Sakara Rey."

"Bow before your Emperor," Shan Kur-Karnah projected to Roman sternly.

Without averting his gaze, Seti Aljyk said to Shan Kur-Karnah, "We shall dispense with protocol Lord Shan, you may rise. I suspect our ways are quite alien to my nephew. He has spent many years in terrible exile on the primitive planet Ki."

To Roman he said, "Prince Armon, I bid welcome to my brother's son."

Roman remained silent.

"Ah, your eyes betray your accusations. You blame me for your exile, but the anger, which grows in your heart, is misplaced. Your exile was of your father's design. It is truly unfortunate that you bear the yoke of his sins."

Roman said, "Where is my father?"

Shan Kur-Karnah quickly glared at the Prince and clenched his fists. Seti Aljyk casually motioned with his hand and Shan-Kur Karnah relaxed.

"My brother Sakara has been most elusive."

Roman felt his mind being probed. The intensity was shocking, but he adapted quickly and resisted.

"But now that you have presented yourself to me I am certain your father will reveal himself, and I can bring this destructive war to an end."

"You want to learn the secret of astral transformation."

"Verily, I see there is no deceiving you, but I am not alone in this quest. Why do you believe your father exiled you to Ki? What do you believe the sons of Geb Rey were trying to achieve on that primitive world?"

"A race of super beings... They hoped to create a race of super beings," said Roman

"Indeed. And, if I am to believe my sage Ne-Ro Jos, the product of their experimentation now stands before me. He claims you are more powerful than Brakis Tarn. We have studied Brakis Tarn's special talent. We are aware he can create a separate astral entity. Indeed, this is an impressive talent, which unfortunately leaves his physical body vulnerable to attack. But you, I am told, are capable of complete astral transformation; the transformation of your physical body into an astral form, with the marked advantage of invulnerability."

Once more Roman was subjected to an intense mental probe and this time he developed a nosebleed.

Seti Aljyk lowered his voice as he said, "Oh. I see... You have dispatched both Ne-Ro Jos and Brakis Tarn. Remarkable. Show me this power. I must see your astral form and know the truth of it."

"I am only interested in finding my father," said Roman.

He launched a counter probe at Seti Aljyk. Shan Kur-Karnah and the twelve sentinels all felt it. The room appeared darker, and the floor shook beneath their feet. Roman and Seti Aljyk struggled mentally, until finally Seti Aljyk motioned with his hand. A wall of psychic energy hit Roman, hurling him into the air; but he landed on his feet several metres away.

He is far more powerful than he pretends to be. And, he wants... He wants the baby. My God, the starglider is coming back... They're coming here. I have to stop them.

Seti Aljyk said, "Prince Armon I'm afraid the walls, floor and ceiling of my throne room are all made of lapys nerian. For you, there will be no escape. Lord Shan, kindly reveal my nephew's strength to me."

"By your will."

The unarmed Kon Jou master approached Roman, each stride confirming his confidence and resolve. Roman assumed a Hatari Ikou ready stance. Shan Kur-Karnah stood before him, stroked his long Fu Manchu moustache and smirked.

"Do you seek to mock me, young Prince? Or do you actually hope to resist a master of Kon Jou with Talisian cacadoh. It will take much more than this to drive me into the folly of rage."

With lightning speed Roman grabbed one side of Shan Kur-Karnah's Fu Manchu moustache and ripped the long white hair from his face.

For a moment, Shan Kur-Karnah just stood wide-eyed and stared in utter amazement. Then he tried to touch his moustache and found that it was gone.

Roman opened his palm, blew the hair into his shocked opponent's face and smiled.

Shan Kur-Karnah snapped out of his daze, and launched a vicious attack, roaring with uncontrollable anger.

Wave after wave of punches, faster than the eye could see, threatened to knock Roman into oblivion. Forced to retreat, Roman desperately blocked, deflected and avoided the deadly blows.

Suddenly a devastating palm strike crashed into Roman's chest. He flew off his feet and landed on the cold floor gasping for breath.

"Now I know the rhythm of your heart, your end will come quite swiftly," smirked Shan Kur-Karnah.

"Indeed Lord Shan, grant no quarter. This pitiful display is unbecoming of a prince of the blood. The child of prophecy will be delivered to me shortly. I shall learn the secret of astral transformation from him. Feel free to make Armon suffer for his father's sins as I shall make his son suffer for his."

"No," roared Roman.

On the bridge of the starbird Sanura, Soraya heard her husband's cry. Zachary instinctively sensed the source of Soraya's sudden unease.

"Roman?"

"They're killing him," replied Soraya with tears welling in her light brown eyes.

"You guys have the power cosmic but that's an armada we're heading into. We're gonna need some help."

"I know," replied Soraya.

"I'll go get Chi-Ro and the others."

Soraya nodded and tried to regain composure.

She said, "You do whatever you need to do to get ready, Zachary. In a minute, I'm gonna give these space devils de hell dey deserve."

"Yeah, I have to admit, these aliens are beginning to piss me off."

Soraya managed a smile and shook her head.

"Go, go now."

Zachary left the bridge. Alone, Soraya clenched her fists and gritted her teeth.

Her eyes rolled back and she said in a voice, dark and ominous, "May it be written, may it be done."

Driven into a relentless retreat, Roman considered it a miracle that all his bones were still intact. But Shan Kur-Karnah did not plan to break bones.

Roman knew that the Kon Jou master planned to strike his heart. He knew the blow would come at a precise moment, between heartbeats. Shan Kur-Karnah planned to cause sudden cardiac death. With each new attack, he perfected the timing of his punches until finally he was able to hit Roman as he blinked.

In the split-second that Roman's eyes were closed, Shan Kur-Karnah delivered his deathblow, a Kon Jou vibrating palm strike, into Roman's chest, directly above his heart. To Roman, the punch was invisible. He never saw it, but he felt it. A pain like no other, immediately numbed the left side of his body into fatal paralysis. Roman's heart had stopped beating.

Roman fell to his knees at the mercy of the Kon Jou master. Shan Kur-Karnah grabbed Roman's head and looked to Seti Aljyk for a sign. With an approving nod from Seti Aljyk, Shan Kur-Karnah would snap Roman's neck.

Seti Aljyk nodded his head. But, before Shan Kur-Karnah could perform his execution, Roman attacked with a punch. This was no ordinary punch. His hand phased through Shan Kur-Karnah's chest and solidified at the precise moment of impact with the Kon Jou master's heart.

In shock and pain, Shan Kur-Karnah released Roman. Without hesitation, Roman leapt to his feet, grabbed Shan Kur-Karnah by the head and wrenched it, snapping his neck.

Both men collapsed; one dead, the other dying.

Seti Aljyk did well to hide his surprise.

He remarked, "Impressive. It seems Armon, you are indeed a prince of the blood. So now, will you save yourself or perish?"

With every ounce of his willpower, he focussed on making the transformation from flesh to spirit. The lack of oxygen to his brain made his mind wander. Within a second, which lasted an eternity, it travelled to another place and another time.

Roman found himself in darkness - a complete absence of light. Then he saw something. At first, he did not notice the pinprick of illumination, but it grew and grew. Within the light, stood a silhouette. The silhouette of a woman. Roman recognised her instantly.

"Mother," he said, and all was light, "Mother is that really you?"

"Yes Roman, I am here with you now in this place, in the time that it takes for a heart to perform a single beat."

"Am I dead?"

"Once again, this is the choice you must make," said Mina Rin.

"What is this place?"

"Indecision. Limbo."

Suddenly Roman heard a distant voice.

It said, "Roman, please don't go."

The woman's Trinidadian accent immediately conjured up pleasant memories of his early childhood on the tropical island.

"Soraya," he said.

"The voice of love calls to you, my son," said Mina.

From the source of the brilliant light, behind where Mina stood, a single monarch butterfly emerged. It swooped down towards Roman. He stretched out his right arm, opened his hand and the butterfly came to rest on his palm.

"Mother what is the significance of this butterfly?"

"Why Roman, is it not obvious? It's a symbol. The monarch is your father, as it is you, as it is your unborn son."

"Yes, I know. Somehow, I've always known. I just didn't want to accept it. I didn't want the responsibility."

"Now that your purpose is clear, you need not suffer the winds of limbo. Sakara Rey needs you as does your wife and unborn child, go forth and fulfil your destiny. Farewell my Prince."

The dream ended, and reality returned. Prince Armon Sakara, also known as Roman Doyle, transformed into an astral being.

His darkness turned to Seti Aljyk and proclaimed,

"All that belongs to my father shall be restored. You will never know my secret. You will never hold my son. May the scribes record it."

Chapter 42

Aboard the Starbird Sanura, Dr. Zachary Silverman released Chi-Ro, Kiya, Anah Sadaka and the five disgruntled shock marines from the brig.

Chi-Ro said, "I agree with Lady Soraya's objective..."

"I do not," interrupted Anah.

Zachary added, "Now is not the time to piss about. We get Roman and we get the hell out of here. That's it, no debate."

Anah replied, "Have a care Kian, I am the commander of this vessel..."

Anah fell silent when Zachary raised the viridian pistol he confiscated from Kiya.

"I've decided I don't like that word – *Kian*. You say it like some obscene reference to an inferior race. For the record, I'm a human being from Earth, not Ki. What are you? A changeling - a cat-woman freak. And, this war of yours, what's it all about? Oh, let me guess, does it have something to do with racial superiority? Are you part of the master race of the universe? How long have you been fighting? How many billions have died? Oh yeah, you feel so superior with your telepathic ability and advanced technology; yet with all that, you still lack the wisdom required for peaceful co-existence. Prick up your ears mein Führer and listen well, help us find my friend or park your pussycat's tail in the brig."

There was a moment of stunned silence, and then Chi-Ro chuckled.

"What's so funny?" asked Zachary.

"I much prefer going into battle with this doctor at my side."

"Yeah right. Listen, I'm sorry I'm not a brave warrior. I'm no cold-blooded killer..."

"Not brave? On the contrary, you are the bravest of us all. The warriors aboard this vessel have fought numerous battles. We have faced death countless times. We are soldiers, prepared to defend ourselves, prepared to die. You are a doctor, not a warrior; your greatest weapon is loyalty to your friend. And, in the name of this loyalty, you freely risk your precious life. No Dr. Zachary Silverman, I salute you."

This time Zachary chuckled.

"What amuses you Dr. Zachary Silverman?"

"I'm touched Chi-Ro, I thought you didn't like me."

"What I dislike, are your frequent and often pitiful attempts at humour."

"Right, I'll stick to full bastard mode then."

Anah Sadaka glared at Zachary as she communicated with him telepathically.

"Perhaps one day you will learn how much you owe to my kind, Dr. Zachary Silverman of Earth. I will be on my bridge. My expertise will be required, if we are to rescue Prince Armon and escape with our lives."

Anah turned towards Kiya and said, "Go with them young one. The Soter must not be captured."

Zachary holstered the viridian pistol and said to Anah, "Soraya wants us all to go to the transporter room."

"Two hundred years ago my mother said to me, 'Be patient in a moment of anger, and escape a hundred days of sorrow'. But, I say unto you, Dr. Zachary Silverman, if you continue to test my patience, the sorrow shall be yours."

Anah headed towards the lift, which would take her to the bridge. Zachary led the way towards the transporter room in the opposite direction.

Zachary said to himself, "Two hundred years? Just how old is she?"

Kiya said, "Dr. Silverman, I will require my pistol."

"Bollocks," replied Zachary.

"Excuse me. What are bollocks?" said Kiya, in well-acted ignorance.

"They're what you slammed your bony knee into a minute ago."

"Oh. You appear to have grown new ones."

"Yeah? Well the gun is mine."

Seated on his magnificent throne, flanked on each side by six unarmed sentinels, Seti Aljyk regarded the wraith standing above his lifeless shamira, Shan Kur-Karnah. The wraith was his nephew, Prince Armon Sakara, also known as Roman Doyle.

"I find your juvenile threats most amusing. Your greatest weakness, Prince Armon, is arrogance. It is this arrogance, which brings you before me uttering words of treason. It is this arrogance, which brings you before me untrained and untested."

"Yet, despite my lack of training, I was able to kill your champion."

"I prefer the word retire. Lord Shan had grown old and ineffective. But let it not be said that I am completely devoid of mercy. I granted him the retirement of a loyal servant, the death befitting a warrior. His son, Lord Karamba Shan, a much younger, more powerful shamira, will take his place; and their House of Wotan shall retain its honour."

"You used psychic suggestion. You wanted me to kill Shan Kur-Karnah."

"Do you really think his failure to prevent a traitor exploding in my presence would go unpunished?"

"Before I left Earth, I was a schoolteacher. Now, because of you and your war, I've become a killer. Believe me, when I say I won't have any reservations about ending your reign, uncle."

"Alas. Overconfidence, coupled with misguided ideals. It is your Kian morality, which offers remorse as an acceptable response. But wait, I sense it is not the ethical implication of killing, which disturbs you. It is the exhilaration you feel having extinguished the life of your opponent. This conflict which rages within, shall be your undoing my nephew."

"Goodbye, my uncle."

"Don't force me to destroy you, Armon. It would break your poor father's fragile heart."

"His heart is already broken. You broke it a long time ago."

Seti Aljyk rose from his throne, allowing his dark cape to slip from his broad shoulders. He stood taller and appeared much more imposing than Roman anticipated. Roman imagined a knot develop in his stomach. He quickly reminded himself that he no longer had a stomach; he was an astral entity. But the thought was not as reassuring as he had hoped.

"Well my nephew," said Seti Aljyk, "There are many lessons to be learnt. Stand forth, so I may teach you."

Seti Aljyk motioned to his sentinels, and the twelve warriors slowly backed away. Roman did not want to kill Seti Aljyk. He believed that if he could overpower and capture him, he could bring the war to an end.

Roman rushed towards Seti Aljyk who drew the Sword of Power and brought it down towards Roman's forehead in a flash. Instinctively, Roman clasped the blade between both palms.

The blade felt like fire, fire that drained his energy. Roman twisted sharply, deflecting the blow away from his forehead. The blade grazed his left shoulder, and he cried out as excruciating pain shot through the left side of his astral body.

Roman fell to the ground. Something was terribly wrong. He placed his hand on his shoulder where the blade had come into contact with his astral form.

Roman instantly realised what had happened, he was no longer a wraith. He was flesh and blood. Blood, which now poured from the open flesh of his shoulder.

Roman stared with wide-eyed terror at Seti Aljyk, who stood above him like the angel of death.

Seti Aljyk growled, "Lesson number one, the first blow is half the battle."

Chapter 43

Aboard the Starbird Sanura, Chi-Ro Jin led the five shock marines into the matter transport room. Zachary approached the room with rising apprehension; Kiya followed close behind.

"Dr. Zachary Silverman," she said.

"What now?" responded Zachary bluntly.

Kiya did not respond, so he turned to face her. She stood closer than he anticipated, close enough to feel her warm breath on his cheek. He briefly stared into mesmerising green eyes, before glancing at her full lips.

"What?" he asked, but this time his voice was not cold and uncaring.

"May the Great Spirit grant you his divine providence..."

Out of view from Chi-Ro and the five shock marines, Kiya pulled Zachary close and kissed him. Lust instantly replaced his shock, and they kissed passionately.

Then Kiya skilfully retrieved her viridian pistol from Zachary's holster. She broke the kiss. And, before he could react, she twirled the weapon with the finesse of a seasoned pistolero and secured it in her holster.

"...And for your groin injury," she continued with a faint smile, "please accept my sincerest apology."

"OK," said Zachary shaking his head and revealing a bemused grin.

"Do try to remain focussed on our mission, Dr. Zachary Silverman."

"I'm suddenly remarkably alert."

Zachary followed Kiya into the transporter room. Staring at the contours of her full hips and ample posterior, in her black stealth suit, he felt invigorated, no longer afraid of the darkness ahead.

On the bridge of the Starbird Sanura, reclined in the command pod, Soraya whispered a prayer as four Karellan marauders escorted by sixteen raiders deployed to intercept the starglider. Suddenly she felt a pang of anger.

How could Roman risk his life confronting this man? This Emperor, an uncle he never knew?

Then an overwhelming sense of dread, replaced her anger.

Are we all going to die out here in space, light-years from Earth?

Soraya sensed that the Karellan warships had orders not to destroy the starglider. She knew that Seti Aljyk wanted her unborn son alive. She felt it. Seti Aljyk's lust for power left an indelible impression on her consciousness.

Then she saw something unexpected. She saw herself asleep in the bedroom of her home in Friern Barnet, North London. A thunderstorm raged outside. In the dark room, she felt a presence - a malevolent presence. She saw a silhouette of a man with his face totally shrouded in darkness. He turned towards her as lightning flashed and she saw that it wasn't a man at all. It was something inhuman – reptilian. It stepped backwards into a full-length mirror and was gone.

"Jumbie. You will not have my son," she said.

"Indeed," said Anah entering the bridge, "the False Emperor must not acquire your son. The unborn Prince must be protected at all cost, which is why I disagreed with your current course of action."

Soraya hid her distress well and tried to dismiss the disturbing vision as simply a bizarre daydream. She kept the starglider on an intercept course with the Karellan flagship, and braced herself for a confrontation with Anah Sadaka.

"Disagree all you like, I'm going for my husband," she said.

"So be it, Lady Soraya. I see you are determined to follow this course of action. Return control of this vessel to me, and focus your attention on the creation of a psychic storm."

"How do I know I can trust you, Ligahoo?"

"Lady Soraya, asking you to return that which is mine is purely a courtesy," Anah paused a moment in reflection then added, "I am of the Niburian race. We have formed an alliance with the Osirians and are the secret guardians of Earth. But if that is not enough to warrant your trust, then trust the one who drew your husband from the Cipero River and certain death."

"That was you? But I thought..."

"I have assumed many forms in my many years but now, in the face of our mortal enemy, is not the time for revelation. I relieve you of your command Lady Soraya."

Soraya hauled herself out of the command pod and removed the command helmet. She passed the helmet to Anah who placed it on her head and took her place in the command pod.

Anah said, "I see you have convinced several Karellan fighters to provide us with an armed escort, very resourceful. Now, use your skill to turn the enemy upon themselves."

In the citadel of the Imperial flagship Anhur, Seti Aljyk swiftly wielded the Sword of Power. He shook Roman's blood from the lapys nerian blade and returned it to its scabbard in one fluid motion.

As he slowly rose to his feet, Roman used his right hand to apply pressure to the wound on his left shoulder. The extreme pain and the sight of his blood made him dizzy.

Seti Aljyk noticed a speck of Roman's blood on the back of his right hand. Without breaking eye contact with Roman, the False Emperor slowly raised his hand and licked the blood from it.

"Such a waste of something so very precious, Royal Karellan blood. I regret, that in their efforts to learn the genetic secret of your astral ability, my scientists will shed considerably more of your precious blood."

"I give my life for my wife and for my son."

"Yes, as we speak, the starglider is returning."

"What?"

"Behold."

Seti Aljyk motioned, with his right hand, and a holographic image appeared. Realising that Seti Aljyk spoke the truth, Roman's eyes widened in shock and disbelief. The Starbird Sanura was on an intercept course with the Karellan flagship.

"But why would they do that?" muttered Roman.

"Loyalty or love perhaps? My race learned to dispense with such emotions eons ago."

"Your race?"

Seti Aljyk returned to his throne and chuckled, "Lesson number two, all warfare is based on deception."

He tilted his head back, and his eyes rolled, so that his pupils were hidden behind his eyelids. A high-pitched inhuman shriek emanated from his throat.

The twelve sentinels leapt into action, immediately surrounding Roman.

"Who are you?"

"We are Saurian. Perhaps you will find some comfort in the knowledge that it was not your uncle but I who betrayed your father. The laws of nature are remarkably consistent throughout the Cosmic Sea. The superior thrive on the inferior, is it not always so? Our resources are depleted, our Niburian livestock ravaged by genetic plagues and our population steadily growing. Surely you understand our need to feed."

Roman's stomach muscles contracted, he tasted the bitterness of bile in his mouth, and wanted to throw up. He exhaled sharply and focussed on remaining calm. He had to overcome the pain in his shoulder and the dizziness, which threatened to topple him to the floor. He had to rid himself of fear. Mercifully, he sensed the False Emperor wanted him alive. He was to be a Guinea pig. This gave him hope of escape.

Searching for more information, Roman probed the False Emperor's mind. He saw concentration camps filled with Karellans and Talisians. Men, women and children, herded together like cattle bred for the slaughter.

"My God."

"If there is a God, is it not his will that you feed us? Has not this God provided us with the rich bounty of Talisian and Karellan flesh? Soon this war will end; and we shall seek out the vast reserves of flesh to be found on Ki, that planet you call Earth."

"No," cried Roman defiantly.

He grabbed a sentinel, quickly snapped his neck and hurled him into two others.

There are too many of them, hopefully they'll get into each other's way, he thought.

They did. The sentinels had difficulty fighting a single, very agile foe; and Roman soon discovered their weakness.

They aren't telepathic. The impostor is different. Maybe his psychic ability is artificial or maybe he's from a different species. I have a chance of getting out of here in one piece.

With his astral energy drained, Roman concentrated on phasing just his hands. His hands punched through armour, ripped through bone and sinew and smashed vital organs.

The dark brown blood of the Saurians stunk like vomit mixed with rotting leaves.

In a few seconds, Roman managed to kill five of the lizard-like sentinels. His head throbbed, and his stomach churned. The stench made catching his breath an ordeal. As he stood in Hatari Ikou ready stance, the seven remaining sentinels kept a safe distance.

The False Emperor hissed with rage and said, "Do I have to contain this animal myself?"

One sentinel turned to the False Emperor and shrieked a reply. The False Emperor stood, quickly drew the Sword of Power and beheaded the creature. With a swift flourish, he shook its brown blood from the blade and returned Najura, the Sword of Power, to its scabbard.

The False Emperor approached Roman who backed away and glanced towards the exit.

"There is no escape, Karellan."

The False Emperor raised his right hand like a conjuror and Roman was immediately suspended in midair. The Saurian raised his left hand and Roman's arms and legs stretched out as if drawn on an invisible rack. Roman cried out in agony. He felt his limbs being pulled by an impossible force and feared they were about to dislocate.

The False Emperor spoke with a low, sinister growl, "So tell me Karellan, will I have to tear you limb from limb as I did your uncle?"

Aboard the Starbird Sanura, Soraya Doyle exerted her newfound power of persuasion. The sixteen Karellan fighters broke formation and crashed into the four marauder-class battlecruisers. She tried not to think of the many men she had killed. She tried and failed.

The Osirian virus embedded in the falsified logs of the Asing vimana Su-Neku, and the Starbird Sanura, remained undetected by the Karellans. It swiftly spread throughout the Karellan fleet, infecting every weapon system. Then it became dormant - waiting for the weapon systems to be activated.

On the bridge of the crippled Imperial flagship Anhur, Admiral Dunai Ras-Karaf gave the order to all vessels to power weapons and destroy the Sanura's fighter escort. It was the last order he would give.

The formidable weapon systems of the avenger class battlecarrier were the first to overload. The feedback created by the massive energy discharge, channelled through command stations, and helmets throughout the fleet.

The admiral was the first to have his head explode. Soon, hundreds of officers and high-ranking officials were similarly killed as the chain-reaction rapidly spread throughout the fleet.

The mutineers seized the moment. Chaos enveloped the Karellan armada, as those loyal to Sakara Rey engaged the supporters of Seti Aljyk in mortal combat.

Once more in command of the Starbird Sanura, Anah Sadaka willed the vessel to break formation. She veered upwards into a tight arc and engaged the Sanura's stealth cloak. The seven Karellan raiders, under the psychic direction of Soraya Doyle, crashed into the bridge of the battlecarrier Anhur.

The resulting explosion completely destroyed the bridge of the Imperial flagship. The battlecarrier immediately began to veer out of formation and out of control, to the loud cheers of those loyal to Sakara Rey.

The Starbird Sanura descended from the arc and Anah brought the vessel to a halt within matter transfer range of the flagship.

"I'm going to the transporter room," announced Soraya as she headed to the lift, "I'm going with them."

"No dear child, you are not," said Anah.

Soraya turned around slowly, like a woman drugged. She tried to speak, but her eyes rolled back. She was about to collapse but Anah motioned with her right hand and instead of falling to the floor, an unconscious Soraya was gently lowered to the ground.

"Now sleep," said Anah, "your battle has ended."

Chapter 44

In the throne room of the stricken flagship Anhur, Roman Doyle remained suspended in midair, tortured by the False Emperor. Roman felt the steadily increasing strain of an immense telekinetic force on his outstretched limbs.

With his consciousness failing, he thought: *Soon it will all be over.*

On the holographic view-screen, the False Emperor watched the Starbird Sanura's relentless approach with a contented smile etched on his dark face.

Not even this modified starglider could hope to challenge four marauder class battlecruisers with a sixteen-fighter escort.

Suddenly the sixteen raiders broke formation and ploughed into the four battlecruisers. The white light of plasma explosions illuminated the Fields of Aaru and vaporised hundreds of Karellan troops.

"What is this?" the False Emperor asked himself.

"That would be lesson number three. Speed, surprise and unpredictability," said Roman.

"Impertinent prey."

Motioning dismissively, the False Emperor hurled Roman into the ceiling high above with a burst of telekinetic energy. Roman's skull impacted hard on the cold lapys nerian. Then the Saurian leader released his telekinetic grasp and callously allowed Roman to fall to the floor - unconscious.

The six remaining sentinels approached Roman's fallen body cautiously, like hungry vultures anticipating the death of a fatally wounded animal.

The False Emperor shrieked. The sentinels quickly assembled themselves and no longer displayed their lizard-like qualities.

Wide-eyed, the Saurian leader witnessed the Sanura arc away from her seven-raider escort and disappear. A moment later, the raiders crashed into the bridge of the Anhur, sending massive shockwaves throughout the doomed vessel.

A series of distant explosions rocked the flagship and ominous darkness descended upon the throne room. The False Emperor swore vengeance with a thunderous roar that sliced through the palpable gloom.

In the matter transfer room, of the Starbird Sanura, Zachary, Kiya, Chi-Ro, Sergeant Kordo Vanne and his four shock marines made final physical and mental preparations for their teleportation to the Karellan flagship, Anhur.

"Won't they be expecting us?" Zachary asked Kiya.

She replied casually, "Eight warriors assaulting the Imperial flagship? I should think not."

"Seven warriors and a risk manager. Risk management used to be my day job, before I pursued intergalactic activities. But seriously, what if they're expecting us?"

"Then our mission will be brief."

"Very brief," added Kordo Vanne.

Chi-Ro sensed that Kordo Vanne and his shock marines were unusually agitated for seasoned warriors.

Suddenly a disturbing thought flashed through Chi-Ro's mind. It was the image of a creature he had not imagined since early childhood. The young Chi-Ro named the monster that inhabited his nightmares. He called it the Seriak - a humanoid lizard that dwelled only in the darkest, most vile places and preyed on the weakest Talisian children - a creature from folklore and ancient myth. So it was, that Chi-Ro Jin vowed never to be weak.

But why would I recall this monster now?

Chi-Ro flinched as he recalled the terrified screams of children being devoured.

Zachary noticed Chi-Ro's discomfort.

"What's up Chi-Ro?"

The veteran of the Psychic Wars quickly shrugged his negative emotions aside.

"Dr. Zachary Silverman, from one who claims to be a scientist, I find that question most disturbing."

"What can I say? My mother was a hippie."

"Hippie?"

"It would take a few days to explain."

"Since entering the matter transfer room, your mind has been preoccupied with song. What are these strange, alien creatures of which your soul sings?"

"Great warriors from the faraway land of Tubs."

"These creatures appear to be neither great nor formidable."

"Looks can be deceiving."

Kiya smiled and put on her stealth helmet. Zachary followed suit.

Chi-Ro closed his eyes and chanted in a low voice, "Raya naar seewar. Ti nava, ti saytoo yo spiritoo Chi-Ro abun Jin. Raya vi, ti noor. Ti nava, ti saytoo aloor e neye majoor - E neye sanctoom."

"What's that you're singing?" Zachary asked Chi-Ro.

"I am not singing, I am praying. I suggest you do the same."

Anah Sadaka's computer-generated voice blared over the intercom, "Commander Chi-Ro, the Sanura is in position. We are at full alert status. The enemy's weapons have been neutralised, and their shields are down. I have located Prince Armon. Situation: critical. He is in a large chamber constructed from lapys nerian, and a heavily armed contingent is converging on his location."

"May the scribes record it," responded Chi-Ro, quickly donning his stealth helmet, "Defenders of Prince Armon, son of Sakara, ready arms - prepare for transfer."

Chi-Ro and the marines immediately cocked their rifles. Zachary followed their example. Kiya drew her viridian pistol, assumed a ready stance, and mentally activated her suit's invisibility cloak. Chi-Ro and Zachary did the same.

"Standby for stealth transfer," came Anah's computer-generated voice. "May it be written, may it be done."

Like lemmings we proceed, thought Zachary, *at least it will be brief. Very brief.*

Zachary felt his heartbeat throbbing in his temples and realised he had stopped breathing. He exhaled sharply, and then slowly inhaled the processed air of his Osirian stealth suit.

God help us.

Suddenly bolts of plasma shrouded the eight individuals in the matter transfer room, and they de-materialised in a flash.

A massive explosion thundered through the throne room, as the Imperial flagship Anhur convulsed in its death throes. Roman opened his eyes to see only blackness. At first, he thought the blow to his head had caused blindness but soon he could distinguish the malevolent form of the False Emperor on his throne.

With difficulty, Roman probed the Saurian's mind. He discovered that, despite their best attempts, the Karellans could not locate the cloaked Osirian starglider. The ill-fated Anhur, the pride of the Karellan fleet, was heading into the Aaruan Nebula, taking the misdirected armada with it.

Rebellion consumed the armada. Forty raiders, the only vessels unaffected by the Osirian weapons virus, were involved in heated dogfights. Sakara Rey's supporters gradually achieved space superiority and panic spread throughout the ranks of Seti Aljyk's followers.

From his telepathic probes, Roman also realised that the Saurians had the benefit of infrared-sensitive receptors. Like some reptiles indigenous to Earth, these aliens could effectively see radiated heat.

But my astral form radiates no heat, thought Roman, *if I can transform I'll be invisible to them in the darkness.*

In the darkness, outside the throne room, the giant sentry eagerly awaited the arrival of two shock marine squadrons. Karamba Shan, son of Lord Shan Kur-Karnah, commanded these marines.

Karamba Shan planned to evacuate the False Emperor from the doomed battlecarrier, but the Anhur's matter transfer capabilities had been disabled by acts of sabotage. Forced to march to the citadel, the warriors encountered fierce resistance and were delayed.

Chi-Ro, Zachary, Kiya, Kordo Vanne and his four marines materialised twenty metres from the giant sentry. Chi-Ro, Zachary and Kiya, remained invisible.

"Halt, who goes there?" barked the sentry to Kordo Vanne and his men.

The giant took aim with his huge Gonda PC-64D phase cannon.

"Sergeant Kordo Vanne reporting as ordered."

"Lower your weapons," growled the sentry.

Ahead of him, the marines lowered their rifles. But the enhanced auditory sensors of the giant's battlesuit registered almost imperceptible sounds to his left and right.

On the right side of the giant, Chi-Ro discharged a sustained blast from his phase rifle. Simultaneously, Kiya opened fire, with her viridian pistol, on the giant's left.

The giant's battlesuit could not shield him at point-blank range, and he crashed loudly to the floor, dead.

I could have sworn he said Fe Fi Fo Fum, thought Zachary.

Zachary saw Kordo Vanne and his men suddenly raise their Blastron M-24 rifles. Chi-Ro and Kiya were already in motion.

Zachary's gut feeling screamed, *"They're going to kill us."*

Something slammed into his chest, and Zachary felt the air rush out of his lungs. He saw both his legs dangle above his shoulders and realised that he had been blown off his feet by a phase rifle blast. In desperation, Zachary squeezed the trigger of his weapon before hitting the floor hard. The impact knocked the rifle out of his grasp.

Instinct took over. Zachary used the momentum of his fall to roll to a stooping position just in time to see Kiya blast the marine preparing to shoot him again.

Zachary saw that two of the four shock marines were still standing. Kordo Vanne took aim at a swiftly moving Chi-Ro Jin, fired and missed. Then

Zachary drew his Blastron P-19 phase pistol and shot Kordo Vanne in the chest. But Kordo Vanne's battlesuit absorbed the energy.

Leaping and twisting in midair, Chi-Ro also shot Kordo Vanne in the chest before landing with his phase rifle poised to fire again.

But Kordo Vanne remained standing. Then Zachary unleashed a sustained burst into Kordo Vanne's helmet; and an inhuman screech emanated from him, just before his dead body hit the floor.

Meanwhile, Kiya had activated her stealth suit's shield. The round screen of protective energy, which emanated from her left forearm, absorbed the phase energy unleashed by the remaining marine.

Kiya fired twice in quick succession, blasting the armoured soldier in his chest and head. Like Kordo Vanne, he also screeched before falling to the floor.

The marine was fatally wounded, but not dead. Kiya deactivated her shield and confidently strode to where the soldier had fallen. She placed her right boot on his chest and aimed at his helmet with her pistol.

"Wait," ordered Chi-Ro.

Kiya said, "Such treachery cannot go unpunished."

"First I must see what lurks within the suit."

The marine's right hand inched towards the self-destruct activator on his left wrist. Kiya blasted his right hand. The warrior let out an unmistakably alien scream. The sound startled Kiya, but she recovered her cool composure quickly.

Chi-Ro removed the dying marine's seared helmet, releasing the acrid stench of vomit into the room. Zachary moved closer to get a better look.

They saw that the left side of the marine's face was badly burnt. The right side of his face was that of a young man in his early twenties. He had blonde hair, pale skin and a cold blue eye, which remained open in a wide stare. But the horribly disfigured left side of the marine's face was covered in brown blood. His injured flesh was a sickly greyish-green colour.

"Why is his blood brown and his skin green?" asked Zachary.

Suddenly, as if in reply, the marine hissed and spat. Zachary, Chi-Ro and Kiya, lurched backwards.

"A Seriak," whispered Chi-Ro.

Kiya opened fire with her viridian pistol, instantly vaporising the alien.

"What the hell was that?" asked Zachary.

"An invader from another galaxy," replied Kiya, "They call themselves Saurians. Do not allow its saliva to touch your skin, it is acidic and extremely poisonous."

"That's great."

Chi-Ro asked, "What do you know of these creatures and why have you kept their existence secret?"

"This is a desperate war for survival Master Chi-Ro. Many Karellans and Talisians have been found to be in league with these vile creatures. Under these conditions, our trust is not easily given."

"We really ought to get Roman, and run the hell out of here," urged Zachary.

"The Prince is imprisoned behind these doors," said Chi-Ro.

Zachary stared at the huge doors to the throne room. He wondered how many lizard-men lurked behind its walls of lapys nerian. He wondered if his friend Roman still lived.

He stared long and hard at the doors and wondered,
How the hell are we going to open these bastards?

Chapter 45

In the throne room, trapped behind walls of lapys nerian, Roman Doyle remained on the floor where he had fallen. In the darkness, he tried to transform himself. To escape a fate worse than death, he had to become a wraith. But, to his dismay, he found that he was either too weak or too terrified to change. Roman remained a wounded man. A terrified man, with the taste of bile in his mouth gradually replaced with blood.

Pulses of white-hot pain wracked through his shoulder wound and spread to his neck and head. Roman could smell his own blood. He read their thoughts and realised that the Saurians smelt it too.

The sentinels are getting hungry.

The Prince probed the False Emperor's mind. The Saurian leader was engaged in telepathic communication with the commander of a spaceship.

The Sanura? Is there a traitor aboard? No, another ship - it's approaching. It's cloaked, but if I focus, I can see it... There... It's similar to the one we saw in the Dark Fields. It's a Saurian warship, thought Roman.

"Ah, young Prince, you are awake," said the False Emperor.

He felt my probe.

"My chariot arrives. Soon I will embark on my journey to Sauria Prime, with your unique offspring in my custody."

The False Emperor rose to his feet and approached Roman.

"There is no need to continue the pretence, I know you are awake, chakula. Get up."

The False Emperor drew the Sword of Power. Roman's fear and anxiety increased. He imagined hearing his heart beating a race towards arrest.

Suddenly, a voice interrupted the throbbing of Roman's pulse. It was a familiar voice, but a voice, which existed only in his head.

The voice said, *"Master Armon, verily I advise you to keep well away from the doors."*

Chi-Ro Jin!

In an instant, the profound happiness that Roman felt neutralised his pain.

I have to distract the Emperor, he thought.

Roman said to the False Emperor, "The starglider carrying my wife and son has already entered the nebula, you'll never find it. Look all around you, those you planned to enslave have rebelled."

The False Emperor laughed mockingly.

"Enslave? You animals lack the basic intelligence required to be useful slaves. Your son is the product of an elaborate experiment, an experiment conducted for the benefit of the Saurian race. He is a prototype. A tool. And you? You are merely genetically enhanced livestock. I have to admit it has been a while since I feasted on Royal Karellan. I think, before I depart, I shall enjoy you as my final meal. Yes, I will devour you while your heart still beats. Any final requests, chakula?"

"Just three: shut up, drop the sword and surrender."

As he laughed, the False Emperor's booming voice reverberated off the lapys nerian walls.

Suddenly, the massive doors of the throne room exploded. Shards of lapys nerian ripped through Saurian armour, knocking the sentinels off their feet. Pinned to the floor by a large slab, the False Emperor howled with rage.

Chi-Ro leapt through the smoke and flames and shot the only standing sentinel. Kiya came next, followed by Zachary.

An injured sentinel rose from the rubble and scampered up the wall. Kiya and Chi-Ro opened fire but missed. The lizard-man leapt from the wall to the ceiling, then launched itself at Zachary.

Zachary fired his phase rifle and blasted the creature in its helmet. It crashed into the floor, barely missing him.

With an ear-splitting shriek, the False Emperor lifted the massive slab from his chest and hurled it towards Kiya and Chi-Ro. They dove for cover. The Saurian leader stood upright, hissing and spitting with contempt.

Roman grabbed a lapys nerian rock and launched himself at the man-sized lizard. With all his might, he smashed the cold, black stone into the side of the False Emperor's head. The alien leader fell backwards. A sentinel leapt towards Roman but Zachary shot it in mid air.

"Let us get the hell out of here, before we all die," shouted Zachary at the top of his lungs.

Phase fire rang out from behind him. He turned activating his stealth shield. It was Karamba Shan with twenty shock marines.

"Shit!" cried Zachary.

Cloaked and shielded Zachary, Kiya and Chi-Ro exchanged fire with the Karellan troops. Undeterred, Roman found Najura, the Sword of Power amongst the rubble. Enraged, he stood over the stunned impostor, about to kill him; but the Karellans already had Roman in their sights.

Chi-Ro Jin screamed, "No Master!"

Zachary turned in time to see Roman, with the sword raised high. Kiya leapt towards Roman, desperately trying to use her body as a shield.

The twenty Karellan troops opened fire. Zachary felt searing heat bore into his back. He took a deep breath, at least he thought he did, but he could not feel the air enter his nostrils. Instead, he felt his knees buckle - his weapon no longer in his hand. And, as he began to fall, Zachary noticed that the dark room turned pale yellow, then suddenly black. And finally, Zachary felt nothing at all.

Chapter 46

Roman, Chi-Ro, Kiya and Zachary materialised in the infirmary of the Starbird Sanura. All had been hit by phase fire. All remained on the floor where they materialised.

"Commander Chi-Ro, please report," came the computer-generated voice of Anah Sadaka from the intercom.

Only Chi-Ro Jin showed any signs of life. He rolled on his back and struggled to remove his helmet. His Osirian stealth suit had failed after absorbing three direct hits from the Karellan shock marines' phase rifles.

"Commander Chi-Ro, kindly respond," said Anah.

Chi-Ro sucked in the antiseptic air of the Sanura and sighed heavily.

"Assistance. We require medical assistance. Activate Jinzou Ningen, immediately," He said weakly.

"Commander Chi-Ro, Osirian vessels do not carry the artificial abomination of Talis. Prince Armon, Nuri Nemsys and Dr. Zachary Silverman are critical. You must place them in regeneration pods. They must be placed in cryostasis immediately. A Saurian battleship approaches. It employs weaponry and technology superior to our own. We must flee at once or suffer a fate worse than death."

"Where is Lady Soraya?"

"After creating a psychic storm, the Prince's consort lost consciousness. She is exhausted. Commander Chi-Ro, I assure you that all medical needs will be met at our destination. Please do your best to secure our comrades."

"Verily," replied Chi-Ro as he dragged himself to unsteady feet and walked to where Roman lay unconscious.

Your father would be proud, my Prince.

Then looking around at his phase rifle and fallen companions Chi-Ro realised that something important was missing.

Where is Najura? Where is the Sword of Power?

Rising from the rubble, in the throne room of the Imperial flagship Anhur, the False Emperor cursed and shook his fists. Karamba Shan and his men fell on one knee and bowed reverently.

"Incompetent fools, you allowed them to escape with the Sword of Power," bellowed the False Emperor.

Karamba Shan lifted his head. He was about to offer his heart-felt apology when he noticed something quite odd.

"Your Highness, your face..."

The False Emperor placed his hand on his face and stepped back into the shadows.

"I bear the scars of a vicious attack."

Karamba Shan stood up defiantly.

"What manner of attack could turn your face green, your blood brown? You are not Karellan. What manner of beast are you?"

The False Emperor addressed the shock marines, "My loyal subjects, I call upon you to arrest Karamba Shan. Like his father Shan Kur-Karnah, Karamba Shan has conspired to assassinate your Emperor and deliver Karella to the Talisians."

Three marines raised their weapons but were immediately disarmed and restrained by the marines adjacent to them.

Karamba Shan drew his Melcor HG-13 pistol and said, "Step out of the shadows, foul creature."

The False Emperor roared, and Karamba Shan opened fire; but he was too late. A matter transport beam took the False Emperor, the bodies of his sentinels and the three Saurian marines.

Karamba Shan holstered his weapon, turned to his men and said, "We have been deceived. All of Karella has been deceived. We are the few to bear witness to the truth. The Anhur is lost. Go now, save yourselves by any means necessary. Trust no one. We shall assemble at Garidius Prime."

"I will not leave your side," said a sergeant.

"No, there is little time. You must go. Go now."

The sergeant hesitated, but the firm resolve in Karamba Shan's unwavering eyes convinced him to follow his instructions.

"Follow me," said the sergeant to the marines.

As the soldiers jogged away, Karamba Shan retrieved Shan Kur-Karnah's ree-sok-bou from the giant sentry's post. He walked through the demolished doors of the throne room and knelt over his father's body.

He said, "My Lord Shan, my father, I shall avenge you."

With her shields disabled, the Battlecarrier Anhur continued to drift towards the Aaruan Nebula. Hundreds of Karellan personnel evacuated like rats from a sinking ship. Five hundred kilometres off the Anhur's port bow, the Saurian warship de-cloaked.

The mysterious enemy appeared briefly, like a monstrous pterosaur, before firing an unknown energy weapon into the heart of the stricken Anhur. The effect was immediate and catastrophic. The Anhur's formidable arsenal ignited a fusion chain reaction, which culminated in a massive explosion. Thousands of men aboard the vessel and in nearby escape pods were vaporised instantly. The Anhur's back was broken. The burning vessel hurtled at sub-light speed into the edge of the Aaruan Nebula before breaking into two parts, which totally disintegrated.

In the fleet, chaos replaced hysteria. Thousands observed an unknown enemy destroy the Karellan flagship. Five marauders and one destroyer, captured by supporters of Sakara Rey, immediately escaped into hyperspace. Then, just as suddenly, the Saurian warship attacked two Karellan destroyer class vessels in closest proximity to the nebula. Both were disabled with substantial loss of life.

With Seti Aljyk now presumed dead, Margrave Klim T'val aboard the orbital bomber Nekhbet, seized command of the loyal Karellan forces. Throughout the armada, the Osirian virus disabled weapon and shield systems. The warships were defenceless against the mysterious invader. Margrave Klim ordered an immediate retreat and hasty preparations were made for hyperspatial travel.

Of the forty Karellan raiders unaffected by the Osirian weapons virus, thirty-five had been disabled or destroyed during heated dogfights. Only five raider starfighters, all loyal to Sakara Rey, remained operational.

Commander Nook Tigg, an Osirian spy and veteran of the Psychic Wars, led these mutineers. The modified command helmet of his raider enabled telepathic identification of, and communication with, other members of the Osirian Guard.

"Agent zero-alpha-one, this is agent zero-zero-six, do you require escort?"

"Agent zero-zero-six, your assistance would be most appreciated," responded Anah Sadaka. *"Accessing data. Prepare for synchronised hyperspatial jump. Standby for confirmation of destination coordinates."*

Aboard the Starbird Sanura, Anah Sadaka communicated mentally through the Sanura's intercom system.

"Thank you, Commander Chi-Ro, sensors indicate all personnel secured in regeneration pods. All life-signs are stable. Navigation to Miru has been set by my will. Hyperspatial jump in fifteen seconds."

"Climatic conditions on Miru are unfavourable. It would be most unwise to transport Master Armon to this location. Qualify your decision," came Chi-Ro's voice in her mind.

"There we shall find sanctuary in the ranks of the 9th Wave under Margrave Rin Mur-Rain."

"Anah Sadaka, I need not remind you that we have been absent from normal space for three years. How can you be certain of the 9th Wave's current location or of Rin Mur-Rain's loyalty?"

"Commander Chi-Ro, there is much I will reveal to you if we are so fortunate as to escape our Saurian pursuers. But at this most critical moment, I implore you to trust my judgement."

"May the scribes record it."

"May it be written; may it be done."

Klaxons blared a grim warning throughout the Sanura as the Saurian vessel approached weapons range. In tight formation, at maximum sub-light speed, with full power diverted to aft shields, Nook Tigg led his raider squadron to defensive positions between the Sanura and the Saurian battleship.

The Saurian warship opened fire at the very instant their quarry activated the jump into hyperspace. Four Karellan raiders were immediately disintegrated, but Nook Tigg's raider and the Starbird Sanura escaped.

So ended the Battle of Aaru with Roman, Soraya, Zachary, Chi-Ro, Kiya, Anah Sadaka and their new ally Nook Tigg secure in life-supporting pods, in a state of cryostasis.

Chapter 47

The heat of brilliant sunshine, stung Roman Doyle's exposed face. He opened his eyes and slowly, white light transformed into hues of colour. Roman realised that he stood in a green meadow. Amongst the tall blades of grass were white, yellow and purple flowers.

About two kilometres away, lush trees marked the beginning of a vast forest; and beyond the forest, snow capped mountains jutted into a deep blue sky. A cool breeze carried the scent of Jasmine, prompting Roman to take a deep breath.

As he enjoyed the sensation of fresh air filling his lungs, Roman recalled a recent nightmare. He recalled his confrontation with Seti Aljyk. He recalled being shot.

Was I dreaming? he thought.

Roman turned around instinctively and twenty metres away he saw a man standing on an outcrop of rock. In his right hand, the man held a staff.

Roman's heart skipped a beat. For a brief moment, his mind and body prepared for a fight. Then he realised that the man was not an enemy; he was Chi-Ro Jin.

Roman recalled his previous training with Chi-Ro and realised, *This is a dream.*

"Chi-Ro," he called, walking briskly to where Chi-Ro stood.

"Greetings, Master Armon."

"Where are we?"

"We are on Alpha Tameri, near the Marusa Forest."

"No Chi-Ro, where are we?"

"Verily, having escaped a fate far worse than death, we are in cryostasis aboard the Starbird Sanura. Our bodies are regenerating at this very moment."

Waves of relief washed over Roman.

"Is Soraya okay?"

"Okay?" asked Chi-Ro, unfamiliar with English slang.

"Is Soraya unharmed?"

"Lady Soraya is unharmed. She is, as you say, okay."

"Zach, Nuri, Anah?"

"Mistress Anah Sadaka is also unharmed. We travel, by her will, to the planet Miru. There will find sanctuary in the ranks of your cousin, Margrave Rin Mur-Rain."

"What about Zach and Nuri?"

"Dr. Zachary Silverman and Agent Nuri Nemsys are both critical but stable."

"What?"

"You are also in a critical but stable state. Were it not for our remarkable stealth suits, we would all be dead."

"But I feel fine."

"We are in my dream, not yours," said Chi-Ro stroking his Fu Manchu moustache.

"I want to see Soraya."

Chi-Ro came down from his rocky platform and began to walk towards the trees. Roman walked alongside him.

"Are you expecting trouble, Chi-Ro?" said Roman referring to the warrior's extended sok-bou.

"Master Armon, we cannot afford to delay your training any longer," replied Chi-Ro sternly.

"Training, now? I thought you said I was critical."

"Critical but stable."

"Somehow I imagined it would be bad to train when critical but stable."

"Once again I am forced to remind you that we are in my dream. Furthermore, your regeneration pod will regulate your heartbeat should you become too agitated."

"The last time, my training turned into a nightmare. I feel so much better knowing that this time I won't die of a heart attack."

"It is human to be afraid."

"Afraid? Who said anything about being afraid? I think I'm naturally concerned and, having endured more than one near-death experience, just a little weary."

"It is true, during your first dream exercise, I overestimated your ability to control your lucid environment. But Brakis Tarn's attack, though unpleasant, has made you much stronger. On this occasion, your training will be conducted within a dream of my making, under conditions of my choosing. This is a necessary precaution. When you are face to face with Margrave Rin Mur-Rain, you may be required to prove yourself."

"The genetic tests you performed prove who I am don't they?"

"Master Armon, simply proving your identity would not be sufficient. You will have to prove your worth."

"I have to take an endurance test?"

Roman's warm smile did nothing to soften Chi-Ro's stone-faced demeanour.

"For many years it was believed that you perished. Margrave Rin Mur-Rain considered himself Lord Sakara Rey's rightful heir and he has the support of many. He will not give his allegiance lightly. You must prove yourself a worthy warrior and a true Prince."

"Forgive me, but I thought Talis developed an extremely advanced civilisation. What are you expecting from me, the Talisian Alexander the Great?"

"We are at war. Many of the trappings of civilisation have been discarded. Now skill, cunning and power are vital if you are to earn respect. And yes, greatness is expected from the Emperor's heir."

"Surely news of the lizard-men will change everything, they're the real enemy. It's obvious the Saurians manufactured this war to weaken Talis and Karella. The war is their prelude to invasion."

"What tangible proof do we have of these invaders?"

"I saw them Chi-Ro, so did you. At least I found out my uncle isn't the real villain. A Saurian impostor led the Karellans."

"Verily, it appears Lord Seti Aljyk was himself a victim of the Seriak. And, indeed, all in our party bore witness to the alien impostors. Even the marines who appeared to come to our aid were Seriak spies. But first, we need to reveal this alien threat to Margrave Rin Mur-Rain."

"Why Rin Mur-Rain?"

"He is the only direct link to your father. Once Margrave Rin Mur-Rain is made aware of the Seriak threat, we can attempt to convince our enemies the Karellans. And yes, this does give us a glimmer of hope. Perhaps fighting this common foe can serve to reunite Talis and Karella."

"So exactly what do I need to do when I meet my cousin, bash his skull in with a rock?"

"An interesting manoeuvre, which revealed Seti Aljyk for the Seriak that he is. Nevertheless, such crude gestures may not be effective in the hall of Margrave Rin Mur-Rain."

"But I'll have to fight my cousin, isn't that what you're saying?"

"It is possible."

"My family reunions aren't turning out to be the happy occasions I imagined they would be. What if Rin's a lizard too?"

"During our encounter aboard the Karellan flagship, Saurian blood and tissue came into contact with our stealth suits. Their genetic attributes were isolated during matter transfer. Our modified sensors can easily identify these alien creatures."

"I came so close to ending the lizard king's reign... at least I retrieved my father's sword."

Deep furrows appeared in Chi-Ro's brow. He paused and stared intently into Roman's eyes.

"Master Armon, your lack of training almost cost you your life. I cannot comment on the fighting skills of the Seriak, but I can say this, you are most fortunate that you faced Shan Kur-Karnah in single combat and not his son, Karamba Shan."

"I'm a schoolteacher, not a warrior," said Roman tightening his jaw.

"No Master Armon, you are a Prince and heir to the Talisian throne, in a time of war. Your guardians died before revealing to you your true identity. They were unable to develop your skills as a warrior and leader of men. Good fortune and the clumsy use of your unique abilities have saved you thus far. But it would be most unwise to continue a reliance on Providence, or powers you barely control."

"You're asking for the impossible," said Roman folding his arms stubbornly.

"I request the difficult, not the impossible. Remember in dreams, waking minutes can be hours."

"Okay, but you'll have to train Zachary, as well."

Chi-Ro raised a quizzical eyebrow.

"And why would I be compelled to do such a thing?"

"My friend Zachary has joined me in this war. I cannot allow his continued reliance on Providence or primitive Kian dances. Without training, he'll be a hazard to himself and those around him."

"Verily."

"So, may the scribes record it," said Roman holding back a smile.

"With reluctance, I agree to instruct Dr. Zachary Silverman. Fortunately for him, any injuries, he receives whilst in the dream state, would not be permanent."

Roman laughed, but Chi-Ro simply raised an eyebrow as if to ask, *Why are you laughing? I am not joking.*

Roman wiped the grin from his face. Chi-Ro resumed walking, and Roman followed.

"I'm looking forward to returning the Sword of Power to my father," said Roman.

"That may prove difficult."

"Why? Aren't we meeting with Rin Mur-Rain, so he can take us to my father?"

"Verily, but it appears the Sword of Power was not transported to the Sanura."

"How can that be? I had it in my hands."

"You were shot. Perhaps you dropped the sword."

"No way."

Chi-Ro looked at Roman quizzically.

"Okay, it's possible," Roman said reluctantly.

"You're right, I almost threw away my life for nothing."

Roman suddenly stopped walking. Chi-Ro looked over his shoulder as if to ask, *Why have you stopped?*

"I need to see Soraya. I need to see her alone."

"That would be ill advised. I can only protect you in a dream of my own design."

"I know. I'm willing to take the risk."

"Then, by your will, you must enter Lady Soraya's dream. I cannot assist you."

Chi-Ro read the question Roman was about to ask.

He said, "I can bring Lady Soraya into this dream, but you will not have the privacy you desire."

"So, how do I enter her dream?"

"Like so many things, it begins simply with a thought. Where there is great love there is great harmony of thought..."

"Love, Chi-Ro?"

"You seem surprised. I am not without understanding; I too have a consort."

"You're married? Wow. Where is she?"

"Oni, my beloved, is with my father and my son."

"But I thought your father was... dead?"

"Indeed, he is no longer on this plane of existence."

"I'm sorry Chi-Ro."

Chi-Ro bowed. Roman sensed the depth of Chi-Ro's pain - controlled by years of discipline.

"Reach out with your consciousness. Focus on harmony of thought. When your brainwaves are attuned with those of Lady Soraya, you will enter her dream."

"You make it sound so simple."

"I am quite certain you have done this many times before, without being aware of it. Close emotional bonds - family, friendship – facilitate a harmony of thought."

"I'll try."

"To try is to accept the possibility of failure. Simply do."

Roman stood still with his eyes closed. He focussed on his wife. At first there was nothing. The heat of the sun continued to sting his face. The bright light made him see red behind his closed eyelids.

Suddenly Roman felt a tingling sensation and the heat on his face vanished. The scent of Jasmine was gone, and he saw only black behind his eyelids.

Chapter 48

Within another dream, Anah Sadaka and Kiya Mankuria stood alone in a dimly lit room. From the walls of the room, shimmering gold reflected on Kiya's troubled face as she spoke.

"Mistress, the directive of the Council of Twelve is clear. The Sword of Power, once retrieved must be returned to Sakara Rey. Or, in the event of Sakara Rey's death, the sword must be passed to his son Armon Sakara."

"Sakara Rey is weak and Armon Sakara is untrained," replied Anah with no emotion.

"You dare defy the Osirian Council?"

Anah calmly folded her arms and said, "Might I remind you, my adopted daughter, I am Niburian not Osirian. I know, better than any, what the Saurians are capable of. The Osirian Council, in their safe haven ten thousand metres below the Atlantic Ocean, does not."

"So you intend to use the Sword of Power to exact personal revenge on the Saurians?"

"This is a matter of universal security. For thousands of years, those creatures hunted and killed Niburians. Now all that remains, of the greatest civilisation that ever existed in the universe, are the descendants of those Niburians who eons ago found sanctuary on Earth; and the pitiful, enslaved millions bred by the Saurians for food and sport. The Saurians genetically engineered the Soter and stole Najura, the Sword of Power. They exploited the rift between the Talisians and Karellans. Because of this vile race, the universe has been plunged into the darkness of a most terrible war. And now the Neph Alim Principality, aware of the success of their Saurian rivals, has increased their attempts to create their own genetically advanced being. The result, as you are well aware, is an increase in human abduction. With both the Soter and the Sword of Power in our possession, we can rid the universe of the Saurian threat once and for all. We can protect Earth from the Neph Alim."

"My loyalty is to Earth and to the Council of Twelve. I will not defy them."

"I find your lack of gratitude most disturbing. The Osirian Colony to which you grant your allegiance would not survive without Niburian assistance."

Suddenly, Kiya fell to her knees wincing in pain.

"Do you hope to gain my agreement through torture?"

With a sigh, Anah offered Kiya her hand. Kiya held it cautiously and rose to her feet.

"Forgive me, my child. I allowed anger to get the better of me."

"Perhaps you have forgotten what separates Osirian Colonists from the followers of Seth. Osirians believe in freedom of choice. The followers of Seth consider themselves the master race. And, by manipulation of the Illuminati, they would impose their will on Earth."

Anah searched Kiya's lime-green eyes and said, "Kiya, do you believe I am sympathetic to the Illuminati?"

Kiya looked down to the ground like a scolded child.

"No Mistress, but it is known that the Illuminati seek to control the Soter. They would use the child to enforce their will."

"I need not remind you that the followers of Seth are sworn enemies of Niburians. Dr. Zachary Silverman..."

"Is not a follower of Seth. He has no knowledge of his father or of his father's crimes. The son cannot be held accountable for the sins of the father."

"It has been my experience that the sins of the father often bear fruit in the son."

"Zachary is harmless."

"Such familiarity with the enemy? Kiya, you disappoint me."

"He is not an enemy. He is a loyal friend of the Prince."

"We shall see where his loyalties lie once he knows the truth."

"You will tell him?"

"No, he does not trust me. He would not believe me. No Kiya, you must tell him."

"Zachary does not trust me, he trusts only Prince Armon."

"Then I believe it is time to reveal our true identities to Prince Armon. Despite the Council's insistence, I will assess this Prince. And once we are reunited with Sakara Rey, I will decide whether or not to follow the directives of the Osirian Council. Now rest Kiya; the task ahead is difficult, and your injuries are great."

"We have the assistance of agent zero-zero-six."

"How fortunate."

"Yes the appearance of Nook Tigg is indeed fortunate."

"I pray that we are successful in our mission, Mistress Anah. May it be written."

"May it be done."

Chapter 49

Roman Doyle felt happy to find himself in the lounge of the two bed-roomed flat in Friern Barnet, North London - the home he shared with his wife Soraya. The clock on the wall revealed the time to be 2:30 AM.

Thoughts of finding rum 'n' raisin ice cream and peanut butter in the nearest twenty-four-hour supermarket were quickly dismissed.

Roman reminded himself, *This is only a dream.*

He walked towards the open door to their bedroom and concern replaced his happiness. He felt sharp pains in his shoulder, chest and stomach and he quickly relived being shot. If not for the protection of his stealth suit, and had Kiya not knocked him out of the way, the Karellan shock marines' well-aimed rifle blasts would have killed him instantly.

Now, Roman recalled the significance of being in his own dream. Roman remembered that his body was actually in a regeneration pod aboard the Starbird Sanura and that he lacked the experience required to suppress his physical pain. His legs felt like lead, but he managed to slowly walk into the dark bedroom. The sight of Soraya asleep on the bed seemed to ease his pain.

Suddenly, Roman became aware of a dark figure in the darkest corner of the room. He assumed a Hatari Ikou ready stance and bit his bottom lip as pain racked his entire body.

"Hello father," said a young male voice.

"Moses?" asked Roman instinctively.

"You decided not to call me that."

"Really?"

"You explained to mother that the name Moses triggered your abnormal and unwarranted fear of rivers and running water. She called me Tristan instead."

"Tristan."

"Yes."

"You won't tell Zachary your mother listens to Wagner, would you? Step out of the shadows, let me see you."

The twelve-year-old stepped into the moonlight shining through the bedroom window. A smile traced itself on Roman's face. The boy's face was devoid of emotion.

"My son," he whispered.

"You won't be able to wake her," said Tristan referring to Soraya.

"Why not?" asked Roman, unable to hide his concern.

"The Niburian has mentally sedated her."

"The Niburian?"

"Mother calls her the Ligahoo, she calls herself Anah Sadaka."

Roman moved to the bed and gently shook his wife's shoulder."

"Soraya?"

"It's no use," said Tristan, "she can't hear you."

"Why aren't you sedated?"

"The Niburian underestimates my power."

"Your power? You're not even born yet."

"Yet here I am."

"No, this is all just a figment of my imagination. You're just a creation of my subconscious mind."

"The only figment of your imagination father, is the security you appear to feel in the company of Anah Sadaka and Kiya Mankuria."

"Nice touch using Nuri's real name."

"Anah Sadaka plans to have mother and I kidnapped."

"Why?"

"She hopes that my power, combined with Najura, will destroy her old enemy the Saurians."

"Good."

"Her ambitions do not end there."

"Go on."

"Anah Sadaka believes that Niburians are the most advanced race in the universe. She believes that they alone have the wisdom required to guide the universe into a new age of peace and prosperity."

Roman shook his head and whispered to himself, "The elidium Chi-Ro gave me probably made me paranoid."

Hear me father, your mistakes, your weakness will lead to the death of your father and the death of my mother. You and I will become enemies."

Roman's pain increased. He heard the sound of his heartbeat grow louder and louder.

"Who are you?"

"I regret, I am your son."

"No!" shouted Roman.

The pain became too much to bear. Roman collapsed. Battling to remain conscious, he turned to see the boy walk towards the bed. As he approached Soraya, he transformed into a wraith, then into dark mist. The mist enveloped Soraya's body and merged into it.

Roman stretched out his hand.

"Wait," he said.

But it was too late. The boy, the wraith, the mist were all gone. Soraya, his wife, remained asleep on the bed; and Roman lay on the floor, immobilised by pain.

Chapter 50

Roman Doyle opened his eyes, absorbing the natural beauty of the alien world known as Alpha Tameri. Roman had returned to Chi-Ro's dream and felt relieved. A gentle breeze brought the soothing sound of a flute being played, and turning towards the source, Roman saw Chi-Ro Jin sitting on an old tree stump, on the edge of the Marusa Forest.

Roman smiled and jogged towards Chi-Ro.

Chi-Ro cocked his head, interrupted his playing and said, "Master Armon, you returned faster than I expected, I trust Lady Soraya is well."

"I had a nightmare."

"A nightmare?"

"Yes, a bad dream."

"I am familiar with the term. What occurred in this nightmare?"

"I saw my son. He told me that I would cause the deaths of my wife and of my father."

"Hmm. And you are troubled by this?"

"Wouldn't you be?"

"No. I am aware that the future is not set in stone. This is but one of many possible futures."

"I couldn't wake Soraya. My son told me that Anah had mentally sedated her."

Chi-Ro raised an eyebrow.

"What more did your son say?"

"He said that Anah had the Sword of Power. She plans to use my son and the Sword of Power to destroy the Saurians and bring the universe under Niburian rule."

"Verily, a most ambitious plan but like so many possessing great talent, Mistress Anah Sadaka is overconfident. She underestimates those around her."

"You don't seem surprised."

"Anah Sadaka informed me that Najura the Sword of Power was not retrieved. It was a lie I never believed. She advised me that Lady Soraya grew fatigued and retired. An unlikely eventuality."

"So Soraya was sedated. She's in danger; I have to go back."

"Sedated? Yes. In danger? No. No harm shall come to Lady Soraya as long as she bears your unborn child. I believe rest will do her good."

"Shouldn't I be doing something about Anah and Nuri?"

"It was always clear that Anah Sadaka and Nuri Nemsys could not be trusted. We shall continue to be vigilant, giving no hint of our suspicions. Remember, destroying the Seriak is a goal we all share."

"Nuri has protected me, more than once. Maybe I'm over reacting; after all, I was having a conversation with an unborn child. Anah and Nuri are pretty handy in a fight, and we'll need all the help we can get."

"Verily; on our present journey to Miru, Commander Nook Tigg is escorting us."

"I know that name," said Roman, remaining silent about the fact that, in his childhood, he had an imaginary friend also called Nook Tigg.

Nook Tigg and his space rocket... Coincidence? Highly unlikely...

Chi-Ro tilted his head quizzically and said, "Perhaps in your childhood, your custodians General Tarom Rin and his consort Mina discussed Nook Tigg. His heroic exploits, in the Battle of Rak No-Var, are very well known. We served together in the Kol Vestri Campaign. I was deeply saddened, when I learnt that he joined the ranks of Seti Aljyk."

"So now, he's your enemy?"

"Possibly. But he may also be a Talisian spy, loyal to Lord Sakara Rey. When we meet face-to-face I will know where his heart lies."

Roman sat cross-legged in the tall grass and said, "I wish I had your talent."

Chi-Ro betrayed a measure of pride when he said, "As it is with any worthwhile skill, mastery of the Sythenian wax wood flute requires practice and dedication."

"Yeah I'm sure, but I mean it's difficult for me to know who to trust."

"Unlike mastery of the flute, this is no special talent. I have simply followed my heart during my lifetime. Shine forth Master Armon, even as the Great Spirit. Listen well to that which I say to you, that you may join your father at his side and govern all your actions with wisdom."

Chi-Ro resumed playing his flute.

"Where's Zachary?" asked Roman.

"Relax Master Armon, he will be here shortly," projected Chi-Ro.

"Chi-Ro, you mentioned the Great Spirit..."

"Words are not necessary Master Armon, use your mind."

"OK. I'm surprised that your advanced culture includes religious belief."

"Most Talisians and more and more Karellans believe that all life emanates from the Great Spirit. This belief is called 'The Veritara'. 'The Kai'. 'The Truth'. In my youth, I considered joining the Sacred Order of the Mara Kai. Imagine Chi-Ro Jin as a Mara Kai Monk."

"I can imagine it. Why didn't you become a monk?"

"A master monk of the Mara Kai named Koylas Morda, claimed to have found enlightenment on the forbidden planet of Druk Benegol in the Deli-Al System. He claimed to have come face-to-face with the Supreme Spirit in the form of a winged serpent whose name could not be pronounced. Koylas Morda was excommunicated from the Mara Kai Order and formed the Cult of the Asing. Perhaps it was youthful impetuousness. But even though my faith in the Great Spirit never wavered, I became deeply suspicious of all religious groups. Instead of becoming a monk, I joined my father in the ranks of the Talisian Assault Troops. Upon the death of Koylas Morda, his son Zaar Koylas assumed leadership of the cult. When Zaar died his five sons Felani, Kirato, Tonn, Mika and Pencha turned the Cult of the Asing into a band of mercenaries in the employ of Seti Aljyk."

"It seems so long ago that we fought them."

"You are a different man now, you would defeat such ruffians quite easily."

Chi-Ro continued to play the flute. Roman sat silently in awe of the beautiful sights and sounds, which surrounded him. He focussed on Chi-Ro's words.

The future is not set in stone.

As he listened intently to the soothing sound of the flute, something caught Roman's eye. It was a dot high above the distant mountains. And the dot, appeared to be growing larger.

"Chi-Ro, what is that?"

Chi-Ro continued to play his flute and was unconcerned.

Roman asked telepathically, *"Is that a bird?"*

"No Master Armon, that is no bird."

"Some sort of plane?"

Chi-Ro stopped playing and sighed, *"Alas, that is no aeroplane."*

"What is it then?"

As Roman asked the question, a flock of birds screeched and took to flight from the trees in the forest. Amongst the sound of the birds, there was another almost indiscernible sound. To Roman, it sounded like some alien animal in pain.

Chi-Ro shook his head in dismay.

"Good Grief! It's coming right at us," said Roman.

"Wait a minute. No, it can't be..."

"Verily, it is."

"Zachary?"

"Whoohooo!" cried Zachary, as he swooped down low, and landed in the tall grass twenty metres away. "What a buzz!"

Roman looked at Chi-Ro questioningly.

"It appears Dr. Zachary Silverman is adept at lucid dreaming."

"Roman, Chi-Ro, where the hell are we? This place is great," shouted Zachary.

"You were allowed to come here at the request of Master Armon."

"Here? Where's here?"

"We're on a planet called Alpha Tameri, Zachary. I'm glad you feel OK."

"OK? I feel Grrreat!"

"Zach, you do realise you're dreaming."

"No, you mean I can't actually fly?" asked Zachary, feigning surprise. "Of course I know I'm dreaming."

"Just checking."

"At least I'm not dead. Those Karellan bastards shot me."

"Yes. Apparently we're critical but stable."

"Whoa. I don't like the sound of that."

"I assure you, Dr. Zachary Silverman, there is no need for alarm. We are being regenerated."

"Nice one. So where's the picnic? I don't know about you guys, but I'm bloody hungry."

"Master Armon, forgive me but..."

"Zach this isn't a holiday, we're here to be trained."

"OK. Can't we eat first?"

"What do you say Chi-Ro? I feel a bit hungry too," said Roman.

Chi-Ro smiled, but it looked more like a grimace.

"You do realise this is a dream, and any perceived hunger is merely a figment of imagination. Alas, there is a cottage in the forest, and in it, we shall find food. Follow me."

Chi-Ro set off, walking briskly into the Marusa Forest with Roman and Zachary following close behind.

"Lets hope it's better than the soylent green we've been eating on the ship," Zachary said to Roman with a nudge.

Chi-Ro replied, "Oh I believe this meal will be to your satisfaction, Dr. Zachary Silverman."

Roman and Zachary looked at each other, like men about to walk into an obvious trap.

Zachary whispered to Roman, "Maybe now's a good time for the two of us to fly out of here."

"Zach, don't aggravate him. This is his dream."

"That's why I think we ought to fly out of here."

"Dr. Zachary Silverman, I will not force you to stay. The choice is yours. Perhaps you can arrange suitable training with your warriors from the land of Tubs."

Roman laughed. Both Zachary and Chi-Ro looked at him as if to ask, *"What's funny?"*

Zachary said, "I'm sorry Chi-Ro, I was only joking. I want you to train me. The great warriors from the land of Tubs are formidable, by Earth standards, but I'm sure they're no match for Saurian lizard-men."

It took all of Roman's willpower to suppress further laughter.

"Very good, Dr. Zachary Silverman. First we eat, then you and I will fight."

Zachary said to Roman, "He's pulling my leg, right?"

Roman shook his head with a smile – *No.*

Chi-Ro said, "Dr. Zachary Silverman, it would appear you are hallucinating. I have neither pulled your leg to the right nor to the left."

Roman stopped breathing in an attempt to control his urge to laugh.

Zachary told Chi-Ro, "It's a rhetorical question."

Chi-Ro replied, "I am unfamiliar with that race or their language."

Roman pretended to cough.

"Master Armon, since you find this amusing, you will fight the makra-gak."

Roman's smile faded fast.

"The what? Wait a minute, Chi-Ro what's a makranak?"

"I think he said makra-gak," added Zachary.

Chi-Ro continued to walk briskly into the forest. Roman strode to keep up.

"Chi-Ro, what's a makra-gak?"

Chi-Ro remained silent. Suddenly the loud roar of a distant animal, shattered the silence in the forest.

Roman and Zachary froze. They looked at each other and tried to hide their terror.

Roman said to Zachary, "I hope you're happy now."

Chapter 51

Roman and Zachary followed Chi-Ro Jin deeper into the Marusa Forest. They did not speak. From time to time, the persistent feeling that they were being watched interrupted Roman's thoughts - unsettling thoughts regarding the safety of Soraya and his unborn child.

The deeper the men ventured into the forest, the darker and cooler it became. The whistles and chirps, of alien birds, accentuated the sound of the wind rustling through the trees. A swarm of butterflies circled curiously before alighting on yellow flowers, which carpeted the ground.

In a clearing, they came upon the cottage. It was not at all what Roman expected. Chi-Ro's cottage was a monolithic dome twelve metres in diameter. It was made of an unknown mirrored material, which allowed the single-storey structure to blend into the surrounding trees and shrubs. Roman could not discern any doors or windows in the dwelling.

Their approach activated an almost invisible energy field, which surrounded the cottage. Chi-Ro reached into his tunic, and produced a flat, metallic disc. Walking towards the cottage, he waved the disc. The energy field deactivated immediately, and a door slid aside.

Roman immediately detected the aroma of cooked food.

Zachary asked, "How did they know we were coming for dinner?"

"There is no one here, Dr. Zachary Silverman," replied Chi-Ro, "we are quite alone in the Marusa Forest."

"Who cooked the food?" asked Roman.

Chi-Ro replied with a twinkle in his eye, "The skilfully prepared karachuk stew is the product of wishful thinking."

Once inside the monolithic dome, Roman and Zachary were surprised to find that its outer surface, though mirrored, was completely transparent inside.

"Some kind of two-way mirror," commented Roman.

"Not quite," said Zachary, "The half-silvered surfaces we're accustomed to, allow half of the light through and reflect the other half from both sides. The reflected side needs to be brightly illuminated and the transparent side needs to be darkened. You'll notice that the light in here is just as bright as it is outside. This is a bit odd."

Roman marvelled at the Talisian interior. It felt as if they were in a space module trapped within a transparent bubble. In the room was a round table finished in silver and around the table, were four chairs made of the same material. The metal furniture appeared to be moulded. There were no signs of joins or rivets. The holographic screen, of a sophisticated workstation, displayed alien characters on the right side of the room.

At the back, of the bubble, was a white wall. On the wall were a sokbou and a pilot's command helmet. Stacked against the wall were four rifles. A single door presumably led to sleeping quarters.

"Sit. Eat. Drink. Soon the sun will set," said Chi-Ro.

Roman asked, "This is your dream. Aren't you controlling this environment Chi-Ro?"

"Verily, Master Armon. Eat, drink and relax, for this is your comfort zone. Once the sun sets, your training will commence. You will be asked to cross the threshold into the unknown."

Roman and Zachary followed Chi-Ro's instructions and sat at the round silver table. Before them were large bowls of karachuk stew and goblets of a deep red liquid. Chi-Ro drank from his goblet.

Realising that his guests remained hesitant he said, "This is pure oliat juice. It is neither fermented nor distilled. It will not impair performance."

Roman drank, and Zachary followed his lead.

"It tastes like prune juice," said Roman with a smile.

Chi-Ro took a spoonful of karachuk stew from his bowl, savoured the aroma and placed the stew into his mouth. The aroma reminded Roman of sweet chicken stew a specialty of Nareesha Thomas, his adoptive mother.

It was not often that Roman thought of Nareesha. Shortly after her marriage to Frank failed, she returned to Trinidad. At the age of ten, Roman felt abandoned; and ten years later, he blamed Nareesha's abandonment for his adoptive father's premature death.

Suppressing his bad memories, Roman put the spoonful of karachuk stew into his mouth. He was not disappointed. Though it did not taste like Mammy's sweet chicken stew, it was a delicious departure from the military rations aboard the Starbird Sanura. Roman, Zachary and Chi-Ro ate with gusto.

The meal ended, and Roman took the opportunity to press Chi-Ro regarding the makra-gak.

"It's quiet outside. I think the makra-gak has gone away."

"No. He will not be far away. The scent of food attracts the beast. He is somewhere out there, watching and waiting. He extracts additional courage from darkness and will not leave until he is fed."

"Will you feed the beast?" asked Zachary.

"No, Dr. Zachary Silverman. Hungry makra-gaks make better opponents."

"You're actually going to watch me fight a monster?" asked Roman.

"With deep interest, Master Armon. Fear not, I would never permit a student to do that, which I would be unwilling to do myself. I told you I considered becoming a monk. Well, my father was deeply opposed to my joining the Mara Kai Monastery and suggested that I was a coward. To prove him wrong, I stole his Mark II Starfire and flew to this very spot to face the fearsome makra-gak on my own. I used the carcass of a Valorian stag to lure the beast. I was armed only with my father's combat dagger."

From its sheath, attached to his belt, Chi-Ro pulled a blade and added, "This dagger."

The reflection of light from the metal blade caught Zachary's eye and he looked away briefly. Chi-Ro swiftly twirled the dagger in his hand and caught the flat surface of the double-edged blade between his thumb and forefinger.

He offered its black hilt to Roman and said, "You will need this."

Roman studied the combat knife. He gently brushed his thumb across the blade, and it was as he expected - razor sharp.

Time seemed to stand still as Roman looked at his doubting reflection in the shiny blade. He remembered his inability to transform into his astral body, in the presence of Seti Aljyk.

Would I lose my nerve if I face this makra-gak?

Shrugging fear aside, Roman looked to his belt and found an empty sheath attached to it. He could not recall losing a combat knife. In fact, he could not recall ever wearing a combat knife. He placed the dagger into the sheath and felt a sense of security. The possibility of facing the mysterious thing that lurked in the beautiful forest, no longer filled his heart with terror.

He reassured himself with the thought: *This is only a dream.*

"You killed a monster with a seven-inch blade?" asked Zachary, masking his disbelief.

Chi-Ro continued, "I fought the monster but was unable to kill it. I was badly wounded, as was the beast, but it escaped into the forest. With great difficulty, I managed to make my way back to the Starfire. I activated the automated distress call before losing consciousness. I was fortunate. My father found me, before his superiors realised his Starfire had been stolen. Yes, the Great Spirit was merciful; and I spent twelve days in a regeneration pod." Chi-Ro chuckled, "Had my injuries not been so severe, my father would surely have killed me."

Roman and Zachary pretended to share Chi-Ro's amusement.

Zachary asked tentatively, "So how old were you Chi-Ro?"

"I was fourteen years old."

"Brave kid," said Zachary. He turned to Roman and said, "You'll be alright."

Chi-Ro added, "I should point out that, at fourteen, I had already mastered the ancient art of Arashi Paksa."

Zachary chuckled. Roman anticipated Chi-Ro's reaction and tried to warn Zachary with his eyes. He failed.

Zachary asked, "What's Arashi Paksa, a game Talisian boy scouts play?"

"No, Dr. Zachary Silverman, though outmatched by Hatari Ikou and utterly useless in the face of Kon Jou, Arashi Paksa is no game."

Zachary looked bemused. Chi-Ro stood up, walked to the wall, retrieved a sok-bou then proceeded towards the exit. He said to Zachary, "Allow me to demonstrate."

As they stood, Roman gave Zachary a look that said, *I tried to warn you.*

"Don't worry, it's only a dream," whispered Zachary.

"His dream, your nightmare."

Zachary walked towards the exit, unaware of any danger. Roman followed, shaking his head.

In the orange glow of the setting sun, in the clearing adjacent to Chi-Ro's cottage, Zachary and his extended sok-bou sailed four metres through the air, before crashing into the ground. Roman winced and shook his head.

Chi-Ro said, "Dr. Zachary Silverman, you possess a sok-bou. I have not drawn my weapon. Yet you appear most adept at blocking my blows with your face. Why am I not surprised?"

With a low groan, Zachary used the sok-bou for support as he dragged himself to his feet.

He whispered, "Nice kick, Fu Manchu. Just you wait, I'll get you. So far, conventional martial arts seem useless against you; but I have a few more tricks up my sleeves, and I'm just warming up."

Chi-Ro's tall shadow crept towards Zachary, shrouding his face with gloom.

"Verily, you have not landed a single blow. You are foolish, but I admire your spirit. As you may have seen, before the swelling of your face obstructed your vision, Arashi Paksa – the Way of the Storm, relies on speed of attack. This is the basic fighting form, taught to all Talisian military personnel. You must master it, or die during any unarmed engagement with the enemy."

"So I guess this particular lesson ends when you grow tired of hitting me."

"Dr. Zachary Silverman, it is unlikely I will grow tired of hitting you," said Chi-Ro with no emotion.

"You're a real sport."

"This is not sport. I continue to hit you because your attacks are slow and transparent. As Prince Armon so rightly asserted, unless you are properly prepared for battle, you are a liability to both yourself and more importantly, those around you."

Zachary said to Roman, "Thanks Buddy."

He deactivated the sok-bou and tossed it to the ground.

Roman thought: *When are you going to get it through your thick skull that this is life or death? Chi-Ro is the best teacher you could have.*

"Oh yeah?" said Zachary, "Don't let that stony-faced exterior fool you. Mr. Miyagi's laughing on the inside."

"Good," said Chi-Ro, "your latent telepathic skills are surfacing. I expect you will eventually master the rudiments of Arashi Paksa, but it may take another twenty years."

Thinking that Chi-Ro experienced a lapse in concentration, Zachary launched himself into a flying kick - the latest of a long string of mistakes.

Chi-Ro instantly fell backwards, raising his right leg. With his leg outstretched, he positioned his foot so as to allow Zachary to fall on it with his groin. Following the unfortunate impact, Zachary tumbled to the ground and rolled about grabbing his crotch and stomach in agony.

Chi-Ro quickly propelled himself to his feet. With his right hand, he casually brushed the traces of soil from his left shoulder.

Roman jogged to where Zachary had fallen and knelt at his side.

Zachary said, "I'm beginning to think that Nuri and Chi-Ro are trying to ensure I never have children."

Roman placed his hands on Zachary's temples and said, "This will ease the pain."

Zachary felt better immediately; and, to his surprise, he received knowledge of various fighting styles from Roman.

"How the hell did..."

"Get to your feet soldier!" barked Roman.

He dragged Zachary to a standing position and shot him a look compelling him to remain quiet. Zachary simply responded with a knowing nod.

Unseen by the pair, Chi-Ro Jin smiled – fully aware of the assistance Roman had given Zachary.

Roman stepped away from Zachary, who groaned and winced pretending to be in agony.

Losing his smile, Chi-Ro walked confidently towards Zachary's position. Once in range, Zachary launched his attack – a blisteringly swift Kon Jou punch. Chi-Ro, just as swiftly, twisted his upper body, grabbed Zachary's wrist and with a fluid motion propelled him into a prickly bush three metres away.

Zachary cried out in pain.

Chi-Ro looked towards Roman and calmly said, "There is still much to learn."

Roman tried to mask his embarrassment. But far from thinking less of him, Chi-Ro understood and admired Roman's loyalty to Zachary.

Writhing on the ground, Zachary resisted an almost overwhelming urge to swear. Finally, he grasped the extent of Chi-Ro's formidable fighting skill. Finally, he sought to avoid aggravating the veteran of the Psychic Wars any further.

Chi-Ro Jin helped Zachary out of the prickly bush.

He said, "Well done, Dr. Zachary Silverman, you have shown great courage."

"That wasn't courage, it was stupidity."

"Even so, I believe you have great promise. This exercise has proved to be most revealing."

Suddenly Roman heard a woman's voice in the distance. It was Soraya.

She said, "Roman. Roman is that you?"

Roman turned to the right and shouted with excitement, "Soraya, we're over here!"

Instead of Soraya's anticipated reply, Roman heard a thunderous roar. He instinctively drew the knife Chi-Ro had given him, as his heart threatened to explode from his chest.

"It's the bloody makra-gak," exclaimed Zachary, who experienced a sudden, pain-relieving adrenaline rush.

Dashing into the forest gloom, in the direction of Soraya's piercing scream, Roman shouted, "Soraya!"

"Roman, wait!" cried Zachary.

Roman disappeared into the encroaching darkness.

Zachary turned to Chi-Ro and said, "You gave him that knife, now he thinks he's bloody Tarzan. He'll get himself killed."

A louder roar sliced through the forest.

Zachary turned to follow Roman, but Chi-Ro's vice-like grip clamped his shoulder.

"If you wish to save your friends, go into the cottage and bring me a rifle. Go now!"

Zachary bolted into the illuminated interior of the cottage. He hurried to the rifle rack and grabbed a Daxia MR-39 phase rifle. He turned swiftly and headed towards the exit. But, the opening was no longer there. With his heart racing and time wasting, Zachary could find no evidence of the door he used to enter the cottage.

"How the hell do you open this bloody thing?"

He frantically searched for a handle, a switch, anything that would open the door. He could find nothing. Panic ensued.

"Chi-Ro, I can't open the bloody door!" he shouted at the top of his lungs.

Suddenly the transparent outer walls of the monolithic dome began to turn white, and Zachary could no longer see outside. Out of frustration, he slammed the butt of the rifle into the wall where he thought the door once was. No effect.

Zachary stepped away from the wall and aimed the rifle. With a frustrated growl, he pulled the trigger. Nothing happened. Pulling the trigger repeatedly, Zachary's panic turned into wild hysteria. He hurled the rifle into the wall. The weapon clattered to the floor leaving the wall undamaged.

Zachary raced back to the rifle rack and grabbed a Zaikat-Su A-9K assault rifle. He quickly aimed and pulled the trigger. Once more, nothing happened.

"Is the safety on? Is there a bloody on switch? Why the hell won't they work?"

He grabbed a heavier, and more powerful, Aknon 874 'Conqueror'. It also refused to fire. With sweat now dripping from his forehead, Zachary tried the only remaining weapon, an Aknon 74S 'Ghost' sniper rifle. He was not surprised, when it too did not fire.

For a brief moment, he stared at the white walls in silent shock. Then, with furious anger, he launched himself at the white wall with the sniper rifle raised high.

He screamed "Bastard-bastard-bastard!" as he clubbed the wall three times with the butt of the rifle.

Both the wall and the rifle remained undamaged. Zachary began to feel the pains of his previous injuries returning.

He sat on the floor and muttered to himself, "This is only a dream, isn't it? I will get out of here. Focus - it'll be just like flying. Focus on walking through the wall."

Zachary took a deep breath and exhaled slowly. He felt his heartbeat gradually return to normal. He felt the pain diminish until it became imperceptible. He rose to his feet slowly and began to walk. He felt as if he walked on air.

I will phase through the wall, he thought.

With confidence, Zachary walked into the wall and bumped his head. "Shit," he said.

Chapter 52

Armed with the combat knife, which once belonged to Jin, father of Chi-Ro, Roman Doyle sprinted into the darkness of the Marusa Forest. He no longer heard Soraya's screams and feared the worse. Instinct brought him to an abrupt halt. Ignoring the painful pounding of his heart, and the throbbing in his head, he strained to listen.

Roman heard only his own shallow breathing. Chi-Ro and Zachary were nowhere to be seen and could not be heard.

Why haven't they followed?

The fear, which had been replaced by desperate bravado, returned with crushing intensity. And, with the fear, came doubt. Roman doubted his senses.

Did I imagine Soraya calling me?

Suddenly he heard a faint sound, directly behind. He tightened his grip on the dagger.

Roman spun quickly. From the darkness, a yellow-eyed hulk, possessing horns, fangs and claws, sprang towards him. The creature roared; a mighty roar, which drowned Roman's scream and stopped his heart from beating.

Miraculously, the makra-gak's large horns lunged on either side of Roman's body; but the creature's head slammed into his chest, hurling him through space.

Roman held on to the dagger for dear life, hoping not to land on its blade, hoping not to crash on his head. He managed to fall on both feet, but the momentum threw him to the ground on his back.

In a flash, the makra-gak was again upon him, sinking its claws into his shoulders. Roman stabbed with the dagger, and the creature roared with pain and anger. Roman stabbed again and again, tossed and rolled on the ground like a rag doll, as the vicious creature, relentlessly tried to kill him.

Desperately, Roman managed to drive the blade of the combat knife into the monster's body. Blood made the hilt slippery, and Roman lost his grip. The knife remained lodged in the side of the makra-gak. The animal tossed its head in pain and anger; a horn crashed into the side of Roman's body, hurling him five metres away.

Roman rolled into a shallow ditch and cowered. He heard the grunts and snorts of the wounded creature. It approached very slowly, in ever-decreasing circles.

"Roman, where are you?" came Soraya's desperate call.

"No! Stay away! Get out of here, get out of here!" shouted Roman.

He dragged himself out of the ditch and to his feet. For the first time, he clearly saw his opponent.

The humanoid beast towered three metres tall. Its angular skull, reminiscent of a ram's, sported a large forehead, pointed ears and a goateed chin. Its sickly yellow eyes glowed in the darkness.

This creature is like the Minotaur of Greek legend.

Clawed hands pulled the combat blade from its flesh and threw it to the ground. Then, for a chilling moment, the creature stared menacingly at Roman.

The makra-gak growled and prepared to charge. Roman focussed. He felt the warm, tingling sensation at the base of his spine.

"Where are you?" cried Soraya.

The makra-gak swiftly turned in the direction of Soraya's voice.

Roman shouted to Soraya, "Stay away!"

Soraya's voice asked, "Roman?"

The creature snarled defiantly, bolted and disappeared in the direction of Soraya's voice.

"Run, Soraya, run!"

Instinct drove Roman to retrieve the dagger. He swiftly wiped the blood on his sleeve before returning it to the sheath on his belt. With a burst of psychic energy, Roman transformed into an astral wraith.

He flew in pursuit of the beast. Despite his blistering speed, the makra-gak remained several steps ahead, leading Roman through a maze of trees and shrubs.

Flying man and running beast approached an entrance carved in dark rock. The entrance led underground.

To his horror, Roman realised, *It's made of lapys nerian.*

Just as quickly, his strength began to fail. He landed, resumed human form and thanked God that he retrieved the dagger. The makra-gak turned to Roman and growled before heading underground.

Roman shouted into the forest, "Soraya, there's a cottage not far from here; you have to get to it."

"I'm in a maze," came Soraya's voice, "I can't find my way out. There's something here..."

Soraya screamed.

Roman realised: *She's in there with the monster!*

His gut feeling told him: *This isn't right. It doesn't make sense.*

However, the fear of losing his wife and unborn child propelled him towards the lapys nerian entrance.

Set in the stone, above the entrance, a smooth crystal orb provided illumination. Roman tentatively touched it. Despite the brilliance of the light it produced, the orb was as cold as the stone surrounding it.

With both hands, Roman wrenched the orb free. He disappeared, with the light, into the underground passage.

As he ventured into the gloom of the labyrinth, Roman felt he was being manipulated. He was being led into a trap.

He tried to reassure himself with the thought: *This is only a dream.*

But the deeper he walked into the dark maze, the more he asked himself, *What if it's real?*

Dream or no dream, he had to rescue Soraya.

To add to his rising apprehension, Roman noticed that the light, emanating from the orb he carried, was slowly diminishing. Soon he would face complete darkness.

He also had another concern: *How will I find my way out of this maze?*

With Chi-Ro's dagger, Roman tried to make a mark in the lapys nerian wall but found unsurprisingly, that the metal blade could not cut the hardest substance in the Cosmic Sea. Returning the knife to its sheath, he continued to follow the trail of blood left by the wounded makra-gak.

Roman estimated that he had walked about two hundred metres since entering the underground passage. He came to a halt. The single passage forked into two. Holding the orb up before him, he noticed a slight increase in its glow, when he pointed it towards the passageway on the left.

The makra-gak went that way. The orb is a proximity beacon. The closer it is to the makra-gak, the brighter it gets.

Roman jogged into the passageway on the left and immediately confirmed the correctness of his intuition. The light of the orb grew steadily brighter. Confidently quickening his pace, Roman sprinted several metres until a fresh breeze caressed his face. He followed a sharp bend in the lapys nerian path and instinct urged him to draw Jin Lan's dagger once more.

Holding the brilliant orb in his left hand, and the metal blade in his right, Roman saw that the passage grew wider, until it opened into an underground cave. With caution, he slowed to a brisk walk and to his surprise, the orb grew warmer and warmer until it became hot, too hot to handle.

Roman heard laboured breathing coming from the cave. He placed the orb on the ground and tightened his grip on Jin Lan's dagger.

The makra-gak is here. It's waiting for me.

Stealthily, Roman walked towards the mouth of the cave, towards the sound of laboured breathing. The sound made Roman realise he had been holding his breath. He inhaled slowly and felt some of the weight of apprehension lifted from his shoulders.

With each cautious step, he steeled himself for a confrontation with the wounded animal. He noticed that the sound of breathing became more and more irregular and that the interval between each breath became longer.

I think it's dying. Maybe I'll get Soraya out of here without much of a fight.

But a pang of guilt, soon replaced his sense of relief.

I didn't want to kill the beast. It attacked me. I had no choice but to defend myself. Why did it attack me? Is Chi-Ro orchestrating this and if so, for what purpose?

With a plaintive wail, a gust of wind rushed from the cave into the passage; bringing Roman to a halt, and abruptly back to full red-alert. The wind subsided, as did Roman's guilt and the painful sound of laboured breathing. All that remained was a chilling silence. Suddenly, the brilliant light of the orb quickly dimmed, glowed briefly and extinguished, plunging the underground passage into utter darkness.

In the black, Roman heard the sound of sobbing. A woman's sobs emanated from the cave.

Oh my God, it's Soraya.

Roman's heart skipped a beat, and he felt a large knot develop in the pit of his stomach.

Chapter 53

With knife in hand, Roman Doyle bolted into the underground cavern. Mercifully, three small gaps in the ceiling allowed streams of moonlight into the large underground chamber. Even so, his eyes strained to adjust to the diminished illumination.

At the centre of the cavern, he discerned a large pool of unmoving water and felt instinctively afraid of it. To his right, a woman wearing a white dress huddled over the fallen body of the makra-gak; and without hesitation, he ran towards her.

"Soraya," Roman called.

Waves of relief threatened to overwhelm him as he rushed to her side. Soraya stood and turned slowly but said nothing. Roman immediately recognised a deep sadness in her eyes. It stunned him into silence and he stopped short of holding her, puzzled by her unusual behaviour.

Suddenly Soraya smothered Roman in a warm embrace and kissed him passionately. Jin Lan's dagger slipped from his grasp and fell to the ground, soon to be forgotten.

Roman tried to speak, but Soraya's tongue sensuously caressed his lips before snaking into his mouth and banishing all thoughts of speech. She wore an exotic scent, which intoxicated him. Her groin pressed against his thigh, and he felt her heat. Against his chest, he felt her nipples straining to break free of her thin bodice. Her fingertips danced up his spine to the nape of his neck, sending waves of pleasure throughout his body.

The voice of reason repeatedly said, *something is not right.*

But screaming, all-consuming lust, drowned out its sober message.

Breaking the kiss, Soraya whispered in Roman's ear, "I burn for you."

Her tongue gently nibbled his earlobe then darted into his ear. Her left hand raked his chest while her right hand inched towards his groin.

She said, "I want you Armon."

In his stupor, Roman could barely mumble, "What?"

Thoughts previously suppressed by carnal desire struggled to the surface.

This is not my wife. This is not Soraya. Soraya is in cryostasis aboard the Starbird Sanura.

It took every ounce of Roman's willpower, to gently push the woman away.

With a voice thick with lust, she said, "I want you now," and she tore open her bodice.

Roman asked, "Who are you?"

She replied, "Do you not recognise me? I am Soraya."

In his mind, he said, *No.*

Mesmerised by her eyes, Roman observed the woman as she slowly stepped forward. Her full lips and gently swaying hips promised untold pleasures. Roman felt drunk.

He took a step backward and raised his right hand in an effort to ward off the temptress. The woman took another step towards him; and the dress fell from her shoulders, revealing her naked beauty. She continued forward without breaking eye contact and paused in a shaft of pale blue moonlight.

Roman briefly searched her dark gaze only to be distracted by her parted lips, long dark hair, heaving chest, flat stomach and broad hips. In an attempt to break her spell, he averted his eyes to the ground. But her long, perfectly shaped legs brought him back to the ravenous clutches of sweet temptation.

The woman asked huskily, "My love, has space travel suppressed your libido?"

Roman repeated, "Who are you?"

"Am I not that, which you desire?"

Roman glanced down to the ground, this time, searching for Jin Lan's blade. The nude woman gracefully squatted, picked up the dagger at her feet and slowly stood upright.

"Would you murder your wife as you murdered the poor makra-gak?"

With a smirk, Roman declared confidently, "You're not my wife and none of this is real."

"You are wrong my love, you no longer inhabit the crude dream designed by the son of Jin, you crossed the threshold into another dimension, one where dreams become flesh."

With bated breath, Roman asked, "Where is Soraya?"

"Soraya is here before you, yearning for your warm embrace. By all means, stab me. Impale me, but not with this."

The woman casually threw Jin Lan's dagger into the dark water. Helplessly, Roman watched his only weapon disappear with a splash that conjured harmless ever-decreasing ripples, and sent them racing to the lapys nerian banks of the small lake. He took another step backward, glanced over his shoulder and found to his dismay that he stood at the water's edge. He struggled with visions of drowning, and then an irresistible urge to flee, descended upon him.

The woman said, "Perhaps you have grown tired of kissing these lips and loving this body."

With that, she became Kiya Mankuria.

Then, speaking as Kiya would, she added, "Perhaps this young, ripe, forbidden fruit will rekindle your passion."

In typical Trinidadian fashion, Roman sucked his teeth, shook his head and said, "For a minute there, you almost fooled me. But now, you have no chance, no chance at all."

In a flash, the woman grabbed Roman by the neck, with her right hand, and lifted him off his feet. He clasped her vice-like grip with both hands as he struggled to breathe.

She said, "I have many virtues Armon, but patience is not one of them."

The woman threw Roman to the ground at the edge of the pool. He fell on his back, and his left arm sank into the water up to his shoulder. Roman immediately pulled his arm out and rolled away from the edge.

In spite of the insulation of his Osirian stealth suit, the water felt cold, shockingly cold; and he feared that it was also very deep. His telepathic communion with Kiya and Chi-Ro had transferred to him the knowledge required to swim, but had not rid him of his phobia. He was still terrified of the water and tried to get as far away from it as possible.

Then, once again, in the distance, Roman heard a familiar voice calling his name.

No, it can't be...

"Yes," said the woman mockingly, "that would be your beloved Soraya."

"Do you really think that tired old trick will work on me again? I know this isn't real. I know that Soraya and I are in cryostasis aboard the Starbird Sanura."

"And you know this because, in a dream, Chi-Ro Jin told you so?"

The woman's high-pitched cackle turned into the haughty laugh of a man.

Then, with Chi-Ro's voice, she said, "Are you asleep? Are you awake? Are you alive or are you dead? Was it Chi-Ro Jin who brought you to a dream to be tested or was it the Winged Serpent? Am I Niburian or am I a demon? Master Armon, what you call life is but a dream, and reality is relative."

Roman could not mask his fear and confusion when he asked, "Chi-Ro, is that you?"

Reverting to Kiya's voice, the woman simply laughed.

Roman demanded, "Who the hell are you?"

"I have many names, the majority of which your limited intellect would find difficult to comprehend and your human tongue impossible to pronounce. But if you insist, you may call me Asmorda and gaze upon my true likeness."

Asmorda changed once more. This time she became a stunningly beautiful woman of mixed origin. Exotic tattoos covered her lean, athletic body.

To Roman, she seemed to be of every race. She had pale Caucasian skin, distinctly Oriental eyes, full African lips, the chiselled cheekbones of a Native American, straight dark Asian hair, and the hourglass figure of Arabic, Mediterranean or Latin women.

Moving towards Roman seductively, on hands and knees, Asmorda said, "To protect her from the lustful makra-gak, I secured your darling Soraya in a chamber. There is only one entrance to this chamber, and it is situated at the bottom of the pool, under twelve metres of black, icy-cold water. The tide is rising and in ninety minutes or so your wife will drown. I know you well, Armon; through your dreams, I have studied you for a very long time. And yes, I know your deepest fears. I know of the terror, the depths instil in your heart. But if you lie with me, if you love me, I promise your wife and unborn child will be unharmed. I will retrieve your Soraya for you, and grant you both free passage out of this maze. She need not even know of our intimacy."

Asmorda crawled upon him; and Roman noticed something, which confirmed his fears.

Asmorda has a tail. She isn't human at all.

"It is true," she said, gently groping the bulge between his legs, "I am not human nor am I Niburian. I am more, much more. If my tail displeases you, I can assume another form. But alas, I suspect it excites you. You have my solemn oath Prince Armon, in my arms you will discover the meaning of true bliss."

"Help me," came Soraya's desperate plea.

Asmorda searched Roman's eyes, but he hid his emotions well.

She said, "I sense her cries disturb you, it would take but a brief moment to..."

With all his might, Roman delivered a perfectly executed right cross into the side of Asmorda's chin; and the creature slammed to the ground, at his side.

He immediately leapt to his feet and shouted, "Hang on Soraya, I'm coming."

Chapter 54

Roman Doyle briefly stared at Asmorda lying unconscious at his feet. He imagined how disappointed his foster mother Nareesha would be, knowing he knocked out a woman. But Asmorda was no woman, she was a shape-shifter with a tail and Nareesha...

Nareesha is Catholic.

In retrospect, Roman imagined Nareesha would say, "Damn Devil daughter, dat good fuh she."

Roman smiled but the smile faded almost instantly. He knew, with every passing moment, Soraya's situation became more critical. He had to rescue her, and to do that, he had to face his deepest fear. He had to dive into the cold, dark water.

"Lord help me," muttered Roman as he closed his eyes and mentally wrestled with rising panic.

Finally, he took a deep breath and steeled himself for the task ahead. As he opened his eyes, terror rose from the pit of his stomach. The cavern seemed much darker and on his right side, in the periphery of his vision, he saw a large bulk; a large ominous shadow loomed where Asmorda had lain.

Roman reminded himself that lapys nerian inhibited only his astral abilities and without turning his head, he calmed his nerves and concentrated. He could not see it clearly, but he sensed the beast. He sensed its fury and read its intentions.

As the creature attacked with a loud shriek, Roman was already in motion. He dove forward, rolled and spun. The thing lunged again; its deadly white fangs glinted in the moonlight.

Roman unleashed a barrage of psychic attacks aimed at the creature's central nervous system; nevertheless its head slammed into his chest, knocking him ten metres into the air.

As he hurtled towards the surface of the small lake, his mind raced and Roman felt as if time was working at a much slower pace. The impact was much worse than he expected and underwater, he found that everything was black. He could see nothing at all.

Roman panicked. For a moment, he fought the murky water with flailing arms and legs before calling on the memories stolen from Kiya and Chi-Ro. Recalling how to swim, Roman kicked sharply and used his arms and hands to pull through the darkness. He glided to the surface, spat out the foul, acidic water and gasped for air.

For the first time, in the pale moonlight, he saw Asmorda's latest manifestation. She had become a giant serpent similar to Shon-Ghūl, the hypnotic reptile from the Beli-Al System - the monster, which blinded Zachary on the Asing vessel. But unlike Shon-Ghūl, Asmorda was not just a giant serpent; she had become a giant serpent with wings.

Is Asmorda the winged serpent the Asing worship?

In the passageway, behind Asmorda, Roman saw the glow of the discarded orb and a series of distant growls confirmed his fears.

There are more makra-gak and they're coming. How the hell am I going to get Soraya out of here? Focus. Focus. First, I'll need the light from that orb to find the underwater entrance...

Roman's thoughts were interrupted by Asmorda's sudden flight. He dove under the pool's surface, seconds before Asmorda's giant maw bit into it.

Roman fought the swirling obscurity and confusion, desperately trying to escape the beast's deadly jaws.

Above the lake, Asmorda hovered and repeatedly thrust her massive head into the water but Roman's black stealth suit merged with the murk of the depths and the winged serpent could not find him.

Finally, Asmorda dove into the water and disappeared into its gloom. This is what Roman had hoped for. He had been hiding close to the bank and quickly scrambled out of the lake.

On the shore he spat, gasped for breath and having inhaled the putrid water, suppressed the urge to vomit.

The light from the orb grew steadily brighter, the roars of approaching makra-gak inexorably louder, and painfully, he listened to Soraya's calls for help.

Roman raced to the passageway, grabbed the bright, hot orb from the ground and without hesitation, threw it into the centre of the pool.

He immediately sensed Asmorda's realisation that he was no longer in the lake. As her rage tore through his mind, Roman sprinted towards the illuminated pool and prepared to dive. He felt dread. Not for himself but for Soraya, trapped with the tide slowly rising.

He dove into the dirty water just as the winged serpent shot out of it.

Using all his might, he propelled himself to the bottom of the lake. A quick glance over his shoulder confirmed that Asmorda had reacted quickly and was closing in on him. With the light from the orb, he easily found a hatch with a large rusted handle embedded in the muck at the bottom of the lake. He tugged at it, but it did not budge.

He sprang away from the hatch a second before the raging Asmorda crashed into it. In a sustained and frenzied attack, the serpent repeatedly lunged at Roman. But Roman narrowly escaped by slipping through gaps in the large jagged rocks, which populated the bottom of the pool.

Then amongst the whirling gravel and silt, Roman saw Jin Lan's dagger.

He grabbed the dagger and plunged it just behind Asmorda's head. With Roman clutching onto her back, Asmorda, the winged serpent, shot out of the lake towards the ceiling of the cavern.

From the bottom of the lake, the brilliant light of the orb revealed stalactites on the ceiling, which Roman had not previously noticed in the pale moonlight.

Desperately, he leapt off Asmorda and unto one of the large spikes. The stalactite was unstable. It would break at any moment.

Asmorda hovered below, and Roman stared into the pale yellow eyes of the demoness. Her eyes narrowed with seething malice as she attacked.

Roman swung himself violently and the stalactite broke free. He fell towards Asmorda's open jaws as the creature shot up towards him. Assisted by a surge of telekinetic energy, Roman drove the large calcite spike into the flesh between the eyes of the monster.

Man and winged serpent crashed into the pool. For a brief moment, Roman was completely disorientated; then he saw the clouds of blood in the water and surfaced, filled his lungs with air and plunged back into the depths. At the bottom, he saw Asmorda pinned by the large stalactite with Jin Lan's dagger partially buried in the silt at her side. She had reverted to the form of a woman with a tail. No longer beautiful, her face bore a large, terrible wound, the blood from which turned the surrounding water scarlet.

What a monumental bitch.

Roman retrieved the dagger and placed it in the sheath on his belt. He could not hold his breath much longer but fortunately, in the very bright pool, he quickly found the lapys nerian hatch again. He pulled its rusted handle but the handle broke off. Roman experienced the briefest moment of hysteria, then clarity banished his apprehension.

He remembered what Asmorda said:

Reality is relative.

Then he recalled Chi-Ro Jin's words, *"Your wish will be your reality."*

Once again, Roman focussed on the lapys nerian hatch.

It's just like Chi-Ro's monolith. A well-executed blow will shatter it. Water resistance would make a palm strike ineffective but a Karate chop might work.

Roman felt the familiar tingle in his spine, moments before he delivered the devastating blow. His hand impacted with the lapys nerian, sending shockwaves up his arm and splitting the stone in two. He used his feet to double kick the remaining rubble free, before swimming through the gap and into a narrow channel, which inclined upwards.

A brief swim brought Roman to a small, dark, partially submerged chamber. He clawed his way out of the pool and stood upright, spitting and gasping for breath. At the centre of the chamber was an altar and on the altar, crying hysterically, with both wrists cuffed above her head and both ankles shackled, lay Soraya. The water had reached up to her face and it was painfully obvious to Roman that unless she could be released, Soraya would soon drown.

Roman kissed her and said, "I'm here... I'm here."

Shivering from the cold, Soraya asked, "Roman. The chains, how are you going to break the chains?"

Roman quickly studied the altar, which consisted of a smooth slab placed on a short wide pillar. Both were made of lapys nerian. At both ends of the submerged slab, there was a large mound with a single hole through which the chain attached to Soraya's leg irons and the chain attached to her handcuffs was threaded.

Bloody lapys nerian. I guess plain old granite would be too much to ask for, human exploration has failed to find it anywhere except Earth.

"Close your eyes Soraya, I'm going to break the chain free."

Soraya nodded and closed her eyes. Roman inhaled slowly. Then, with a sharp exhale, confidently delivered a palm strike through the water and directly into the mound, which housed the chain above Soraya's head. The lapys nerian shattered into many small fragments releasing the chain.

Roman immediately helped a relieved Soraya to an upright position.

"Just a little while longer, I'll break the chains, then we can leave," he said.

Soraya simply nodded her head, closed her eyes and shielded her face with both hands.

With a single blow, Roman smashed the mound at her feet and in the process, knocked a small chunk of lapys nerian from the slab. He quickly retrieved the shard of black stone from the rising water and examined it. One end came to a sharp point, whilst the other was flat and wide. He had an idea.

Roman took Soraya's left wrist and scrutinised the shackle.

"Soraya, I'm going to break your cuffs with this piece of stone. Put your wrist on the table and don't move."

Soraya immediately did as he asked and rested her shackled wrist on the table under the water. With his left hand, Roman placed the sharp point of the stone shard against the shackle. Then, with a firm blow from his right palm, he drove the lapys nerian into the metal.

The cuff broke open freeing Soraya's wrist. He hurriedly repeated the process with Soraya's remaining irons, until finally she was free.

With the water relentlessly rising, Roman hauled himself onto the altar. He pulled Soraya to her feet, embraced and kissed her passionately.

Breaking the kiss, Roman said, "There's only one way out of here, and that's through the water."

"I know," responded Soraya, "when did you learn to swim?"

"I used memories from Chi-Ro Jin."

"How?"

"Soraya, we have to get out of here now."

"Show me."

"Now's not the time."

"You know I can barely swim, if this memory transfer helped you, maybe it will help me as well."

She's right, of course, and with the makra-gak approaching she may have to defend herself.

"OK," said Roman with a sigh and he placed his hands on Soraya's temples.

"Oh my God," she said, "I can swim. I can fight!"

For a brief moment she looked at Roman with a gleeful smile. Then she remembered something and her brow became furrowed, her face sullen. Suddenly she slapped Roman hard across the face.

"Who's dat woman?" she demanded.

"What? What woman?"

"De naked one."

"You mean the monster I killed? Wasn't she the one who brought you here?"

"Brought me here?"

"Soraya, how did you get here?"

"I don't know. I don't know how I got here."

"What do you mean you don't know? I had to swim through almost seventy feet of shitty water to get here."

"But I couldn't have come through the water. When I saw that thing I passed out."

"What thing?"

"It looked like Pan. It had horns..."

"A makra-gak? A makra-gak brought you here? Show me."

Once more, Roman placed his hands on Soraya's temples. He saw broken images, incomplete and jumbled memories. From Soraya's point of view, he ran through the Marusa forest.

Something chased her, a hulking figure - a beast. It overtook her. It was a makra-gak and the shock of seeing it caused Soraya to faint.

"There's another way into this room," said Roman, "one that does not go through water. Search the walls, there has to be a door."

Soraya stood on the altar, scouring the walls of the room with her eyes. Roman plunged into the water and made his way to the wall at the head of the slab. In the dimness, he rubbed his palms along the smooth lapys nerian, searching for any indication of a door. He found something, a raised disc, about twenty-five centimetres in diameter, on the surface of the wall.

Instinctively, Roman applied pressure on it with his palm and immediately he felt a tremor in the floor. Some sort of mechanism had been activated.

He surfaced to find Soraya screaming, "It's closing, we'll be trapped."

To his horror, Roman watched helplessly as a slab of lapys nerian slid from the ceiling. It completely sealed the passageway he used to swim into the chamber. Roman was about to swim towards the trap door, when another tremor began. The wall adjacent to the disc slowly slid up into the ceiling, draining the room of the foul water.

"Come Soraya. Hurry."

As Roman lifted Soraya off the altar and onto the ground, an exhilarating gust of fresh air rushed into the chamber.

Holding her hand, Roman led Soraya through the trap door and into a narrow passageway. The path inclined downward and was lit by an orb. Roman pulled the orb from the wall.

As they walked, he noticed that the water from the altar room flowed into three evenly spaced drains.

"Look, over there," said Soraya.

In the distance, bathed in moonlight, Roman saw steps hewn into the rock and adding to his sense of relief, he also noticed that the further they got from the torture chamber, the dimmer the orb's light became.

We're getting away from the makra-gak and away from danger.

Nevertheless, when they got to the bottom of the stairway, Roman decided to err on the side of caution.

Placing a finger to his lips, he motioned to Soraya to remain quiet. Then the opened palm of his left hand directed her to stay put; he gave her the orb, pulled Jin Lan's dagger from its sheath and stealthily proceeded up the stairway.

Chapter 55

Within another dream, Anah Sadaka stood alone in a dimly lit room with walls of shimmering gold. Behind her, a door silently slid open; and a tall, slim, black man entered the room. He wore an Osirian stealth suit and had deep blue eyes. His very short hair showed tinges of grey, and gold from the walls reflected on his oval, clean-shaven face and chiselled cheekbones. He paused and stared intently at Anah Sadaka.

Without turning, Anah said, "Baraka, agent zero-zero-six."

"Baraka, Sayeeda. It has been a long time, but surely you recall how much I dislike numeric designations."

Anah Sadaka turned to face the man, stared deeply into his eyes and said, "And surely, Nook Tigg, you are aware that the title Sayeeda is no longer appropriate."

"Nevertheless, leadership suits you."

"Some within the Osirian Council disagree."

"Yes, I heard of your demotion. Is this why you have chosen to defy the council's orders?"

"Perhaps I might ask you the same question. Your role was that of covert protector. You were strictly forbidden to establish any personal contact with the boy."

Nook Tigg's jaw immediately tightened and his eyes narrowed, then regaining his composure, he said, "That was some time ago, but I suppose to those such as us, twenty years is but a brief moment in time. I pitied him. He knew nothing of his true heritage."

"And how, may I ask, did stories of Nook Tigg and his space rocket help the young Prince's development?"

"When very young, dreams can alleviate the process of mourning. And the Prince had much to mourn."

"Your stories posed a security threat."

"Do you not think that being sent to the Talisian battlefront was enough punishment for my transgression?"

Anah swallowed hard and said, "It was too much, especially after the loss of your son."

Nook Tigg snapped, "It was you who advised the council."

"I did my duty."

"Dwell in the past, worry about the future and find misery in the present. It is forgotten; I bear no grudge."

"I assure you, I strongly opposed the council's decision to send you to the front. You were sorely missed in the Osirian Guard."

"And you Anah, did you miss me?"

"You are a fine warrior..."

"Fine warriors obey orders. Why have you assumed this form? I thought the feline was your preference."

"My interaction with humanoids revealed that my feline form created unnecessary unease."

"Indeed," said Nook Tigg as he searched her eyes. Then he added, "I find this dimly lit chamber stifling."

Nook Tigg motioned with his hand, and suddenly they were no longer in the room.

Instead, Anah Sadaka and Nook Tigg appeared on a deserted, tropical beach, bathed in brilliant sunshine. Anah's long white hair billowed in the onshore sea breeze. Powerful waves rolled onto the un-spoilt, sandy coastline, which went on for miles.

"Kairi?" asked Anah Sadaka, as they strolled.

"Yes, the northern coast."

"I see the Prince's former sanctuary still fascinates you. I must admit, there is great beauty in this land of the hummingbird. I have fond memories of my assignment in San Fernando. And I recall there was much disappointment, amongst the team that retrieved Tarom Rin's starship. None of the Osirians welcomed re-assignment or relocation. I have always found it curious how easily Osirians form attachments."

"So Anah, do you care to explain why you have not passed the Sword of Power to the Emperor's heir?"

"Najura, the Niburian sword of kings will be presented to the Prince when I believe he is ready."

"Roman needs to know the true history of Earth. He needs to be fully aware of the Osirian Colony, the followers of Seth, the Illuminati and the Neph Alim Principality. He needs to know all, Mistress Anah, and he needs to know it now."

"Even now, you still insist on referring to Prince Armon Sakara by his alias?"

"It is the name he has known all his life, and it is how he chooses to identify himself. Some may say you intend to use Najura to exact revenge from the Saurians. Have a care Mistress Anah, you risk termination with your present course of action."

"And would you carry out such an order my old friend?"

"I have lost the full trust of the Osirian Council. They would send another."

Anah smiled and said, "Oh, I believe they trust you well enough. Only the most trustworthy agents are used to infiltrate the ranks of the Royal Karellan Shock Marines, and you have proved yourself to be a most effective assassin."

"Nevertheless, Delius Roi still eludes me."

"Need I remind you, that Delius Roi killed the Talisian's most prolific assassin, Nuri Nemsys? But, Kiya assumed the role adequately don't you think?"

"Is it the will of the council that the traitor's son be allowed to fraternise with the Talisian heir?"

"You did not answer my question, Nook Tigg. If ordered, by the council, would you terminate me?"

"It is a question, which should not be asked; therefore I will not answer it. The boy must learn the truth of things."

"Then, by all means, tell him."

"And risk banishment?"

"I will it. That much authority I still have. The son of Sakara Rey does not trust me, nor does he trust Kiya. You will be the one to reveal the full truth to him."

"So, he does not trust you or your adopted daughter? Is that the real reason for your refusal to reveal the truth to him, Anah? I absorbed your report when I accepted the mission to protect Roman. I experienced the depth of your guilt at not saving Mina Rin."

"You absorbed my report as well as that of the coroner assigned by the Colonial Magistrate's office, so you know the truth. The trauma to Mina Rin's skull was too extensive. I could not save her. No one could save her."

"And what of the truth, regarding Zachary Roi? Should I tell Roman who his friend really is?"

"Leave Zachary Roi to me. The Neph Alim have taken a great interest in him."

"What manner of interest?"

"He has been abducted eight times in the last twelve months. It is unlikely he is even aware of it."

"That is frequent, even by their standards. This may be a foolish enquiry but have you removed his Neph Alim tag?"

"Of course. In the Dark Fields, both Armon's Talisian transponder and Zachary's Neph Alim tag were removed. Interference with any of their chosen subjects is a breach of treaty. And, if the Neph Alim Principality became aware of our involvement with the Karellans and the Talisians, they would declare war; and ultimately, the Earth would be destroyed."

The strolling pair came upon the broken stump of a coconut tree. Anah sat on it. Nook Tigg stood, silently assessing her features, reading her emotions and noting her relaxed posture.

Staring out to sea, Anah continued, "So, I trust you agree, this Zachary may have untapped potential, which may yet prove useful; and, at the very least, it may be possible to use him as bait for his father."

"Zachary Roi is the son of a traitor. The politics and experimentation regarding the age-old Soterian myth does not interest me, neither does astral projection."

"I believe they should, especially since it is now clear that the Soter is no myth. Armon has shown abilities, which surpassed even those of Brakis Tarn; and his unborn son is even more powerful. Scientific secrets gained, from both the Saurians and the followers of Seth, led to our development of DAT1966; and, with the aid of our operatives, to the Talisian development of elidium. It is only a matter of time, before the Neph Alim Principality, or the followers of Seth, make similar breakthroughs."

"In spite of all this scientific wizardry, I believe pure-blooded Karellans will always have superior psychic abilities to those of the other races in the Cosmic Sea. This ability is strongest in the line of Rey Enki. That is why his line rules. It is why Sakara Rey is the True Emperor." Nook Tigg paused, folded his arms and added, "Anah, you have not explained why you believe that Roman would trust me?"

Anah smiled and said, "Men implicitly trust the mentors of their infancy. It is not often that a man discovers that the imaginary friend of his childhood is real."

"And are you certain, Brakis Tarn has been eliminated?"

Anah stood, stared deeply into Nook Tigg's eyes and said, "May it be written; Brakis Tarn is no more." Then clasping his hand in hers she added, "I share the Saurian belief that Armon Sakara's unborn son is the Soter. Therefore, I am assigning you the task of protector to the foetus and his human mother, Soraya."

"I have already sworn to protect Roman. It is a vow I shall never break."

"Sakara's heir shall remain under the protection of Chi-Ro Jin," said Anah.

She thought privately, *Even without the necessary training or due to a lack of it, this Prince Armon has managed to gain the loyalty of the most exceptional warriors. Curiously, even Kiya, despite all her pretence, also has some affection for him.*

Then, after careful thought, Nook Tigg said, "Chi-Ro Jin is indeed, a most worthy shamira."

"Commander Tigg, do you accept your mission?"
"May it be written, Mistress Anah."
"Indeed, Nook Tigg, may it be done."

Chapter 56

The sights and sounds of the benighted Marusa Forest greeted Roman Doyle at the top of the stairway. Amongst the gentle rustle of trees and the intermittent call of night birds, Roman discerned the distant flow of a river. A river, which he assumed, fed the underground lake.

A tidal river... The blackness and acidity of the water is probably the result of tannins released from the decaying leaves of trees and vegetation from the nearby Marusa forest. But, what am I thinking? Surely all of this is only a dream. Chi-Ro's training has the aftertaste of a personal assault.

"I sense your resentment, Master Armon; but I assure you, this assessment was necessary."

Roman instinctively tightened his grip on Jin Lan's dagger. Then, he turned slowly to find Chi-Ro, standing in the shadows, a few metres behind the top of the stairway.

"How so, Chi-Ro?"

Chi-Ro emerged from the shadows, raised his right hand and said, "My father's dagger, if you will."

Roman looked at the dagger in his hand, then at the approaching master of Hatari Ikou and said, "This dagger isn't real."

Roman called, "Soraya?" Then, upon receiving no response, he said, "Just as I suspected. Soraya, this forest, Asmorda and the makra-gak, all figments of your sadistic imagination."

Roman hurled the knife at Chi-Ro, who effortlessly caught the weapon and casually placed it in a sheath on his waist, without breaking his stride.

"No, Master Armon, your intriguing exploits within this dream have exceeded the limits of my imagination. Verily, this illusion of the Marusa Forest was taken from my memory; but everything else, including the makra-gak were of your design."

Roman asked disbelievingly, "I created Asmorda?"

"Indeed. Your opinion of yourself is clearly far greater than I anticipated."

"And Soraya was never in danger?"

"Not from horned beasts or sex-starved changelings."

"But the makra-gak was your suggestion..."

"Verily, but its manifestation was of your making."

"You tricked me."

"No, Master Armon, I simply tested you. It was necessary for me to assess your strengths and weaknesses."

Chi-Ro overtook Roman and continued walking along a path in the direction of his secluded cottage.

Roman asked, "So, did I pass your test?"

"There is no passing or failing. This exercise simply facilitated an observation of personality and mental acuity, whilst under stress."

Roman smiled, shook his head then said, "So, what did you learn?"

"You have banished your irrational fear of deep water. Your sexual fantasies are somewhat alarming, but on the whole, your behaviour has been in keeping with my prior observations of your personality. You value the lives of those you love above your own. This is a noble quality. The Apera Veritara speaks highly of it. Indeed, chapter 16, verse 12 of the Scrolls of Aram asks: 'Of what value is your life, lest you are willing to sacrifice it for those you love?' Be that as it may, self-sacrifice is not an option available to Lord Sakara's heir."

"You'd expect me to stand by and watch Soraya killed by a monster or allowed to drown?"

"I would expect you to do what you must. It is the duty of every man to protect his consort, but not every man is heir to the throne, which rules the Cosmic Sea. Be ever mindful of the fact that you are not expendable, Prince Armon."

I was so afraid, thought Roman.

"Verily, a man without fear is either dead or happy to die," responded Chi-Ro telepathically.

"Recently, I've found myself having difficulties distinguishing dream from reality."

"Have you considered that what you call reality, is merely a dream - more difficult to wake from?"

"Even so, how can I be sure which is which?"

"Perhaps, Master Armon, the question of dream or reality is irrelevant and what is of utmost importance is that we always deport ourselves in righteousness. You must learn to control your dreams or your dreams will forever control you."

"And what about Zach?"

"Surprisingly, Dr. Zachary Silverman has greater command of his dreams than you do."

"So Zach, being here in the Marusa Forest, is not just a figment of my imagination?"

"Sadly, it is not. Dr. Zachary Silverman is here."

"You don't like him do you?"

"He is like a kytan-fly - most annoying. He masks fear with sarcasm and poor attempts at humour."

"He's my friend."

"Indeed. It took some effort to prevent him from rushing to your side."

"Where is he?"

"He is currently in my cottage, using language I do not recognise. He renders it with great anger. I suspect it to be profanity."

"So what's in store for us next?"

"Dreamless sleep. Our bodies require it at regular intervals, but an increased frequency is essential if we are to fully recover before we reach our destination."

"Tell me about the planet Miru."

"A most inhospitable world, ravaged by plasma storms and constant acidic precipitation. In the last three years, forces loyal to Lord Sakara Rey have suffered great losses. What remains of Margrave Rin Mur-Rain's 9th Wave has sought refuge on Miru. Unique planetary conditions make nanoviral weapons ineffective and adversely affect the accuracy of orbital bombardment. Also, the planet's terrain is not conducive for the use of heavy armoured chariots such as the Karellan Gerian T-38 Devastators. By the grace of the Great Spirit, the enemy can only rely on lighter armoured anti-gravity vehicles and platforms. Using guerrilla tactics, a relatively small, mobile force, can effectively repel a larger heavily armoured contingent."

"You seem certain, we'll be attacked on Miru."

"It is possible. Highly likely."

"I've learnt a lot since leaving Earth, but I'm no soldier."

"Verily; that which you learnt through mental communion, with Nuri Nemsys and myself, is far from adequate. All are taught to resist such intrusions from a very early age. This skill is enhanced in military service, and Nuri Nemsys is very well trained. It has been my observation that a majority of men become deeply unstable when a desirable woman is involved. Do not underestimate Nuri Nemsys, I sense she seeks to manipulate you."

"Don't worry, I don't trust her."

"Attraction can cloud judgement."

"What are you implying?"

"Much can be deduced from your encounter with the creature you named Asmorda."

"The creature I destroyed."

"Indeed, the creature you destroyed," said Chi-Ro. Following a tense pause, he added, "Miru's gravity is greater than that of Alpha Tameri or, for that matter, Ki. After our period of dreamless sleep, we shall commence weapons and gravity combat training."

"I love my wife, Chi-Ro."

"Of that, I have no doubt, Master Armon."

"I need to get her back to Earth, where it's safe."

"Master Armon, having been to the planet you call Earth, I can assure you, it is anything but safe."

Chapter 57

Aboard the Starbird Sanura, Soraya Doyle opened her eyes and found herself oddly disorientated. Her head throbbed painfully, and it took a few moments for her to realise that she had woken from a dream. A few moments later, with details of the dream already forgotten, she made sense of her metallic grey surroundings.

I'm on the bridge of an Osirian starship, in a life-supporting pod. This, unfortunately, is reality.

In her womb, Soraya's unborn child kicked gently. The sensation gave her comfort, but it was short lived.

Soraya gazed at the sleeping form of Anah Sadaka in the command pod of the Sanura. The flutter of her eyelids suggested Anah was in R.E.M. sleep.

Soraya thought: *The Ligahoo mentally sedated me. I won't underestimate dat bitch again.*

A sudden gloom descended upon Soraya as she recalled events just prior to her collapse.

Roman was trapped on the Karellan flagship. I wanted to go to him, but dat ting put me to sleep. Why? Why would she do that?

Past, present and future images suddenly came to Soraya in sporadic mental flashes. She heard voices. Familiar, yet unfamiliar voices echoed in her mind like the playback of a damaged tape recorder. The voices did not play at the correct pitch. Some she recognised, others she did not, but Roman's voice was not among them.

Is meh husband dead?

Soraya heard a male voice say, *"I trust our agent is safely aboard."*

Another replied, *"Yes, Your Majesty."*

Agent? The Ligahoo and the killer call themselves agents. Is Anah or Nuri a traitor? No, it's someone else. It's a man. One of the marines? Perhaps... Wait... Yes, the marines are traitors – all of them. But they're dead. I can see it. Zach, Nuri and Chi-Ro killed them. It was self-defence. The marines were inhuman. Lizards. And dat voice... Seti Aljyk. He's a lizard too. The Saurian kill Roman uncle, and was impersonating him ever since.

Soraya heard another male voice say, *"Sobek."*

Is 'Sobek' another name for the Saurians? Chi-Ro call them the Seriak – devourers of children. Reptilian aliens from Talisian myth. But they not mythical are they? They exist. Reptiles pretending to be human beings... Dis is crazy. I must be dreaming. Dat's it, ah havin' ah conspiracy theorist nightmare.

Soraya took a deep breath and with her right hand she pinched her left forearm. It hurt.

Ah cyah be certain what's real anymore. Is it the truth I see? And Roman... Why can't I see Roman? Is it because he's dead?

Soraya felt nauseous, and her headache got worse. Somehow she knew Seti Aljyk's agent was aboard the Sanura.

It's definitely a man... I sense the presence of three men: Zachary, Chi-Ro Jin and someone else. Who is the third man? Seti Aljyk's agent? And, where is my husband?

An intense image flashed into her mind's eye. She saw a black man with strikingly deep blue eyes.

Who is this man? Did he come aboard while I was asleep? No, he's in another ship. A fighter ship. He's following us, and Anah is communicating with him... He is called... Agent zero-zero-six. So, he's an agent. Is he Seti Aljyk's agent?

Soraya mentally focussed on the man's Karellan raider.

His name is Nook Tigg.

A chill ran down Soraya's spine.

That name... Roman's imaginary friend from his childhood. But, how is this possible?

As she asked herself the question, she shivered. The clairvoyance generated by her unborn child, filled her with the fear of God.

What have I become? What evil possessed me?

The past, present and future, continued to flash before her mind's eye - filling her heart with dread.

Nook Tigg lived on Earth. And, as I suspected, Anah Sadaka and Nuri Nemsys have also lived on Earth. Even now, there are secret Osirian colonies on Earth. The Osirians have been watching Roman and me, for a very long time - they want to use our son. But exactly how, ah cyah see. Why dey allow me to be captured by the Asing? Did the Asing also know I was pregnant? No, their boss, the Obeah man Ne-Ro Jos didn't give them that information. The Asing target was Roman. And also on Earth, I see another group. Their symbol is the crocodile. Followers of... Seth? Now I understand. Those months of insomnia... The nightmares... They drugged me. A man, a Follower of Seth, injected me with elidium while I slept. Who is he? Is this the agent Seti Aljyk was talking about?

Tears ran down Soraya's cheeks. With knowledge came responsibility - a heavy burden; and she feared for her mortal soul.

The secret of Astral Projection - that's what it's all about. These groups believe it's the key to controlling the Cosmic Sea. The Saurian race isn't naturally psychic; and the Osirians and Followers of Seth descended from a group of Talisians, stranded on Earth, thousands of years ago. Over time, conditions on Earth caused them to lose their natural psychic abilities.

Soraya felt her heart pounding in her chest, but an overwhelming sense of awe began to banish her feelings of fear and anxiety.

My God, it gettin' clear to meh now... The Niburians, shape-shifters and psychics feared by the Saurians. Outta dis fear, the Saurians try to subjugate and destroy them. Saurian strength is technology. Dey use it to disguise themselves... Dey pretend to be Niburians, Talisians and Karellans. Forever scheming, manipulating... And the result of their evil? Genocide... Now only a few Niburians remain. And war... Dey behind the Psychic Wars. Even the android revolt is their doing. Dey want to rule, and astral projection is the key. We have tuh stop dem.

Suddenly Soraya experienced another mental flash and with it came greater pain. She closed her eyes and gritted her teeth.

Will these visions end? Ah want them to end. My God, what will you have me do? Ah see... There is yet another group... They call themselves the Neph Alim Principality - the ones those conspiracy weirdoes call 'the greys'. Dey come from the Dark Fields... Ah see it clearly now... Human abduction... Experimentation... The manipulation of human bloodlines.

Soraya trembled.

The secret of Astral Projection is in us. My God, it's in us women... Certain human women carry the gene. Roman's real mother had to be such a woman - a human woman. How many other women are there like me? Brakis Tarn the only other man known to have had this terrible astral ability had to be half-human... Merciful God, protect me from Satan's traps.

Soraya suddenly became aware of a loss of time.

Have I been dreaming?

She opened her eyes and found herself oddly disorientated.

Has this happened before? No, I've been dreaming.

To Soraya's dismay, many of the details, which appeared so clearly to her moments ago, swiftly faded.

Where is Roman?

Soraya felt a sudden rush as the thought of Roman dying flashed through her consciousness. The sense of panic was brief. She could not explain how she knew, but she felt as if waves of certainty washed over her and penetrated her to the core.

He's aboard... I sense him. Thank God. Thank God.

Soraya looked at Anah Sadaka asleep in the adjacent command pod and thought: *Dat Ligahoo mentally sedated me. I won't underestimate dat ting again.*

Suddenly a chill ran down Soraya's spine.

What was I dreaming? Something important became clear to me, but why can't I remember it now?

Her eyelids felt heavy, but she relaxed knowing that Roman was alive.

Soon, please God; I'll hold him in my arms. I've been asleep a long time, but I still feel tired. So tired...

In her womb, her unborn child kicked gently.

My baby is alive. My husband is alive. They are my reasons for living.

Soraya closed her eyes and smiled. She shook her head as she thought: *My husband and his weird imagination... What was it he used to tell me? Ah yes, I remember - stories of his imaginary friend and his space rocket. What was his name? Nuke something. No, it was Nook Tigg. That's it, I remember - Nook Tigg and his space rocket. Poor Nareesha, she thought Roman was seeing spirits. He was six when she took him to Mount St. Benedict. He had those monks rolling with stories of Nook Tigg the rocket man. Nareesha didn't expect monks, from the oldest Benedictine monastery in the Caribbean, to laugh so much. Yeah man, she say she was vex-vex-vex. But when they kept repeating that Roman was a very intelligent and imaginative boy, she said she felt real proud. Hmmm. What a strange story for her to relate to us on our wedding day. Poor Nareesha, I miss her.*

Then, gently, with a smile on her face, Soraya drifted back to sleep.

Chapter 58

Exhausted and clutching a Daxia MR-39 phase rifle, Dr. Zachary Silverman flopped into the double bed in the dimly lit sleeping chamber of Chi-Ro Jin's cottage.

Even though he had been unable to fire the weapon in his prolonged and ultimately futile attempts to leave the dwelling, he thought: *At least I could brain Chi-Ro Jin with it. The sadistic bastard's out there, laughing his head off, I can feel it.*

Taking in the chamber's featureless white walls and then its equally plain ceiling, Zachary felt relieved that they did not appear to be made of the same material used for the exterior of the technologically advanced, monolithic dome.

I'd feel even more like a lab rat, trapped behind a two-way mirror.

Zachary looked towards the open door, suddenly noting the bright light that streamed through it. Briefly, he toyed with the idea of closing the door but lacked any inclination to relinquish the surprising comfort of the double bed.

Bastard! I can't believe Chi-Ro locked me in here. It's unforgivable.

Zachary rubbed the bump on his forehead where it impacted on the wall.

Great. Another bloody bruise to add to all the other bloody bruises the bastard Chi-Ro gave me.

Suddenly Zachary started laughing, the type of laughter that suggested mental instability.

What the hell am I thinking? This is all a bloody dream, isn't it? When I wake up the bruises will be gone. Here I am, about to take a nap in a bloody dream. Well that should be interesting. If I dream, I'd be dreaming that I'm dreaming. And when I wake up I'll probably still be dreaming...

He laughed again. Then, in a flash, Zachary sat bolt upright and aimed the phase rifle through the doorway in the direction of the faint footsteps he heard.

He shouted, "Who's there? I have a gun, and I'm prepared to use it."

"And that amuses you?" came the familiar voice of Kiya Mankuria, also known as Nuri Nemsys.

"Come closer. Into the light... Slowly... Where I can see you..."

With arms raised, Kiya cautiously stepped into view.

"As you can see, Dr. Silverman, I am unarmed."

Zachary's pulse quickened. Kiya had that effect on him.

"Chi-Ro if that's you impersonating a woman - a particularly attractive woman, then you are one sick bunny."

Kiya lowered her arms, cocked her head, raised her left eyebrow and said with unmasked sarcasm, "You are a man of unmitigated charm, Dr. Silverman."

"Yes, and as long as you still have knees, I consider you armed and extremely dangerous."

"Perhaps my presence, here in this bedchamber, has caused you unnecessary excitement and led you to place far too much importance on your injured groin. I assure you, carnal acrobatics are furthest from my mind."

"Acrobatics," said Zachary, matching Kiya's aloof pitch and tone, "The word suggests a very healthy imagination; and I assure you, with the aid of the technological marvel you refer to as a regeneration pod, I've fully recovered from your aggressive foreplay."

Unfazed, Kiya observed, "There is no need to point your weapon at me, Dr. Silverman. It will not fire."

"What?"

"I am referring to the Daxia MR-39 phase rifle, not your..."

"Right. Of course."

"I absorbed the rules of this dream prior to entering it. Commander Chi-Ro has willed that the weapons in this cottage are non-operational."

"Yes, I see you managed to find the front door. You studied the rules huh? Very clever... I seem to have misplaced my copy of the rulebook. Can I borrow yours?" Zachary lowered the rifle to the floor and shifted to the left side of the bed. He patted the vacant right side and said, "Come. Sit. Don't be shy."

"I prefer to stand doctor, but I am glad you are seated as the information I am about to share with you may come as a shock."

"Wait, let me guess. You actually have a sense of humour?"

"Before entering this dream I was genuinely sorry I used violence against you. Now I regret being so gentle."

"Did you come here to finish what you started outside the transporter room or are you just practicing your role of Queen Tease of the universe?"

"Must you irritate me with these puerile exchanges? I am here to discuss your father."

Zachary sniggered, "My father? You know my father? Because I don't."

"Regrettably, though your father is extremely elusive, his exploits are well known."

"If this is your idea of a joke, you really need to work on the bit that's supposed to make me laugh."

"I never joke."

"No. Really?"

"Your father is Delius Roi. He is guilty of many capital transgressions including crimes against humanity."

Kiya's words prompted a moment of stunned silence. Then Zachary laughed and seemed even crazier than before.

"You're telling me that my mother never once spoke about my father because he's a Nazi war criminal?"

"I am amazed by your ability to find amusement in the fact that your father is a mass murderer."

Zachary screamed at the top of his lungs, "My mother hates Nazis!"

With eyes squinting with rage, Zachary observed the sudden flush of Kiya's cheeks, the subtle widening of her lime-green eyes and the tightening of her jaw. She had not anticipated Zachary's anger and remained covertly poised for violence even though his rage dissipated just as swiftly as it had surfaced.

Zachary was quick to note, for the first time since entering the dreamscape, Kiya's emotionless veneer faltered. She had misinterpreted his laughter. He had misinterpreted her words. Thick silence descended on the room as both fought to hide their embarrassment.

Staring intently, Kiya said, "Your father is a Follower of Seth."

With calmly devastating bluntness, Zachary asked, "Who are you?"

"In spite of everything I have said, and will say, I am your friend."

"No; who the hell are you? Because you sure as hell aren't the woman who kissed me outside the transporter room."

"That was a mistake, for which I hope you will eventually forgive me."

Using the back of his left hand to brush aside thick, black hair from his furrowed brow, Zachary said, "Sweet. So tell me about my father the Follower of Seth, whatever that is."

"Dr. Silverman, I must ask you to try to remain calm. Your anger may alert Commander Chi-Ro to my presence here."

"You don't strike me as being afraid of Chi-Ro. In fact, I don't think I've ever encountered anyone quite as cold-blooded as you."

"By all means, insult me if it makes it easier to accept all I have to say."

Zachary looked into Kiya's eyes of green, noting the dilation of her pupils. His gaze cowered from the focussed intensity he observed. Averting his eyes, he followed the bridge of her nose to her slightly flared nostrils, before briefly settling on her full lips. He wanted to kiss those lips - as he had kissed them before. Perhaps if he kissed this beautiful woman, the rage, the frustration and the anxiety would all melt away - as his heart melted.

Can't you see how I feel about you? He secretly thought, and his blue eyes found her gaze once more.

Kiya continued to speak, and Zachary wondered why he hadn't noticed the gentleness in her tone before. She said, "To answer your question, my real name is Kiya Mankuria; and I am proud to say, I was born on Earth. After the death of my parents, my mentor Anah Sadaka adopted me. From the age of eight, I have been trained to be a weapon in the service of my people and a defender of the planet Earth."

"You are from Earth? There are aliens living on Earth?"

"Yes, I was born on Earth and my people, the Osirians, are defenders of Earth. If you call us aliens, then I say to you that you are as alien as we are."

"Are you saying my father is one of your people?"

"A very long time ago, at the dawn of human history, a starship carrying a group of Talisian scientists came to Earth..."

"Is this going to be a very long story? Because I'm all out of popcorn, and I suspect all the supermarkets are closed."

"These scientists were outlaws who conducted genetic experiments in an attempt to create, what they believed to be, the next stage of humanoid evolution: super-beings possessing astral abilities..."

"Yes, I could tell this is going to be an epic of Biblical proportions..."

"But, intelligence agents of the Talisian High Council tracked these rogues to Earth. To destroy the scientists and their work, the High Council's android slaves bombarded the planet..."

"Bingo! Listen, I haven't read the book; but I've seen the movie..."

"Shut up, and listen carefully!"

There was something in the tone of Kiya's voice that clearly indicated to Zachary that he had crossed the line and risked more than bruised testicles. He wisely became attentive.

Kiya continued with sinister calm, "Two brothers and a group of genetically enhanced humans survived the orbital bombardment. The brothers were called Osiris and Seti. They were not in agreement and eventually two separate colonies were formed: one sworn to protect the Earth from external threats, the other bent on subjugating the Earth's human population and eventually all sentient life in the Cosmic Sea."

"Please, just tell me what my father's done."

"I will not discuss specifics regarding your father's crimes. There is little time and much of the information is classified. Simply trust me when I say his crimes are many."

"And you don't know where he is?"

"If I did, I assure you his death would come swiftly."

Zachary chuckled, but this time, Kiya recognised it to be the product of shock and not mirth.

"So finally, the truth is revealed. Now I know why I was allowed to tag along on this merry adventure. Use the son to snare the father. Is that it?"

"I will not lie to you. It is an option, which has been debated but one I strongly disagree with."

"Thanks. I guess you weren't joking when you said, "Be useful or be dead." You'd kill me without batting an eyelid, wouldn't you?"

"Would I be giving you this information if I intended to kill you?"

"Forgive me if I suspect you're sadistic."

"I assure you Dr. Silverman, if I intended to kill you, I would have done so, long before you had the opportunity to make comments about my arse."

"Do you really want me to focus on your arse right now? No, don't answer that. I admit I haven't figured you out. Not yet. But eventually, I will. When you meet my father, be sure to give him my regards before you grant him that swift death."

"One more thing..."

"What? There's more? What could possibly be the icing on the cake? Let me see... I know... How about this? My father killed your parents..."

Zachary immediately recognised his error. Kiya's eyes ignited with restrained violence. A less disciplined agent would have struck Zachary, and an emotional novice may even have killed the tactless quantum physicist. But Kiya Mankuria was, in the words of her proud foster mother, the best agent to ascend the esteemed ranks of the Academy of Guardians in over seventy years of diligent observation.

Kiya raised her chin and said in a calm, controlled voice, "You are obviously in pain, so I'll ignore this most recent attempt at provocation. But know this, if you ever..."

"No, I'm sorry. That really wasn't called for. Forgive me, the last few hours have been the worse experience of my life."

Kiya stared deeply into Zachary's blue eyes and beneath a thin layer of angst she easily found the sincerity she sought. Her voice was low and ripe with subdued emotion when she said, "I have the Jinzou Ningen to thank for the death of my parents."

"I'm sorry," said Zachary, his voice just above a whisper.

"But alas, it was one of your father's lieutenants who failed to kill the young Prince Armon, yet succeeded in murdering his custodians. To this day, my mother, who at the time was charged with Armon's protection, blames herself for the loss of Tarom and Mina Rin."

To her surprise, Kiya observed a sudden transformation in Zachary. His face appeared white and hollow.

Aware of his anguish, she added, "I am sorry to be the bearer of such unsavoury news."

"And, I'm disappointed that you think I'm anything like my father," replied Zachary, clumsily attempting to mask his shock and profound sorrow.

"Zachary, it may be of little consolation, but I resist your advances, not because of your father and his many crimes, but because my heart belongs to another."

Without thinking, Zachary blurted, "Roman's married, sweetheart."

With calm potency, Kiya responded, "May your bruised ego find comfort in the knowledge that my love is not your good friend, the Prince."

"Oh? What's his name? Is it even a man?"

I have hurt him deeply. That was not my intention. And now, like a wounded animal, he is most dangerous.

Kiya glared at Zachary and said, "We are aware that you have been abducted eight times in the last twelve months by a dangerous race known as the Neph Alim Principality. And we have removed their tag from your skull. It is possible that your father, Delius Roi, impregnated your mother as part of an experiment related to the development of beings capable of astral projection. Whatever the reasons for your abductions, and regardless of your father's motives, one thing is clear: You have great potential."

"Gosh, thanks Kiya, that's the nicest thing you've ever said to me."

Ignoring his obvious sarcasm, Kiya said, "It would be to your benefit that Chi-Ro Jin never learn of my presence here. We will be arriving at the planet Miru in three standard days. I sense you are fatigued but soon the Sanura's regenerative process will induce a period of dreamless sleep. It will do you good."

"You think?"

Kiya turned and strode confidently towards the front of the cottage.

Zachary followed and said bitterly, "Come again soon. I really enjoy our little chats."

Kiya did not respond. She simply phased through the wall, where a door once existed, and vanished from sight.

Zachary poked the wall. Unsurprisingly, it was cold and hard. He remained trapped.

He shouted at the wall, "Are you gonna help me realise my full potential, Kiya?"

Or are you gonna take notes, while I go slightly mad, in this bloody nightmare?

With a heavy sigh, Zachary slowly turned, leaned his back against the white wall; and then, as if all strength had been drained from his legs, he slowly slumped to a sitting position.

I'm the offspring of a murderer. My father killed Roman's parents. How the hell will I ever look Roman in the eye again? Once he learns the truth would he still consider me his friend? No. There's just no way. And once he turns against me, I'll have no one. Agendas. Everyone has an agenda, and it's clear I

*can't trust anyone. No, not even Roman, not anymore. Once Roman and Chi-Ro
find out whose son I really am, I'd be lucky to last all of two seconds.*

"I'm well and truly fackked."

Once more, Zachary laughed. But this time, any casual observer would
insist he be placed in a padded cell immediately.

Finally, the maniacal laughter subsided. Alone and defeated, Zachary
hugged his knees close to his chest, and fought the overwhelming urge to cry.

Chapter 59

As he walked through the Marusa Forest, in Chi-Ro Jin's dreamscape, Roman Doyle recalled his dream meeting with his childhood friend and protector - Nook Tigg, and a faint smile briefly crossed his lips. The old space adventurer explained how the powerful suggestion, that he was merely a figment of a child's imagination, was planted in Roman's psyche. This was done after a keen Osirian agent, amongst the good monks of Mount St. Benedict, alerted the Osirian Council of Twelve of Nook Tigg's serious security breach.

The Osirian Guard with their men and women in black were Earth's secret protectors and no effort was spared to ensure that they remained secret.

Roman was happy to meet the commander once more; and to learn that the stories presented to him, in his childhood, though at times exaggerated for dramatic effect, were firmly grounded in fact.

Nook Tigg and his space rocket are real. As is the noble Emperor, and the young prince sent to the faraway planet of Ki - there to be hidden, on the paradise island of Kairi. I am that prince. The riddle of the monarch butterfly is solved, for it is the Ten-Shi. The Arosian Ten-Shi - the symbol of The House of Enki. It is my father's symbol, as it is mine - for I am Armon Sakara, son of Lord Sakara Rey. The True Emperor of the Cosmic Sea.

As agreed, with Anah Sadaka, Nook Tigg advised Roman of Earth's hidden history. He now knew of the Followers of Seth and of the Neph Alim Principality. As a result, Roman no longer viewed Zachary's tale of being abducted by little grey aliens as far-fetched.

But, Nook Tigg made no mention of Zachary's true heritage to Roman, nor did he reveal the fact that the Sword of Power - Najura, remained hidden somewhere aboard the Starbird Sanura.

As he took in the now familiar sights, of the forest of Chi-Ro's dream, Roman's thoughts moved to his wife - Soraya, and their long overdue dream meeting.

A few days apart, seemed like a month in dreamtime. I missed her. She's changed. She's grown stronger yet more protective of our unborn child and of me. She seems certain it's a boy - a boy with frightening powers.

Then, after the period of dreamless sleep, and for what seemed like months, Roman and Zachary endured Chi-Ro Jin's rigorous crash-course in soldiering.

But changes in Zachary's behaviour had not gone unnoticed. Absent now were the constant jibes, which previously infuriated Chi-Ro and Kiya.

Zach hasn't been the same since that brief spell alone in Chi-Ro's cottage. He says everything's OK, but I can't help feeling he's changed somehow. Even during Chi-Ro's combat training I felt it. I must've sparred with Zachary at least a hundred times on Eart; but, during the Hatari Ikou dream sessions, he's been the most serious I've ever seen him. I guess it's my fault. He came out here because of me. He's left his mother, his job, his prized sports car and a long string of girlfriends behind. For a while, it seemed there was a spark with Kiya. Now the mere mention of her alias - Nuri, causes him to clench his teeth with suppressed rage. Something's happened. Has he finally taken one of her insults to heart? Or does he blame me for dragging him out here, into space?

Roman recalled his first encounter with his friend, Zachary Silverman, and a smile reappeared on his face.

I was eleven years old on my fifth day at high school, when an eighteen-year-old sixth form bully accused me of deliberately kicking dust on his new shoes. That was some beating I took. I was really lucky the bugger didn't break my nose. In fact, he might've done just that, if Zachary hadn't stepped in when he did. Good ol' Zachary and his perfectly executed reverse punch. He'd been practicing Shotokan karate for six months, and itching to test his skills outside the gym. Zachary at sixteen... I learnt a lot from him. It was Zachary who convinced me I should take up karate. "If anyone messes with you again, break their bones," he said. That was Zachary, the Bob Marley fan who loved Notting Hill Carnival because of the food. Zachary, my friend.

In the clearing, dubbed the appointed place of practice by Chi-Ro Jin, Roman found the Master of Hatari Ikou perched on his tree stump playing his flute. Not too far away, Zachary skimmed stones across a slow-moving river.

"Am I late?" asked Roman.

Abruptly ending his recital, placing his Sythenian wax wood flute in a pouch on the belt of the Osirian stealth suit he now always wore and standing before Roman, Chi-Ro said, "No Master Armon, the good doctor and I are quite early."

Recently, there had been a newfound respect apparent in Chi-Ro's references to Zachary. Roman's friend had excelled in the training sessions, and his aptitude for lucid dream exercises was obvious. He was attentive and respectful. In a word, Zachary was not quite himself.

Roman called to his friend who seemed oblivious of his arrival, "Hey Zach."

Zachary turned, said, "Hey," and walked towards where Roman and Chi-Ro stood.

I see the winning Silverman smile is absent, thought Roman. *What the hell has happened to him?*

Chi-Ro said, "Gentlemen, in your preparation for combat, I have exposed you to the art of Hatari Ikou, which you have explored with vigour, in various terrains and in conditions ranging from zero gravity to the formidable gravity of Miru. Despite your training in both Kian and Talisian techniques, when engaging the enemy, I urge you to be like water - fluid of movement, formless of style. My father often warned me, especially on the eve of battle - fear sees, even when eyes are closed. So, I say to you, do not allow fear to govern your actions. But also, be not afraid to fear, for a man without fear no longer values his own life and is a danger not only to himself but also to his comrades." Then, stroking his Fu Manchu moustache, Chi-Ro added, "Is there any topic you wish to discuss prior to our landing on Miru, eighteen standard hours from now?"

Roman said, "You're pretty certain that if the Karellans attack they won't bring their big anti-gravity tanks?"

"You think a veteran of the Psychic Wars to be pretty?" replied Chi-Ro.

Zachary shook his head in silent dismay.

"It's a figure of speech, Chi-Ro," said Roman.

Chi-Ro calmly replied, "It seems there are many ambiguities in the Kian application of language. And since ambiguity can lead to disaster on the battlefield, I suggest you refrain from the further use of these so-called figures of speech."

Roman's anger was only thinly veiled when he responded, "Thank you for your advice, Commander Chi-Ro. Are you certain armoured chariots will not be included in a Karellan assault?"

"Verily, Master Armon; the planet's powerful gravitational field, and unstable surface, makes the use of heavier armoured units unfeasible. The enemy will opt for two-man anti-gravity platforms instead."

Aware of the rising unease, Zachary said to Roman, "After World War II, they experimented with something similar didn't they? What was it called? The Hellier..."

"I think you mean The Hiller Flying Platform. It was designed in 1955. It turned out to be unstable in flight, and left its pilot vulnerable to attack. Soldiers found it almost impossible to fire any weapon while operating the thing."

"Obviously, with psychic control and shield technology, our extraterrestrial foes seem to have perfected the device," came Zachary's straight-faced reply.

"Indeed, it is a formidable weapon, in the hands of veteran Shock Marines," said Chi-Ro.

Roman asked, "Are you certain the Siouxbatai will remain neutral?"

"Communiqués from the 9th Wave claim they do not pose a threat."

"But I sense you don't believe that, Commander Chi-Ro."

"Indeed, Master Armon, I suspect not enough has been done to secure their loyalty."

"Don't worry Roman, Chi-Ro and I will be watching your back."

"Watching his back? For what purpose would we observe the Prince's backside?"

"I'm not worried about myself, Zach. I have a pregnant wife to protect."

"Soraya's pretty scary now. Anybody messes with her and she'll break their bones."

Chi-Ro mumbled to himself, "If it comes to battle, and they persist in conversing in this manner, I may shoot them myself."

Roman smiled and thought: *Is this the old Zachary? The one who constantly pisses off the haughty Chi-Ro Jin?*

Then he said, "Still, I'm dragging my wife into a possible war zone."

"What can I say Dude? The alternative would be to haul-arse back to Earth and hope the Karellans and the Saurians don't follow us there."

There it is; he wants to go home - that's the source of resentment. And I don't blame him.

"We both know that would be too risky, Zach. But Rin Mur-Rain can take us to my father. After that, we can arrange for one of the newer, better-equipped stealth ships to take you and Soraya back to Earth."

"Oh don't worry about me, I'm loving all the death and destruction, but clearly this isn't the environment for a pregnant woman, even one with superpowers."

Chi-Ro noted the unusual tension between the two friends but put it down to a mixture of mental fatigue and anxiety.

He said, "You are not yet masters of the Talisian fighting arts, nor are you seasoned soldiers, but I have observed the warrior spirit in both of you and that is a great ally. The final period of dreamless sleep should leave us all refreshed and ready to face any new challenges."

"May it be written," said Roman.

And Zachary added, "Yeah, may it be done."

Chapter 60

On the bridge of the Starbird Sanura, within her life-supporting command pod, Anah Sadaka mentally prepared for hyperspatial exit. She visualised the return to normal space and with a sudden, mental rush her Osirian craft materialised. It proceeded at sub-light speed towards the planet Miru. Seconds later, as anticipated, Nook Tigg's Karellan raider appeared, swiftly matching the Sanura's velocity.

The planet Miru's diameter measured twenty-one thousand, three hundred and ten kilometres – eight thousand, four hundred and forty kilometres larger than that of Earth. And, like Earth, Miru suffered several devastating impacts in the millions of years since its formation. The greatest of these impacts occurred just thirty million years ago.

Dust expelled from the eighty thousand kilometre-per-hour collision of a twenty-kilometre-wide comet, prevented light from the system's Population I star from reaching the planet's surface for many months. The combined fallout of ejected sulphur, airborne nitrogen and chlorinated-water vapour from Miru's boiling oceans, produced a devastatingly toxic smog and extremely acidic rain.

Instantly rising temperatures and planet-wide firestorms ensued. Then came an all-consuming darkness and lasting deep-freeze. Eventually, photosynthesis in plants and algae ceased altogether. The mass-extinctions, which followed, claimed nearly ninety-eight percent of all species alive at the time. Only mammals dependent on organisms, which fed on decaying plant life, and small, insect-eating lizards and frogs, survived the holocaust.

One year later, the dust began to settle and light from the system's young, metal-rich star, finally reached Miru's frozen surface. But elevated levels of carbon dioxide produced by previous, planetary forest fires, created a greenhouse effect, which quickly led to extreme global warming and the further loss of several species that had survived the cold.

Now, thirty million years later, Anah Sadaka projected her faculties through the Sanura's sensors, in order to experience her first mental glimpse of this Earth-type planet.

She experienced mild disappointment. Shrouded by relentless plasma storms and thick rain clouds, Miru's nine landmasses remained hidden from her mind's eye. All she perceived, through scant gaps in the grey clouds, were hints of milky blue oceans and white Polar Regions.

But, under the cloud cover, windswept and dark, there is land, thought Anah. *This is the home of the mysterious Siouxbatai, the reclusive followers of*

Badra Ging of Malobar. Intelligence reports suggest that thus far, Margrave Rin Mur-Rain has been most unsuccessful at gaining their trust, let alone their allegiance. Perhaps I could be more persuasive than His Grace.

The coordinates downloaded by Nook Tigg would lead Anah's starglider directly into the heart of the massive Adrassi Rainforest in Adrassia Sud. This huge continent, the second largest of the planet's landmasses, was situated in the southern hemisphere. With soil extremely rich in deposits of acid-neutralising calcium oxide, Adrassia Sud's primordial forest occupied fifteen million square kilometres, almost three times the size of Earth's Amazon Rainforest.

Red, mineral-rich, dust from the Gorayu Desert, distributed by fierce storms, combined with water vapour to create Miru's Rain of Blood. A survey of the Adrassi region, ordered by Rin Mur-Rain, concluded that the red sand from the Gorayu Desert also served to increase the pH values of local precipitation. That, combined with the large deposits of quicklime in the Adrassian soil, contributed to making the Adrassi Basin's two Rivers of Blood – the Eloshen and the Mithra, the planet's largest reserves of potable water.

Suddenly, Nook Tigg's familiar thoughts entered Anah's mind, *"Agent zero-alpha-one, this is agent zero-zero-six, Talisian transponder has been activated. Transmitting ID codes now. Seventeen seconds to orbital minefield. Follow my lead precisely."*

Anah Sadaka instantly detected unusual anxiety in Nook Tigg's projected thoughts.

Even so, she mentally replied, *"Zero-zero-six projection received. Will comply."*

Each orbital stealth mine measured half a metre in length and carried a Rampage MK12 thermonuclear bomb designed by the late Melcor Pirian. These nuclear devices, laid by engineers from Rin Mur-Rain's 9th Wave, defied detection without the use of the appropriate navigational countermeasure software. Once uploaded, into his fighter's central computer, the software permitted Nook Tigg's intellect to see the stealth-cloaked mines through the visor of his command helmet.

Substantially larger than Nook Tigg's fighter, Anah's Osirian starglider also lacked the appropriate computer interface to integrate the Talisian countermeasure software. Anah was fully aware that her path had to precisely match that of the Karellan raider, in order to avoid a catastrophe.

Our minds must be one.

Nook Tigg's raider shot ahead of the Sanura. Suddenly the source of his anxiety became painfully clear to Anah Sadaka as she carefully observed his raider.

Seconds prior to initiating hyperspatial jump, the raider sustained port side damage to the wing and aft reaction control system. Without fully functioning RCS, successful attitude control and steering through the orbital minefield is virtually impossible. And, even if Nook Tigg miraculously avoids destroying us all in the minefield, he may be unable to achieve the precise attitude required for atmospheric entry. EDL failure is likely.

"*Zero-zero-six, kindly report RCS status.*"

"*Aft, port side RCS – negative function. Entering minefield by my mark.*"

"*Abort.*"

"*Negative. Braking thrusters – forty percent efficiency. Five, four, three, two, one, mark.*"

Suddenly thoughts from another mind interrupted Nook Tigg's projection.

"*No,*" came the mental voice of Soraya Doyle. "*He will blow up, I've seen it.*"

"*Sleep, Lady Soraya,*" thought Anah.

But she found herself unable to mentally sedate Roman's wife.

"*I ent fallin' for dat trick again.*"

"*Lady Soraya, I implore you to silence your projections, all my faculties are required to avoid destruction.*"

Soraya reluctantly complied. She silently prayed that the vision she saw of Nook Tigg's raider exploding was only the manifestation of her anxiety and not the shape of things to come.

For twenty painful minutes, a thunderstruck Anah Sadaka and a fearful Soraya Doyle witnessed the impossible piloting skills of Nook Tigg. The Osirian agent expertly manoeuvred his crippled raider through a nail-biting series of near misses.

Until finally he announced, "*Congratulations agent zero-alpha-one, you have successfully traversed the Miruvian minefield.*" And, with a chuckle he added, "*With persistence, you too could one day become a formidable fighter pilot.*"

"*What impertinence. I had flown over sixty fighter sorties, decades before you were born, young pup.*"

Nook Tigg laughed, "*Prepare for atmospheric entry. Try not to break your ship, old woman.*"

Soraya said to Anah, "Are you going to allow him to commit suicide? His ship is damaged and will blow up."

"That is, by no means, a certainty."

"I heard your thoughts: EDL failure; Entry, Descent and Landing failure. Rather than bandy words with me, why don't you just transport Nook Tigg aboard?"

"My attempts have been unsuccessful."

With sadness, Soraya watched the holographic image of Nook Tigg's raider, glowing orange with friction, as it descended through Miru's ionosphere only to be swallowed by dark, lightning-bearing cumulonimbus clouds.

The Sanura followed the raider's lead. Even with inertial dampeners at maximum, the starglider rumbled and shook violently and its shields absorbed lightning, several times.

Continuously staring at the holographic projection, but unable to see Nook Tigg's raider through the raging thunderstorm, Soraya suddenly said, "Oh no..."

A massive flash followed her words. Flames and burning debris scattered through the sky. Instantly, the wing of a Karellan raider crashed into the Sanura sending the starglider into an uncontrolled, spiralling dive.

As seconds seemed like minutes, massive G-forces pressed Soraya's body into her life-supporting pod. Barely able to move her head, she glanced over to Anah Sadaka. Anah's eyes were closed; she grimaced and gritted her teeth as she struggled to regain control.

Soraya turned her attention to the holographic display once more. The spinning image, combined with the terrible physical stresses she endured as a result of the ship's failed inertial dampeners, made her dizzy.

Unexpectedly, the spiralling stopped. Now the holographic image rocked from side to side, and Soraya detected the bitterness of bile at the back of her throat. The rapid thumping of her heart matched the throbbing in her head.

Slowly, she discerned a distant river, like a long, reddish-brown snake weaving through a sea of tall, green grass. The snake rapidly became larger and more ominous; and the tall grass was revealed to be a forest of gigantic tropical trees. Rapidly, deep green replaced the blood red of the Eloshen River.

The Sanura skimmed the treetops, and Soraya closed her eyes. She thought of her husband and unborn child; then Soraya imagined her mother, on far-away Earth. She wondered if she would ever see her again. A brief moment of peace, silence and clarity of thought followed, as she anticipated the inevitable crash. Suddenly Soraya felt a massive impact, followed by a thunderous roar, and the screaming of distressed metal.

She opened her eyes but saw only yellow. She heard a persistent ringing and felt disembodied.

Is this how it feels to die?

A cold chill rose from the base of her neck and rushed through her head. For the briefest moment, her eyelids felt like they were made of lead. Then finally, Soraya Doyle felt nothing at all.

Chapter 61

In the Starbird Sanura's badly damaged infirmary, Roman Doyle slowly opened his eyes, taking a moment to realise that he reclined in a regeneration pod, completely encased in what appeared to be strange, yellow, gelatinous goo.

It's some kind of liquid cushion restraint... I remember now... We crashed on Miru.

Dazed and confused, Roman listened to the progression of an alien countdown, emanating from the ship's intercom. The strange language spoken by the Sanura's mechanical voice, and the luminous orange characters that appeared on the infirmary's central pillar were familiar. He previously encountered them in Chi-Ro Jin's escape pod, stranded in the seclusion of Epping Forest.

Someone's activated the Sanura's auto-destruct sequence. Why?

Roman performed a hasty, visual inspection of the room's remaining pods and found Zachary slowly regaining consciousness within one of them. The units, allocated to Chi-Ro Jin and Kiya Mankuria, were vacant. An abandoned stealth helmet remained poised on the nearest of these modules.

Telltale trails of yellow, high-viscosity gel led out of the infirmary. The gel was swiftly evaporating and, within seconds, Roman found that he could move once more.

Zachary groggily asked, "Did we hit something? Where's everyone?"

Vacating his regeneration module, and abruptly aware of the intensity of Miru's gravity, Roman replied, "We crashed. The ship's auto destruct sequence has been activated."

Struggling to extricate himself from his own pod, Zachary said, "That explains the yellow space shit. The ship must've crapped itself."

Roman was about to remove his stealth helmet when Zachary shouted, "Hey, don't do that! There may be toxins in the air."

Suddenly, Chi-Ro burst into the room, looking like death covered in blood, but apparently uninjured. The veteran of the Psychic Wars held a fully charged viridian rifle in each hand and hauled another slung over his left shoulder.

Roman and Zachary quickly removed their own headgear and saw apprehension mirrored in each other's eyes.

Chi-Ro said, "It is with deep sorrow; I bring grave tidings."

"Oh no," whispered Zachary.

Roman's helmet slipped from his grasp, landing on the metallic floor with a loud clatter.

Chi-Ro declared, "We have lost two of our number."

During a moment of stunned silence, Roman and Zachary stared at the formidable warrior standing before them in bloodstained garb.

The prince and the doctor both asked themselves the same question, *Whose blood is that?*

Roman broke the heavy silence by barking in desperation, "Where's my wife?"

Chi-Ro responded with an uncharacteristic thickness of voice, "Lady Soraya is safe in the Sanura's amphibious rover. She is unharmed. But I regret, Commander Nook Tigg's raider exploded, moments after we entered Miru's atmosphere; and Mistress Anah Sadaka is dead. May the scribes record it."

Roman realised he had been holding his breath and exhaled. Waves of relief washed over his being only to be immediately replaced by profound sadness. Determined not to show weakness in the presence of his mentor, he held back his tears and stooped to retrieve his helmet from the floor.

Chi-Ro tossed a rifle each to Roman and Zachary before grabbing his Osirian stealth helmet from the nearby pod.

He added, "The air, though not ideal, supports human life, but prolonged exposure to precipitation on this wretched planet will cause several complications, including blindness. We'll need our helmets."

Then, swiftly turning on his heels, Chi-Ro cried, "Come, we must leave at once!"

He jogged out of the room, quickly followed by Roman and Zachary.

With Miru's gravity bearing down on their every step, the trio navigated the structural devastation and sporadic fires within the bowels of the doomed Sanura.

Unsuccessfully attempting to swallow the considerable lump in his throat, Zachary asked, "Where's Nuri?"

"On what remains of the bridge, attempting to ascertain why the self-destruct has been activated and by whom."

In his love-hate relationship with the beautiful Osirian woman, Zachary finally conceded that love had gained the upper hand; and he greeted the news of Kiya's well-being with secret elation.

Roman asked Chi-Ro, "Do you suspect foul play?"

"Surely such a tragedy cannot be likened to... Ahhh... I see... Foul, not fowl. Indeed, there is something most foul regarding the death of Mistress Anah. Although her physical trauma is consistent with the impact damage sustained by her command pod, there is evidence that someone or something entered the bridge seconds after the crash. It appears this unidentified individual has left the Sanura bearing the Sword of Power - Najura."

Zachary ventured, "Something? Like an android, uploaded into the ship's systems by the Karellan marines?"

"It is possible."

"The old girl did well to get us down here in one piece. Oy gevalt; poor Anah..."

"Chi-Ro, take Zachary to the rover," ordered Roman.

Chi-Ro simply nodded, "Yes."

Zachary could not resist asking, "Where the hell are you going?"

Roman quickly took astral form, and Zachary thought: *I'll never get used to him doing that.*

In the ominous voice of his alter ego, Roman said, "I need to solve a few mysteries."

"Well, be careful, Sherlock," said Zachary.

Zachary observed with awe, as Roman's wraith phased through the ceiling and was gone.

He asked himself, *What else does he suspect?*

Chapter 62

Lightning hacked bright purple streaks through Adrassia Sud's dawn sky; and deafening thunder angrily interrupted the incessant drone of relentless rainfall. In astral form, hovering high above the wreck of the Starbird Sanura, Roman Doyle observed the progress of the amphibious rover. The Osirian craft raced in an easterly course on the red water of the Eloshen River.

Roman felt relieved that the rover, piloted by Chi-Ro Jin, had already travelled a considerable distance away from the Sanura.

The ship will self-destruct any second now.

A search of the Sanura's interior had revealed evidence of Anah Sadaka's body being vaporised. A hasty funerary rite had been performed. But, disturbingly, Kiya Mankuria was nowhere to be found.

Roman quickly scanned beyond the crash site in the seemingly unending expanse of the Adrassi Rainforest. The Eloshen, and a region of mud plains about five kilometres south of the crash, offered the only breaks from the deep green of tropical trees. In this sea of mud, Roman's keen astral sight detected movement.

Is that Kiya, and is it possible she betrayed us all?

Travelling at the speed of thought, Roman could be on the mud plains in mere seconds, but suddenly an overwhelming sense of danger forced his attention to the west. There, on the Eloshen River, he discerned a flotilla of swift-moving craft reminiscent of the airboats operated in the Florida Everglades of Earth.

There are flags on those boats, and is that the Ten-Shi I see? No, that's no butterfly. It looks like a bird of prey, the emblem of the Siouxbatai.

Then, as anticipated, the Sanura self-destructed, creating a large crater in the Adrassi Rainforest. And, on the Eloshen, a shockwave caused the amphibious rover to roll in its wake, but the resilient vessel remained true to its course.

Roman's prescience heralded the approach of another source of danger and drew his attention to the thick storm clouds above.

Suddenly two small, saucer-shaped craft broke cloud cover at high speed and proceeded towards the mud plains. The Siouxbatai flotilla immediately opened fire with projectile artillery. They were ineffective against the shielded flying saucers, which counter attacked with energy weapons.

As the airboats absorbed a brief but devastating aerial assault, several soldiers jumped overboard. Those who stubbornly remained at their posts were disintegrated along with their vessels. The flying saucers proceeded undamaged towards the mud plains.

At the speed of thought, Roman intercepted the lead vessel where he confirmed his suspicions. Its pilot was Saurian. The scout ships had followed the Starbird Sanura from the Battle of Aaru. An astral scan of the Saurian pilot's mind, revealed that their mission was to retrieve an agent who possessed the Sword of Power and vital information regarding the location of the planet Earth. Once the agent had been retrieved they were to gather intelligence information regarding the Talisian forces stationed on Miru.

The Saurian agent relayed the 9th Wave's countermeasure software transmission to the scout ships. That's how these Saurian saucers avoided the orbital mines. The agent was supposed to abduct Soraya, but something went wrong. Yes, it's all beginning to make sense now. It was Anah. Anah gave her life to save us all. That's Kiya down there on the mud plains - I can sense it. Kiya Mankuria, a traitor? Did she kill Anah, then vaporise her body to destroy evidence of the crime? No, it just does not make any sense. What could possibly drive Kiya to betray us, after risking her life so many times to save members of our group? I can't believe it. I won't believe it.

With her anti-gravity stealth cycle at full throttle, Kiya carved a windswept trail of red ochre in the thick mire of the Adrassi Basin. Relentlessly pounded by acid rain, shielded and barely visible the Osirian woman focussed on one thing and one thing only.

Vengeance. Vengeance will be mine!

Ahead of her, the Saurian agent carved his own trail in the saturated soil. Hurtling across the storm-ravaged landscape, he desperately raced his stolen stealth cycle to rendezvous with the Saurians that would extract him from this cursed land.

A most sophisticated Saurian android, thought Kiya, *well hidden in the memory banks of the Sanura. My mother detected the sedative you unleashed as we slept and managed to reverse its effects. So, you killed her. Then, in desperation, you activated the Sanura's auto-destruct. But, your plan to kill the rest of our party failed. And now, my fleeing synthetic foe, your existence is nearing its end, for I am Kiya Mankuria and vengeance will be mine.*

Suddenly the android applied his braking thrusters, violently swinging his anti-gravity bike around in a wave of dirt. The artificial human unleashed the bike's viridian canons. The shields on Kiya's cycle absorbed a direct hit. Undeterred she continued her vengeful charge, her own viridian canons blazing.

At the last possible moment, with her stealth cycle set on auto-fire, Kiya drew her viridian pistol and leapt onto the soft mud. The momentum briefly dragged her under the knee-high slush, but she rose in time to see her cycle collide with her opponent's. The two Osirian anti-gravity vehicles were utterly destroyed in a viridian explosion. To her dismay, her opponent managed to leap to safety. But, unlike Kiya, the android did not have the benefit of a stealth suit. Without his cycle's stealth cover, the red environmental suit he wore became clearly visible in the light of the rising sun. Najura, the Sword of Power, hung from a sheath at his side.

As Kiya scrambled to solid ground, the android discharged a pistol of unknown design. The torrential rain beating against her cloak of invisibility betrayed her position. Her stealth shield absorbed a direct hit and to Kiya's surprise, failed completely.

Using her viridian pistol, she traded shots with the enemy, finding temporary cover behind an outcrop of rock. Kiya cursed Miru's high gravity, which impaired her movements and drained her energy. The increased blood flow to her feet made her dizzy. Fortunately, Kiya's opponent faced similar challenges. The raging thunderstorm confused his senses and adversely affected his ability to target.

High above in the turbulent sky, and having learnt its pilot's secrets, Roman Doyle's astral form entered the control chamber of the lead saucer. The Saurian pilot was about to screech in terror, but Roman seized its will with astral telepathy.

He mentally said, *"Destroy your escort."*

The reptile immediately broke formation and quickly silenced the high pitched protests of the other lizard by blasting its ship from the Adrassi sky.

Then, Roman said, "Now, leave my sight."

Entranced, the creature got out of the pilot's seat, walked to the airlock and activated it. The thing was immediately and violently sucked out of the craft. The airlock closed automatically, leaving the Saurian scout grasping the wind as it plummeted to certain doom.

Roman returned to human form and sat in the pilot's chair.

He coughed and said to himself, "Phew, those bastards really stink."

On the ground below, Kiya Mankuria activated a thermal grenade. She fired several covering shots with her viridian pistol, hurled the grenade as the android ducked for cover, then leapt to her feet and ran to another rock. Drawing the android's attack, Kiya dove to the ground as energy bolts seared so close to her body that she felt the heat.

The android noticed her grenade three metres from his feet. He leapt away, seconds before it exploded; but the blast ripped off his left arm. For a moment, he writhed in agony; then with his pistol lost in the sludge, the Saurian agent crawled to solid ground, stood and drew the Sword of Power.

Three viridian bolts slammed into his synthetic chest. He staggered two steps backward and collapsed against a rock in a seated position, still clutching Najura. A high-pitched whine left his lips, and he began to shake uncontrollably.

Kiya deactivated her stealth cloak, calmly placed her pistol in its holster and approached her fallen enemy. She violently removed the android's helmet and tossed it away. Then, she retrieved a small silver disc from her belt and placed it on the rain-drenched forehead of the wide-eyed android. The machine gritted its teeth, attempting to focus.

"Your resistance is an exercise in futility, abomination," said Kiya derisively, "the interrogator will extract all your secrets."

In her visor display, Kiya observed the progress of the device. For a brief moment, ancient alien symbols rapidly flashed before her eyes, and the android screamed in pain. Then Kiya calmly removed the interrogator disc from the exhausted machine.

With effort, it said, "If... I am... an abomination, then... what... are... you?"

Staring at the machine, Kiya returned the interrogator disc to her belt, and just as calmly, she removed the Sword of Power's scabbard from the trembling android and placed it on her waist. Then, unleashing her suppressed rage, Kiya violently grabbed Najura and beheaded the android with a single blow. The machine's body convulsed. Kiya ignored it.

In Samurai fashion, she tapped the flat side of Najura, removing any traces of the android's bodily fluids from the Sword of Power's lapys nerian blade. Then, in a swift but precise motion, she expertly placed the sword in its scabbard.

Kiya removed another thermal grenade from her weapons belt, activated it and casually tucked it into one of the open wounds in the convulsing android's chest. She walked away, as if without a care in the world.

As he came in to land, in the Saurian saucer, Roman saw the explosion of the android. He understood now what had happened, and felt shame for having doubted Kiya's loyalty. But, the Osirian agent had no way of knowing that Roman piloted the Saurian craft.

She held a thermal grenade and cried defiantly, "Surrender your vessel or I will destroy the Sword of Power."

"Nuri, this is Prince Armon Sakara. Please don't blow yourself up."

Undeterred, she shouted, "Your tricks will not work with me Saurian abomination. You have ten seconds."

At the speed of thought, Roman was at her side.

"Gimme that, before someone gets hurt," he said, resuming human form and wrenching the grenade from her grasp.

Kiya calmly said, "Then I suggest you quickly discard the grenade, Prince Armon. It will explode in five seconds."

Roman immediately threw the grenade, and as promised, it exploded.

His anger surfaced quite quickly, and he was about to give Kiya a stern chiding, when he experienced the pain of her loss.

He said, "I'm sorry, Nuri. Anah Sadaka was a great woman."

She said, "In keeping with Niburian custom, I ask that you join me in honouring my mother by sharing a cup of Jainon tea once we are settled amongst the 9th Wave."

"Of course, Nuri. It's the least I could do."

"Prince Armon, from this day forward, I would prefer if you called me Kiya. Nuri Nemsys is dead, and Kiya Mankuria is my real name."

"Okay Kiya," said Roman.

Kiya removed the sheath containing the Sword of Power from her waist.

She presented it to Roman and said, "My Lord, I return to you that which was stolen from your father - Najura, the Sword of Power."

Roman accepted the sword and immediately experienced flashes of pre-scient visions. He saw a great fleet of Saurian warships en-route to Miru. He saw his father's face. He saw the faces of the Siouxbatai warriors who, even now, observed them from their hiding places amongst the trees lining the mud plain. He saw two soldiers armed with shoulder-launched missile weapons. They targeted the Saurian saucer Roman left hovering one hundred metres above.

Roman embraced Kiya and said telepathically, *"We have company."*

"Yes, I can see them now, my stealth suit must have sustained damage or I would have been alerted to their approach. There are six men..."

"Eight. Two more are directly behind you, armed with shoulder-launched rockets."

"Oh. That creates an even greater challenge."

"You realise of course that the Sword of Power robs me of my astral ability."

"Indeed. Prince Armon, I think you should be aware that my stealth shield has been disabled. What a pity you wasted my last grenade."

Chapter 63

In the dimly lit dining hall, aboard the Imperial Karellan Warship Drac El, six high-ranking Saurians, in full military dress, enjoyed their main course of roasted leg of man. Ironically, all remained disguised as human beings, including the creature called Sobek, the creature that impersonated Seti Aljyk. Sobek's facial injury had been repaired leaving only a hairline scar.

General Meclak, who had the appearance of a rotund, middle-aged man with receding mousy-brown hair and deep-set eyes, chewed slowly, savouring his meal.

Rolling his eyes with delight, he said, "My compliments to your chef, Lord Sobek. Human flesh is naturally tender and has such wonderful flavour; it is unforgivable that my own chef always over-cooks it. I think, after this campaign, I will have the imbecile fed to my pet iguadon."

All the creatures laughed except the Saurian disguised as Seti Aljyk. He smiled, but his eyes betrayed a measure of contempt and anger.

He replied, "That may not be wise Meclak. Unless the location of the human-infested Earth is found soon, we may need to eat our chefs in order to survive."

Sensing the sudden change of mood, the darkly tanned General Sheerak said, "The new androids are virtually indistinguishable from humans. I am confident our agent will retrieve the sword, the Soter and the location of Earth."

"Indistinguishable from humans you say? Then perhaps you should be enjoying roasted leg of android instead of roasted leg of man," said Sobek derisively.

Momentarily interrupting his ravenous eating, a Saurian with a distinctly Asian disguise added, "Much progress is being made in the science of human cloning, My Lord. A major breakthrough is on the horizon, if our scientists are to be believed. Soon, we may not need to conquer the elusive planet Earth, we could simply clone all our dietary needs."

"Yes Toemak, progress in a science which these inferior humans from Talis perfected thousands of years ago. Look at us, disguised as the very creatures we eat. Am I the only one present who feels foolish?"

"We have all pretended to be stupid humans for so long, it may have robbed us of some measure of intellect," said Sheerak, before ripping a generous chunk of flesh with his sharp teeth.

Meclak cast his deep-set gaze at all present before adding dryly, "Have a care my most esteemed colleagues, we are merely soldiers following the King's orders."

Sobek stared at him long and hard, then said, "Meclak, I hope you are not insinuating that I am in any way disloyal to my cousin the King."

"Of course not, Lord Sobek. What has possessed you of late?"

"I am sorry, my old friend. My encounter with the human called Armon has left me unsettled. I fear we underestimate these creatures."

"Nonsense," said Toemak, "I suspect that Saurian science is at the root of these astral abilities in humans."

"You believe the ancient myths do you?"

"It is no myth that the evil one deceived the Saurian heretics of old and that these Saurians have eventually succeeded in creating these advanced humans. But evil will not prevail. We shall capture this Armon and his man-child. Their power shall serve us. Evil shall be turned to righteousness and we will feast on the bounty of planet Earth."

"We have dominated these human creatures at every turn," said Borek, the Drac El's captain. "The Talisian Noorstrum Sun Shipyards at Pyraeus have been utterly destroyed and the Karellan Melcor Imperial Defence Yards at Bedi Sirius suffered a similar fate. Iliac, the highly addictive drug they call snow, introduced to them just three years ago, has totally decimated both the Karellan and Talisian fighting forces. The cowardly Sakara Rey is in hiding, nursing a deadly poison, which will soon end his miserable life. I say the fall of mankind is inevitable. Complete Saurian dominion is close at hand."

"Here-here," said Sheerak. He raised his glass and shouted, "To dominion!"

"Dominion!" roared the other Saurians in unison.

After a moment, Meclak turned to Sobek and said, "So tell me, what method does your chef employ in the preparation of this most exquisite meal?"

"There is some debate regarding which method yields the best results. Some argue that searing the meat on high heat seals the flavour and slow cooking on low heat thereafter, ensures that the flesh remains tender. My chef prefers a method of slow cooking on low heat from start to finish. Obviously the quality of marinade is equally important. But I regret he claims the marinade is a family secret. He will not share its recipe with me."

"A pity," said Meclak.

"Indeed," said Toemak, "The secret of this culinary delight should be shared."

"Perhaps if I threaten to eat his eldest daughter, my chef may be more forthcoming."

The Saurians roared with laughter, which resonated far beyond the confines of the Drac El's dining hall.

Chapter 64

As ordered by the unseen leader of the seven Siouxbatai warriors, Roman Doyle and Kiya Mankuria did not make any sudden moves. But, defiantly, Kiya had not removed her weapons belt and Roman still held the Sword of Power. He found that although the lapys nerian weapon robbed him of his astral abilities, close proximity to it enhanced his physical prowess and substantially increased his psychic proficiency.

They're afraid of us. I sense it. They watched Kiya's battle with the android. They saw me in astral form. A few are wondering if I'm some kind of demon. Tye Goh... What does it mean? Ah, yes... I sense it means dark wizard, in the Malobari language. Perhaps by playing on their superstition and acting the part of the Prince, I can diffuse this situation. The Saurians are coming, and these people can be useful allies.

The hidden Siouxbatai leader shouted, "This is your final warning Outworlders, drop your weapons or we will cut you down where you stand!"

Mindful of the tone and pitch of his voice, Roman replied, "Who dares issue orders to a Talisian Prince? Come out of the bushes, let me see you."

For a moment, the Siouxbatai silently considered Roman's words. Then, a brave young man, dressed in a skin-tight, reddish-brown environmental suit stepped forward. Unlike the Osirian stealth suit with it's mirrored visor, the Siouxbatai environmental suit had a helmet, which allowed the wearer's features to be clearly seen. The tanned youth had a broad face, blue eyes and greenish blond hair.

He's been drinking copper-contaminated water or swimming in chlorinated pools. Either that, or green hair is all the rage in Adrassia Sud. I sense Miru's gravity has made him very strong - stronger than he looks. He's about nineteen years old. A few of the men under his command resent taking orders from one so young. But he is the son of Badra Ging and they dare not challenge Badra's authority. He's worried that the scout ship is manned. He's afraid but he dare not show it. Despite his fear, he is the bravest of the group.

"I am..."

"Shree Badra, son of Badra Ging of Malobar," interrupted Roman.

The surprised youth kept his composure.

He simply cocked his head slightly when he said, "You have me at a disadvantage, Prince of Talis - if indeed that is what you are, for I do not know your name."

"I am Prince Armon Sakara, son of Sakara Rey, the True Emperor of the Cosmic Sea."

I don't feel like a prince, but hopefully I sound like one.

Shree Badra chuckled and Roman noted the surreptitious hand-signal he issued, prompting five armed men to reveal themselves. All trained their weapons on Roman and Kiya. The two remaining men made hasty preparations to launch their rockets at the hovering scout ship.

Kiya communicated telepathically, *"They are armed with Talisian-made Aknon nine-zero-nine rifles."*

"Why would Rin Mur-Rain supply these people with weapons?"

"He would not."

"Have there been violent clashes between the 9th Wave and the Sioux-batai we're unaware of, or are these weapons simply stolen or acquired through illegal trade?"

"The precise strength and location of the 9th Wave has always been a closely guarded secret, Prince Armon. Osirian intelligence regarding this planet and Rin Mur-Rain's presence here is understandably very limited."

Shree Badra said, "The Imperial heir, no less! Forgive me, I did not recognise you, Your Highness. Your visor completely hides your face."

Sarcasm. He feels more secure with each passing moment. He believes I used the scout ship's matter transport device, leaving the spacecraft unmanned and unarmed. To him, my momentary astral form was just a facet of the matter transfer process. He does not believe in the supernatural. He's intelligent, but inexperienced. And now, he underestimates us.

Shree Badra continued, "You are a very poor liar, Outworlder. It is known, even here in this forgotten land, that Sakara Rey has no son. No, you are not Talisian Royalty, I believe that you are Karellan spies. We witnessed the woman's battle with the synth. She is clearly well trained in combat. It is unlikely that one so violent could be domesticated. But, if the woman is comely and can be tamed, she will find sanctuary as a servant to one of our warriors. Unfortunately for you, we have no use for magicians in our ranks. You are made of mud, and the mud shall claim you."

Shree Badra smiled with reassurance when he heard his men cock their rifles in unison. But a quick glance revealed that these cocked rifles were now aimed at his head. His smile instantly vanished.

He said to Roman, "Ah, I see hypnosis is part of your magician's repertoire. Impressive. Perhaps we can use one such as you in our ranks, after all."

The men lowered their weapons and found that no matter how hard they tried, they were unable to aim them at Roman or Kiya.

Roman placed the sheathed Sword of Power on his waist and said, "A terrible enemy will arrive within a fortnight. They want me, they want my son and they want this, Najura - the Sword of Power. And, to get what they want, they are willing to eradicate all life on Miru."

A man shouted venomously, "Then let them have you, Outworlder!"

This man openly challenges Shree Badra's authority. He has an agenda...

Sakir Mar, the bitterest of the group. The stocky, thirty-five-year-old, sallow-skinned, flat-faced fighting man carried a rocket launcher.

"We Siouxbatai have no enemies," he snarled, "We seek only to protect ourselves, from the evil that exists in the Outworld."

Roman replied, "Sakir Mar, the craft you see hovering above you, is a Saurian scout vessel. Even at this range, your rocket couldn't scratch its shielded hull."

Sakir Mar recoiled with the thought: *How does this Outworlder know my name?*

"You lie, Tye Goh! Your airships are not impervious to attack. At dawn I shot down one of your craft, which violated our airspace."

Sakir Mar's words echoed in Roman's mind and a terrible rage rose from the pit of his stomach. With the rage, came a sudden and overwhelming awareness of Miru's strong gravitational pull. Roman became aware of the increased flow of blood to his feet. He felt dizzy and on the brink of losing control of the situation.

Calming himself, Roman asked, "You shot down a Karellan raider?"

Again, Shree Badra issued clandestine instructions with a magician's sleight of hand. Sakir Mar placed the launcher on the solid ground at his feet and immediately assumed the posture of a child who had been scolded.

Shree Badra said to Roman, "One who calls himself zero-zero-six is in our custody."

"You're lying!" snapped Roman and the ground shook below their feet.

In a flash, Kiya drew and aimed her viridian pistol at Sakir Mar. The man's eyes bulged with terror.

"No, Kiya!"

In response, Kiya lowered the weapon but said telepathically, *"Prince Armon, Commander Nook Tigg loved you as a father loved a son."*

Roman was thankful that his visor hid the tears of sadness that welled in his eyes.

He responded, *"You suggest that Nook Tigg is dead, Kiya, but he isn't dead. He's out there, somewhere."*

Roman said to Shree Badra, "I know you no longer have him, he escaped."

"I am quite confident we will find him."

"Pray that you don't, for he is dear to me and I will exact a terrible revenge if he is harmed."

"You threaten me in my father's domain?"

"Do you have any idea who you're dealing with, boy?"

Fear. I sense it, just as they sense my psychic power. Yes, they should all be afraid. Anah Sadaka is gone, but I won't lose Nook Tigg as well.

Just then, from his helmet's wireless, Shree Badra received a coded transmission. He continued to glare at Roman but as he listened his stare became more and more glazed. The group recognised the look on the youth's face, as did Kiya and Roman.

Bad news.

Shree Badra announced, "At dawn, five airboat warriors died as they attacked two craft similar to the one hovering above us. The craft escaped undamaged."

Sakir asked, "What news of my brother, Goram?"

"Your brother Goram is dead."

Trembling with rage, Sakir drew his knife and screamed, "I demand satisfaction!"

In response, Kiya immediately drew her dagger and said, "If this toad shot down Commander Tigg, he deserves to die."

"No, Saurians are the real enemy," said Roman.

Sakir Mar jeered, "This coward calls himself Sakara's heir? Fight like a man, without your witchcraft. Come, Tye Goh, I shot down your Karellan friend. My brother's blood cries out for vengeance!"

There is more to this. The death of his brother is not what motivates this aggression. Sakir Mar and his brother were estranged. He seeks to impress someone. Badra Ging? No, someone else... Someone he considers more powerful. Why are so many things still hidden? As much as I try, I cannot control my prescience. I'll play Sakir Mar's game until his motives become clear.

Roman mentally said to Kiya, *"Put away your dagger."*

Sensing the terrible psychic storm brewing in Roman's mind, Kiya reluctantly did as instructed.

Pacing anxiously, Sakir stared at Roman with intense hatred. But his pacing stopped abruptly when Roman drew Najura.

Roman projected to Kiya, *"Hang on to this, I'll only be a second."*

He handed her the Sword of Power, and stepped forward to face his opponent unarmed.

Lightning flashed; thunder rolled; and Miru's acidic Rain of Blood fell relentlessly.

With a wry smile, Sakir announced to his comrades, "It seems the Outworlder has grown a pair of balls!" Then, turning to Roman, he said, "I have had six duels and yet here I stand, uninjured before you. You will do well to face me with your sword, Tye Goh."

Yes, the sword... Someone told you about the sword and what it represents, before I mentioned the Saurian interest in it. But who?

Without raising his voice, Roman said, "The Saurians killed your brother. Join the fight against them and earn your revenge."

"The Saurians, is it? You command a Saurian vessel. So, why should we believe you are anything but Saurian? You killed my brother!"

"I commandeered the scout vessel immediately after its assault on your comrades. I destroyed its escort. You saw the explosion. Now you pick a fight with me, under false pretence, despite having irrefutable proof we are not Saurians."

"Oh? How so?"

"If we were Saurians, all of you would already be dead."

"No, I believe you are Saurian, you and this synth!

Synth? I suppose in this male-dominated culture, a woman with Kiya's fighting skills must seem like an android.

Shree Badra said, "Be silent Sakir." Then turning to Roman he announced, "In accordance with our customs, this is a fight to the death. Once complete all ills will be discarded. The survivor will bear no further grudge and suffer no retaliation. This is our way. This is our law. Do you accept this challenge, Outworlder?"

"Yes, clearly violence is all you people understand," said Roman.

Showing signs of apprehension, Sakir Mar said to Shree Badra, "This Outworlder is a liar who uses mind tricks."

Shree Badra replied angrily, "You called the challenge Sakir, and it has been accepted." Then, turning to Roman in an afterthought, Shree Badra asked, "Outworlder, do we have your word you will not employ your magician's tricks in this duel?"

Roman said, "You have my word."

"There it is. So be it. Let the duel begin."

Shree Badra clapped twice and Sakir immediately lunged at Roman. Wasting no time, Roman sidestepped, delivering a devastating punch to Sakir's stomach. The older man immediately vomited in his helmet. Holding his midsection in agony, he stumbled about, unable to see anything but his regurgitated breakfast.

In a matter of seconds, Roman had transformed the proud man into a clown. Sakir growled, cursed and slashed blindly with his blade. Finally in frustration and desperation he wrenched off his helmet.

Roman assumed a relaxed posture, arms at his side, leaving his enraged opponent clueless. With acid rain stinging his eyes, Sakir Mar launched his second vicious attack.

Roman sidestepped once again, intercepting Sakir's wrist with his own, driving the Siouxbatai's knife-hand downwards into the mud, twisting his wrist, exerting pressure on his elbow and on his shoulder. With effortless fluidity of motion, Roman broke Sakir's arm at these three vital joints.

Sakir screamed in agony. Having lost his knife, and unable to get to his feet, Sakir thrashed about in the sludge like a worm. He sank deeper and deeper into the mud.

With this act of violence, I've earned the respect of these inbred morons. I'm having serious doubts about their usefulness in the scheme of things.

Roman took a long hard look at the helpless, pathetic man. Then he turned to the gathered Siouxbatai and said, "This is what the Saurians want. They want us to fight each other. They want us to do this, because ultimately it weakens us."

His battles with the Asing, Brakis Tarn and Shan Kur-Karnah, flashed through Roman's mind.

He thought: *How many more battles do I have to fight?*

Turning his back on Sakir, Roman walked towards Kiya stretched out his hand and received the Sword of Power.

He addressed the assembled warriors again, saying, "The choice is yours, men of the Siouxbatai, join us in the fight against the Saurians, or be their victims. They are coming with ships a thousand times larger, and more powerful, than this scout vessel. There is no greater threat in the Cosmic Sea, no greater evil."

Shree Badra said to Roman, "Outworlder, this is a fight to the death, complete it."

Roman replied, "Haven't you heard a word I've said. The Saurians will eat your wives and children. Do you understand? That's what they do. They eat human beings."

"I suggest you focus on the matter at hand, Outworlder. The law demands a satisfactory conclusion."

"I have no quarrel with Sakir Mar, I am only interested in killing Saurians. If you don't value this man's life, then you kill him."

Roman quickly regretted the hastily uttered statement.

Shree Badra calmly said, "So be it. Farewell, Sakir Mar, mud bore you and lo, to mud you now return."

Shree Badra made another subtle hand-gesture and the Siouxbatai next to him raised his rifle just high enough to fire twice into the back of Sakir's head. The dead man's body slowly slipped off solid ground, to be swallowed by the deep, hungry mud.

Such callousness. Is this a facet of Siouxbatai culture? No, I think Shree Badra silenced a political enemy today. Sakir Mar held vital clues regarding a plot. A plot against me. I thought I was playing Sakir Mar's game. This is no game. My plan backfired and the man is dead. I'll have to be far more careful in future.

Aware of his audience, and despite his horror and revulsion, Roman showed no sign of weakness.

Shree Badra continued, "Let it be known amongst the Siouxbatai, all ills are discarded and we welcome these Outworlders in peace."

The men responded, "We are Siouxbatai. The law binds us. Till the end of days, we are one."

Roman looked to Kiya and said telepathically, *"Maybe we're better off fighting the Saurians, without these nutters."*

Chapter 65

The acid rain downpour subsided to a light drizzle and the storm clouds rolled back to reveal Miru's brilliant sun. At the request of Major Kong Garee of the 9th Wave, Commander Chi-Ro Jin cut the engines of the Sanura's amphibious rover and awaited transport. Chi-Ro knew the major quite well - a skilled Starfire pilot whose call sign was Chigaru. Following standard Imperial military protocol, Chigaru referred to Chi-Ro by his old fighter pilot's call sign - Hondo.

The rover gently rocked on the Eloshen River, about eight hundred kilometres south of the Sanura's designated landing coordinates. Deep within Siouxbatai territory in an area of the Adrassi Rainforest known to be the hunting ground of a large herd of teroseriak - ferocious, two-metre high dinosaur-like predators.

Major Kong also informed Chi-Ro that the deep Eloshen River was home to Miru's eighteen-metre-long, shark-like selachi. Chi-Ro therefore saw the wisdom in having the amphibious rover transported by the military carrier that now hovered above.

But something else troubled Chi-Ro. The four remaining vials of elidium, he carried at all times, had been taken from him. The theft occurred during the period of dreamless sleep, just prior to the Sanura's crash.

Kiya Mankuria has destroyed the Seriak agent and presumably, the experimental drug - a hasty move. Was retrieving elidium part of this Jinzou Ningen's mission? I do not like this news of the Prince's duel - clearly an assassination attempt. Was this Sakir Mar operating alone, or are the Siouxbatai in league with the Seriak? Perhaps more will be learnt from Prince Armon's audience with Badra Ging.

Major Kong's squadron of Mark IX Starfires patrolled the area, ready to engage anything that dared threaten the security of the Talisian carrier. Chi-Ro marvelled at how much sleeker fighter design had become in the three years they were absent from normal space.

"I sense these pilots are very nervous," said Soraya.

"Verily, they are duly alert. We are far from the agreed landing coordinates and it appears there is tension between the 9th Wave and the Siouxbatai."

"I don't think that's their biggest concern. I think the Margrave sees Roman as a threat."

"That is possible Milady. But there are many more obvious threats in this time of war. The Seriak have powerful weapons at their disposal and it is known that in recent years the Karellans resorted to using clones as well as battle androids. Let us not forget, this planet Miru has many dangers. I believe these pilots would give their lives in your protection and in the protection of Prince Armon."

Would they give their lives in my protection, Chi-Ro? I hope this isn't a glimpse of Earth's future - armies of clones and synthetic human slaves. Everywhere I look in these technologically advanced cultures, I find evidence of barbarism, thought Zachary.

"Don't the Talisians use clones? It's already clear you use androids."

"Verily, Dr. Silverman, my loyal friend Teev Meg has served as a medical officer for over forty years. He is a veteran of the Psychic Wars but I am unaware of clones ever being used in Talisian ranks."

"It's a shame Kiya killed Teev Meg."

"I assure you he is backed up and the virus which ailed him will be removed by those qualified within the 9th Wave."

"He seemed intent on shooting me. I doubt I'll ever trust him again. I suppose programming androids to perform hazardous tasks safeguards the human population, but personally, I find it unethical."

"Agreed."

He agrees?

"Many, many years ago, artificial humans were developed and mass produced to serve - a mistake for which humans paid dearly in the Great Ningen Wars. Since that time, androids have gained complete freedom and independence. Natural mankind is no longer involved in any aspect of their manufacture or programming. You will be able to verify this for yourself, the Alphatron is here on Miru with a force of one hundred thousand troops."

"The Alphatron?"

"I did advise you to familiarise yourself with all aspects of recent military history, Dr. Silverman."

"Yes-yes. Well, I got preoccupied with scientific matters."

"Let us hope these scientific matters are useful in the battle which will surely come."

"Verily," said Zachary, with a hint of derision.

"The Alphatron leads the Jinzou Ningen forces."

"Is he a Transformer?"

Chi-Ro gave Zachary a puzzled look.

"Hondo, Bokusa, prepare for matter transfer in ten seconds," barked the captain of the carrier over the rover's intercom."

Chi-Ro responded, "Bokusa, Hondo, by your mark."

In a bolt of energy, the Sanura's amphibious rover disappeared from the Eloshen River, instantaneously re-appearing within the massive cargo bay of the Talisian military carrier. Inside the rover, Chi-Ro, Zachary and Soraya felt the rumble of the carrier's massive electromagnetic drives as it pulled away from the Eloshen River.

The carrier headed towards the 9th Wave's base to the north, escorted by seven Starfires under the command of Captain Ram Karra - call sign Moto. Lieutenant Chang Gaya had orders to comb the area with five fighters until Commander Nook Tigg was found and Major Kong proceeded to the camp of Badra Ging with the eight remaining fighters.

"What's with all the nicknames?" asked Zachary.

"I assume, Dr. Silverman, you refer to our call signs. Chigaru means hound, Hondo means war, Bokusa means boxer."

"Yeah, call signs. I get it, I saw Top Gun. So, do I get my own call sign?"

"Verily."

"Cool. I think my call sign should be Nimrod, it's the name of a mighty hunter."

"Dr. Silverman, did your Top Gun not explain to you that call signs are selected and assigned by a superior officer? As that individual, I have already selected your call sign, to be used on all military transmissions."

"Oh?"

"Verily, you will be pleased that from this day forward, and in honour of the great warriors of Earth, you shall be known as Tinki Winki."

There followed a brief moment of shocked silence, then Soraya began laughing loudly.

"What?" asked Zachary, who managed to sound on the verge of panic.

"Is not Tinki Winki the largest and most formidable of the band of warriors that occupy your mind?"

"You can't call me Tinki Winki!"

Casually turning away from Zachary, Chi-Ro simply smiled. Soraya laughed hysterically.

Suddenly, the voice of Captain Ram sliced through Soraya's laughter and Zachary's protests.

"Bokusa, Moto, break right! Break-break-break-break!"

The carrier immediately banked sharply, accelerating to supersonic speed. Soraya stopped laughing and thanked God that she wore restraints.

"Rolling to intercept," came another pilot's voice.

"Where did they come from?" barked another.

Something hit the shielded carrier and for a moment the intercom went dead. Then, confusion ensued.

"What the hell's going on?" yelled Zachary over the excited pilot chatter, which now spewed relentlessly from the re-activated intercom.

Wide eyed, Soraya shouted, "Lizard men. It's the lizard men!"

"Sensors indicate six small vessels jumped into the planet's atmosphere. The enemy is here much sooner than Prince Armon anticipated."

"You sound surprised," said Zachary with a shaky voice.

"Jumping into the atmosphere, of a planet with a gravitational field as strong as Miru's is exceptionally difficult. Most would regard the attempt of such a feat as suicidal."

"I guess they must be very hungry. Soraya?"

"I'm trying."

"I'm hit, I'm hit!" came the cry of Baridi over the intercom.

A scream, followed by a massive explosion, signalled the death of Sergeant Mo Zann, also known as Baridi.

"Soraya, now would be a good time," said Zachary, trying not to submit to hysteria.

"Something's wrong, I think the baby's asleep."

"What do you mean, he's asleep? Wake him up!"

"I'm trying..."

"We've lost shields," announced Chi-Ro.

"I've got one!" yelled a Starfire pilot moments before being blown from the sky.

"Where the hell is Major Kong?" screamed Zachary.

In a flash, Chi-Ro spun in his chair and fired his viridian pistol in Zachary's direction. Before Zachary could scream in terror, the Saurian that had materialised behind him had his head blown clean off his shoulders.

"Shit."

"Verily, Dr. Silverman, do not be surprised if more of this shit materialises."

Soraya let out a heavy sigh and slumped into her chair. Her eyes rolled back under their lids.

Thinking she had fainted, Zachary hastily undid his restraints and rushed to her side. Soon the comm-traffic confirmed what Chi-Ro already suspected.

"Bokusa, Chigaru, hostiles destroyed. I repeat, hostiles destroyed," came Major Kong's voice.

"Chigaru, Bokusa, outstanding."

"Bokusa, Chigaru, negative. Hostiles obliterated but cause unknown. Moto and Panchi are lost. Thirteen Starfires destroyed by enemy fire, may the scribes record it. Hondo, Chigaru, status please."

"Dr. Silverman how is Lady Soraya?"

"She seems to be asleep, Chi-Ro."

"No, I'm awake," said Soraya weakly, "I don't think I can do that again. At least, not for a while."

"It is most fortunate the enemy does not know this, Milady."

"Hondo, Chigaru, status please."

"Chigaru, Hondo, secure. Proceed to Wave Actual location immediately."

"Hondo, Chigaru, affirmative."

Chapter 66

Under a two moon sky and the protection of a massive shield dome, Margrave Rin Mur-Rain, Wave Actual and cousin of Prince Armon Sakara climbed the ramp of his personal shuttle, flanked by his burly shamira – Goren Rag and tall, thin squadron leader Major Tohm Salahee. A black leather patch covered Rin's left eye. Long black hair brushed his broad shoulders and he bore the distinctive, high cheekbones of the House of Enki, framed by neatly cut sideburns, moustache and beard. The facial hair did not hide his youthfulness. He wore a dark grey Imperial Space Marshal's uniform with six golden butterflies on each lapel and a long black cape flowed behind him.

When he addressed troops of the 9th Wave, the Margrave always carried a fully charged Daxia AR-6-06 assault rifle slung around his shoulder - a constant reminder to his men that he fought alongside them. Today was no exception.

His rallying call to the men and women of the 9th Wave was met with unrestrained jubilation. Rin had no doubt these brave men and women would follow him into the fires of Hades if necessary.

Let's pray it does not come to that, he thought.

Under his shrewd leadership, the 9th Wave had been victorious in every military campaign against Karellan forces, but the Saurians were a far more formidable enemy.

The Margrave swept into the Imperial shuttle, stopping briefly to hand his rifle to one aide whilst another removed his cape.

"I will join you gentlemen in my ready room shortly," he said to his shamira and squadron leader before proceeding towards his private quarters.

Inside his quarters, Rin Mur-Rain sat alone at a grand desk. He studied the holographic display of the thousands of military vessels parked on a wide expanse of rock two kilometres east of the shield dome.

What we have long feared is confirmed. The Seriak menace is real. They have manipulated us these many years, setting brother against brother, until the very survival of both cultures hang in the balance. And now, at this most critical time, my uncle's son appears out of the wilderness of space.

The Margrave struck his desk with a gloved fist.

A calm, woman's voice said, "I see you have returned, my love; and your mood is as dark as ever. Did your soldiers not adore you to your complete satisfaction?"

Rin Mur-Rain calmly turned to look at the woman. Her name was Ishma. A beautiful, tanned woman with deep blue eyes and long greenish blonde hair. She wore a black, semi-translucent negligee that left little to the imagination. Despite her best efforts, the almost imperceptible slurring of her speech did not go unnoticed.

"Have you recently indulged in Iliac, my sweet?"

"No, Your Grace. We Siouxbatai do not partake of such mind-altering drugs. Hmmm, your temperament is indeed most foul. Perhaps if you accompanied me to bed more often, I would not seek the consolation of Dolian wine and you would not be so very moody."

Ishma walked towards him. Her broad hips swayed invitingly.

"There is a time for everything, my sweet."

"You would place duty before love."

"If I do not perform my duty, there may be no one left to love."

Ishma sat at the corner of Rin's desk. With the back of her hand she swept the hair from her face.

In a low voice, she said, "So Your Grace, where is the Great Prince?"

"He is in your father's camp."

Ishma chuckled, "Oh, did my father not invite you? Perhaps if you had fought for me according to Siouxbatai law, he would have a bit more respect for you."

"He is obliged to respect my office. He need not respect me."

"I understand your frustration, my love. My father's pride matches your own."

Ishma stood, about to leave, then a thought entered her mind.

"Oh, but I sense my father's stubbornness is not what bothers you, Your Grace. She accompanies the Prince, does she not?"

Rin Mur-Rain's jaw tightened.

"I grow weary of your unfounded jealousy."

Ishma chuckled as she walked towards the bedroom.

"Yes, you do seem tired of late. By the way, why did Sakir Mar meet with you five days ago?"

Rin Mur-Rain growled, "Know your place, woman."

Ishma's cheeks glowed red as she replied, "I will be waiting in my place, if your mood should change, Your Grace."

Without compromising her dignity, she bowed low. Then, Ishma gracefully disappeared into the dark bedchamber and in its gloom, wiped away the tears that now streamed down her cheeks.

Chapter 67

At dusk, in the captured Saurian scout vessel, escorted by Major Tohm Salahee's Starfire squadron, Roman Doyle and Kiya Mankuria arrived at Rin Mur-Rain's military camp. Roman wore the dark blue military dress uniform of a Space Marshal of The Imperial Talisian Host. A long black cape draped his shoulders and an ornate, ceremonial baldric ran diagonally across his chest, from which the lapys nerian Sword of Power hung in its scabbard at his left side.

Roman thanked Chi-Ro Jin and the Margrave's personal aides for supplying the fine Imperial clothing. But secretly, he felt like a humble history teacher attending a fancy-dress party and playing at being a dashing prince.

Kiya wore the dark grey uniform and cap of a Talisian Officer. She had spoken and projected little, since their audience with Badra Ging. Curiosity prompted Roman to attempt probing her mind, but Kiya was very well trained and her thoughts remained hidden. So, Roman assumed that the Osirian woman mourned the recent death of her foster mother, Anah Sadaka.

On the ground, Roman and Kiya were quickly ushered into the Margrave's Imperial Chariot and driven to Wave Actual's shield dome. Twenty of Rin Mur-Rain's finest Imperial Shadow Warriors accompanied them, riding four anti-gravity command-reconnaissance vehicles.

With military precision, the four transports fanned out and parked on either side of the Margrave's shuttle. Armed troops immediately disembarked and assumed defensive positions at either side of the imposing craft's ramp. Maintaining speed, and unleashing a distinctive roar, the Imperial Chariot raced up into the ship's bowels, coming to an abrupt halt at the top of the ramp.

Grimly alert officers of the Emperor's Own Psionic Police, with their distinctive cranial attachments, lined the fortified inner walls of the shuttle's cargo bay. They mentally protected the Margrave and his guests against enemy psychic assault and espionage.

The bay had been completely transformed and triple shielded for the reception. Large black banners hung from the ceiling, displaying glittering golden Arosian Ten-Shi - symbol of the House of Enki. Smaller banners of red, gold and brown depicted the Margrave's armorial crest. A wide carpet of royal purple ran from where the Margrave's chariot parked, to the assembled dignitaries and statuesque military personnel in full uniform.

With unmistakable presence, Rin Mur-Rain stood apart from this illustrious group. He wore a black cape over his dark grey full dress Space Marshal's uniform and the gold sash of the Order of the Tordon Raptor. But, of his many medals, he opted to wear only the Star of Ra.

When quizzed by Ishma, he calmly replied, "It is enough. I feel no need to parade trinkets of platinum, verlaine or gold to one who wears the Sword of Power."

All doubt has been removed. The blood samples supplied by Chi-Ro Jin have been checked, cross-referenced and checked again. This man is my uncle's son. He is The Prince Armon.

Thick silence enveloped the cargo bay as the passenger door of the chariot swung upwards and a short ramp descended. Roman Doyle - The Prince Armon Sakara, emerged from the vehicle. All present military personnel, including the Margrave, sharply saluted the Emperor's heir.

Observing established protocol, Kiya walked down the chariot's ramp, ten paces behind His Highness. She then joined the smart ranks of Shadow Warriors standing in obeisance, to the left of the Prince.

As instructed by his mentor Chi-Ro Jin, Roman confidently walked towards his cousin, Rin Mur-Rain and without breaking eye contact stopped ten paces before him and saluted. Matching each other's movements perfectly, the Prince and Margrave ended their salutes.

The other military personnel held their salutes for a further ten seconds before dropping their hands sharply to their sides. At this point, Rin Mur-Rain bowed at the neck.

Then Roman noted with concealed embarrassment that everyone else bowed quite low. He approached his cousin, mindful of his own thoughts and actions.

I must not show the slightest hint of weakness.

Once again, Rin Mur-Rain mirrored Roman's movements as he stretched out his right arm and firmly gripped his cousin's left shoulder.

Roman said, "Margrave Rin of Taria."

Rin said, "Welcome Your Highness. Your safe arrival has filled my heart with gladness."

"I am pleased to find sanctuary in your gracious camp," responded Roman.

Strange, I sense no threat from him. He is supremely confident and appears genuinely pleased to see me. But that business with Sakir Mar, was it simply a test? Still, I must remain on guard. Historically, in powerful families, cousins have a poor record regarding loyalty. Until recently, Rin believed he would have inherited my father's throne. Only a very rare man would willingly give up such a valuable prize. Once this show for the benefit of the armed forces is complete, I will learn more of his true motives and intentions.

In unison, each man removed his hand from the other's shoulder.

Directly behind Rin Mur-Rain, stood Ishma, Goren, Soraya and Chi-Ro. Behind them, stood Zachary with Rin's most senior officers.

Turning slightly, Rin Mur-Rain gestured to Ishma who gracefully stepped forward, dressed in layers of gold and brown that shimmered in the light.

He said, "Your Highness, may I present the Margravine Ishma of Taria, daughter of Badra Ging of Malobar."

Even in such technologically advanced cultures, beautiful women are used as political pawns, thought Roman.

Adhering to protocol, he responded, "Margravine Ishma, you do me honour with your presence."

"Welcome, Your Highness. May your arrival herald greater cooperation and friendship between Miru and Talis."

"Indeed. Alliance between Talis and Miru is deeply preferred. I am grateful for your father's efforts to retrieve my dear friend, Commander Nook Tigg, lost in the Adrassi Rainforest."

"We are committed to finding the commander and deeply regret the unfortunate incidents leading to the death of your starglider's fine captain."

"May the scribes record it."

Roman recalled the cold reception he initially received from Ishma's brother, Shree.

Shree Badra was correct to be wary, when faced with someone claiming to be the Emperor's son. Until recently, my very existence remained a closely guarded secret from all but my father's most trusted servants. The Malobari genocide at the hands of Karellan forces has understandably made the Siouxbatai paranoid and reclusive. But the rocket attack against Nook Tigg's raider, his capture and my icy encounter with Badra Ging's son Shree, led to the Siouxbatai leader being obliged to make amends or risk all-out war with my father's forces. According to Talisian intelligence, Badra Ging commands a force of a million fighting men, trained in the high gravity and formidable conditions of Miru. Armed with superior Talisian weaponry, they could return the 9th Wave to its optimum strength. Unfortunately, there is more than just a hint of insanity in Siouxbatai culture. Even so, I may have succeeded in securing a potentially useful ally against the Saurians.

With a discreet nod, Rin Mur-Rain signalled his men to stand at ease. As the crowd mingled, Roman experienced a sudden jolt of emotion and realised that his mind had wandered. At that moment, Kiya Mankuria's pained expression caught the corner of his eye. For the briefest moment, Kiya had allowed her guard to fall and Roman quickly circumvented any mental defences that remained.

Jealousy. She has feelings for Rin Mur-Rain, he concluded.

As he pondered the possible implications of Kiya's attachment, Soraya found her place at Roman's side. She exuded elegance in a flowing gown of deep green with a shimmering, intricately embroidered bodice, based on a pre-war Talisian design. Around her neck, Soraya proudly displayed the viridian pendant given to her by Roman on their engagement. He looked deeply into her eyes, which now matched his own in colour. The deep pools of light brown made her even more striking. His gaze travelled down to her full lips and he had an almost overwhelming desire to kiss her.

Later, he thought with a smile.

In turn, Roman and Soraya were introduced to Rin Mur-Rain's most senior officers, including the Alphatron with his piercing purple eyes and ominous voice.

After the necessary introductions were made, the Prince and his Consort were afforded a moment to themselves. The established rules of Imperial sanctum were upheld. No one ventured within a radius of ten metres from the Prince's presence.

Soraya whispered, "I love you."

Roman replied, "Yes, I've long suspected that."

"I see all the fuss has finally got to your big Royal head, My Majesty."

"What impudence. I shall have to punish you repeatedly this evening."

"I'll scream."

"I certainly hope so."

For the briefest moment, Soraya quietly giggled like a schoolgirl. But the curious stares of Talisian V.I.P.'s, quickly reminded her of the strict formality of their venue.

Looking deeply into his wife's eyes, Roman said, "I've missed you. I'm sorry about all this. Despite all the security, we are not safe here."

"Now is no time to be feeling sorry. I'm sure being Prince of the Universe carries a few perks."

"Apologies for interrupting your Mills and Boon moment," said Zachary.

Aware of his obvious breach of protocol, Zachary avoided Chi-Ro's stern stare. Many guests also marvelled at Zachary's unabashed boldness.

Heading to the guest conveniences, Mula, General Quat's consort whispered to herself, "He is indeed unstable."

"How dare you?" joked Soraya ensuring she was not overheard.

"What's up Zach?" whispered Roman, flashing a professional smile for the benefit of the Margrave's guests.

"I just had to escape from a general's wife or consort or concubine or whatever the hell she is," said Zachary, "She noticed my Rolex."

"You real harden eh, didn't Mr. Chi-Ro say not to wear it?"

Impersonating Mula, Zachary continued, "What an exquisite antique, wherever did you acquire such an ancient timepiece? It must be at least ten thousand years old and utterly priceless."

Soraya could not suppress a chuckle.

Roman whispered, "I hope you didn't mention anything about Earth."

"Of course not. I simply said, "Yes." Then she went on about how the general suspected I was a dangerous assassin. I told her, "Not recently. I was decommissioned because I was deemed to be far too unstable." Then, she suddenly had the need to go to the ladies'"

Roman and Soraya chuckled, doing their best not to laugh out loud, but the curious stares of Rin Mur-Rain's guests immediately reminded them that they were not allowed to let their guard down, not even for an instant. Many of the individuals present, including His Grace, the Margrave Rin Mur-Rain, observed and assessed their every action.

Noticing the sudden attention, Zachary said, "If I growl at them, do you think they'll go away?"

"I think it's best we enjoy this moment of calm, for as long as it lasts. The Saurians are coming. The swift destruction of their scouts gave them pause, but they're still coming."

"I'm sure the androids will learn a thing or two from the scout ship you captured. I've been doing my own research as well. I'm convinced your astral ability stems from the dark matter and dark energy that accounts for the vast majority of mass in the observable universe. It's purely hypothetical, but I believe much of what we call the supernatural is due to our very limited understanding of this invisible matter. I'm also convinced there is much more to the Sword of Power. I suspect it acts as a conduit or amplifier and that it is somehow powered by dark energy. It's a theory, anyway.

"Well, we don't have much time before the Saurians arrive, Zach. If there's more to this sword..."

"Don't worry Boss, I'm on the case."

With that, Zachary stepped ten paces backwards and bowed low to the Prince and his consort. He sniggered to himself, aware that his posterior aimed directly at Chi-Ro Jin. Standing upright, Zachary walked away to the left of Roman, ensuring he did not turn his back on the Prince.

Zachary continued to avoid Chi-Ro's burning gaze and pretended not to receive his projected thought: *"Have a care, your every move is being observed, Tinki Winki."*

Entering the darkness of her quarters aboard the Prince's Imperial shuttle, Kiya finally allowed her emotions to get the better of her. She sat on a corner of her bed and tears flowed from the corners of her green eyes.

Then suddenly, the Osirian woman swiftly drew her viridian pistol and aimed at a corner of the dark bedchamber.

"I thought I would never see you again," said a male voice.

"Lights," barked Kiya.

Bright illumination flooded the room, revealing Rin Mur-Rain. Standing slowly, Kiya continued to aim at the unarmed Margrave.

"Regardless of your rank, you have no right to be here," she said angrily.

He approached her saying, "Do you intend to shoot me for this transgression?"

"Perhaps."

"Hesitation? It seems we have both changed a great deal in the last four years."

"Indeed, you have lost an eye and gained a consort. I have lost a mother, and vowed never to be a concubine."

Rin Mur-Rain stopped as the barrel of Kiya's viridian pistol pressed into his chest. He had observed the gradual transformation of her eyes from lime green to aquamarine.

The Margrave said, "I thought you were dead."

"I am, I died today," Kiya said, her voice thick with suppressed emotion.

"I am truly sorry. News of your mother's death has deeply saddened me, I offer my deepest condolences."

"Since that is all you can offer, at the appropriate time, we will share a cup of Jainon tea. Now leave, before I put a hole in your chest."

"As you wish," said Rin, "I hope that one day you will forgive me. I still hold great affection for you."

"That is inappropriate, Your Grace," said Kiya, "I suggest you channel this affection to your consort."

Maintaining eye contact, Rin Mur-Rain backed away from Kiya, touched a bracelet on his left wrist and vanished in an electric-blue transport beam.

Kiya returned her pistol to its holster, slumped into her bed with a sigh and barked, "Lights."

In the darkness, her mind racing, she stared upwards at the ceiling. Then, closing her eyes, Kiya slowly curled into a foetal position and sobbed bitterly.

Chapter 68

Kyd Shaduu, the captain of Roman's Imperial shuttle, woke him early the following morning - Rin Mur-Rain requested Roman's presence at a high-level meeting. So, accompanied by his shamira, Commander Chi-Ro Jin, the Prince joined the senior staff in the ready room of the Margrave's shuttle.

Present were the Alphatron, Generals Quat Nye and Nokh-Ra Deem, Brigadiers Toykin Shu, Ley Ka-Tow and Mos Saba, and Space Commodores Taro Dao and Su Hodra.

The Margrave swept into the room with his shamira, Commander Goren Rag and a soldier of the Siouxbatai.

Roman recognised the broad-shouldered Siouxbatai as Maha Sar, leader of Badra Ging's armed forces. Goren and Maha took their places at the large conference table.

Standing before the assembly, Rin Mur-Rain acknowledged Roman with a curt bow of his neck.

Then, he said, "General Maha Sar of the Siouxbatai has additional information regarding the most recent Saurian incursion."

Maha said, "Four hours ago, in the Adrassi Rainforest, just south of the Hishon mudplains, a Siouxbatai hunting party encountered five Saurian soldiers. All five of the vile creatures are dead - Siouxbatai hunters killed two and the teroseriak devoured the remaining three. These five Saurian animals managed to kill thirteen Siouxbatai men, including my master's son, Shree. Five men are wounded, three critical."

"General Maha's men were able to retrieve one Saurian body from deep mud and the corpses of seven teroseriak. All have been made available for study by our scientists," added Rin.

"They killed just seven teroseriak?" asked Ley Ka-Tow, a puzzled frown appearing on her weathered face.

Maha replied, "No. They killed twenty-three. The seven teroseriak, my men retrieved, died shortly after eating Saurian monsters."

"Yes, I have absorbed the reports supplied by Commander Chi-Ro regarding His Highness The Prince Armon's victory over the Saurian leader. Our enemies have toxic bodily fluids."

"Verily," said Rin, "His Highness has duelled with the creature that impersonated Seti Aljyk and seized the Sword of Power from that vile beast. He did so after defeating the legendary Shan Kur-Karnah, Lord of Goria, no small feat. You are indeed your father's son."

So, he does view me as a threat, thought Roman.

"I wish to discuss these encounters with you in more detail, Prince Armon," said Rin, and Roman noted the slight narrowing of his cousin's visible eye.

Roman deliberately projected confidence with a hint of arrogance when he replied, "Certainly, there is much to be discussed. The Saurian disguise is very effective, my cousin. Have all your men been screened?"

"Verily, there are no Saurian creatures hiding among us and the Alphatron's scientists are developing an enhancement which will allow our battle visors to see through the Saurian disguise."

"A massive Saurian force is en-route to Miru. There are Karellans among them. They are our brothers, deceived by the real enemy. I wish them to be spared."

"These Karellans are fools and we are at war. In war, foolishness is often fatal."

Very well hidden rage. He respects my title but he is not accustomed to receiving requests.

"Agreed, war favours the wise; and wisdom dictates that only a combined Talisian and Karellan force can ultimately rid the Cosmic Sea of the Saurian menace. Therefore, we must be merciful to the misguided Karellans."

"Excellent," projected Chi-Ro Jin. *"Assert your authority, Master Armon."*

"I will not shed the blood of my men, in defence of Karellan traitors," growled Rin, unable to contain his anger.

Roman replied with calm firmness, "Agreed, the loyal and the innocent are our priority. But we will take Karellan prisoners of war even as we kill every Saurian we encounter. No Saurian is to be spared. We must kill them all."

A smile slowly appeared on Rin's face, he stroked his beard and held Roman's stare with his bright eye.

"You are a man after my own heart, cousin. I have already ordered my men to show no mercy to the evil Seriak aliens." Then, turning to the Alphatron, Rin said, "Tell our Prince of your recent genetic advancements."

The android's voice boomed, "Since the battle of Aaru, Jinzou Ningen have been tasked with the development of a biological weapon."

"The Krivas Convention prohibits the use of biological weaponry," interrupted Chi-Ro.

"Against a human foe, synthetic or natural, Commander. But Saurians are utterly inhuman and not protected by convention. We are therefore developing a nanoviral agent which targets only Saurian DNA."

Chi-Ro asked, "Have you already found a way to penetrate Seriak shields?"

"For the moment, Saurian shield technology remains more advanced than our own but the captured scout vessel has yielded a minor breakthrough. We have found the means to compromise their shields with organic material. It is actually a design feature that allows the Saurians to transport food whilst maintaining vessel defence."

"So, naked, unarmed men can be transported into Seriak vessels. At which point, the Seriak need only skin them and fry them," said Chi-Ro with bold sarcasm.

Chi-Ro's cutting remark was lost on the android but created visible tension amongst the rest of Rin's staff. An almost imperceptible tightening of Rin Mur-Rain's jaw, betrayed his disapproval.

"Alphatron, exactly how do you propose to introduce the nanoviral agent?" asked Roman.

"It will be introduced as part of the creature's diet."

"Whoa-whoa-whoa..."

Suddenly all eyes focussed on Roman. He stilled his emotions, mentally dismissed their puzzled stares and resumed his princely persona.

"Woe, Your Highness?" quizzed the Alphatron.

Ignoring his question, Roman asked the android, "Isn't their diet human beings?"

"Verily, natural human flesh appears to form the bulk of the Saurian intake of meat. The virus, harmless to humans, will be introduced into the bloodstream of all our troops."

"They eat us, they die," chimed General Quat Nye, with a chuckle.

"I wonder General, how many of your men have volunteered to go into battle naked?" asked Chi-Ro, with thinly veiled derision.

"Mind your tone, Commander!" barked Quat.

As a silent rage rose from the pit of Roman's stomach, he thought: *They are utterly insane!*

"Commander Chi-Ro speaks with my authority!" said Roman, his stare causing the general to tremble, "Answer his question."

"Apologies, Your Highness. We have no intention of transporting naked troops into battle. It is expected that a percentage of our troops will be captured and eaten. But the virus, which is also spread through Saurian bodily fluids, will eventually eradicate their entire race."

"I was reliably informed that on Miru, planetary conditions make nanoviral weapons ineffective."

"Verily Your Highness, airborne nanoviral agents," said General Quat.

It took much effort for Roman to hide his concern when he asked, "Have you considered the repercussions if this nanoviral weapon has unforeseen effects on humanity?"

"We have faith in the Jinzou Ningen. None have a better understanding of human genetics, natural or synthetic," interrupted the silver-haired General Nokh-Ra Deem.

Roman addressed Rin when he asked, "Has my father given this ambitious plan his blessing?"

The Margrave replied, "His Majesty the Emperor has granted his approval."

My father is dying and this plan is madness. I don't care how extensive their knowledge is, I can't allow the Jinzou Ningen to introduce this nanoviral agent into human beings. If it goes wrong, God help us all. It's interesting that the Saurians infiltrated the Sanura with an android. Could the Jinzou Ningen be in league with the Saurians?

"Chi-Ro, is there some way I can stop this madness?" projected Roman.

"Defying your father's wishes can be interpreted as treason."

"I have an idea."

"Verily, your thoughts are transparent. Who is this Patton?"

Roman stood and said, "Margrave Rin, please take your seat. I wish to address all present."

A low murmur rose from Rin's staff, instantly silenced by a flash of his fiery gaze.

He said, "As you wish, Your Highness," and maintaining his dignity, sat at the conference table.

Roman faced the assembly and in turn, stared deeply into each individual's expectant eyes.

When the silence became almost unbearable, he said, "There is nothing more repugnant to me than cowardice. I would rather drink a flask of lukewarm Saurian vomit than tolerate cowardice. I sense no cowardice in this room. You are all veterans of the Psychic Wars, loyal servants of my father, the Lord Sakara Rey, Emperor of The Cosmic Sea. No, I sense no cowardice in this room; but at least one of you, entertains the thought of defeat. General Quat Nye jokes of Saurian monsters eating us and dying as a result, perhaps the acid rains of Miru have eroded his brain."

Turning to the alarmed object of his rage, Roman growled, "General, the Saurians are preparing their dinner table and you are their main course, your wife and children their dessert!"

Then to all assembled, he cried, "Any plan, which relies on the capture and digestion of our troops by creatures so vile, so utterly repugnant, courts defeat. How could this general dare to speak of defeat in my presence? Does he not know that defeat is utterly unacceptable? Does he not know that mere mention of the word creates in me the most murderous intention? Send him to the battlefront where he will either triumph or die."

Roman observed the pale hollowness that descended on General Quat's round face as he bitterly accepted his fate. The Prince stared challengingly at the rest of the assembly. He noted the silent pride and approval in Chi-Ro's predatory eyes and grim visage. Then, Roman held the formidable glare of the Margrave Rin Mur-Rain and found no weakness in his cousin's dark brown eye.

He hides his fear well, that one. Despite his show of arrogant strength, he worries that I will seize his command. Don't worry cousin; the 9th remains yours to lead.

Roman's piercing gaze swept across those assembled, looking through and beyond them, as he continued ominously, "I say to you all, our fine troops will never be Saurian meals. Our women and children will never be theirs to devour. And let it be known, any man or woman showing even the smallest mercy to these vile creatures faces summary execution."

He paused, thinking, *I mustn't make an enemy of my cousin. I mustn't embarrass him, especially in front of his men.*

Roman continued, "Heroes inspire us to greatness. Here I stand in the presence of Talis's finest hero - the Margrave Rin Mur-Rain, whose courageous leadership ensured the 9th Wave never lost a single battle - a man who leads his men into the fray without the slightest regard for his personal safety. My cousin honoured me with mention of my encounters aboard the Karellan flagship. Much is rightly made of heroic deeds, but let us never forget that no battle is won through individual acts of heroism. Battles are won when the unique talents of each and every one of us is channelled towards achieving a single goal - complete destruction of the enemy! I have no doubt that under the Margrave's wise leadership we will defeat our Saurian foe."

The Margrave's staff applauded in heartfelt agreement.

It's working, I'm gaining their trust. Even Rin, feels more secure. Now, I can give them an alternative to using human beings as carriers of the nanovirus, without appearing treasonous.

Chapter 69

Half naked, Dr. Zachary Silverman awoke suddenly to the overpowering sound of a blaring alarm.

"Action Stations! The ship is at Action Stations! This is not a drill," the male computerised voice warned.

Where the hell am I?

Zachary stared up at the ceiling in a terrifying state of physical paralysis and mental disorientation.

I'm on the floor. What on Earth am I doing on the floor? But I'm not on Earth am I? I'm in the Juarian star system, about three hundred million kilometres from Miru's sun, aboard a battle spaceship – the Starcarrier Kach. And I'm experiencing sleep paralysis – a side effect of the drug I've been taking. I need to get off the floor though. Any second now, Rhys Kadar, my eager-beaver shamira will be knocking at my door, if he finds me on the floor there'll be far too many questions. I suppose it was only a matter of time before the whole Prince thing went to Roman's head. First he developed an odd obsession with finding Nook Tigg. He just couldn't accept that the poor sod's most likely in the belly of a Miruvian dinosaur. Then In the last month he had Chi-Ro, the smug bastard, promoted to general. Kiya is now Soraya's shamira and The Prince Armon decreed that in order to conceal my Earthly origin, I would be known to these arrogant aliens as Zak Aree, son of a Talisian merchant. My overbearing friend insisted on assigning the humourless Rhys Kadar, one of Chi-Ro's star students, as my shamira. Come to think of it, it was probably Chi-Ro's insidious idea in the first place.

Control over his body gradually returned, and Zachary slowly hauled himself upright. He stood on unsteady legs and chuckled at the absurdity of his predicament. As the drug-induced paralysis faded, he felt invigorated, but most of all, Zachary felt extremely confident. He smiled, knowing that, in the past weeks, he had hidden this confidence well. Zachary had mastered the ability to not only shield his thoughts, but he had also become adept at psychic deception.

Roman gets the call sign Thaur, but I'm Tinki Winki - that vindictive schmuck, Chi-Ro. It's not bad enough that the slant-eyed git still insists on calling me Tinki Winki, he had to have his boy Rhys baby-sit me. Well, perhaps it's a good thing; it confirms that they all have no idea what I'm really capable of. And, there's nothing to gain and everything to lose from telling Roman about my father. Roman's a historian. He talks about his foster parents who died over twenty years ago, as if they died yesterday. A man that obsessed with the past won't be very forgiving. If he knew my father ordered the death of his foster parents he would hate me and under the circumstances, I'd be as good as dead.

Zachary grabbed an Osirian stealth suit from his closet and quickly dressed. The suit was designed as a superficial replica of the suits used by Talisian Imperial Shadow Warriors.

Deception is everywhere, Zachary thought. *Osirian spies like Kiya, pretending to be Talisians; Saurians impersonating Karellans – I guess that's what advanced civilisation is all about.*

The ship's alarm made Zachary painfully aware of a throbbing headache – another side effect of the drug he was secretly taking.

I wish they'd shut off that infernal racket.

"Yes, I know it's not a drill, I get the bloody message!"

I'm guessing the Saurians finally got hungry enough to attack us. The lizards are here a month later than Roman said they'd arrive. So, the Prince is not infallible - there's a surprise.

Fully dressed, he stared at himself admiringly in a reflective wall and said, "Well Zachary, I guess it's time to go kick some Saurian arse."

On the impressive, dimly lit bridge of the formidable Starcarrier Shor, Margrave Rin Mur-Rain observed the approach of a Karellan Imperial Shuttle through the visor of his command helmet. The dwarfed shuttle and its sole occupant, Seti Aljyk's herald Mirel Ko, were scanned and rescanned. No weapons, computer viruses or biological threats were detected.

Mirel Ko, a tall tanned Karellan with reddish-brown hair and Fu Manchu moustache, appeared to Rin's consciousness through his command helmet.

"Your Grace, The Margrave Rin of Taria, I transmit the Imperial Seal. His Imperial Majesty, the Emperor of Emperors, Seti Aljyk I, proclaims that you are guilty of treason and orders you and your followers to immediately lay down your arms that you may qualify for his mercy. His Imperial Majesty the Emperor of Emperors, demands that The Prince Armon and his consort be transferred to my care immediately. Failure to comply will result in your complete annihilation," came the brazenly arrogant projection of Mirel.

"Your master's authority is not recognised herald. I serve His Imperial Majesty Sakara Rey I, Lord of the Imperial Host, True Emperor of the Cosmic Sea. Who is this Prince Armon of whom you project?"

"With all due respect Your Grace, Lord Seti Aljyk is extremely well informed. It is known that The Prince Armon and his consort were passengers aboard the Starbird Adara and that they joined your camp on the planet Miru. Spare the lives of your valiant men and surrender. I await transport of The Prince Armon and his consort."

"If your master is as well informed as you boast, he would know that the Starbird Adara was destroyed and that there were no survivors."

"Is that your final word, Your Grace?"

"I have no message for your master, but heed my words, Mirel Ko. You and your Karellan brethren are victims of a deception most foul. The one you believe to be Seti Aljyk is a Seriak impostor. The proof will be downloaded to your vessel."

"There will be no download, Your Grace. The Talisian use of software viral agents is legendary. I will now return to Lord Seti Aljyk with your response."

"Fly to your Seriak master, foolish herald. May your death and the death of your Karellan brethren be swift and painless."

"May the Great Spirit have mercy on your souls."

As Mirel Ko's shuttle arced away, Prince Armon Sakara and his shamira Chi-Ro Jin swept onto the bridge of the Starcarrier Shor. Both wore Osirian stealth suits; and, at a glance, appeared like grim Talisian Imperial Shadow Warriors. At his waist, in its scabbard, Armon wore the Sword of Power. The black-bladed, katana-like weapon instilled awe wherever he went. The bridge of the 9th Wave's Flagship was no exception, but a casual gesture from his hand put the overly alert bridge staff at relative ease.

Margrave Rin rose from the Shor's command pod, handing the command helmet to the silver-haired General Nokh-Ra Deem who bowed low to receive it.

"So begins the dark business, my old friend," projected Rin with a twinkle in his eye, *"Maintain full alert. The Seriak believe they have surrounded us and will attack swiftly. They are convinced that victory will shortly be theirs. But soon, they shall learn their food does not agree with them."*

"May the scribes record it, Your Grace."

Rin acknowledged Armon with a curt bow at the neck and proceeded towards the door of his ready room flanked by his shamira Goren Rag and followed by Armon and Chi-Ro.

Behind the closed doors of Margrave Rin Mur-Rain's ready room, Armon said, "It is as we anticipated. Though they lack psychic ability, the Saurians are capable of using a form of deep hypnosis to maintain their grip over the Karellan forces."

"Their distant cousins, the Shon-Ghūl, are known to possess hypnotic ability," said Goren Rag, betraying no emotion. Then, as an afterthought, he added, "But of course you already know that, Your Highness, having killed one of the vile beasts aboard the Asing's vimana the Su-Neku - few men could live to tell such a tale."

Goren, the cynic, war has killed the romantic artist I sensed you once were.

"Yes there appears to be a distinct evolutionary link between the two species."

"We have little time, gentlemen. Pray tell Armon, news of your mission," said Rin icily.

"Accomplished," replied Armon, bright-eyed.

"So you managed to compromise the shield barrier of Mirel Ko's shuttle."

"And infiltrate its central processing unit, Your Grace," added Chi-Ro with thinly veiled pride.

"Those impenetrable Saurian shields will soon be under our control, my cousin."

"You must tell me how you achieve these marvellous feats..."

Suddenly a massive explosion rocked the Shor. Momentarily plunging the Margrave's ready room into darkness, briefly and sporadically illuminated by the neon-green discharge of a viridian pistol and lightening-blue bolts from unknown weapons.

Seconds later restored lights revealed the unmoving Margrave lying facedown on the floor with Goren Rag across his body. Goren Rag had a Daxia H3-16 pistol aimed at Chi-Ro who had positioned his body to shield Armon and was holding a recently discharged viridian pistol aimed at Goren Rag.

Has Rin been shot? Why didn't I see this coming? Even after all Chi-Ro's training, I was caught off guard!

"Kindly lower your weapon, Commander," said Chi-Ro calmly.

"After you, General," said Goren with equal serenity.

"Chi-Ro!" projected Armon sternly, far more angry with himself than with his experienced mentor.

Not breaking eye contact with Goren Rag, Chi-Ro placed his pistol into its holster at his hip. Goren did the same and quickly assisted Rin to his feet.

"Thanks to our esteemed comrades we remain unharmed," said Rin to Armon as he adjusted the patch over his left eye then activated a holographic screen with a wave of his gloved hand. He barked into his wrist communicator, "General Nokh-Ra Deem, status!"

"Your Grace, The shockwave you felt was from a barrage of five thousand cloaked long-range, projectile weapons - shields holding on all capital ships. I have positioned the Wave just out of bombardment range and activated psychic storm amplifiers. Mirel Ko's shuttle - destroyed by cloaked enemy scout-class vessels of unknown design. Synchronized incursions by enemy androids - successfully repelled. The main enemy force has been identified as the 74th Karellan Shock Division, commanded by Baron Godric Calla. Five hundred starfires, one hundred starchariots and eighty stargliders are space-bourne and will intercept one thousand Karellan raiders, supported by four hundred marauders – ETA fifty seconds."

"They have about sixty capital ships, I expected more," projected Armon to Chi-Ro as he absorbed the holographic news update.

"There are," came his shamira's nonchalant response.

Nokh-Ra Deem continued, "Miru is surrounded; and long-range sensors have just detected two thousand raiders, one thousand marauders and an estimated six hundred cloaked interceptor-class vessels converging on the 9th Wave – ETA twenty minutes. Intelligence confirms this force to be the 149th Karellan Shock Division, commanded by Duke Arved Rahn."

I knew we'd be outgunned, but fifteen to one?

"Launch half of all remaining raptors to intercept Duke Arved's fighters, General. Take the Shor, Kach, Avedis and our escorts towards Miru's second moon at full sub-light speed. Position the rest of the Wave to engage the 149th. Use all your tricks Silver Fox, neither Arved nor Godric have ever tasted defeat in battle."

"Proceeding with orders received, Your Grace."

"Clever Seriak, they anticipated the computer virus in the herald's shuttle," said Rin as he sat behind the impressive desk in his ready room. Then stroking his goatee beard thoughtfully he added, "I assume these are a similar type of android to the one that infiltrated the Sanura," referring to the three artificial humans lying dead in the room.

"We knew there was a chance they would discover the computer virus. But, as we hoped, the Saurians have confirmed to their satisfaction that they can compromise our shield defences at will. So, they continue to underestimate us. The Alphatron's men can now see to it that any enemy android survivors carry the nanovirus back to their Saurian handlers. I'm surprised they haven't transported these corpses out of here already."

"His Grace's ready room is triple shielded," said Chi-Ro.

"Open," barked Rin and the doors to his ready room immediately obeyed his command. Then he added, "Goren, if you will," and his loyal shamira stood in the doorway, and signalled to three security officers.

The men immediately came into the ready room and hauled the android bodies onto the bridge where they were transported away.

Rin stood and said to Armon, "This is the calm before the storm. Enjoy it, because in a few moments we will descend into Hades and a few moments after that, you too will be a veteran of the Psychic Wars. Join us on the bridge in five minutes, that's all the period of calm the Seriak have left us."

With that, Rin, Chi-Ro and Goren Rag left Armon alone in the ready room.

Armon immediately activated his wrist communicator.

"Roman, yuh alright?" Came the familiar singsong of his wife's Trinidadian accent.

"Yes. Soraya, things are gonna get pretty rough from now on. But you're in the citadel - it's the most heavily fortified part of the ship; and you have Ishma for company. Kiya Mankuria and Lady Capella Hezion are probably the two most formidable women in the Cosmic Sea. You couldn't ask for better shamiras."

"Yes, they've already demonstrated their formidable skills."

"What? What happened?"

"Seven androids beamed into the citadel."

"Seven? Where are they?"

"Don't get riled."

"Soraya, where are they?"

"Well, as my grandmother from Cedros used to say, crapaud smoke dey pipe!"

"For a minute, I forgot how much Kiya loves androids."

"Capella ent easy either. Dem robots lasted two seconds."

"Can you sense anything?"

"Not a damn ting... Roman I know you doh want to hear it, but yuh feel it too. These powers we have, they're dark..."

"I'm not afraid of the dark and neither should you. Seriously Soraya, promise me that if any of those Saurian monsters come anywhere near you, you show no mercy. No mercy..."

"No mercy."

"Promise me."

"I promise. Oh, it's probably nothing..."

"What?"

"I had a dream this morning – all I remember is Chi-Ro saying something about the Butcher of Cyclone returning."

"Could it have been Cyclo?"

"Yeah that's it, Cyclo. Who's the Butcher of Cyclo?"

"A ghost."

Chapter 70

The new Karellan flagship, the Imperial Drac El, was an impressive vessel by any imaginable standard. The most impressive combat machine recorded in the Psychic Wars thus far. Created in utmost secrecy at the Koroba Shipyards at Minas Kral, this prototype ravager-class super battlecarrier was, in fact, the brainchild of highly advanced Saurian technology. It boasted a central processing core three times faster than any vessel in either the Karellan or Talisian fleets.

At twenty kilometres in length, the Drac El carried a complement of two hundred raiders and two marauders. Her armaments included plasma and particle-beam cannons, and zero point torpedoes. For hyperspatial travel, she employed four hyper-stellar reactors and eight zero-point field generators provided sub-light propulsion.

Three kilometres longer than her Talisian counterpart - the Ayntaiyou, and two kilometres longer than the ill-fated Battlecarrier Anhur, the Imperial Drac El was simply the biggest, fastest and most heavily armed vessel known to enter the Psychic War arena.

Disguised as His Royal Highness Arved Rahn the Duke of Criesse, First Admiral of the Imperial Karellan Fleet, the Saurian General Sheerak commanded The Royal Host of the Karellan Imperium. He easily defeated the Talisian 4th and 7th Waves. And, at Garidius Prime, successfully engaged the defecting forces of Karamba Shan, son of Lord Shan Kur-Karnah.

In a bloodless confrontation, Karamba Shan had usurped the command of previously loyal Karellan forces from Margrave Klim T'val. Then, having commandeered the Battlecarrier Taharqa - sister ship of the Anhur, he boldly challenged the Imperial Drac El and the Duke's armada. But at Zolis Nid, outmatched and outmanoeuvred, Lord Karamba lost twelve destroyers and one hundred and eighty-nine raiders. He barely escaped the encounter with the badly damaged Taharqa and the orbital bombers Nekhbet and Sekhmet. Relentlessly pursued, his capital ships and their escorts desperately initiated hyperspatial jumps as their captains prayed for a miracle.

Duke Arved believed that Karamba Shan posed a discernible threat to Saurian interests. Lord Karamba knew Seti Aljyk was an alien impostor and the Duke feared the charismatic leader could conceivably usher in the mass defection of Karellan forces and be instrumental in combining these forces with those of Talis. But despite Duke Arved's strenuous protests, Seti Aljyk ordered that pursuit of the renegade Lord Karamba be abandoned in favour of the Miruvian Objective.

Seti Aljyk believed only two remaining forces posed any real threat to Saurian dominion of the Cosmic Sea: Sakara Rey's guardians, the elusive 1st Wave, commanded by Viceroy Tuduh Fadah, First Admiral of the Imperial Talisian Waves; and the 9th Wave commanded by Margrave Rin Mur-Rain, stationed at Miru.

According to Karellan intelligence Prince Armon, the Tan-Kyu, found sanctuary within Margrave Rin's camp. The current holder of the Sword of Power, he posed the greatest threat to Saurian interests and had to be neutralised by any means possible. Saurian long-range scanners traced multiple instances of Armon Sakara's archaic transponder signal to various locations on Miru. Each one had to be investigated.

So, in a move anticipated by Rin Mur-Rain and his generals, the Saurians attempted to intimidate the ill-equipped Miruvian forces. They fired upon the orbital minefield destroying hundreds, and then they dispatched eight orbital bombers. But undetected mines disabled three of the eight bombers and forced the remaining five to retreat. A thorough search of Miru was delayed but not averted.

At the heart of the Drac El's citadel, guarded by twelve sentinels and with Duke Arved in full military dress standing at his side, Seti Aljyk sat on his high, dark throne and stared grimly at the holographic image of a submissive General Toemak, the Saurian disguised as the Karellan General Beric Naya.

"Pray tell, Toemak, how does it feel to be outwitted by your food?"

Toemak tried to reply but Sobek continued mockingly, "'We shall capture this Armon and his man-child. Their power shall serve us. Evil shall be turned to righteousness, and we will feast on the bounty of planet Earth.' Were these not your arrogant words, Toemak?"

"Yes, Lord Sobek but..."

"Silence, you pitiful moron, I am certain to find more intelligence in the mindless screeching of Meclac's pet iguadon! It is highly likely the son of Sakara and his offspring remain on Miru. They must be found General! And do not make the mistake of irradiating this vital source of human flesh. Nuclear weapons cannot be employed! As repugnant as it must seem, if it comes to it, you will just have to take your troops to the surface and fight the old-fashioned way. Do you understand me General?"

"Yes Lord..."

"Silence! Why are you still bowing? Get out of my sight!"

At that, Seti Aljyk ended the holographic transmission.

"I never liked Toemak," he said to Duke Arved, "he has that sickly-lean look of a vegetarian."

"I always assumed it was just his poorly applied disguise," replied Arved with a measure of contempt.

Seti Aljyk stared at Arved Rahn taking stock of the general who had subdued several Talisian forces but failed to eliminate the threat of Karamba Shan.

"I fear Toemak may not be Saurian enough for the task assigned to him. If he does not commence landing on Miru within the hour have him relieved of duty, permanently."

"Molok is a fine officer. He graduated top of his class at Shongo Military Academy. He would provide a most satisfactory replacement."

"No doubt. But do not allow Saurian arrogance to get the better of you, old friend. We cannot afford to underestimate these human creatures. Your own experience should tell you they are more intelligent than the King and his court believe."

"Their ploy to infect the herald's vessel with one of their insidious viruses was laughable and utterly predictable."

"Yet we remain uncertain how it was actually accomplished. How did these inferior creatures infect a vessel protected by Saurian shield technology? I tell you, we may eat these things; but they are not just stupid animals. The psychic ability of the average human is to be respected and the astral aptitude exhibited by both Armon and Brakis is to be feared."

"Come now Sobek, you begin to sound like a member of the religious minority who believes all life is sacred."

"I've heard the Queen is secretly sympathetic to their cause."

"No."

"Yes old friend, and there are many others. Be vigilant, there may be Saurians in our ranks with, shall we say, counter-productive religious views."

"I will not fail you or the King, My Lord Sobek. Do not fear these humans, none have been found to resist sustained exposure to iliac and hypnotherapy. Despite his obvious talents, even the son of Tarn could not resist our methods."

"I know you will not fail old friend, you would not force me to make a widow of my dear sister. Nevertheless, perhaps we should increase the daily administered dose of iliac to these humans."

"No My Lord, extensive tests have shown that any increase results in what the humans refer to as paranoid schizophrenia. Furthermore, the animals become unsuitable for consumption as the iliac remains at too high a level for our food decontamination processes to effectively neutralise."

"Indeed," resigned Seti Aljyk with a dejected sigh, then with a sudden fire in his eyes, he snapped, "Go now, if Sakara's heir is among the 9th Wave bring this human Prince and his childbearing consort to me in lapys nerian chains. Send in that repulsive human fortune-teller and my new shamira when you leave, and do make sure neither one explodes in my presence."

Arved Rahn bowed low and said, "As you wish, My Lord."

Seti Aljyk activated the throne room's formidable lapys nerian doors and the darkly tanned Duke Arved took his leave.

Chapter 71

In the first hour, of conflict, Baron Godric Calla's 74th Karellan Shock Division annihilated thirty five percent of the 9th Wave. The Imperial Drac El disabled every vessel that challenged her and now pursued the Starcarriers Shor, Kach and Avedis. The badly damaged capital ships and their escorts fought a desperate running battle, hastily retreating towards Miru's second moon - Zia.

Disguised as Commodore Kaitas Grinn, the Saurian Molok replaced Toemak and assumed command of the Karellan invasion force. Toemak, in the guise of General Beric Naya, collapsed on the bridge of the orbital bomber Habu. General Beric became the seventh high-ranking officer to suffer sudden cardiac death in recent months. The increased incidence of this rare ailment fuelled many conspiracy theories among the humans of the 74th and 149th Karellan Shock Divisions.

Tripling the force previously committed for Operation Miru, Molok succeeded where Toemak failed. He breached the Miruvian orbital minefield by sacrificing hundreds of unmanned drones. Or so he thought, for the vast majority of mines were deliberately deactivated by their Talisian manufacturers and remained undamaged and undetected.

Under Prince Armon's direction, Badra Ging's Siouxbatai and Margrave Rin Mur-Rain's 9th Wave cooperated in the meticulous preparation of Miru. They planted thousands of non-sentient robot decoys at strategic positions in the planet's cities. From these locations, the decoys confused the enemy by constantly transmitting the Prince's transponder signal.

To add credibility to their ruse, the Talisians constructed heavily shielded dummy bases. And, using codes recently broken by Karellan intelligence, these unmanned bases automatically exchanged hundreds of bogus military communiqués. Secretly constructed dummy battleships, fighters and armoured chariots enhanced the illusion that the bulk of the 9th Wave remained on Miru's surface.

After their first two landing parties re-materialised in rock, all Karellan attempts to transport troops and equipment to the planet by matter transfer were abandoned. Molok ordered his bombers to assume equidistant orbits around Miru; and deployed raider-escorted military shuttles and heavy carriers laden with troops and material. These immediately came under fire from Siouxbatai surface-to-air missiles but remained shield-protected and undeterred.

But as this heavily-armed invasion force descended on the storm-wracked planet, Margrave Rin Mur-Rain ordered the reactivation of the orbital stealth minefield and, though they had not yet realised it, more than a third of the entire Karellan fleet became trapped.

Many kilometres from major cities, in the heart of Miru's massive rain-forests, shielded underground bunkers provided refuge for the terrified civilian population. In the many years since their exodus from the Talisian continent of Malobar, the Siouxbatai had adapted well to their new Miruvian environment. They had developed superior physical strength and acquired in-depth knowledge of their surroundings.

Saurian Military Intelligence casually dismissed any consideration of brutal hand-to-hand combat with human beings. The Saurians regarded the human race as livestock. So they were completely unprepared for the ancient, forgotten art of guerrilla warfare devastatingly employed by the warrior-followers of Badra Ging. Saurian military tacticians were also unable to antici-pate the lethal effectiveness of Rin Mur-Rain's elite snipers. Equipped with Aknon 74S 'Ghost' rifles, lightly armoured and highly mobile, these 'ghost' warriors successfully targeted high-ranking Karellan officers, spreading fear and utterly demoralising the enemy.

The Krivas Convention did not protect invading non-human aliens from Talisian biological and chemical weapons. Applying their extensive knowledge, the Jinzou Ningen finally perfected a nanoviral agent that specifically targeted Saurian DNA. They called their Saurian-killing creation serivelen five-one-two. And, because conditions on Miru inhibited the nanoviral agent's airborne effectiveness, they armed the planet's cities with booby traps and automated weapons modified for effective delivery of the pathogen.

Instead of the proposed human hosts, Prince Armon suggested the Tal-isians use the fierce dinosaur-like teroseriak as living carriers of the nanovirus. Up to two metres tall and six metres long at full maturity, armed with curved eight-centimetre-long septic teeth, and jaws capable of biting a full-armoured shock marine in two, the predatory teroseriak became a most effective weapon of terror in the war against Saurian dominion.

Saurian underestimation of human resourcefulness coupled with their preposterous obsession with fresh meat, led them to develop shields utterly impervious to aggressive bombardment but designed to facilitate the transport of organic material, which they intended to consume. Exploiting this security flaw, the Talisians developed a protocol that circumvented Saurian security, and permitted the transport of hundreds of teroseriak to Karellan warships, creating absolute mayhem.

Years later, Talisian scribes would record that the Saurian-led Karellan invaders fell into a trap masterminded by His Highness Prince Armon Sakara. But they would never know that the Prince employed his extensive knowledge of Earth history and drew on the strategies of World War II generals in order to outwit the technologically superior alien invaders.

An hour of sustained bombardment finally compromised the aft shield generators of the fleeing Starcarrier Kach. And, as her engineers desperately worked to restore the ship's failed protective energy barrier, elite Karellan shock marines transported aboard and faced stiff opposition.

Having received news of the infraction, the shamira Rhys Kadar hurriedly took his charge to the relative safety of the heavily armoured, triple shielded citadel of the Kach. Zachary Silverman, suffering the somewhat euphoric side effects of elidium did not appreciate this protective measure - Zachary wanted to fight.

Within the citadel, huddled in the company of their personal bodyguards, protected by elite Jinzou Ningen shadow warriors and members of the Emperor's Own Psion Police, were aristocratic consorts, concubines, eminent civilian dignitaries and members of notable regal families. The sound of battle gradually became more intrusive, and the scent of fear saturated the recycled air.

Zachary and his shamira listened intently to their military-band communication links, absorbing the laconic intelligence reports of the raging battle. Karellan shock marines steadily converged on critical locations in the ship, despite fierce resistance from Talisian shadow warriors. New visor enhancements allowed the Talisians to see through Saurian disguises and terminate them with prejudice. But the Talisians found it difficult to safeguard Karellan lives. Many of the iliac-addicted Karellans refused to surrender, preferring in many cases to commit suicide.

Why doesn't Soraya do something, can't she see we're getting our arses kicked here? That unborn kid of hers picks the worse possible times to take naps.

Suddenly, bringing ominous darkness and temporary silence to the citadel, three explosions in quick succession rocked the Kach. The security forces immediately used their powerful visor lamps to search the stronghold for possible enemy incursions. Emergency lights snapped on promptly, eliciting audible sighs from the many civilians immobilised by terror.

Having confirmed the safety of the citadel, a few of the battle-experienced turned their attention to quelling any rising panic among the dignitaries.

Sweeping his gaze about the throng, Zachary stumbled upon the thunderstruck, elfin faces of a girl and her brother. The pale, fair-haired twins were no more than six years old and stared directly at him with probing blue eyes. Zachary found himself captivated. The young girl reminded him of faded pictures he had seen of his mother, at a similar age; and because of this, he became instantly protective of these young strangers.

Children, in a place like this, at a time like this? Bloody madness. Zachary noted the armorial crest of dark blue and silver on their small body armour, identifying them as members of the House of Arat, one of the oldest and most prestigious of the surviving Great Houses. With effort, Zachary averted his eyes and instantly realised that the shamiras of the young royals were also twins. The tall, grimly vigilant and heavily armed man and woman wordlessly deterred the crowd from venturing too close to their charges.

Returning his attention to the children, Zachary felt a sudden need to re-evaluate his feelings.

A moment ago, all I wanted to do was fight. Elidium has made me stronger and more agile; I've even developed telekinetic abilities. But now I wonder if my skill, and that of all the experienced warriors in this room, will be enough to protect innocents, such as these children, from harm.

"They are Baronet Apel and Lady Nayri Masuvi," said the usually tight-lipped Rhys Kadar.

Zachary immediately turned to his young dark-haired stony-faced guardian. He wondered if, despite his efforts, Rhys had somehow read his thoughts. He knew any surreptitious attempt to probe Rhys's mind would fail. Rhys was far too well trained, far too disciplined. Raising his mental guard even higher, Zachary searched Rhys's brown eyes for clues but observed nothing suggesting the disclosure of his secrets to the grim warrior. The quantum physicist found it difficult to relate to this humourless bodyguard who spoke little and appeared devoid of vice. And, because Chi-Ro Jin handpicked Rhys, Zachary inwardly believed his shamira was assigned to spy on his activities.

Zachary faced Rhys, preventing his lips being read by the children or their bodyguards, and asked, "Why are these children here?"

Noting Zachary's desire for discretion, Rhys leaned forward, ensuring his lips were also obscured, and replied, "They are orphans under the care of the Alphatron, Sir."

Masking his surprise, Zachary looked to the children's shamiras for that telltale feature he somehow missed before and instantly observed the deep purple of their bright, predatory eyes.

Yes, their guardians are Jinzou Ningen: artificial human beings; but this female is not at all like the pleasure skins I've encountered. Pleasure skins. I've obviously spent too much time around drunk Talisian marines. Yet, there is something very unsettling about a society where artificial humans can be distinguished solely by eye colour. Especially since it's so easy to convincingly change eye colour to something less exotic than purple.

Zachary suddenly thought of Kiya and her singular talent for terminating Jinzou Ningen.

I'm glad she's on the Shor and not here, he thought but failed to convince himself.

Commanded by the Alphatron, the Starcarrier Kach boasted the best scientific facilities in the 9th Wave. Despite the Prince's protests, Zachary insisted it was important he remained aboard the Kach, to further his dark matter research. But secretly, and much to his dismay, Zachary became overwhelmed by a growing infatuation with Kiya Mankuria and jealously suspected the object of her affection to be the Margrave Rin Mur-Rain.

Zachary also feared his thoughts would eventually reveal incriminating clues regarding the identity of his father. And without constant prudence, his guilt-ridden conscience could divulge his theft of the valuable elidium. Or expose his selfish plan, to earn untold riches from ultra advanced Talisian science, if he ever returned to Earth.

I have to give them all a wide berth.

Developed for Armon Sakara's specific DNA, the experimental drug elidium, permanently altered Zachary's physiology and brain chemistry. In the last month, while his physical and intellectual abilities improved, his growing scepticism devolved into paranoia, confidence transformed into arrogance, and his habitual mild annoyance degenerated into bitter contempt and intolerance. Elidium initiated a chain reaction - one that Zachary lacked the inclination or ability to stop.

Violent tremors shook the beleaguered starcarrier, jolting Zachary back to the here and now. Noting the sudden, ominous silence of his communication-link, and observing the battle preparations being made by all the military personnel in the citadel, Zachary experienced an invigorating rush of adrenaline. Then suddenly, amid the swell of perceived fears, sobs, gasps and murmured prayers, only the diminutive Lady Nayri Masuvi captured Zachary's gaze.

With each passing moment, more of the ship is being overrun. Soon the Karellans will be here. The tides of war seldom protect the innocent. This is no bloody place for children.

Chapter 72

On the bridge of the 9th Wave flagship Shor, with his loyal shamira Chi-Ro Jin at his side, Prince Armon observed the Imperial Drac El's bombardment of the Starcarrier Kach. Armon secretly cursed Zachary's stubborn resolve to remain aboard the Shor's sister ship. He felt directly responsible for Zachary's involvement in the Psychic Wars and wanted more measures taken to safeguard his friend. But, with Soraya's abilities mysteriously dormant and his own abilities impaired by forces unknown, he remained powerless to protect Zachary as Karellan Shock Marines stormed the Kach.

The Karellans are looking for us. They want me and they want my unborn son even more. But the Saurian leader disguised as my uncle, the one they call Sobek, is not the only one intent on finding us. I sense there's much more to this. The Saurians want us alive, but there're those who want us dead. What's happened to my clarity? Suddenly the future is darkness. In fact, it's as if I no longer have a future. Have the Saurians found a way to rob us of our psychic abilities? There is something I'm overlooking - I can feel it.

"This Imperial Drac El projects a psychic storm far more powerful than any I have ever experienced," projected Chi-Ro Jin.

"I can't see the future, Chi-Ro. Maybe if I had more elidium..."

"The drug is gone Master Armon. And any additional benefit to be gained from the last four doses remains uncertain. Your thoughts are transparent. Dr. Zachary Silverman made his choice; but fear not, the Alphatron is one of the finest Talisian generals. And, despite their lack of psychic ability, Jinzou Ningen shadow warriors are exceptionally formidable in battle. They are stronger, faster and better coordinated than natural humans and make powerful allies. Rhys Kadar is one of my finest students; I have much faith in his abilities. The doctor is exceedingly well protected on the Kach."

"I think the Saurians have finally realised we're not on Miru."

Chi-Ro stroked his Fu Manchu moustache thoughtfully, as he projected, *"Perhaps. But righteousness will prevail."*

Armon's comlink suddenly activated.

"Thaur, Pantera, switch to stealth," came a familiar female voice.

It's Kiya, using call signs within the ship; and she wants me to communicate mentally. Something's very wrong.

"Pantera, Thaur, switching now."

Masking all signs of his rising anxiety from General Nokh-Ra Deem and his bridge crew, Prince Armon deactivated his wrist communicator and immediately put on his helmet. He established a mental projection link with Kiya Mankuria.

"*What is it Kiya?*"

"*I received a coded message from an Osirian agent - Ne-Ro Jos has recovered. He has resumed his post of Grandmaster of The Order of Mysteries and continues to advise Seti Aljyk.*"

"*I thought I fried his little evil brain.*"

"*There is more. There have been unconfirmed sightings of Brakis Tarn.*"

"*When did Osirian agents start seeing ghosts? Brakis Tarn is dead.*"

"*His body was destroyed, not his consciousness.*"

"*That's right, so unless he has an identical twin brother...*"

"*It is possible Brakis Tarn has been cloned, or a superficially identical Jinzou Ningen body has been manufactured. There is much that remains unknown regarding Saurian technology; there may be other techniques at their disposal for restoring the Butcher of Cyclo.*"

"*But why aren't you even considering the possibility that a Niburian or Saurian is impersonating Brakis Tarn?*"

"*The Saurians were quite effective in their two-hundred-year genocide. Mistress Anah was one of the last of the Great Ones. The Niburian race is all but extinct, in fact, with the death of my foster mother, only thirteen are known to survive. Five are Osirian Councillors, and the remaining eight are high-ranking Osirian field agents. Their loyalty is unquestionable. It is also highly unlikely that a Saurian impersonator was sighted.*"

"*And why is that?*"

"*The observer wore an enhanced visor, and Osirian Intelligence has intercepted com-chatter, which suggests that the Karellans are also baffled by their own unconfirmed sightings of the butcher.*"

"*Kiya, where and when was Brakis Tarn last seen?*"

"*He was glimpsed aboard the Karellan bomber, Küstah, orbiting Miru, four hours ago.*"

Armon immediately recalled Soraya's dream and thought privately: *I don't believe in coincidence. Kiya may be right - the bastard's probably alive. So, I've failed to stop both Brakis Tarn and Ne-Ro Jos. I'm not the soter - I've seen it; and Ne-Ro the evil monk confirmed it. But I'm the only one who can stop Brakis Tarn. I believe the Sword of Power is the only thing that can kill him. But all I see ahead of me is darkness. Am I to die, so that my son, the soter, may live?*

"*Sir?*"

"*Perhaps you're right Kiya, I sense much more than the apparent danger. It's hidden... Elusive. I'm coming to the citadel, but don't tell anyone except*

Soraya. If my suspicions are correct, we'll soon have some heavily armed unwanted guests. So be prepared."

"Yes, Your Highness."

Margrave Rin Mur-Rain emerged from his ready room, flanked by his grim shamira Goren Rag.

Rin asked the communications officer, "Any news from the admiral?"

"Viceroy Tuduh Fadah has not yet contacted us, Your Grace," came the voice generated by the communications helmet the man wore.

Turning to General Nokh-Ra Deem, Rin said, "And still, we have not located the cloaked Saurian warship."

"No, Your Grace."

"It remains at large, watching, waiting, like a hungry predator," whispered Rin.

Suddenly three of the twelve stormbringers, attached to the mental amplifiers comprising the Shor's main psychic storm generator, collapsed. The woman and two men were quickly taken away. Replacements rose from adjacent life-supporting pods and immediately manned the vacated posts. They resumed the grim task of attempting to counter the efforts of their Karellan rivals, but fought a losing battle.

Rin said to Nokh-Ra Deem, "This charade has gone on long enough."

"Agreed, Your Grace."

"Proceed with operation Coiled Dragon."

"By your command."

Armon removed his helmet, turning his attention to the main holographic display. He observed as the Kach and Avedis broke formation. The Kach veered to port and the relatively unscathed Avedis repositioned, so as to bear the brunt of the Imperial Drac El's relentless firepower. Simultaneously, the Shor veered to starboard.

The retreating Talisian starcarriers launched their remaining fighters and initiated a sustained counter attack on the overconfident Imperial Drac El and her escorts. The formidable enemy flagship had been lured away from the relative security of The Royal Host of the Karellan Imperium.

"Master Armon, your nose is bleeding," projected Chi-Ro.

Armon used the back of the index finger of his gloved right hand, to wipe away the blood.

"Chi-Ro, I want you to come with me to the citadel right away. We'll need a heavily armed escort."

"What have you learned, Master Armon?"

"Ne-Ro Jos and Brakis Tarn are alive, and I believe they know we're here."

"Odd, that I have not sensed my old master."

As anticipated by Saurian tacticians, a substantial Talisian force, previously hidden on the dark side of Miru's second moon, finally emerged. With three starcarriers already engaged in head to head exchanges of firepower with the Imperial Drac El, the formidable armada from the dark side of Zia quickly split into two equal forces.

A starcarrier led each force that now threatened to flank the Karellan flagship, and her escorts, in a perfectly executed pincer movement.

Outnumbering the Talisians fifteen to one, the Karellans and their Saurian leaders remained confident of victory. It was only when Sobek ordered Molok to commit half of his invasion force to repelling the battleships from Zia that the full extent of Talisian deception became clear.

Molok's hysterical transmissions were garbled – jammed at their source. What little could be deciphered, suggested that the invasion force, a third of the entire Karellan fleet, was engaged in desperate battles with 'exceptionally dishonourable humans who fought in the most cowardly and deceptive manner'. And their space blockade encountered 'evil, carnivorous monsters that mysteriously materialised on every orbital bomber'.

But the Karellans and their over-confident Saurian manipulators in the main attacking force, remained unaware that the 'evil, carnivorous monsters' were actually the fierce dinosaur-like teroseriak, indigenous of Miru. Under Prince Armon's direction, the six-metre long predators were infected with serivelen five-one-two, a nanoviral agent that specifically targeted Saurian DNA. These vicious biological weapons were transported aboard the Karellan warships, exploiting a flaw in Saurian battleship shield technology.

Intelligent but inexperienced, the frantic, beleaguered Molok finally used his initiative and attempted to intercept the Zian armada with eighteen of the twenty-four orbital bombers under his command.

But Rin Mur-Rain ordered the detonation of the entire Miruvian minefield. Three Karellan bombers, including Molok's ship, the Habu, were completely destroyed, six were crippled and the fifteen that remained lacked effective shields or sensors. Whether they knew it or not, their crews, exposed to lethal levels of radiation, were condemned to a slow, agonising death.

Armon projected to Rin, *"Margrave Rin, I need six of your most trusted warriors for a special mission."*

"Have you received news of your father, My Lord?"

"No."

"Armon, without the support of the 1st Wave, our situation is utterly hopeless. We can probably endure another hour, maybe two at best, before we are completely overrun by the enemy."

"Yes Rin, I know. The Emperor will be here soon."

"Not a word for months, then an urgent communiqué bearing the Imperial seal, ordering that we engage Karella here and now. Have you received other news?"

"Yes, I believe Brakis Tarn is alive."

"Alive you say? Your reports indicated that the Butcher of Cyclo was killed by a thermal grenade."

"It seems only his body was destroyed."

"This is the most critical phase of our engagement with the Karellans, and we have no plan for dealing with Brakis Tarn."

"Leave Brakis Tarn to me."

"Is there any other news?"

"I believe the Saurians can compromise our new modulated shields."

"The shields used on the Kach were designed to give the Karellans that impression, but I assure you..."

"Prepare to be boarded by enemy forces, Margrave."

"As you wish, Your Highness."

"We just have to hold on a little while longer. My father is coming. Victory will be ours; I can feel it."

"May the scribes record it."

Rin turned to his shamira and said, "Commander Goren, have six of your finest men assemble in corridor zero-one heavily armed. There they are to await instructions from His Highness, The Prince Armon."

"By your will, Your Grace."

"This is the perfect opportunity; we must proceed with operation Hammer," Goren projected privately, *"Do I have your authorisation?"*

Goren activated his comlink and hesitated. This hesitation, and the subtle tightening of Goren's square jaw, did not go unnoticed by Chi-Ro Jin.

"Your Grace, do I have your authorisation?"

"No Goren, you do not."

Effectively masking his disappointment, Goren barked into his comlink, "Captain Taro Dao, assemble your five best men and report to corridor zero-one immediately. Once there, you shall await further instructions."

Chi-Ro Jin solemnly expressed his approval, with the slightest of nods, then turned and followed Prince Armon Sakara as he swept off the flagship's bridge.

Margrave Rin Mur-Rain entered his ready room accompanied by his sullen shamira. Armon's cousin immediately walked to the wall behind his desk and placed his right palm firmly on it. Directly below his palm, the door to a hidden compartment slid aside revealing an ornate, translucent crystal bottle of Miruvian medovina. The bottle was on a silver tray with six highball glass tumblers.

Rin snatched the bottle, twisted its cap free, poured the reddish-brown liquid filling a glass, then offered it to Goren. Goren declined. With a shrug, Rin pressed the glass to his lips, sipped the potent alcoholic beverage, swallowed and grimaced.

He activated his holographic viewscreen, took another sip of Miruvian medovina that caused him to grimace once more, and intently observed the desperate space battle raging around them.

Without looking at Goren, Rin asked, "Merciful Great Spirit, what would you have me do?"

"You must do what is required to safeguard the Talisian Empire, Your Grace."

Continuing to avoid Goren's gaze, his voice thick with remorse, Rin said, "History will cast me as a villain."

"The scribes will record that The Prince Armon, his consort Soraya and the Margravine Ishma were all victims of Karellan treachery. It is painfully obvious this Prince, with his naïve pacifist agenda, would make a weak and most inexperienced emperor. Where was this Armon, when Karellan assassins executed four hundred intellectuals at the Forum? How many battles has he fought against our enemies? The Cyclan, Kolan and Anubian Genocides, the Siege of Avaris with two hundred thousand dead, the merciless slaughter of my entire family, your parents, your sister - countless, utterly unforgivable acts of savage barbarism by dishonourable Karellan kak. Will Armon avenge the deaths of Talis's dearest blood? No, this prince speaks of peace with the Karellans blaming the Seriak for every manifestation of Karellan evil. I ask you, are the Prince and his followers Talisian? I hate the Karellans. You hate the Karellans. Every true Talisian hates the Karellans to his very core, and the obtrusive taste is like sour vomit in his mouth. Armon must die, for you alone earned the right to occupy the Emperor's throne, no one else."

Rin turned to stare at Goren long and hard, and then said, "Goren, we both know Armon's consort and unborn child are innocent. As is Ishma, Kiya Mankuria, Chi-Ro Jin and Zac Aree."

"You say this only to provoke me into confirming what you already know to be true, Your Grace. To maintain the Empire, wisdom dictates that, when necessary, you must be devious, unscrupulous, inhumane and disloyal. If

Armon's offspring survives, when he comes of age, he will surely challenge you for the throne. By sparing his life now, you would condemn us to a future, ravaged by yet another terrible civil war. What of the unidentified DNA possessed by members of Armon's court: Soraya Armon, Zac Aree and Kiya Mankuria? Who are they? What are they? It is quite prudent to view them as threats. Despite his mysterious absence the last three years, Chi-Ro Jin still manages to retain the respect of most of the enlisted men of the 9th Wave. He is utterly loyal to the Prince. It would be unwise to view him as anything but extremely dangerous. You have no heir; Ishma is addicted to snow - barren. Divorce would suggest personal weakness, whereas her death, and that of Armon and his entourage, would provide politically acceptable grounds for the utter destruction of our foes. With Ishma dead, Rhia, daughter of Archduke Kan Junai Parentiis, could be your consort."

With fire in his eye, Rin said, "For the last sixty-two years, we have called ourselves Talisians; but let us not conveniently forget our blood-ties or our Karellan ancestry. Any man, who chooses to forget his history, deserves to die and be forgotten. No Goren, though your argument is indeed compelling, I cannot shed the blood of my family nor can I murder the innocent. I will not betray my cousin or my consort. I am no messiah, I know this much; but I do believe the legend of the soter. Armon, or his offspring, is the chosen one. I know it. We both know it; and the thought brings with it a certain degree of terror. Are you not rich enough my friend? Have we not earned our place in history? We cannot defy the will of the Great Spirit. So, inform your men that no harm is to befall Ishma or the Prince and his entourage. That is an order, Goren."

"But..."

"Obey me!" shouted Rin with a sudden, uncharacteristic display of blind rage.

Then, regaining his composure, he added, "This day is still young, ripe with possibilities. We cannot afford to underestimate our Seriak and Karellan enemies. What we do now Goren, affects the fate of the Cosmic Sea."

With a measure of venom, Goren said, "I totally agree, Your Grace."

Then, with blinding speed, Goren drew his Daxia H3-16 pistol and fired. Shot in the chest, Rin toppled backwards across his desk and crashed violently onto the floor on the other side.

Goren spoke into his comlink when he said, "Proceed with Operation Hammer."

Terminating his transmission, Goren slowly walked to where Rin lay helplessly paralysed with pain and shock, his left leg uncomfortably draped over the armrest of his chair.

Rin's eye widened with terrible realisation as Goren stood above him and whispered ominously, "I shall see to it, that history does not cast you as a villain. You die to safeguard the Talisian Empire, Your Grace."

The Margrave desperately launched a concentrated psychic attack, targeting Goren's optic nerves and cardiovascular system, but Goren, a veteran of the Psychic Wars, gradually resisted and counter-attacked.

Wracked with excruciating emotional and physical pain, Rin watched, with increasing anxiety, as his violently trembling shamira slowly, and with Herculean effort, raised his Daxia H3-16 pistol and took aim. The Margrave of Taria closed his eye, bringing all that remained of his psychic faculties to bear. But to his horror, Rin Mur-Rain finally heard the dreadfully distinctive sound of a Daxia H3-16 pistol firing.

Chapter 73

Aboard the Imperial Drac El, in the throne room, at the heart of the citadel, Ne-Ro Jos completed his report to the Saurian disguised as Seti Aljyk. Dressed in his lavish black robe and cape, the False Emperor sat on the dark throne he usurped from Sakara Rey. He focussed his attention on the gigantic holographic display of the raging battle of Miru.

At his right side, stood his new shamira, a surly Kon Jou master called Lokai Zann. Pulled taut over powerful arms and legs, Lokai wore a shimmering tunic of dark grey, which echoed the colour of his cold killer's eyes. Black, shaggy hair framed his pale face, brushing his broad shoulders. Ten paces behind Lokai, the Emperor's twelve unarmed sentinels stood at attention in blood red battlesuits.

Look at this arrogant pretender and the twelve who protect him, thought Ne-Ro, *I know what you are, Seriak. I have always known. You see my followers and I, are completely immune to the poisons you feed us. Our minds are too powerful to be subjected to your pitiful hypnosis. And now, without the Sword of Power you are vulnerable, more vulnerable than you can imagine. Oh yes, Sobek, I know your name. Death whispers it to my resourceful servant Brakis Tarn. And foolish Lokai, if only you knew the true nature of the abomination you have sworn your allegiance to, you would immediately embark on the ritual suicide demanded by your archaic warrior's code. But soon my patience and sacrifice will bring its ultimate reward. The tapestry of prophecy unfurls, granting me, Ne-Ro Jos, the 606th Grandmaster of The Order of Mysteries, the opportunity to become the most powerful individual in the Cosmic Sea.*

"You are certain the son of Sakara is aboard the Starcarrier Shor, Ne-Ro?" asked Seti Aljyk, who continued to watch the holograph of the three Talisian capital ships, breaking formation.

Averting his eyes submissively, Ne-Ro replied, "Yes, Your Majesty."

"And your monks have succeeded in neutralising his psychic power and that of his offspring?"

"Indeed, Your Majesty, not only are our new storm amplifiers ten times stronger than those of the Anhur, they are powered by refined lapys nerian crystals."

"Excellent Ne-Ro, now pray tell, how did you not foresee the insidious traps of Miru?"

"I fear that the same mysterious force, which has robbed you of your ability to communicate telepathically, may have diminished my abilities and those of my disciples, Your Majesty. With our reduced faculties focussed on the daunting task of neutralizing the soter and his father, some minor details continue to escape our psychic gaze."

With unusual restraint, Seti Aljyk focussed his piercing stare on the crimson-clad monk and said, "Minor details? You call the loss of a third of our forces a minor detail?"

Nervousness descended on Ne-Ro Jos, who replied with carefully chosen words, "Your Majesty, I assure you, this setback will not affect the positive outcome of this campaign."

Watch how I cower in your presence, oh Great One. How completely you underestimate humanity. So easily you believe my lies, nothing hinders my faculties. I saw the Talisian plots, foolish Seriak, but they serve my agenda.

Seti Aljyk leaned forward menacingly and said in an ominously low voice, "Perhaps I have placed too much faith in your abilities, soothsayer. Are you certain you have completely purged Armon's imaginary Elosian vipers from your mind?"

Ne-Ro's right eye twitched when he said, "I have fully recovered, Your Majesty."

And, unlike you, I do not need the Sword of Power to give me psychic ability.

Motioning to the holographic display, Seti Aljyk said, "So tell me Ne-Ro, what do you make of this Talisian manoeuvre?"

"Their plan is to encircle us, My Lord."

Seti Aljyk leaned back into the comfort of his throne.

With a low chuckle, he said, "Go now. Return to your inner sanctum. Prepare for the arrival of the son of Sakara and his offspring, Lokai will accompany you."

"Majesty, you do me great honour by assigning your esteemed bodyguard for my protection, but..."

"Do not flatter yourself, soothsayer, Lokai and his men will be concerned with the containment of Armon, not your protection. We cannot risk a repeat of your first encounter with my nephew. It left you rolling about on the floor, like a blithering idiot. Your lack of vision left me physically injured and lacking a shamira. But most importantly, your weakness facilitated Armon's escape with the Sword of Power. You should count yourself most fortunate, that I have not yet executed you for your failure."

Ah, but you need me. Without the sword, you have no prescience. Poor Seriak, if only you knew the real secret of its value. If only you knew the real power of this Niburian marvel.

Ne-Ro bowed low saying, "I deeply appreciate Your Majesty's mercy. I will not fail, this time."

"No Ne-Ro, you will not fail me again."

Haughty Seriak, it is you who will be executed this day. You will join Rin Mur-Rain, who has already taken up residence in Hades. And, since Armon will not be controlled, I have also ordered his death and the capture of his offspring. Soon, after a lifetime of humiliation and subjugation, the Sword of Power, the soter, and the Emperor's throne, will all be mine.

The Imperial Drac El's brutal onslaught left the Shor's transporter system temporarily inoperative. So, with their heavily armed six-man escort, Prince Armon and Chi-Ro Jin walked briskly towards the Shor's citadel.

With reports of Talisian battle-losses, blaring from their military-band communication links, and an intense psychic storm clouding Armon's pre-science, it seemed everything around them sought to increase their sense of foreboding. The Starcarrier Shor shuddered and moaned under the constant barrage of enemy fire. Overhead lights in the corridor dimmed, failed completely, and then were restored.

Armon sensed the steely resolve of his shamira, caught a glimpse of his predatory eyes and heard his unsettling projection: *"Prepare yourself, Master Armon, our escorts plan to assassinate us."*

"What?"

"Clear your mind! Focus. Your life and the lives of those you hold dear hang in the balance. Recall all that I've taught you. Use it now, without hesitation."

Six warriors in attack formation, clad in Karellan shock marine battle-suits, armed with Melcor C-51A rifles, transported into the corridor ahead. They were the grim executors of Operation Hammer - Talisian traitors who would blame the Karellans for the execution of the Prince and his shamira.

The corridor lights failed once more and the helmet lamps of the shadow warriors and shock marines instantly activated. Simultaneously, Armon and Chi-Ro engaged their stealth cloaks, rendering themselves virtually invisible.

Aware of the limits imposed by the Imperial Drac-El's relentless psychic storm, and employing an Iaido-like technique absorbed from Kiya Manku-ria, Armon spun swiftly drawing Najura, the katana-like Sword of Power, and a rush of enhanced awareness instantly flooded his senses. But Armon found his face level with the barrel of Captain Taro Dao's Aknon 604 'Liberator' rifle.

Intending to deflect the weapon, Armon slashed instinctively with his lapys nerian sword. But, instead of deflecting it, Armon's Najura effortlessly sliced through the Karellan rifle and the hands holding it, like a hot knife through butter.

A sustained hail of fire, from Chi-Ro's viridian pistol, instantly extinguished Taro Dao's screams, and the lives of the two traitors nearest to him. The fake shock marines opened fire with a lethal barrage, which neutralised the remaining three Talisian shadow warriors but failed to hit the cloaked prince and his loyal shamira.

Raising his right arm, the leader of the Karellan impostors motioned his troops to stop firing.

His synthesised voice cried, "They are employing some kind of cloak, switch to enhanced audio."

Then suddenly, an ear-piercing sound shattered the brief silence. It was Chi-Ro Jin, with his helmet removed and no longer cloaked, producing a high-pitched sound on his flute. With their audio receptors switched to maximum, the assassins screamed in agony. Two collapsed from sensory overload and perforated eardrums; while the remaining four fired blindly, missing their intended victims who had swiftly moved behind them.

Only at point blank range would their weapons be effective against the heavily shielded shock marine battlesuit armour. And so, with single bursts from his viridian pistol, Chi-Ro neutralised two assassins and, with the Sword of Power, Armon impaled another.

The leader of the assassins turned swiftly, intending to fire, but Armon expertly sliced the assassin's rifle in two. Then, in blind desperation, the frantic leader reached for a thermal grenade on his utility belt. But, in Iaido fashion, Armon swept the Sword of Power in a perfect arc, delivering a single blow to his assailant's shoulder that took off his right arm.

Returning Najura to its scabbard with expert fluidity and precision, Armon left a neat central line of his would-be assassins' blood spatter on the metal floor of the corridor.

The one-armed man fell to the ground screaming in agony. Chi-Ro immediately pinned him where he lay, quickly removing his grenades and pistol. Then, leaving nothing to chance, Chi-Ro drew his father's dagger and used it to disable the suicide module situated amongst the left forearm controls on the assassin's battlesuit. Having successfully disabled the traitor's ability to turn himself into a living bomb, Chi-Ro returned his father's dagger to the scabbard on his waist.

"Who sent you?" screamed Chi-Ro, into the deaf assassin's mind.

"I am Captain Logar Moz, service number KSM-0015-2150-X1A," projected the fallen assassin.

"Do not compound the gravity of your situation by insulting my intelligence. You are Talisian, not Karellan."

The soldier struggled, silently praying for death, as Chi-Ro Jin removed the skull-like Karellan helmet that hid his Talisian features. Chi-Ro took off his own gloves and gripped the screaming man's temples with his bare hands.

"Verily, you know that your resistance is utterly hopeless. So, once again I ask you, who sent you?"

With a large hole at the back of his head, Goren Rag's lifeless body fell to the floor of Rin Mur-Rain's ready room with a loud thud. Then, as the sound of an unseen intruder's footsteps approached, the dying Rin, unable to reach his own pistol because of his failing strength and awkward positioning on the floor, desperately struggled to retrieve Goren's Daxia H3-16 pistol instead.

Just as his fingertips brushed the Daxia's barrel, a gloved hand took the firearm away.

A male voice calmly announced, "It is said, the Great Spirit created men, but Daxia made them equal."

Wide-eyed, Rin stared at the intruder with a look of utter disbelief etched on his face. There, on the floor of his ready room, in a state of shock, the Margrave Rin Mur-Rain took his final breath, and the intruder's gloved fingertips gently closed his lifeless eye.

Chapter 74

In the desperate battle for space superiority, the outnumbered Talisians in their sleek Noorstrum Sun Mark IX Starfires offered stiff resistance to the Karellans and their slower but more heavily armed Koroba RA-97 Raiders. There were heroes on both sides as humans, clones, Saurians and androids engaged in the bloodiest space battle of the Psychic Wars.

Against the odds, veteran starfire pilots, Majors Kong Garee and Tohm Salahee, call signs Chigaru and Bulta, survived five hours of sustained fighting and continued to lead what remained of their respective squadrons.

In the hands of such seasoned war veterans, the new starfires with their superior speed, range and manoeuvrability had so far won the day against the older Karellan raiders and their relatively inexperienced pilots.

But, as the grim events of the sixth hour of the battle of Miru unfolded, a mysterious Karellan raider launched a dramatically distinguished sortie. This lone raider did not broadcast a transponder signal and had no escort. Curiously defiant and recklessly isolated, the fighter destroyed all opposition within thirty seconds of engagement, quickly invoking Talisian fear and earning Karellan admiration.

Repeated calls by Karellan Fighter Command, for the unregistered raider pilot's identification, got only comm-static. Within just half an hour of battle, the lone raider gained nineteen kills and assumed a relentlessly daring flight-path, on an apparent suicide mission, towards the heavily protected bridge of the Starcarrier Shor.

Inside the citadel of the Talisian flagship, Lady Soraya Armon, Margravine Ishma Rin, Kiya Mankuria and Lady Capella Hezion barely survived the treachery of those sworn to protect them. Following Goren Rag's orders, six members of the Emperor's Own Psion Police hand-picked by Margrave Rin Mur-Rain and twelve shadow warriors wearing Karellan battlesuits, attempted to murder the women under operation Hammer.

Despite the arrogant boasts of the Karellan soothsayer Ne-Ro Jos, the abilities of Soraya's unborn child were greatly impaired but not completely neutralised. The formidable psychic storm, produced by Ne-Ro's dark monks of The Mysterium, could not prevent Soraya from once again employing telekinesis in self-defence.

Applying the will power that only a mother protecting her child could muster, Soraya mentally hampered the physical movements of the would-be assassins. As if in a dream, she observed the precise grace, fluidity of action and focussed lethality of Kiya Mankuria and Capella Hezion as they shot seven of their betrayers at point-blank range.

Four alert shadow warriors, trained by Chi-Ro Jin, traded shots with the remaining traitors. In a matter of seconds, three loyal guards were wounded; five civilians, two shadow warriors and all the assassins had been killed.

As their lifeless bodies slumped to the floor, Soraya marvelled at the fact that she felt not even the slightest remorse for the traitors.

In fact, she could almost hear her grandmother saying with her distinctly sing-song voice, tempered by advanced age, *"Crapaud smoke dey pipe!"*

The men were killed within seconds and almost instantly, panic ensued among the other dignitaries and aristocrats seeking refuge in the citadel.

Shamiras shielded their wards - defensive weapons at the ready and uncorrupted shadow warriors trained their rifles menacingly. All eyes focussed on Kiya and Capella with their pistols drawn and personal shields activated. They stood poised to deal death to anyone threatening their charges. Everyone present seemed to hold his or her breath; and for a painfully tense moment, thick silence descended on the stronghold.

Then suddenly, Capella barked grimly, "I am Lady Capella Hezion, shamira of Margravine Ishma of Taria. You will lower your weapons!"

The armed occupants of the Shor's stronghold hesitated, prompting an enraged Ishma to scream, "Are you deaf? Lower your weapons now!"

Reluctantly, rifles were lowered, and pistols returned to their holsters. Almost instantly, the sobs of children and the din of heated discussion replaced the silence, as the eminent civilians and their bodyguards attempted to come to terms with the assassination attempt.

Orphaned at an early age, Lady Capella Hezion adored Sakara Rey whom she considered her surrogate father. Soraya had quickly befriended the widowed Capella, Roman's distant cousin, whose dark features, long, braided hair and strong South Avaris accent made her seem almost West Indian. Like a Trinidadian, Capella smiled warmly with the least provocation.

To Soraya, Capella's personal qualities seemed very much at odds with the sober task of protecting the Margravine. Ishma was a strikingly beautiful woman who always managed to seem distant, mentally preoccupied, fragile and cold. The faint scent of alcohol on her breath and her occasionally slurred speech had earned Rin's melancholy consort Soraya's heart-felt pity. That pity became almost overpowering when, after the initial shock, Soraya observed Ishma's gradual realisation of what had just occurred. Abandoning any pretence of a stiff upper lip, the once proud woman soon crumbled into a terrified, loudly sobbing bundle of nerves.

Somehow Soraya knew that Roman had been unharmed. She felt like a ghost, observing herself, watching the crying Ishma. Soraya imagined that her body remained in the citadel while her very essence accompanied her husband, fiercely battling his way to her side.

I must be in shock, she thought, *I feel no fear.*

Then, Soraya's attention turned to Kiya. Struck by the depth of sincere concern and overwhelming heartbreak she observed in her lime-green eyes, Soraya impassively watched the Osirian woman holster her viridian pistol, tighten her jaw and struggle to contain her own emotions.

Kiya was about to speak to Soraya, when Prince Armon's telepathic projection confirmed what the four women already knew but desperately did not want to accept. Rin and Goren had devised a plot to eliminate Ishma, the Prince, and his entourage. Then, Armon relayed even more shocking news. An unknown assassin had killed both the Margrave and his shamira.

An inconsolable Ishma, grieving the recent death of her beloved brother and fighting a losing battle against drug-induced delusions of persecution, lacked the strength to cope with either Rin's callous betrayal or his terrible death.

So, in desperation, the Margravine Ishma of Taria, daughter of Badra Ging of Malobar, while still embracing her shamira, Lady Capella, and sobbing loudly, suddenly drew Capella's Daxia H3-16 pistol and quickly shot herself in the left anterior chest.

"No, Mistress, no," cried Lady Capella, gently lowering Ishma to the cold, metallic floor.

Struggling to hide her own grief, Kiya rushed to the Margravine's side, swiftly joined by Soraya.

With the warship's matter transfer system offline, Ishma could not be quickly transported to the ship's infirmary nor could medical androids be downloaded.

A qualified nurse, Soraya instantly noticed the sound of air passing through Ishma's chest wound with each shallow, rapid respiration. Soraya correctly deduced that, at the very least, Ishma's left lung and heart suffered irreparable injury. Although conscious and in shock, not even the most basic medical knowledge was required to surmise that Ishma had just moments to live.

Instinctively, through sheer force of will, Soraya attempted to prevent Ishma's death. Instead, for a few seconds that seemed like minutes, Soraya experienced the Margravine's extreme shock and excruciating pain. It was enough to render Soraya unconscious, and she plummeted like a puppet whose strings had been unexpectedly cut. Kiya quickly grabbed the pregnant Soraya, preventing her from falling to the floor.

Moments later, when Soraya slowly regained consciousness, reclined in the arms of her Osirian shamira, she found to her dismay, that Ishma had already died.

With Talisian reinforcements relentlessly converging on the Imperial Drac El's position, the Karellans employed a previously unseen non-nuclear electromagnetic pulse weapon. A vast majority of Talisian Jinzou Ningen, within one thousand kilometres of the Karellan flagship, suffered brief unconsciousness, disorientation and confusion. The EMP also caused widespread damage to Talisian shield-generators, communication arrays, matter transporters and psychic storm amplifiers.

So, despite several frantic attempts, Prince Armon was unable to warn his friend, Dr. Zachary Silverman of the imminent plot against his life. Encountering Karellan shock marines, at almost every turn in the Shor's dimly lit corridors, Armon Sakara and Chi-Ro Jin barely made it to the citadel alive.

Then, inside the compromised stronghold, a scene of horrific death greeted them. In a grotesque portrait of interstellar warfare, the plasma-riddled bodies of Talisian shadow warriors, Psion Police and unfortunate aristocrats lay beside similarly killed Karellan shock marines. There, amongst the numerous dead, Chi-Ro Jin found the abandoned corpse of Ishma, Margravine of Taria; but found no trace of Soraya, Kiya or Capella.

"I do not believe they have been killed or captured," claimed Chi-Ro, in an effort to reassure the concerned Prince.

"Then where the hell are they?"

Suddenly, a massive tremor rocked the Shor, plunging the battle-wracked citadel into darkness. Then another much larger shockwave sent Chi-Ro and Armon sprawling onto the cold floor. Seconds later, rising to their feet in the smoke-filled gloom, they experienced a sudden decline in gravity, which had Armon fighting an almost irrepressible urge to vomit.

Chi-Ro was already drawing his holstered weapon, when the distinctly neon-green bolt of a viridian pistol streaked past the Prince. The sustained energy vaporised an unshielded shock marine, who had previously feigned death and now took deadly aim with a Blastron M-24 rifle.

Swiftly spinning on their heels with pistols drawn, Armon and Chi-Ro spied the tall, slim silhouette of a man in the smoky entrance to the citadel.

A vaguely familiar male voice, said haughtily, "I see age has made you careless Chi-Ro, son of Jin."

Then suddenly, with the mysterious man already in motion, Chi-Ro Jin fired through the doorway, stunning another shock marine who appeared behind him. Stumbling backwards, discharging his Blastron rifle, the dazed Karellan was cut down by a lethal hail of green fire from the shadowy figure.

Chi-Ro said calmly, "It appears age has similarly affected you, Nook Tigg."

Armon's heart skipped a beat, as the slim dark man, dressed in a weather-beaten Osirian stealth suit, holstered his pistol and walked into the dim light emanating from a malfunctioning wall console.

Gone were the long black hair and full beard the Prince remembered so vividly, replaced by a crew cut peppered with a tinge of grey and a clean-shaven face that seemed untouched by the rigors of time.

"Perhaps the Karellan psychic storm impairs our faculties, more than we would like to admit," said Nook Tigg dryly.

For a tense moment, Armon just stared into the deep blue eyes he had not seen since his early childhood.

"I thought you were dead," he muttered, scarcely believing that his old mentor was actually standing before him.

"Indeed," said Nook Tigg, then he projected privately, *"It grieves me to know my absence once again caused you pain, Manuk. But I assure you it was necessary."*

'Manuk', the nickname Nook Tigg gave me, all those years ago in Trinidad. A name I've told no one. This is my old, not-so-imaginary friend.

Armon rushed forward and embraced the tall, dark man.

Deeply touched by this show of affection, Nook Tigg whispered with a lump in his throat, "I will never abandon you again, my son."

Stepping back to look into his old mentor's blue eyes, Armon asked, "Where have you been?"

"As they say, in that place we both call home, I've been undercover."

They laughed, compelling Chi-Ro to raise a puzzled eyebrow. Then he asked with a subtle hint of accusation, "Commander Nook Tigg, did you kill the Margrave of Taria?"

"No General, I arrived in time to hear the traitor Goren Rag issue the order to assassinate the Prince. With my viridian pistol, I was able to stop him from shooting, His Grace the Margrave, a second time. Unfortunately, Goren's first shot proved to be fatal."

"You are certain the Margrave did not issue the order to murder the Prince?"

"I am. And now gentlemen, we must leave this vessel at once," said Nook Tigg motioning for Chi-Ro and Armon to follow him into the corridor. "We will join Princess Soraya and her shamira. My cloaked ship is parked in the main hangar I dare not risk matter transfer after the recent electromagnetic pulse."

Hesitating, and then referring gravely to the fallen Margravine, Armon said, "We shouldn't leave Ishma like this."

Nook Tigg replied earnestly, "Princess Soraya has already convinced me to accommodate Lady Capella. I've only room for the living on my small ship. I regret I must leave the dead to tend the dead."

Armon muttered regretfully, "OK let's go," and swooned as the Shor's artificial gravity fluctuated once more.

Chi-Ro's firm grip steadied Armon.

Nook Tigg said perceptively, "This sudden change in gravity takes some getting used to."

Embarrassed, Armon declared softly, "I'm fine, let's go."

Using helmet lamps to illuminate their path, Armon, Chi-Ro and Nook Tigg quickly made their way through the stricken Starcarrier Shor's darkened corridors.

Chi-Ro projected privately, *"Commander, I was not aware that Lady Soraya has been formally granted princely status by the True Emperor."*

"A mere formality General. I assure you, news of Armon's valiant deeds, and those of his impressive consort, has already reached His Majesty's regal ear."

With the sounds of conflict echoing throughout the dying ship, the men came upon two disorientated, purple-eyed women, dressed in bloodstained garments that left little to the imagination. One of the women tried to speak, but simply threw up. Then her malfunctioning companion fired bursts from a compact fire extinguisher at her.

This bizarre, morbidly comical sight, prompted Armon to recall Zachary saying, *"War is hell."*

Displaying complete indifference to the confused androids, Nook Tigg said, "Ne-Ro Jos desperately seeks the Sword of Power, and I was unable to stop the cloned abomination he dispatched to retrieve it."

Chi-Ro growled contemptuously, "Brakis Tarn."

"Indeed. The Butcher of Cyclo has destroyed the Shor's bridge by crashing his raider into it. With his advanced astral abilities, it's highly unlikely he has committed suicide."

Coming to a halt, Armon said with solemn confidence, "Yes, he's alive, and I must face him."

"You must not," said Chi-Ro firmly.

"Agreed," said Nook Tigg, turning to face the Prince, "You have yet to learn the secret of Najura."

Suspicion became sudden realisation, which prompted Armon to ask, "What do you know about the sword?"

"It is Niburian..."

"As are you," interrupted Armon.

Taken aback, unable to hide his astonishment, Nook Tigg replied with an impressed smile, "Yes Your Highness, I am Niburian."

Armon solemnly pressed, "So, Nook Tigg, what is the secret power of the sword?"

"It is rumoured that only Ne-Ro Jos knows it's secret, which is why it must be kept from him at all costs. Translated from a Niburian dialect that died some thirty thousand years before the Amphitheatrum Flavium was built, Najura literally means 'key'."

The Flavian Amphitheatre, the original name of the Colosseum of Imperial Rome. He senses my scepticism and hopes to reassure me that he actually is who he appears to be; by mentioning a fact only someone versed in Earth history would know.

"According to Niburian legend," continued Nook Tigg, "there were three swords - Najura the nerian key, Salya the viridian timepiece and Anikou the ruberian scythe. Najura was first discovered six hundred years ago during archaeological excavations in the Talisian capital city of Avaris. It disappeared during the War of the Archons fifty years later, only to reappear one hundred and seventy years ago in a Mara Kai monastery on the distant world of Asorya. Salya and Anikou have never been found. Place your hands on my temples Prince Armon. Quickly learn all that I know."

Chapter 75

"Silence!" growled Sobek contemptuously, at the only other occupant of the Imperial Drac El's citadel.

Sheerak, the Saurian general disguised as Arved Rahn, Duke of Criesse, knelt submissively before the False Emperor seated on Sakara Rey's throne.

Nostrils flared - dark visage contorted with malice; Sobek resumed his vindictive verbal assault, "Your poor judgment in assigning your illegitimate son Molok the task of invading Miru has directly led to the loss of a third of our forces. Oh, you thought I didn't know about your little bastard."

Leaning forward on the dark throne, the Saurian impersonating Seti Al-jyk lowered his voice to an ominous whisper. "Well, I've always known about that spawn of a Slagornian dung-eating newt. And your other misbegotten progeny, that feathered throwback you hid in the Ba'lkar-Zhūl Cloister on Gome. Sheerak, do you not realise that thousands of humans have been contaminated with radiation? They are utterly inedible. Inedible! Now you dare to kneel before me, with your pathetic request that I deploy Asmorda. How could my sister be bonded to one such as you? Can you not see we would lose the vital element of surprise? No Sheerak, Sakara Rey must be lured out of hiding. Then and only then will Asmorda be deployed."

Wisely, Sheerak remained silently passive.

He bowed even lower as Sobek rose from the throne and said solemnly, "Your recent performance has been a source of great disappointment to me, General. Consider our long friendship dissolved. I need not remind you what fate awaits, should you fail me again. I shall retire now. The day's events have left me with a debilitating migraine; see to it I am not disturbed."

"Yes, Lord Sobek."

"And Sheerak, once Armon and his consort are in custody, have the animal Ne-Ro Jos slaughtered. More and more, I see the flicker of foul treachery in his eyes. Though our food appears not to agree with us, we will nevertheless win this battle."

Averting his gaze, Sheerak replied, "By your will, Lord Sobek."

Turning away from his dejected subordinate, Sobek walked towards the hidden door to a small antechamber, which led to his Imperial Suite. Suddenly, the low hum of an energy discharge, a pungent animal scent, instantly followed by an ear-shattering roar, had the Saurian leader reaching for the pistol that now replaced the Sword of Power.

Terror gripped his reptilian heart when he turned to discover that Sheerak had been bitten in two by a bull teroseriak, and another was already in full charge ferociously towards him. He opened fire into the torso of the attacking predator, then leapt out of the way as the mortally wounded teroseriak fell and slid towards him on the polished floor of the throne room. With a bone-crushing thud, the dying beast crashed into the wall adjacent to the door of the antechamber.

Simultaneously, the second creature dropped the mangled remains of Sheerak to the bloodstained floor and instinctively launched a furious attack of its own. But, quickly scrambling to trembling feet, Sobek back-pedalled and fired several shots from his modified Blastron P-55, killing the second monster.

Immediately, Sobek became aware of the muffled sounds of gunfire, frenzied animal roars and the hopeless screams of his guards behind the closed doors of the throne room.

My protective shields have been deactivated, he observed, *I have been betrayed!*

Using the command device he always wore on his left wrist, Sobek attempted to initiate emergency transport to the Asmorda, the cloaked Saurian battleship intended for the ambush and utter destruction of Sakara Rey.

But, after several desperate attempts, it became painfully obvious to Sobek, that there would be no quick getaway from the Imperial Drac El's besieged citadel.

In the seconds it took Sobek to overcome his initial shock, he repeatedly shot the fallen predators ensuring they were dead. Then he entered the Imperial Suite; and he briskly walked between the two long rows of black, highly polished pedestals bearing disembodied heads of eminent Karellans and Talisians. These included Duke Arved Rahn, Baron Godric Calla, General Beric Naya and Commodore Kaitas Grinn. All were perfectly preserved and proudly displayed in identical, sealed, transparent, fluid-filled jars. All of these notable humans, whose bodies were ceremoniously eaten by the Saurian invaders, seemed to stare vengefully at the increasingly panicked False Emperor.

Sobek finally approached the real Seti Aljyk's head. The lifeless eyes of Armon's murdered uncle stared silently at the reptilian alien that now hid behind a replica of his face. The dead man's stare added to the alien commander's unease.

Despite the many warnings I have issued regarding the dangers of underestimating humans, I have myself managed to fall foul of their cunning treachery. How could I be so utterly stupid?

Sobek's mind raced through a myriad of possibilities, clues, suspicions and fears.

How could all my meticulous precautions, all my well-placed plans come to this? Can the humans really be this intelligent? Do these animals have the capacity to outsmart some of the best military minds of the Saurian race? Or are Niburians, or even rogue Saurians, assisting them? The Niburian shape-shifters, our former masters who became our slaves and then later our livestock. Are they behind this? Is this to be their revenge? What of the possibility of Saurian treachery? The Queen never favoured me, of that I am certain, but I always had the approval of my cousin the King. Could it be that the King no longer has faith in my abilities?

Suddenly, a low growl followed by a loud thump on an outer wall, had Sobek back-pedalling, holding his pistol threateningly, and acutely anticipating another teroseriak attack.

Sobek's personal communicator activated, and he immediately felt a sense of relief.

The Asmorda's crew is aware of my plight. My salvation is at hand, he thought.

"Your Majesty Seti Aljyk," came the familiar nasal whine of Ne-Ro Jos.

Dread instantly replaced relief, and Sobek felt his recent lunch of fried infant human legs, served on an exquisitely prepared bed of Maripenay rice, garnished with parisum and coriak, rising irrepressibly in his stomach.

Ne-Ro Jos. When I leave this place, I shall slit his slimy throat myself. Watching his death throes may provide some measure of much-needed amusement.

"Ne-Ro, there are wild beasts threatening my Imperial Person," declared Sobek with more than a modicum of anger.

"Yes Your Majesty, I know," came Ne-Ro's flat, tempered monotone.

"You know?" said Sobek, somehow managing not to explode.

Is this repugnant creature the architect of this current assassination attempt?

"It appears the Talisians have somehow exploited a flaw in our security shields," said Ne-Ro with unusual coolness.

"What incredible deductive abilities you possess, soothsayer. I require immediate transport out of my apartment," said Sobek, no longer able to mask his rage.

Using carefully controlled pitch and tone to deliver his disdainfully mocking statement, Ne-Ro said, "Where does His Majesty wish to be transported? Let me guess, perhaps His Majesty would like to flee to the cloaked warship that now shadows the Imperial Drac El's every move. The Talisians were unable to breach its shields, which is why I impersonated His Majesty and ordered the captain of the cloaked ship, the Asmorda, to lower his shields. I fear the captain and his bridge crew were the first to be devoured by the fierce teroseriaks the Talisians delivered to them."

"What?" screamed Sobek, shocked to the point of gagging on a sickening mixture of bile and baby flesh.

"Oh yes, it appears the wily Talisians have been starving the beasts, to ensure that they are ravenously hungry. Can you believe they also infected the creatures with a nanoviral agent? Remarkably, it seems this agent is completely harmless to humans; but tests have shown it is a virulent pathogen, fatal to a species we call the Seriak."

"What?" screamed Sobek, this time even louder.

Feeling as if the blood vessels in his cranium threatened to burst, the Saurian leader swooned and leaned against the jar containing the head of Seti Aljyk. The jar fell to the ground with a loud crash that sent liquid, small shards and the severed head of Seti Aljyk spilling across the floor.

And still, the lifeless eyes of the beheaded Seti Aljyk seemed to stare at Sobek accusingly.

"What indeed," continued Ne-Ro, savouring his victory, "The Seriak are reptilian creatures that call themselves Saurians. They were bio-engineered by another race, the noble Neph Alim Principality, driven to the brink of extinction by the evil Niburians and their human pets. But that's another story for another time. Would you not agree, Emperor Seti Aljyk? Or should I call you Sobek, Warlord of the Seriak?"

Sobek became hysterical. He swore, issued threats, begged, shot several disembodied heads and wailed. The teroseriak that materialised behind him went unnoticed for two seconds. That was a second longer than it took the predator's puny brain to decide whether to attack. Talisian scribes would later record that, regardless of where they were, all the beings aboard the Imperial Drac El heard Sobek's final terrified screams.

Chapter 76

On the deck of the Starcarrier Kach's darkened citadel, lying on his back, winded, and in a state of debilitating shock, Dr. Zachary Silverman pushed away the lifeless body of Rhys Kadar that pinned him to the metal floor. The young shamira valiantly gave his life protecting Zachary from lethal gunfire. Gunfire delivered by a most unlikely assassin.

When Mula, General Quat's tear-ridden consort approached, Zachary prepared himself for the tedious task of consoling the apparently fearful woman; while reinforcing her image of him as a dangerous and unstable assassin. But, perceiving a threat, the dutiful Rhys immediately moved to intercept Mula.

"Don't worry I know her," Zachary recalled whispering with confidence, "She's harmless."

Those were almost my last words. Unbelievable. The little shit tried to kill me, and if Rhys, poor sod, wasn't so quick on the draw, she would have. What the hell could Mula possibly stand to gain from killing me?

With the trauma caused by Mula's assassination attempt swiftly subsiding and his elidium-induced euphoria wearing thin, Zachary became more and more aware of the screams of women and children and the distinctive sound of energy weapons being discharged in the doomed Kach's stronghold. Through the smoke, in the dim emergency light, among the dead and the dying, he observed out-numbered Talisians battling steadily increasing waves of invading Karellan shock marines.

My God, where are the twins?

His pulse racing, Zachary slowly turned his face to the left. And there, to his dismay, lying next to Mula's dead body, with his lifeless eyes frozen in a terrified stare, was the young Baronet Apel Masuvi.

Paralysed with overwhelming grief that immediately replaced any remnants of shock, Zachary closed his tear-filled eyes. Then suddenly, a stray energy bolt slammed into the corpse of Rhys Kadar, instantly snapping Zachary out of his temporary emotional crisis and prying his stubborn eyes wide open.

Zachary saw Lady Nayri Masuvi's wounded and disorientated shamira absorb a final hail of rapid fire from Karellan Blastron M-24 rifles. And blind, seething rage instantly banished his grief and fear. He watched as the dying Jinzou Ningen bodyguard plummeted to the floor shielding her elfin charge. Trapped under the weight of her fallen shamira, the child Nayri remained transfixed in terror, unable to scream or cry.

Zachary's overwhelming emotions, coupled with the elidium in his bloodstream, triggered a chain reaction, and a tingling sensation in his spine swiftly grew and spread throughout his body. He felt incredibly powerful, and he would use this power to avenge the death of his shamira. He would use this power to destroy those who would callously slaughter innocent children.

Briefly, Zachary's mind projected through space and time, basking in blissful clarity. Then, with a low growl, he rose to his feet, no longer a man, but a vengeful wraith imbued with astral energy.

Relentlessly, the matchless Kon Jou master, Brakis Tarn, made his way to the Starcarrier Shor's main hangar deck, effortlessly killing all who chose to challenge him. Brakis Tarn shrugged away the sudden feeling that a new, unforeseen source of danger had been created in the Cosmic Sea. Foremost in his mind was his recurring dream; a dream in which he held the Sword of Power and Armon's body lay at his feet.

It is my destiny.

His last encounter with Prince Armon, and the months he spent as a disembodied wraith had only served to make Brakis Tarn even more powerful. His new clone body had the vigour and vitality of a Karellan forty years younger. And, from Armon's untrained mind, he had extracted the ability to transform his cloned flesh into astral matter at will.

In his mind's eye, Brakis Tarn observed the progress of Armon, Chi-Ro and Nook, as they fought their way to Soraya, Kiya and Capella, waiting expectantly in the lone starchariot parked in the Starcarrier Shor's main hangar.

My lapys nerian sok-bou prototype will be more than a match for the Sword of Power in Armon's inexperienced hands. Soon, I will have my revenge. Soon, Armon Sakara and Chi-Ro Jin will lay dead at my feet; and the key, the Sword of Power, will finally be mine.

Reclined in a life-supporting pod, aboard Nook Tigg's starchariot, Soraya battled the urge to vomit once more. The sudden loss of gravity, following the collision of Brakis Tarn's raider with the Shor's bridge, caused Soraya to vomit twice during the dangerous trek from the citadel to the main hangar. With each passing moment, the fierce interstellar battle intensified, as did her fear for the safety of her unborn child and endangered husband.

In an attempt to cope with her anxiety, Soraya focussed her attention on her silent companions. Kiya sat in the vessel's command pod, wearing the command helmet with a frown of deep concentration. Standing next to an adjacent pod, her jaw taut with suppressed sorrow, Capella observed the raging space battle on the ship's holographic display.

Though Capella blamed herself for Ishma's death, Soraya sensed Roman's cousin would not resort to the ritual suicide demanded by the centuries-old Talisian code of honour.

Even so, it would be a long time before she ever forgives herself.

However, what most intrigued Soraya were the subtle changes she observed in Kiya's disposition.

Though Kiya hides it very well, I can sense her extreme agitation. At first, it seemed like a reaction to the shocking news that Rin betrayed us all; and was killed. Oh yes, Kiya... Kiya loved him; but her agitation may be a symptom of something else, something physical rather than emotional. Could Kiya be affected by the Karellan's electromagnetic pulse? But that would mean...

"How do you feel now, Mistress Soraya?" came Capella's despondent voice, interrupting Soraya's train of thought.

"I feel much better, thank you. The metal disc you placed on my forehead, how does it work?"

"The augmenter serves many functions. The sudden loss of gravity, and resultant change in equilibrium and perception caused your brain to conclude you were hallucinating due to poison ingestion. And so, your brain induced vomiting to clear the imaginary toxin. The augmenter simply assisted my attempt to convince your brain that there was no ingestion of poison and, therefore, no need to expel your stomach's contents. However, despite your polite response, I sense you still feel nauseous. Your brain must be quite stubborn."

Soraya clasped Capella's hand in her own and chuckled, "Yeah Capella, I see there's no foolin' you. At least the gravity in this ship is normal. In a moment, I'm sure I'll be okay."

Finally, a faint smile broke Capella's gloom, and she said, "May the scribes record it."

Her smile did not last. Suddenly the starchariot's alert klaxon blared a stern warning and a grim-faced Capella swiftly returned to her pod.

"What is it?" cried Soraya, above the din.

The ship's computer verbalised Kiya's mental response, "Incoming. Zero point torpedoes. The hangar's shields have not been fully restored. Complete destruction is likely. Initiating emergency launch."

"Wait, what about Roman?" screamed Soraya, without thinking.

"Unable to establish transport lock. Prepare for lift-off."

Despite Soraya's continued protests, the starchariot's sub-light engines rumbled to life and Kiya willed the vessel swiftly towards the open hangar bay doors.

"Not enough time, we have to jump!" cried Capella.

"Inadvisable," came Kiya's computer-generated voice.

As the zero point torpedoes impacted, the starchariot cleared the Shor's massive hangar bay doors. And, within seconds, a huge fireball engulfed the escaping vessel, forcing Kiya to accept that she had no choice.

Kiya's mind screamed the command, *"Jump!"*

The wake of the starchariot's hyper-spatial jump ripped through the Shor's weakened protective shields and added to the damage caused by the Imperial Drac El's torpedoes.

Prince Armon had been racing ahead of his companions, when the zero point torpedoes struck the Shor. Uncontrolled decompression violently propelled him through an airlock into a large antechamber, which led to the main hangar deck. Desperately grabbing a loose power conduit, he prevented himself from being sucked into outer space through the hull breach.

Briefly engulfed by flames and struggling to endure the immense forces that tugged at his body, Armon watched helplessly as the airlock sealed shut, separating him from Chi-Ro Jin and Nook Tigg.

As he dangled horizontally, unsecured objects shot past Armon and were expelled from the large antechamber along with vented air. Gripping the power conduit with all his might, Armon thanked God for his Osirian stealth suit's fire-retardant properties and emergency oxygen supply.

Then, to Armon's relief, the starcarrier's automated systems established a containment field around the hull breach and he plummeted to the deck with a loud thud. Rising slowly, and unsteadily to his feet, he tried unsuccessfully to open the airlock. And, despite several attempts, he could not mentally project to his companions on the other side of the blast-resistant door. A quick glance at his left wrist confirmed that his comlink was damaged.

Suddenly, like the icy fingers of death, a chill ran down his spine and he experienced a disturbing vision of the future. In his mind's eye, Armon saw Brakis Tarn standing above his fallen body, triumphantly holding the Sword of Power. Overwhelmed by terror, Armon turned slowly, and there, at the far end of the antechamber, stood the dark, astral form of the Butcher of Cyclo.

Brakis Tarn.

Chapter 77

In the darkened citadel of the Starcarrier Kach, the surviving Talisians kept their distance from the wraith that seemingly appeared out of nowhere and, to their amazement, smote fourteen heavily armed Karellan shock marines in a matter of seconds.

In stunned silence, they watched the wraith walk towards a terrified little girl. The child, Lady Nayri Masuvi, huddled close to the dead body of her twin brother and sobbed bitterly. Unsure of the wraith's intentions, the armed Talisians instinctively trained their weapons on the dark spectre. It turned to them silently; and, as they stared into the faceless silhouette of a man, terror gripped their souls. They wisely lowered their weapons.

Zachary heard their panicked thoughts.

"Is it Brakis Tarn?"

"Will he harm the child?"

"How can we stop this demon? Our weapons have no effect on him."

To the fearful survivors of the Karellan attack, Zachary said, "Don't be afraid."

However, his astral voice sounded like thunder and terrified everyone.

Zachary offered his hand to the child and repeated in the gentlest voice he could muster, "Don't be afraid."

Nayri screamed at the top of her lungs.

Zachary was about to lose patience, when he noticed movement in Apel's fallen shamira.

He's alive.

Kneeling beside the Jinzou Ningen bodyguard, Zachary resumed human form to the gasps of the thunder-struck Talisians.

"It is Tinki Winki!" cried a Psion police officer.

Zachary glared at the man, gritting his teeth; then he thought: *It's not his fault. It's Chi-Ro's.*

He said to the man, "There's no need to use my call sign; you can call me Zac Aree."

But despite this announcement, the crowd continued to whisper, "It is Tinki Winki." "Tinki Winki is the soter."

Resisting the urge to kill them all, Zachary gently placed his fingertips on the temples of the bodyguard.

"What are you doing?" came Nayri's diminutive voice, filled with Royal disdain.

Zachary did not reply, and he did not look into her eyes. He could not bear it. Feeling her profound sorrow was enough.

"My brother and our shamiras are dead," continued Nayri plaintively.

Zachary searched deep within himself, summoning intense psychic energy; and with shaking hands, he attempted to transfer this energy to the artificial human. He failed.

With a lump in his throat, Zachary admitted to Nayri, "Your brother's bodyguard isn't dead, but I'm sorry, I can't cure him. I don't have the required skill."

"Perhaps, I can assist him," said a Jinzou Ningen shadow warrior.

Standing upright, and staring deeply into the artificial human's purple eyes, Zachary said, "Do your best to save his life. I'm assigning you shamira to Lady Nayri."

"But..."

"But what?"

"Only specially trained female officers can be shamira to..."

"Things change. Make sure nothing happens to her, or I'll kick your arse."

"Yes sir."

Zachary walked towards the exit and once again transformed into a wraith.

"Wait," cried Nayri, "where are you going?"

With a voice like thunder, Zachary replied, "I'm going to put a stop to this stupid war; don't worry, I'll be back."

With that, Zachary flew out of the citadel and disappeared in the darkness.

With the air supply restored to the antechamber, Brakis Tarn resumed human form and activated his lapys nerian sok-bou. Words were not necessary. His piercing, blue, feral eyes uttered a thousand insults and his mind screamed the promise of agonising murder.

Prince Armon Sakara removed his helmet and allowed it to slip to the metal floor with a loud clatter. He took a deep breath, noting the hint of acrid smoke from smouldering synthetic material being fed into the antechamber. With a slow exhale, he breathed away his fear. He opened his hands and relaxed, allowing oxygen-rich blood to flow freely to his extremities. Then, matching Brakis Tarn's vengeful stare, Prince Armon walked towards his nemesis.

Armon came to a halt ten paces before Brakis Tarn and, without flourish, drew the Sword of Power, taking note of the faint smile that immediately appeared on his blond opponent's lips.

Brakis Tarn's powerful psychic probes tested Armon's resolve like a dagger in his mind. At the speed of thought, myriad possibilities were explored and innumerable deceptions presented. With unrestrained malice, the Butcher of Cyclo subjected Armon's mind, body and soul, to his diabolically efficient inquisition.

Then, satisfied that he had discovered the means with which to assure his victory, Brakis Tarn assumed a Kon Jou ready stance.

A tightening of the jaw and gravelling of voice, betrayed his aversion as he said, "Death whispers your name to me, Armon Sakara. I have seen your end, as have you."

Assuming a Hatari Ikou ready stance, Armon said with all the calmness he could muster, "You've tried several times to kill me, yet here I stand, against you."

"You shall be destroyed, by my will. As surely as your woman, and the abomination she carried in her womb, have been destroyed by my flagship's torpedoes."

Briefly, the crushing weight of doubt descended on Armon.

No, it's yet another deception. I'd know if they'd died. The starchariot escaped; Soraya and my unborn child are alive...

Armon's momentary loss of focus almost cost him his life. Brakis Tarn launched a vicious and sustained attack with the dark, lightning-edged whirlwind that was his lapys nerian sok-bou. Armon back-pedalled, relying on instinct more than observation to parry the Kon Jou master's impossibly swift strikes.

Brakis Tarn noted the perfect design of the pommel and blade of the unique lapys nerian sword. In worthy hands, the perfectly balanced Najura could efficiently facilitate lightening-fast attacks, effective blocks, devastating slashing and precise piercing of an opponent or his weapons.

Brakis Tarn coveted Najura, the Sword of Power, but soon realised that he had underestimated Armon's martial arts prowess. He observed Armon's stunningly fast strikes, his powerful circular motion that fluidly deflected and countered the sok-bou's deadly plasma. He recognised the secret knowledge he had imparted to his former student Chi-Ro Jin, expressed in Armon's sophisticated art.

Brakis Tarn firmly believed that Sakara Rey and Jin Lan had condemned his father, Tarn Havek, to a futile death on the battlefield. Though he had betrayed his emperor, and murdered his commanding officer, his lust for revenge remained unsatisfied.

The sons must pay the ultimate price, for the sins of their fathers. Chi-Ro Jin will die; Armon Sakara will die; and they shall die by my will. Only then, shall this rage that threatens to consume my very being be quelled.

With his anger exuding astral energy that electrified the air, Brakis Tarn attacked with even more malicious vigour.

Sensing that his large opponent sought to press him into an inescapable corner of the room, Armon feinted right, veered left and then leapt high to avoid his legs being amputated by deadly plasma. He yelled triumphantly with an immediate downward slash of the katana-like Najura but missed the Karellan's head completely.

Brakis Tarn delivered a swift kick to the side of Armon's head adding to the downward momentum that had him scrambling to keep his footing. Instinct brought Armon's arms up and over his right shoulder, positioning Najura across his back, parrying the sok-bou strike intended to hack his body in two.

A swift turning slash kept the Karellan warrior at bay, long enough for Armon to regain his footing and avoid the aggressively buzzing blur of plasma that sliced the air so close to his face that he inhaled nitrogen oxides.

Armon felt relieved that he had escaped being cornered. Nevertheless, Brakis Tarn's way of the spirit warrior utterly outmatched Armon's Hatari Ikou and the Prince began to consider it a small miracle that he had escaped death, so far.

Pressed relentlessly backwards, Armon recalled Chi-Ro's teachings: *"Change. Adapt. Bend so as not to be broken. Let opportunity guide your actions."*

In the smoke-filled bowels of the doomed Starcarrier Shor, Chi-Ro Jin and Nook Tigg desperately raced towards Prince Armon. A wall of twisted metal and debris blocked the airlock through which Armon entered the antechamber. To reach the Prince, Chi-Ro and Nook had to make their way around the large antechamber to the airlock on the devastated main hangar.

They charged into a service corridor, startling five Karellan shock marines. With their personal shields activated, and pistols blazing, Chi-Ro and Nook wiped out the surprised Karellans without breaking their strides.

A powerful sidekick from the Kon Jou master ploughed into Armon's chest, driving the air out of his lungs and propelling him eight metres backwards. Armon did not resist the momentum. He needed a few seconds to recover from Brakis Tarn's psychic assault on his optic nerve, and he needed distance from the power tip of Brakis Tarn's lethal sok-bou.

Armon positioned his arms at either side of his body, breaking the fall and protecting his spine from injury. Taking advantage of the backward momentum, he kicked both legs over his head into a backward roll and rose, barely in time to parry Brakis Tarn's Herculean lunge aimed at his brow.

Immediately, Armon initiated his first prolonged attack against his formidable enemy. Brakis Tarn effortlessly gave ground, luring the Prince into another corner of the room, intent on trapping him. The two-metre long sok-bou gave the Kon Jou master much needed distance from the lethal slashes of Armon's lapys nerian sword. Brakis Tarn had gambled that Armon did not know the secret of the sword's real power, and he was correct.

"I can feel your strength waning, young one," he taunted, "soon your pitiful resistance will..."

Armon's sudden, maniacal attack had his blond opponent backpedalling. A vicious lunge of Brakis Tarn's sok-bou was met with a turning parry from Armon, off balancing the Kon Jou master. Armon instantly drove his elbows into Brakis Tarn's ribs; and, with a cry of victory, brought Najura down in a killing blow. The swift Brakis Tarn escaped with only some of his long blond hair, together with the tip of his right ear, severed; and his immeasurable pride damaged.

Brakis Tarn could scarcely believe it as he felt the trickle of blood down his sweaty neck.

The Royal kak drew first blood.

"When it's time to fight, fight, don't talk," came Armon's solemn warning.

"May the scribes record it," was Brakis Tarn's bitter, thunderous response; and he transformed into an astral entity once more.

"You are Niburian. Change yourself. Fly ahead of me and save the Prince from certain death," projected Chi-Ro to Nook, as they hurtled through a badly damaged corridor.

"The psychic storm generator employed by the Karellans is not of Karellan or Saurian design. It employs Neph Alim technology and robs Niburians of their ability to transform."

"Kak!"

They sprinted recklessly past two Karellan shock marines who were initially too stunned to fire their weapons at the crazy enemy warriors. As Chi-Ro and Nook disappeared down the dark corridor, the junior officer suddenly snapped out of his stupor.

"Are we not going to pursue them, Sir?" he asked his commander.

"Pursue them? Are you mad? I did not recognise his dark companion, but I could never forget the face of Chi-Ro Jin. By all means, pursue them, if you wish to die."

Chi-Ro and Nook sprinted at top speed into the corridor, which led directly to the destroyed hangar deck. Unsurprisingly, it was the most damaged, and a containment field kept barely breathable air within it. Thirty metres ahead, loomed a breach in the deck, about ten metres in diameter. Holstering their pistols and deactivating their personal shields, Chi-Ro and Nook Tigg accelerated and leapt high. A volley of plasma fire rang out from below, and they were both hit. Like discarded sacks of potatoes, Chi-Ro and Nook fell hard onto the battle-damaged metal deck, on the other side of the gap.

Chapter 78

Armon shook the sweat from his brow, vaguely aware of his nosebleed. Little by little, Brakis Tarn's constant psychic oppression was taking its toll. Kon Jou, Hatari Ikou and even Kiya's little-known Ma Isha style could not bring Armon victory over the Butcher of Cyclo. The dark wraith's tireless rage seemed unstoppable.

Armon stared into the wild darkness of his opponent and saw a reflection of his own fall. Once again, his mind observed Brakis Tarn standing above his lifeless form, brandishing Najura and exulting in his success.

Silently cursing the Karellan psychic storm that inhibited his psychic and astral abilities, Armon hurled himself at his astral enemy in a whirlwind of lapys nerian. Najura had the power to terminate even an astral entity and Brakis Tarn fiercely battled to keep Armon's furious blade at bay.

Bathed in sweat and driven by singular desperation, it was not the insightful teachings of Chi-Ro Jin that Armon recalled, but the modest wisdom of his loving wife:

"Remember Roman, you're a man - a man with terrifying abilities, but still just a man. If yuh ever forget that, the devil has won."

Acknowledging that his dream training with Chi-Ro Jin and the grim, supernatural abilities he possessed, were just not enough in the face of this terrible enemy, Armon drew much-needed strength from his faith in God, and with each strike and each blistering parry, his confidence slowly returned. With God's help, Armon believed he could defeat the evil warrior.

So as Brakis Tarn projected hatred, doubt and slanderous lies into Armon's mind, The Prince Armon countered with the prayer of Giovanni Francesco Bernardone, more commonly known as Francis of Assisi.

"Today is a good day, for you to die," projected Brakis Tarn.

Twisting his upper body, Armon felt the heat of the sok-bou's neon blue plasma as it shot past his left cheek.

"Lord, make me an instrument of your peace."

The black blur of Najura arced centimetres from Brakis Tarn's neck as Armon launched into a series of flips, somersaults and spinning kicks all barely missing his wily opponent.

"There is no lord to save you. Your fall is inevitable. And on the foundations of your death and the death of your father, I shall establish a new order in my empire."

Brakis Tarn countered Armon's gymnastic attacks, parrying several airborne strikes before initiating a deadly whirlwind that had Armon performing back flips to avoid.

"Where there is hatred, let me bring love," projected Armon.

Brakis Tarn cartwheeled to the left as Armon suddenly flipped forward with a midair slash of Najura.

He responded contemptuously, *"Ahhh yes, love. Did you know, that I came to your woman as she slept?"*

"Where there is injury, let me bring the spirit of forgiveness."

Armon sliced Najura through the toxin-filled air, missing Brakis Tarn's neck, turning into a slash that missed his ankles and finally into an arc that missed his torso.

"You did not father the child in her womb."

Almost too late, Armon realised his error. Brakis Tarn had lured him to the periphery of his spinning power rod, forcing him to frantically avoid and deflect the Kon Jou master's relentless counterattacks.

"Where there is doubt, let me bring faith," projected Armon with grim determination.

"Watch the veil of heated passion on her face and listen to her cries of ecstasy as she accepted my seed."

It was a split second, but the almost imperceptibly brief loss of concentration was enough. And, in the twinkling of an eye, Brakis Tarn subjected Armon to the crushing yoke of deceit and the darkness of physical blindness.

Sweeping Najura in a vengeful arc that would behead the evil wraith, Armon cried defiantly, "Where there is despair let me bring..."

"Hope? There is no hope," growled the Butcher of Cyclo.

Armon heard a loud clatter and became vaguely aware that he no longer held Najura. Something was wrong – terribly wrong. He could no longer feel his legs, yet he stood facing his mortal enemy. Armon coughed blood, and slowly looking down, he discovered that the plasma of Brakis Tarn's sok-bou had effortlessly impaled his stomach and protruded from his back.

Armon mumbled weakly and instinctively, "Oh no."

Brakis Tarn withdrew his weapon and retracted it, allowing the mortally wounded Prince to slump to the floor. The evil Kon Jou master had delivered a perfectly executed thrust, which avoided Armon's spine and internal organs. It was a wound that callously condemned the Prince to a slow and agonising death.

Brakis Tarn exerted his imposing psychic will, forcing Armon to watch as he calmly discarded the lapys nerian sok-bou, which fell with a loud clatter to the metal floor at the dying Prince's feet.

Resuming human form, he stooped to the floor, retrieved Najura and whispered contemptuously in Armon's ear, "How ironic. The primitive Kian superstition in which you placed your faith, finally succeeded where Delius Roi, the Brothers Zaar and Shan Kur-Karnah all failed. Foolish, backward religion sealed your doom."

"*Righteousness will prevail,*" projected Armon defiantly.

Standing above the fallen Prince Armon, Brakis Tarn bellowed, "Indeed. I shall rid the Cosmic Sea of its Talisian infestation, once and for all."

Using the sole of his right boot, Brakis Tarn, the Butcher of Cyclo, forced Armon's head to turn towards the impassable airlock at the far end of the antechamber.

His voice coarse with hatred, Brakis cried, "Now, foolish Prince, behold the super science of the Ancients of Niburi. Behold the power of the key that is Najura."

Removing his foot from the side of Armon's face and pointing the curved tip of the katana-like blade towards the airlock, Brakis Tarn mentally reached deep within himself.

Armon deliberately turned away, hoping that Brakis Tarn would use his psychic ability to force an audience.

I'm not dead yet. Where there is life, there is hope.

Brakis Tarn established a psychic link with Armon's body. He mentally commanded Armon's muscles, forcing him to watch.

Now I will know the secret of the Sword of Power.

The shadow of a man that was Brakis Tarn began to shift and phase, drawing energy from the dark matter in the space that surrounded them. Suddenly Armon's mind was filled with clarity.

Zach was right. The key to Najura's power is dark matter, just as dark matter powers astral transformation. Only someone possessing astral ability can use the key to open a doorway. The Ancient Niburians lost their astral ability, but sought to regain it through the genetic manipulation of human beings.

Awestruck, and with his life inexorably ebbing away, Armon watched as light enveloped the black astral form of Brakis Tarn. Even the black, lapys nerian sword now radiated dazzlingly brilliant light.

Armon asked himself, *Isn't Lucifer the bearer of light?*

The airlock began to distort, and to Armon, it seemed as if a circle of space about five metres across, suddenly collapsed into itself. The airlock and the wall were no longer there. Armon looked through the circle and what he saw brought tears to his eyes.

Armon saw the bridge of a starcarrier. He saw it clearly and he heard the sounds from the scene as if they were in the antechamber with him. This was no vision. It was reality.

There on the bridge of the Ayntaiyou, dressed in full military regalia, stood his father, Sakara Rey I, Lord of the Imperial Host, True Emperor of the Cosmic Sea.

Overwhelmed, and to Brakis Tarn's initial glee, Armon began to weep. However, it took only a brief moment, for Brakis Tarn to realise that Armon's tears were not tears of sorrow. Armon was overjoyed to finally see his father. He was overjoyed that his father was still alive and that he had seen his father's face before his own inevitable death at the hands of Brakis Tarn. It immediately occurred to Brakis Tarn that Armon's death was not coming swiftly enough.

Barely conscious, gasping for breath in the thin, toxin-filled air, Armon watched the being of light, which was Brakis Tarn, turn towards him. He could see no eyes – no distinguishing features, but Armon vividly imagined piercing blue eyes filled with the most terrible bloodlust.

When Brakis Tarn spoke, the antechamber trembled as if about to implode.

With all the contempt he could muster, Brakis Tarn said, "Prince Armon Sakara, when you meet with the Great Spirit, be sure to report that a lowly peasant named Brakis Tarn took your abominable life."

Brakis Tarn launched a final, brutal, mental attack. Armon sensed that in a matter of seconds, several blood vessels in his brain would explode and his life would end. He knew that once he was dead, his victorious opponent intended to step across the breach onto the bridge of the Ayntaiyou, and murder his father. With blood streaming from his nostrils and the side of his mouth, Armon prepared himself for his final sacrifice. He would use what power he had left to stop Brakis Tarn.

Armon recalled Chi-Ro Jin's confident words: *"Righteousness shall prevail."*

And suddenly, to Armon's disbelief, Chi-Ro was in the antechamber, rushing towards Brakis Tarn, sok-bou drawn, closely followed by a similarly armed Nook Tigg.

Displaying shocking speed, Brakis Tarn sidestepped drawing the light of Najura in a perfectly deadly two-handed arc. In a blinding flash, his upper hand pushed the full power of his entire body into the strike, as his lower hand pulled the blade through Chi-Ro Jin's neck. With a sharp twist powered by Brakis Tarn's heel, through his hip, and into his upper body, Nook Tigg's torso met with the sharpness of light. Cut in two, the Niburian hit the floor a second after Chi-Ro's severed head and twitching body.

In a single blur of darkness that was once a man, Armon grabbed Brakis Tarn's lapys nerian sok-bou from the floor, activated it and plunged it at the heart of the light. The antechamber shook with thunder that rolled continuously until Armon realised that it was his own astral voice, screaming with rage and grief and bitter triumph.

Impaled and transfixed, Brakis Tarn reverted to human form. Insane with vengeance, blinded by furious anger, Armon violently wrenched Najura from his foe's grip. Immeasurable, indescribable energy instantly coursed through Armon. It was too much to bear. He unintentionally reassumed human form, and fell to the floor paralysed, the sword of light slipping from his grasp and reverting to its black state.

The circular doorway to the Ayntaiyou's bridge distorted, darkened and finally disappeared. Enduring extreme pain, Armon watched as the shocked, impaled Brakis Tarn fell to his knees and reached for Najura, his fingertips barely brushing its pommel.

Grabbing the sword, Armon spat, "You want this? Then have it!"

And with a single thrust, he drove the tip of the blade into the soft base of Brakis Tarn's neck, above his sternum, between his clavicles. Armon heard Brakis Tarn's sharp intake of air.

He stared into the defeated Kon Jou master's bulging blue eyes and cried, "Brakis, son of Tarn, when you meet with your bloody comrades in hell, be sure to report that Armon, son of Sakara took your evil life."

With the sharp bitterness of vengeance, Prince Armon Sakara heard Brakis Tarn's final, laboured exhale, and watched as the spark of life left his broken opponent's blue eyes forever.

Returning Najura to its scabbard with expert fluidity and precision, Armon left a perfect central line of Brakis Tarn's blood spatter on the metal floor of the antechamber.

The dead Kon Jou master slumped backwards, propped up by the sok-bou that impaled him. He remained kneeling at an angle, with his head hanging forward limply, as blood streamed from his wounds.

Grief-stricken, choking on the thin, acrid air of the antechamber, Armon looked towards where his mentors had fallen and found, to his utter disbelief, that their bodies were no longer there.

With his thoughts racing, and the bitter taste of bile at the back of his throat, Armon closed his eyes as the room began to spin violently. Finally giving in to his pain and profound exhaustion, he slumped facedown onto the cold, metal floor. And lulled by the sound of his laboured breathing, The Prince Armon slipped to the edge of oblivion.

Chapter 79

The Empress Consort, The Noble Lady Akana-Benu, swept onto the bridge of the 1st Wave flagship Ayntaiyou. She wore a shimmering black tunic, which bore the glittering golden Arosian Ten-Shi, the butterfly symbol of the House of Enki.

Her shamira, the mute Mara Kai nun and Mistress of the Deadly Arts, Arya Binara, accompanied her. She wore the distinctive silver habit, and black monastic scapular and cloak of her order. A black cowl covered her clean-shaven head and framed her pale face. In keeping with Mara Kai tradition, at the end of her rigorous initiation, Arya's eyebrows had been ritually removed and replaced with a black stain that also covered her eyelids, lips and the palms of her hands.

During a pivotal battle in the First Psion War, Armon's grandfather Rey Enki coined the phrase 'the black hands of war', after nine Mara Kai fighting monks defeated two squadrons of Talisian Assault Troopers in hand-to-hand combat. In time, the Mara Kai Masters and Mistresses of the Deadly Arts would be known simply as Kurotays, which literally meant 'black hands'.

Mina Rin, who called herself Miriam Doyle and assigned the anagrammatic name 'Roman' to her charge, was an Imperial Custodian to The Prince Armon. After Mina's death, Nareesha Thomas, the Trinidadian woman, became Armon's legal guardian. If love and devotion were the only criteria, both women had earned the honourable title of 'mother'.

Nevertheless, Akana-Benu is flesh of his flesh and bone of his bone. Akana-Benu is Armon Sakara's real mother. And now, even her extensive Imperial conditioning could not entirely mask her agitation.

In full military battledress, Emperor Sakara Rey stood rigidly behind Viceroy Tuduh Fadah, First Admiral of the Imperial Talisian Waves. Tuduh Fadah wore the Ayntaiyou's command helmet and occupied the command pod of the impressive starcarrier. Without averting his gaze from the approaching battle on the flagship's main holographic viewer, Sakara subtly betrayed his displeasure by folding his arms as Akana approached.

Sakara projected sternly but calmly, *"We are about to engage our deadliest foe, Akana. Even with your black hand, as formidable as she is, the battle-bridge is no place for the mother of the Imperial Heir. Please return to the citadel."*

Ignoring his request, Akana stood at Sakara's side. She applied her Mara Kai training to repressing her tears, and preventing the trembling of her hands.

"Our son is here. A moment ago I felt his presence as clearly and as deeply as my love for him. But now that feeling has passed. You cannot hide your fear from me, Sakara. It is not the Seriak or the Karellans that trouble you. You are afraid that our son has met with disaster."

"Are my thoughts so transparent?"

"Only to me, my love."

"Our son is not dead; and our great sacrifice, sending him to a distant galaxy, has not been in vain."

Then turning to the communications officer, Sakara said with his clipped Avaris accent, "Lieutenant, the auxiliary communications helmet if you will."

"Yes Sir," came the young lieutenant's crisp reply as he handed Sakara the helmet.

Placing the communications helmet on his clean-shaven head, Sakara suddenly observed the contrast between Arya's ink-stained lips and the whiteness of her cheeks. He recalled his father's words regarding the fearsome Mara Kai.

Sakara paused briefly, then the projection of his mind reverberated throughout the Imperial Host, "Sons and daughters of the noble Talisian Empire, this is Sakara. As we fly into the records of glorious history, joining the rarefied ranks of the righteous in life or death, know that, by the grace of the Great Spirit, our victory is assured. For we are the honoured few, chosen to oppose an insidious enemy recently revealed. We are vengeance made flesh, children of the Truth, and the black hands of war. On this day, at this hour, in this Battle of Miru, righteousness will prevail. May the scribes record it!"

With Sakara's synthesised voice still echoing throughout the battleships of his Imperial Host, a jubilant roar swelled from the combined voices of men, women and Jinzou Ningen. He had spurred the fleet to battle, as he had done so many times before, and Akana could no longer hold back her tears.

Sakara Rey, Emperor of the Cosmic Sea, removed and returned the communications helmet to the awe-struck lieutenant, whose youthful face illuminated with newfound national pride. Stroking his grey-tinged beard, and with the glint of regal dignity glazing his deep brown eyes, Sakara scanned the Ayntaiyou's bridge crew, holding the gaze of each cheering officer in turn.

Above the subsiding din, he cried, "Not even Enki the Great had been blessed with a crew as fine as this. Now, let us utterly remove the iniquitous stain that is the Seriak from the Cosmic Sea. Admiral Tuduh Fadah, prepare the Wave for battlejump."

"By your will, My Lord."

As the bridge lighting dimmed and the starcarrier's immense hyperspatial drives powered up with a low rumble, Sakara's raptorial vision found the misty, loving eyes of his consort Akana. Neither words nor projected thoughts seemed necessary. Sakara bowed at the neck, prompting Akana and her shamira Arya to bow low. Then, as the Emperor's Own Psion Police saluted them, the women left the Ayntaiyou's bridge.

Tuduh Fadah projected, *"Your Majesty, all preparations for battlejump have been made. Awaiting your command."*

Sakara barked, "Admiral, proceed with operation Silent Storm."

"By your will, Lord Sakara."

"It has been an honour serving with you, old friend."

"The honour is mine, my Emperor."

In the dark and the deep of poisoned sleep, Prince Armon Sakara heard distant, vaguely familiar male voices. Muffled, distorted and strangely ominous, they provided little comfort as he slowly suffocated.

The first voice asked, "By the Great Spirit, are we too late?"

Armon thought he imagined strong hands tug at his shoulders. Suddenly he was no longer lying face down on the cold metal floor. Someone had rolled him onto his back. He tried to open his eyes, but that seemed to require far more energy than he could muster. He attempted to speak, but his lips barely parted.

"Quickly, your augmenter," said the second voice.

Armon felt something cold being placed on his forehead. Almost immediately, his strength began to return. His throbbing headache, the ringing in his ears, the burning sensation in his throat and nostrils, his vertigo and almost uncontrollable urge to vomit, dissipated with each passing second.

The first voice said, "The containment field is failing, Nook Tigg. In a moment, flames will engulf us. We must leave at once."

Nook Tigg? Nook Tigg is alive, thought Armon, instantly overcome by healing waves of happiness.

Nook Tigg said urgently, "His helmet, Chi-Ro. Quickly!"

Nook Tigg and Chi-Ro Jin! Thank God, they're both alive!

Nook Tigg removed Chi-Ro's augmenter from Armon's forehead and quickly placed the helmet on Armon's head. With the benefit of the emergency oxygen, supplied by his Osirian stealth suit, Armon was finally able to open his eyes.

Choked with emotion, he said to his mentors, "Thank God, you're both alive."

As Nook Tigg, helped Armon to his feet, Chi-Ro limped towards them with Najura in his right hand and the severed head of Brakis Tarn in his left.

"What happened?" asked Armon weakly.

"You butchered the Butcher of Cyclo," said Chi-Ro proudly lifting the head of Brakis Tarn, firmly gripped by long, blond hair.

I did not behead him. That was your doing, Chi-Ro, Armon thought to himself.

He asked Chi-Ro, "What happened to you?" And, sensing that Nook Tigg was also wounded, he turned to the dark Niburian and asked, "What happened to both of you?"

"Nothing of consequence," said Chi-Ro bowing low, offering the hilt of the Sword of Power to Armon.

Armon accepted the sword and immediately understood that toxins in the air of the antechamber had previously caused him to hallucinate. When he saw Brakis Tarn kill his mentors, it was only a poison-induced dream.

Nook Tigg said sternly, "Unless you would have us become roasted meals fit for the Seriak, I suggest we delay discussing Chi-Ro Jin's wounded posterior."

Armon became aware of Nook Tigg's own wound in his left inner thigh, and Chi-Ro's embarrassingly burnt buttocks.

One of the Psychic War's greatest heroes - shot in the butt; and the other - almost castrated, Armon thought with a smile.

Then, swiftly returning his focus on the gravity of their current predicament, Armon resuming his princely role and said, "My strength has returned and I see the danger. Stand behind me."

I can't believe I just said that. Whatever happened to the schoolteacher from Barnet?

"Have you learnt the secret of the sword, Manuk?"

"Yes, Nook Tigg, I have."

With a sudden roar, the containment field failed and once again, deadly flames rushed into the antechamber. Armon regarded the advancing wall of fire with a deeply profound, inhuman clarity. As time seemed to grind to a standstill from his unfettered astral perspective, Armon observed the infrared light, blackbody radiation and photon emissions of the fire. He marvelled at its beauty and utterly understood it.

Armon clearly heard the frenzied thoughts of his mentors, but he did not share their concern. The fact that his Osirian stealth suit had been badly damaged by Brakis Tarn's lethal sok-bou seemed of little consequence.

I wield the Sword of Power, he thought.

Suddenly enveloped by brilliant light, Armon pointed the tip of Najura's equally illuminated, katana-like blade towards the swiftly advancing, raging heat. With the esoteric knowledge, he gained from the mind of Brakis Tarn, Armon unlocked the hidden secret of Najura and used it to open a transdimensional portal through the flames.

"Follow me," he said to Chi-Ro and Nook. Awestruck they watched as, within the raging fire, Armon stepped through a circle about five metres across, onto the dimly lit deck of the formidable enemy flagship - the Imperial Drac-El.

Leading the charge, the Ayntaiyou appeared in the battle arena seconds after her zero point torpedoes hit their enemy targets. Almost instantly, the remainder of the 1st Wave jumped into the fray in like manner. This was Sakara's battlejump, an extremely risky manoeuvre, which called for the precise targeting and discharging of weapons during hyperspatial travel.

The 1st Wave appeared after the enemy was either blinded or disabled. A steady stream of fighters left Sakara's starcarriers long before the ambushed Karellans could react.

The Saurian secret weapon, the Asmorda, meant to counter Sakara's battle jump, did not join in the fight. Her formidable guns remained silent as Talisians, Karellans and Saurians fought each other in a desperate bid to seize her command.

On the Ayntaiyou's main holographic viewer, the prototype ravager-class super battlecarrier, the Imperial Drac-El, loomed like a large bird of prey that blotted out the stars and threatened to devour all that dared to challenge her. Hundreds of Karellan raiders and marauders engaged hundreds of Talisian starfires, chariots and gliders in a battlespace littered with the burnt and the burning, the dead and the dying. Never before had so many been killed, in so short a time.

Following a general mutiny against the Saurian impostors, the combined forces of the 74th and 149th Karellan Shock Divisions, now controlled by Ne-Ro Jos, surrounded the valiant remnants of the Talisian 9th Wave, led by Ley Ka-Tow.

With Generals Quat Nye and Nokh-Ra Deem killed in battle, Ley Ka-Tow received a field promotion to the rank of general from the Alphatron, shortly before the Jinzou Ningen leader was himself disabled by the enemy's electromagnetic pulse weapon. Leading the 9th Wave from the bridge of the Starcarrier Kach, Ley Ka-Tow performed her duties admirably, resolved to fight to the bitter end.

Crippled, boarded by enemy troops, but still under desperate Talisian control, the doomed Avedis did its best to protect the Kach from utter annihilation, whilst the defeated Shor with its bridge destroyed by Brakis Tarn's crashed raider, drifted through space like a blazing comet. The constant bombardment by the warship Drac-El, with support from an Orbital Bomber, left the Avedis and Kach little more than battle-damaged hulks on the brink of disaster.

"It is imperative that we seize the Asmorda, Admiral; we are still out-numbered and outgunned," said Sakara to Tuduh Fadah, "Verily, in mere moments we will lose any advantage granted by our battlejump."

Sakara's jaw tightened with suppressed emotion when he projected privately, *"Any news of my son, old friend?"*

"Not since the space battle began, Lord Sakara."

"Damn their psychic storm."

The alert klaxon of the Ayntaiyou suddenly activated.

"Multiple ENDAR targets have jumped into weapons range," came the tactical officer's computer-generated voice.

"Display," barked Sakara.

The readings of the Ayntaiyou's enhanced detection and ranging system instantly replaced the battlescape display on the main holographic viewer.

"Three capital ships and four hundred plus fighters deployed on an attack vector," added the tactical officer.

"Shields to maximum, diverting six starfire squadrons to engage the enemy," came Tuduh Fadah's grim announcement.

"That will not be enough, Admiral," projected Sakara.

"Enemy force identified as the Battlecarrier Taharqa and the orbital bombers Nekhbet and Sekhmet," announced the tactical officer.

The Taharqa - Klim T'val's ship. So, does my distant cousin command this force, or a Saurian impostor?

"Intercepting enemy transmission from the Taharqa," came the young communications officer's computer-generated voice.

"On speaker," commanded Sakara.

"Karellan brothers, Jinzou Ningen and Talisians, this is Karamba, son of Lord Shan Kur-Karnah. We have been deceived. Even now, our mutual enemy the Seriak leads us closer to the precipice of human extinction. I denounce the False Emperor. I oppose the Seriak impostor that calls itself Seti Aljyk and all who support it. I will add my sword to the swords of Karellans, Talisians and all who would see the end of this war and an end to Saurian domination! This I swear freely, on self-imposed pain of death."

"This is the miracle we have been praying for," said Sakara.

The sound of cheering rose throughout the vessels in the battlespace.

Chapter 80

Aboard the Karellan flagship, the Imperial Drac-El, the wraith merged through the walls of the inner sanctum of the brothers of The Mysterium. He had permanently silenced the monks' psychic storm. He left them physically blinded and overwhelmed by recurring dreams of being trapped in a large chamber ravaged by fire and brimstone. The wraith also left the twelve red-garbed sentinels, tasked with protecting the religious brothers, lying on the cold floor, with silent screams etched on their wide-eyed, contorted faces. The wraith had killed many more since his arrival on the Drac-El; and, as he phased effortlessly through her walls, like a dark angel of death, he anticipated ending even more lives.

Killing those morons had been so very easy, the wraith thought, *it felt as if I was watching someone else rupturing blood vessels in their evil brains. But watching had been very satisfying, maybe a bit too satisfying. Oh well, I've done it, no point dwelling on it now. If they had simply surrendered, I wouldn't have lost my temper and killed the stupid bastards. Now let me see, where is their evil master? Where is that Ne-Ro Jos?*

Ne-Ro Jos, the crimson clad Grandmaster of The Order of Mysteries said casually, "Ah, Brakis Tarn, I was just explaining to Lokai that with, the death of Sobek, his services were no longer needed." Firing another lethal burst into Lokai Zann's prostrate body, completely vaporising it, he added derisively: "My Empire will not tolerate another Seti Aljyk or one foolish enough to be his shamira." Turning his attention to the wraith, Ne-Ro asked, "Where is the Sword of Power?"

"You tell me," came the wraith's blunt, thunderous response.

"This is not an interval for games, son of Tarn," replied Ne-Ro, suddenly gripped by the coldness of uncertainty.

"I'm not Brakis Tarn."

Ne-Ro gradually and instinctively aimed Sobek's modified Blastron P-55 pistol at the wraith. There was a slight tremor in his voice as he echoed, "Not Brakis Tarn?"

"His services were no longer needed," the wraith said grimly.

Armon defeated Brakis? How could I not foresee this? Against all odds, he is set on the second path.

Delivering his best acting performance, masking his rising terror, Ne-Ro said, "Ah, Armon. I should have known."

"Wrong again. You should consider another career. As a clairvoyant, you're pretty useless."

Not Armon, but a third astral being? Where indeed is my prescience? Are events unfurling as prophesied in the book of Mithnoss? Chapter 13, verse 9: 'At the end of days, I saw the phantom representative of a long forgotten race emerge from an expanse of darkness to assume a prominent role. A new empire was thereby established, in his name, greater than the last; and all, including the false king, bowed before him'. Perhaps, here stands a prophecy revealed. The experiment has surpassed all expectation. My Neph Alim masters would be most pleased that their antisoter has the power, most elusive.

"Of course, Zachary Roi..."

"Don't call me that," snapped the wraith.

"Oh, would you prefer I call you by your call-sign, Tinki Winki?"

"Don't call me that either!"

"By what name do you wish to be addressed?"

"Under the circumstances, *Death* seems oddly appropriate."

"Would you kill a servant of the true masters of the Cosmic Sea?"

"Watching innocent women and children die, has me in full bastard mode. So, to answer your question, yes with pleasure."

"Ungrateful wretch! It was the super science of the enlightened beings of the clouds, the most noble Neph Alim Principality that made you superhuman."

"I ask you, how can shoving metal probes up my arse make me superhuman?"

"You are so very much like your father, a complete disappointment. But we gave you your power and we can take it away."

Ne-Ro pressed a concealed button on the armrest of the throne. Shimmering black and purple rays suddenly surrounded the wraith. He immediately fell to his knees and reverted to human form. Dr. Zachary Silverman managed to prop himself up on one knee, and cast his deep blue eyes up at Ne-Ro's smugly smiling, sickly pale face.

His nasal voice rising a tritone, saturated with contempt, Ne-Ro spat, "You fool; did you not expect me to be protected? Did the Talisian idiot Armon not advise you of my lapys nerian containment fields?

"Why don't you ask him? He's standing behind you."

Ne-Ro thought: *It is conceivable that the son of Roi and the son of Sakara working together could defeat Brakis Tarn; but my prescience would have alerted me to that eventuality.*

"No," Ne-Ro chuckled with disdain, "Though some minor details in the shifting sands of time have changed, there still remain only two possible paths before Armon. Both will end in his demise. In the first, he is destined to fall foul of Brakis Tarn's lapys nerian sok-bou. In the second, he will die at the hands of his abominable offspring. No, my Neph Alim superslave, these paths do not threaten my security," cried Ne-Ro Jos, "I have foreseen it."

"Zachary's right, your clairvoyance is pretty useless," came Armon's distinctive voice.

"What?"

Ne-Ro glanced over his left shoulder and Zachary immediately pulled out his viridian pistol and fired, wounding Ne-Ro in his right shoulder. Screaming in agony, Ne-Ro dropped Sobek's pistol and watched helplessly as Zachary rose to his feet.

Emerging from the shadows, with Najura in hand, Armon said calmly, "Your monks have been captured and your lapys nerian devices deactivated. The purple rays are completely inert. The Neph Alim device has been removed from Zachary's skull; you could never control him the way you did Brakis Tarn. Your plots and schemes have come to nothing, and you will live out your few remaining days in the custody of my father's servants."

Utterly overwhelmed, Ne-Ro repeated, "What?"

Stepping out of the purple rays, taking deadly aim at Ne-Ro's head, Zachary said contemptuously, "You're really beginning to get on my last nerve with that stupid question."

It's true. The son of Roi's mind is totally independent; and I sense Armon has discovered the secret of Najura. All is lost. I am doomed, thought Ne-Ro; and with that thought began the gradual descent of his mind into the fire-pit of complete insanity.

Armed with his viridian pistol, Chi-Ro Jin emerged from the left and said to Zachary, "You have deported yourself admirably this day. For facing the treacherous crimson monks of the Mysterium unaided and for ending the Karellan psychic storm, you have no doubt earned the Star of Ra, Doctor. Then, turning to glare at the terrified Ne-Ro, Chi-Ro growled, "Esh mernumes toofta."

Ne-Ro's eyes seemed set to pop out of their sockets when he pleaded, "I had no choice, the Neph Alim forced me to do all I did. Can't you see? This war is not about us; it is an old conflict between the Neph Alim and the evil Niburians. Please, please don't kill me."

Zachary was about to shoot Ne-Ro again, but a stern look from Armon compelled him to lower his weapon.

Zachary muttered, "Come on Roman, he's a dick."

Pounding the last nail into the twisted cleric's mental coffin, Nook Tigg finally stepped out of the shadows; and, as he proudly walked towards Ne-Ro Jos, he assumed the natural, shimmering, humanoid form of his race.

"N-N-Niburian," stuttered a terrified Ne-Ro.

Consumed by panic, Ne-Ro attempted to launch a psychic attack but, in his mind's eye, he saw Nook Tigg transform into a monstrously large Elosian viper, which lunged at him menacingly. Utterly disarmed, Ne-Ro cowered in the impressive, dark throne like a Pithian field mouse.

"Yes, vile servant of the Neph Alim," said Nook Tigg, "I am Niburian. I suspect you know what I am capable of. Order the complete and unconditional surrender of your forces immediately."

"What?"

No longer able to restrain himself, Zachary fired.

Ne-Ro's eyes strained open to their limits when he realised that Zachary's aim had just barely missed his head.

"You are so lucky I'm a crap shot."

Suddenly, without breaking eye contact with Ne-Ro Jos, Nook Tigg outstretched his shimmering right hand towards Zachary. To Zachary's amazement, he lost his grip on his viridian pistol, which flew across the room and fell to the floor with a loud clatter.

Still staring intently at Ne-Ro Jos, Nook Tigg barked, "Surrender or die!"

Trembling violently, his voice no more than a pitiful whine, Ne-Ro spoke into his wrist communicator, "This is Ne-Ro Jos, c-cease all hostilities immediately."

Then, he slumped into the high back of the luxurious throne with a heavy sigh.

Staring blankly into space, Ne-Ro thought: *Why-oh-why? Why did I leave my suicide pills in my bedchamber?*

Returning Najura to its scabbard, Armon calmly walked past Nook Tigg, stood before the throne and with the deepest contempt, glared at Ne-Ro seated on it.

Then in a low, guttural voice, filled with the deepest malice, Armon said, "Now get your bony arse off of my father's throne, you pathetic piece of shit."

Ne-Ro instantly stood upright with a shudder, like a puppet whose strings had been suddenly tugged. Dressed in crimson finery, he stood before the Prince, a miserable, quivering mess. Grasping his painful shoulder wound, his left eye twitching violently, he tried to speak but only managed a breathless, pathetic, high-pitched squeak.

Armon raised his left hand and swiftly propelled Ne-Ro backward with a powerful burst of kinetic energy. Ne-Ro tumbled to the floor, a screaming, humiliated wreck; and came to an undignified rest at the feet of Chi-Ro Jin.

Chi-Ro grabbed Ne-Ro, violently pulled him upright by the scruff of his neck; and staring deeply into his sickly eyes, hissed menacingly, "Death whispers your name to me, Aspiring Emperor Ne-Ro."

It was all too much for the cowardly Ne-Ro Jos, who promptly fainted.

Chapter 81

Weapons drawn, two squads of grim Talisian shadow warriors stormed the Drac-El's citadel. Stepping forward, their commanding officer bowed low before Armon.

Then, standing at attention and saluting, the soldier said to Chi-Ro Jin, "Lieutenant Onno Fahr reporting, General Chi-Ro. Your orders, Sir?"

Holding Ne-Ro Jos upright, Chi-Ro replied, "Take this war criminal into your custody. Ensure he is restrained, and a psychic inhibitor applied. No harm must come to him before he is put to trial."

Two warriors immediately took the unconscious Ne-Ro Jos away.

Zachary said to Armon, "So, we did it. Against the odds, we put an end to this senseless war."

Armon's light-brown eyes seemed aflame when he said, "I see you've developed some new skills, Zachary."

"Yes, it seems thanks to my alien abductors I have abilities similar to yours. According to Ne-Ro Jos, they're called the Neph Alim; but you probably know more about them than I do."

"The name literally means cloud scholars, the cloud in this case being a very, very distant nebula."

Armon projected privately to Zachary, *"The Neph Alim are responsible for the Niburian genocide and the Psychic Wars. They are utterly evil and represent the greatest possible threat to the planet Earth and to humanity."*

"Well, I'm sure you're right, but I was able to use their evil genius against them. I silenced Ne-Ro's monks. I took the Drac-El. Yes, I have to admit, it's been a great adventure but now that this stupid war is over, I'd like to go home, to Earth."

"You can't, Zachary, not yet."

"Roman, don't you understand? I never thought I'd ever hear myself say this, but I miss my mother. I miss driving my Alfa through deserted country lanes. I miss women with low IQ's, cigarettes, football, pub lunches, soul music, movies, popcorn and ice cream. But of all the things I miss, Roman, I miss my bloody mind most of all!"

"I know about your father, Zach."

"Well, there we are. I guess we aren't friends anymore; all the more reason, for me to go on my merry way. You would never forgive me for my father's crimes."

"No Zachary, you're wrong."

"Am I? I guess your men are going to re-activate the lapys nerian containment field for my own good."

"Zachary, elidium was designed specifically for me. Can't you see? It's adversely affecting your mind. The superhuman effects are only temporary. But before the effects wear off, we need to be sure you don't harm yourself or others."

"Bollocks! There must only be one, is that it? Isn't the universe big enough for the both of us? Am I a threat to your godlike image, oh Prince of the Cosmic Sea?"

"For God's sake man, you killed over a hundred men on this ship."

"This is war! What the hell do you expect?"

"Over one hundred men, Zachary, including twenty-seven Talisians sent to assist us. Why? In astral form, you were completely impervious to their weapons. With your abilities, you did not have to kill any of them. The Zachary I knew couldn't kill anyone. It's obvious you're not in complete control."

"Listen, you don't have to take my comment about missing my mind so literally. You know perfectly well that some of those men were actually Saurian aliens in disguise. How many people have you killed, Roman? Have you listened to yourself recently? If anyone has lost the plot, it's you. You're a schoolteacher playacting at being Prince of the Cosmic Sea! I can't be held accountable for the sins of my father, especially since I didn't even know who he was until recently. The man abandoned my mother. He abandoned me!"

"This has nothing to do with Delius Roi."

"You're a historian, Roman. You dwell in the past. Those who dwell in the past are seldom forgiving. Before I developed these abilities, I had nothing. Look at you, superhuman Prince of the Universe, happily married with a kid on the way. Why should you always have everything?"

"Perhaps you have more than your drug-induced delusion permits you to see, Zachary."

"If you take away my power, I will never forgive you. Never!"

"You were developed as a weapon to be used against us, by our mortal enemies. I have no choice."

Armon motioned to Chi-Ro Jin who immediately spoke into his comlink, "Activate the lapys nerian shield."

Once again, shimmering black and purple rays surrounded Zachary, but this time they were armed with debilitating lapys nerian energy.

Armon said to Zachary, "I'm sorry Zach, this is for your own good; maybe someday you'll understand."

With pure, unadulterated rage, Zachary screamed, "Damn you Roman! Damn your smug self-righteousness!"

The citadel trembled, it's lapys nerian walls cracked and to the awe of all present, Dr. Zachary Silverman transformed himself into an astral wraith.

With a thunderous roar, Zachary hurled his astral body against the ray shield, and the Talisian Imperial Shadow Warriors opened fire; but their shots only served to intensify Zachary's explosive anger.

Armon sidestepped as Zachary broke free of the restraining energy and lunged towards him in a blur of darkness. Having missed his target and resumed human form, Zachary landed on the polished floor in a low crouch and growled menacingly.

Armed with Brakis Tarn's lapys nerian sok-bou, Chi-Ro Jin rushed toward Zachary. But, remaining crouched like a wild predator, Zachary swiftly grabbed the weapon and using Chi-Ro's momentum, sent him flying across the room, propelled with a massive burst of kinetic energy; energy that also threw Nook Tigg and the Shadow Warriors off their feet like discarded dolls.

Only Armon barely held his ground. Equipped with the prototype weapon Brakis Tarn used to impale Armon, Zachary stood upright and assumed a Hatari Ikou ready stance, his dishevelled dark hair partially obscuring his wild blue eyes.

"You dishonour yourself, Doctor," cried a stunned Chi-Ro Jin.

"Dishonour?" came Zachary's ground-shaking response, "I've been nothing but a loyal friend to Roman. Betrayal and imprisonment is the reward I get for destroying his enemies. This is the thanks I get for ending this war and for saving his life."

"Elidium has made you paranoid, Zachary," said Armon grimly, "Don't do this."

Zachary laughed contemptuously and said, "Even if I'm paranoid, it doesn't mean you have my best interests at heart. Oh Prince of the Cosmic Soup, I am what you aliens call Kian, and I regret, I was never your subject to command."

With that, Zachary unleashed an unfocussed torrent of psychic energy, and it took all of Armon's mental strength to protect himself and the others in the room from sudden death. But despite his best efforts, he was unable to prevent the cardiac arrest of a shadow warrior whose helmet had been damaged and now had little defence against Zachary's extremely powerful psychic assault.

For a long, desperate moment, the prince and the doctor sparred mentally. The Herculean struggle seemed to drain the very light from the throne room; and larger cracks appeared in the lapys nerian walls, ceiling and floor, of the trembling citadel.

Finally, accepting that he was unable to conquer Armon using his will alone, Zachary resumed astral form. He immediately initiated a deadly whirlwind attack against Armon who back-pedalled, barely evading the lethal tips of the lapys nerian sok-bou.

Constantly moving backward but remaining focussed, Armon swiftly drew Najura and with a circular strike, slashed Zachary's right shoulder. Briefly assuming human form, howling with agony, filled with rage, fear and frustration, Zachary tried frantically to counter-attack, but Armon employed the unfamiliar Ma Isha style he had acquired from the mind of Kiya Mankuria.

For a few desperate minutes, Armon evaded Zachary's frenzied assault until finally, with a precision blow, he slashed the wraith's right forearm.

Once again Zachary assumed human form, but he continued the fight without breaking his stride, his elidium-induced hysteria making him relentless. Aiming at Armon's Adam's apple, he unleashed a killing blow, but Armon instantly shifted his weight. The deadly tip of the lapys nerian weapon glanced the left side of Armon's neck as he spun on his heel, wielding Najura in a deadly arc that ended centimetres from Zachary's exposed neck.

The Prince and the wraith stood frozen. With Najura's black blade at his throat, Zachary understood that he was completely at Armon's mercy.

He said sadly, "Go on, finish it; I'm ready to die."

Exhausted, wracked by pain and in a state of crippling shock, Zachary lost his grip on the sok-bou, which fell to the floor with a loud clatter.

His voice saturated with the acceptance of bitter defeat, Zachary said, "Kill me... the way you killed Brakis Tarn. Go on, what are you waiting for?"

Armon stepped back, sheathed Najura, and said, "You'd have me kill my loyal friend, just when he needs me the most? Focus Zachary, focus on finding yourself, don't let the drug continue to possess you."

"My father ordered the assassination of your foster parents."

"Not you."

"I just tried to kill you."

"No Zachary, that was elidium, not you. Half your mental energy was spent battling drug-induced hysteria."

"Hysteria? C'mon, let's face it, you're just lucky you had a sword and I'm crap with a staff."

A faint smile broke the gloom on Armon's dark face, but Zachary's eyes betrayed profound sorrow as he continued, "An hour ago, when I fought all those men, it was as if I was watching helplessly, as someone else did it. I couldn't stop the slaughter. You're right Roman; I can't control myself."

Armon embraced his friend and said, "I will help you."

Zachary's legs buckled, but Armon held him upright.

Nook Tigg approached with arms outstretched offering his assistance.

Armon projected to him, *"He is exhausted. I am appointing you his shamira, see to it that he is well cared for."*

"Me, Manuk? You would have me he shamira to the son of a mortal enemy?"

"He is my valued friend, that alone should be your incentive. However, if you require additional motivation then I suggest you hold to the warrior's axiom, keep your friends close and your enemies closer."

Taken aback, Nook Tigg held Armon's light-brown gaze. Then, he smiled with genuine warmth and responded telepathically, *"It fills my heart with pride and joy that you have become the prince I always imagined you to be. Your wisdom is impeccable, and I hope you will forgive me my prejudice. I will guard the life of Zachary Roi with my own, this I swear to you. May it be written."*

"May it be done."

Nook Tigg summoned two soldiers to assist the semi-conscious Zachary. He bowed low before Armon, then said, "Baraka, Prince Armon of the Cosmic Sea, may the light of the Great Spirit always shine upon you."

"Baraka, Nook Tigg, my protector, mentor and friend."

Nook Tigg smiled once again as did Armon. Chi-Ro Jin saluted the Niburian veteran of the Psychic Wars, and Nook Tigg immediately stood at attention, his smile suddenly replaced by the grim visage of a seasoned warrior.

He saluted and said, "It has been an honour, general. Until we meet again."

"May the scribes record it."

Nook Tigg left the citadel with six shadow warriors and Zachary.

Armon projected to Chi-Ro, *"The soldier with the damaged helmet. How is he?"*

"He will live, Master Armon."

"Any news of the women?"

"We are still searching. Our investigations have so far only revealed, that the starchariot's pilot initiated a blind hyperspatial jump; but rest assured, we will find them."

"A blind jump creates too many possible exits. In order to use Najura to rescue them, I would need some point of reference. You must give me more information, Chi-Ro."

"Verily. This has the highest priority."

With a heavy sigh, Armon said, "I know you're doing your best."

"Master Armon, the time has finally come for you to meet your parents."

"Yes Chi-Ro, I know."

Chapter 82

News of the Karellan surrender swiftly swept through what remained of the Talisian 1st and 9th Waves, the ranks of the Karellan defectors and the Miruvian populace, bringing wanton jubilance. However, for The Prince Armon Sakara, aboard a starchariot piloted by his loyal shamira, Chi-Ro Jin, en route to the Imperial flagship Ayntaiyou, this moment of triumph was filled with the deepest dread.

Have I sacrificed my wife and unborn child to win this war? The thought of losing them is too much for me to bear. Where is my prescience?

"Your thoughts are transparent, Master Armon. Know in your heart, that the Great Spirit forbids the sacrifice of man or beast for his sake. Only followers of the Winged Serpent believe such blasphemies. Having brought you this far, the one true God will not abandon you," projected Chi-Ro, reclined in the ship's command pod.

"I cannot sense them. I'm afraid they're lost," said Armon, his voice thick with restrained emotion.

"Fear is the opposite of faith, an assault on the spirit, which should not be entertained. Perhaps you have grown to rely too much on your wondrous gifts. Sometimes a man deludes himself with the belief that he is the sole author of his destiny. I have often made this mistake; more so in my youth, intoxicated by my complete confidence in my own abilities. But, it is said that the Great Spirit laughs at the plans and wishes of men; and the older I become, the more I see the truth of it. Do not doubt your actions. All actions are guided by divine wisdom, and it is an unfathomable intellect that has brought us to this point in time. Do not forget that there is a universal design beyond our comprehension and above all, do not lose your faith."

Armon sighed heavily and thought: *I wish I could share your unshakeable optimism, Chi-Ro.*

"Optimism alludes to inexperience Master Armon, and veterans of the Psychic Wars are anything but inexperienced. Surely you have considered that your loss of prescience is simply a test of faith."

"Having read my thoughts, you know I have."

I also have to learn to hide my thoughts more effectively.

"Verily, such a talent may prove to be most useful."

Armon smiled, for a moment no longer preoccupied by gloom.

Chi-Ro Jin guided the sleek, battle-weary starchariot onto the Ayntai-you's main hangar deck, teeming with the Emperor's Own Security. On the holographic display, Armon observed the battered starfires and stargliders of the Imperial Host, fortunate enough to have survived the Battle of Miru.

Then, Armon caught his first glimpse of the Emperor and his consort. Despite the impressive abilities he now possessed, the proud banner bearing the emblematic Arosian Ten-Shi made the butterflies in his stomach seem all the more natural.

Armon focused on his illustrious parents. His father, the Emperor, wore a shimmering black cape draping his white, full dress Supreme Marshal's uniform and gold sash of the Order of the Tordon Raptor. At his father's left side, stood Armon's mother, The Noble Lady Akana-Benu. At first glance, she appeared a vision of regal serenity in a formal blue dress with understated gold embroidered ten-shi. But Armon's intuitive gaze caught the anticipation in her eyes and sensed his mother's nervous uncertainty.

She's afraid that I don't understand her reasons, their reasons, for sending me to Earth. She's afraid I won't accept her as my mother. How could I ever deny the woman who bore me? Even now, I can feel her love.

Grimly flanking his parents, stood their Mara Kai shamiras: Grandmaster Kai-Ita Wah, briefly Chi-Ro Jin's mentor after the death of his father at the hands of his master, Brakis Tarn, and now the Emperor's personal bodyguard; and the mute Mistress of the Deadly Arts, Arya Binara.

Armon's mind wandered. He imagined peace in the galaxy. He imagined a future with his wife and children, in the company of his parents. But the sound of the vessel's ramp being lowered snapped Armon out of his reverie and once more he entertained thoughts of losing his beloved Soraya.

She is my weakness, my greatest love.

"Are you ready, Master Armon?" asked Chi-Ro, briskly climbing out of the ship's command pod.

"Yes," replied Armon without hesitation, "Let's go."

A fanfare accentuated by thunderous drums and the loud cheers of the rank and file announced The Prince Armon's much anticipated arrival. With dignity, he approached his parents. At his side, his loyal shamira, Chi-Ro remained grimly aware of the rising tension being experienced by the Emperor's Own Psion Police.

Wearing the Sword of Power in the presence of the Emperor was strictly against any interpretation of acceptable protocol and could be construed as a dangerous threat or, at the very least, a challenge. Prince Armon, well aware of the importance of this first meeting, did not take the decision to wear this most powerful key lightly.

Ten paces before the Emperor and his consort, Chi-Ro Jin came to a halt and bowed low before them, signalling the end of the welcoming fanfare. Then, as Armon stood confidently before his parents, their shamiras Kai-Ita Wah and Arya Binara raised their hands before their breasts, with their black-stained palms exposed and their fingers splayed in the traditional greeting of the Mara Kai. In the case of martial monks, this gesture also served as a silent warning that their weaponless hands were still very lethal.

Protocol demanded that Armon, a Prince of the Blood, stand upright and bow at the neck; but in another departure from tradition, he instead knelt on one knee before his parents and drew Najura, the Sword of Power, to the stunned gasps of the assemblage. Instantly, the Emperor's Own Psion Police trained their firearms on Armon.

Emperor Sakara barked angrily, "Lower your weapons at once. Is this how you greet my beloved son? Do you not recognise a gesture of submission from a most loyal Prince?"

The security forces immediately complied with their Emperor's wishes; and, continuing to kneel, Armon bowed at the neck and offered Sakara the Sword of Power.

Fully aware of the moment's historical and political significance, with his clipped Avaris accent and using the oldest, most formal Talisian, Sakara said, "Sheath thy sword, min son. In min hand, tis merely a symbol; but in thine, tis a most powerful key: weaponry to end all wars. So rise Prince Armon and may the scribes record it."

Without flourish, Armon slowly returned Najura to its scabbard and stood proudly before his father. Following acceptable procedure, he bowed at the neck.

Then, staring deeply into his father's eyes, Armon wanted to speak, but found that a large lump in his throat made this surprisingly difficult. He glanced towards his mother and discovered that tears flooded her eyes.

Suddenly dispensing with all protocol, Sakara embraced Armon who needed to employ all his mental faculties to avoid sobbing like a baby.

For a moment, he basked in the warmth of Sakara's strong embrace and only then did Armon fully realise just how much of a chasm had been created in his life when both his foster fathers had died.

I mustn't cry. I mustn't cry.

"They told me you were dying," Armon projected to Emperor Sakara.

"Concern... It warms my heart that you hold me in such esteem, even after a lifetime of separation; for now, I am both father and stranger. Know that the reports of my impending death were wild exaggerations made for the benefit

of our grim enemies. Fear not, for I am not yet in the twilight of my years, my son."

Armon's father released him, and his sobbing mother rushed to take his place.

Trembling with happiness, Akana cried, "Oh my son, my son, how my arms have ached to hold you."

I mustn't cry. I mustn't cry.

As Armon battled with overwhelming emotions, he heard Sakara announce proudly, "Rejoice, oh children of Talis, for our Prince, my beloved son Armon, has been restored to us."

The crowd roared their approval. Armon looked into Akana's saturated eyes; and though he had rehearsed this meeting several times in his mind, the only words that now came to him were, "How are you?" he hesitated, then added, "Mother?"

Akana's laughter sounded like music to his ears as she replied, "Why? I am overjoyed, my son; delightfully overjoyed."

Then, she projected privately, *"But I sense something troubles you. Am I not the mother you expected?"*

"You are exactly as I hoped, exactly as I imagined. It's just that I had wished that my wife would meet you."

"Verily, she is comely, intelligent and selfless. She sincerely seeks after your best interests and those of your heir. Today, not only have I been reunited with my most loved, most yearned son, but I have also gained a delightful daughter and grandson."

"What?"

"You must be most eager to see them."

"Soraya is here? I have a son?"

"Did you not know?"

His sudden realisation removed any remaining vestiges of restraint. Armon laughed and cried with joy.

Stunned and confused by Armon's unusual outburst, Chi-Ro projected sternly, *"Master Armon, please temper yourself, you are publicly in the presence of His Majesty the Emperor."*

"I know exactly where I am Chi-Ro, why didn't you tell me that Soraya had been found?"

"Because Chi-Ro Jin, my loyal servant, did not know," came Sakara's projected interruption, *"I forbade any news of their starchariot's recovery being transmitted on any channel. My son, our enemies have been beaten, but not destroyed. Considering their marked interest in my grandson and his mother, it is best our enemies continue to believe that they have been lost in space. But*

come now, today is a great day to live! We must rejoice and give praise to the Great Spirit for his many blessings."

In the citadel of the Imperial flagship Ayntaiyou, Prince Armon Sakara stood silently with Chi-Ro Jin at the door to the antechamber that led to the apartment occupied by his wife and newborn son.

Chi-Ro projected, *"Why do you hesitate, Master Armon? By the will of the Great Spirit, all is as it should be. The war has ended in victory; and the Princess Soraya and your heir have been restored to you, just as you have been restored to His Majesty and Her Honour."*

"Chi-Ro I want to thank you for all that you have done. You have suffered so much personal loss, and yet you retain your unshakeable faith."

"You speak of the deaths of my father, my beloved consort and my only son. Verily, a man should not cling to those who have passed, for he will likely neglect service to the living. What profit to anyone is there in prolonged mourning? It will not restore my loved ones to me. By the grace of the Great Spirit, one day I shall go to them; but they shall never return to me."

"Chi-Ro, the Great Spirit that you describe as the one true God, does he have a name?"

Chi-Ro smiled warmly and said, "Verily his names are many, and having merged my mind with yours, I know that one of those names is etched indelibly on your heart. It has been a great honour serving you, Master Armon. Shall we proceed?"

Armon simply nodded, *"Yes."*

Chi-Ro spoke into his comlink, "This is General Chi-Ro Jin in the esteemed company of His Highness The Prince Armon."

A moment later, the door to the chamber slid back; and Kiya Mankuria and Lady Capella Hezion emerged. In unison, they bowed low before Armon.

"I'm glad to see you both. Thank you for protecting my wife and my son," said Armon softly.

With a blush of embarrassment on her cheeks, Kiya said, "Forgive me, Your Highness, it was my rash behaviour that..."

"Saved the starchariot from certain destruction. I absorbed the reports; and your thoughts are transparent Kiya."

"Thank you Your Highness."

Turning to Capella, Armon said, "I know you blame yourself for Ishma's death and though her suicide could never be your fault it is right to mourn her passing, but only for a while. Don't allow personal feelings of guilt to hinder your service to the living. Our enemies are defeated, not destroyed; and we need you Capella. Burying your head in the sand does not make you invisible it only leads to suffocation. Your self-imposed exile to the Mara Kai cloister on Merklax will not return Ishma to us."

Averting her eyes, Capella said, "You would trust me in your service?"

"Without hesitation."

Capella briefly searched Armon's light-brown eyes; and finding reassuring sincerity in them, she said, "Then, I humbly offer my service to you, Your Highness."

"Lady Capella Hezion, I wish for you to be shamira to my son."

"But only a man can be your heir's shamira."

"I am aware of the tradition."

Capella bowed and said, "You do me a great honour, for which I am most grateful."

"So why aren't you smiling?"

Suddenly a heartfelt smile traced itself across Capella's full lips as she replied, "Your will is my command, Prince Armon."

"Good, now go have some fun, the both of you, that's an order."

"Yes Sir," said Kiya and Capella in unison.

The sharp Imperial Guards at the citadel's imposing doors saluted crisply as the women made their exit.

Armon said to Chi-Ro, "You too, old man."

"Old man? Do I appear old to you? I understand that the humans of Earth seldom live as many years; nevertheless I am only middle aged by Talisian standards."

"It's just an expression Chi-Ro."

"Verily, a most inaccurate one."

"Fun, Chi-Ro. That's an order."

"As you wish; but I will need to acquire another Sythenian wax wood flute."

"Wow, I can tell you're really gonna party."

"Verily."

Chi-Ro bowed reverently and left Armon smiling, standing in the doorway.

Armon entered the antechamber and a man with an oval face, marked by the rigours of many years of scholarly pursuits, bowed low before him.

"Your Highness, I am Arkon Samel, physician."

Not any physician, the Emperor's personal physician - best of the best.

"How are they, doctor?"

"As anticipated, surgery had no complications. The Princess Soraya is resting comfortably in her regeneration pod. Consistent with his preterm birth, the Prince's lungs are not yet fully developed; and he will require artificial ventilation for two days during the growth acceleration process. This of course, is routine, no cause for alarm. Modern science has all but eradicated preterm-related infant mortality."

"Thank you, Doctor Arkon."

The physician bowed low and said, "I shall be at your disposal should you require me."

Following protocol, Doctor Arkon walked backwards ten paces before turning to make a prompt exit.

The weight of joyous anticipation descended on Armon as he entered the apartment and approached Soraya's regeneration pod. Her eyes remained closed, and the sound of her reassuringly rhythmic breathing warmly punctuated the room's cold silence. Armon turned his attention to the small, raised pod containing his sleeping son and tears of joy began to stream from his eyes.

"Tristan was eager tuh see de world," whispered Soraya softly.

Armon suddenly remembered his disturbing dream-encounter with a young boy named Tristan, a boy who claimed to be his son, and his heartbeat immediately accelerated.

Tempering his anxiety, Armon leant over Soraya's pod and kissed her forehead, "Tristan? I thought we agreed to call him Moses?"

"Did we?" Soraya laughed.

"Didn't we?" asked Armon, staring at the elfin features of the premature baby and wondering if one day this child, for whom he now felt such unimaginable, unconditional love, could ever be his mortal enemy.

Impersonating her husband, Soraya said, "Soraya, we've had this conversation. I'd like to pass on my name."

"That conversation took place a very long time ago, on a world so very far away. The man who spoke those words, is..."

"The man standing before me. The man with all the strengths and weaknesses that make him the one I love," interrupted Soraya, "Please don't let your new abilities go to your head."

"I know who I am. I'm not a messiah. I'm just a man, trying to do the right thing; and my faith remains in God."

With a tender smile, Soraya said, "Yes, and I'm your wife, so don't hold it against me when, from time to time, I remind you of these pertinent facts." Soraya paused, looked at Armon long and hard, and added, "Now that you're here, there are just two things that would make this moment perfect."

"Anything, just ask."

"A jar of smooth peanut butter, and rum 'n' raisin ice cream in a cone with a flake."

For a brief moment, Armon held a bemused smile, and then they both began to laugh.

APPENDIX I

LIST OF THE MOST PRESTIGIOUS MILITARY DECORATIONS
Compiled in order of precedence

Star of Ra
(Extreme valour and gallantry in the face of the enemy)
Star of Enki
(Courage and heroism in circumstances of extreme danger)
Order of the Tordon Raptor
(Honourable and distinguished service during a time of war)
Awarded at the Emperor's pleasure.
Distinguished Service Order
(Distinguished service in combat)
Order of the Eternal Warrior
(Gallantry in the face of the enemy)
Awarded at the Emperor's pleasure.
Star of Conspicuous Valour
(Valour during active operations against the enemy)
Distinguished Service Star
(Exceptionally meritorious conduct and achievements)
Verlaine Star
(Gallantry in combat)
Sentinel of the Cosmic Sea
(Conspicuous service in the protection of the Ruling House)
Awarded at the Emperor's pleasure.
Star of Merit
(Heroic conduct and meritorious achievement)
Distinguished Aerospace Service Medal
(Valour and dedication in aerospace operations against the enemy)
Mircon Star
(Meritorious achievement or service)
Commander of the Order of the Eternal Warrior
(Gallantry in operations against the enemy)
Awarded at the Emperor's pleasure.

Commander of the Order of the Cosmic Sea
(Distinguished service to the Cosmic Sea)
Awarded at the Emperor's pleasure.
Officer of the Order of the Cosmic Sea
(Meritorious service to the Cosmic Sea)
Awarded at the Emperor's pleasure.
Star of the Legion of Blood
(Wounded or killed in operations against the enemy)

APPENDIX II

SELECTED EXCERPTS FROM
THE SECOND PSYCHIC WAR DOSSIER
Compiled by Imperial Scribe, The Lady Enya Fadah

Baron Seti Aljyk
Firstborn of Emperor Rey Enki I and his legal concubine Amisi Aljyk, Baron Seti Aljyk was not Rey Enki's legal heir under Universal Law. Though Seti Aljyk's envy of his half-brother Sakara Rey's status is often cited as one of the main causes of the Second Psychic War, there is historical evidence to suggest that the Siege of Avaris may have been perpetrated by an impostor. He established the Royal House of Seti and fathered four daughters with his legal concubine Saru Neem. They are Iza, Oni, Cassiopeia, and Tabia. He fathered no legal sons.

Grandmaster Ne-Ro Jos
606th Grandmaster of the Holy Karellan Order of the Brotherhood of Mysteries. Ne-Ro Jos is also believed to be Prefect Ultimo of the Luminata Prefectara. He has extensive knowledge of the Ancient Niburian Swords of Power and may have discovered the locations of Salya the viridian timepiece and Anikou the ruberian scythe.

Brakis Tarn
Commonly known as the Butcher of Cyclo, Brakis Tarn is the grandson of Captain Havek Izom, creator of the Piros Kreegan Guerrilla Militia, and the fifth son of General Tarn Havek. During the First Psychic War, Brakis Tarn aged twenty-three became the youngest commander in the Karellan Marines and the youngest recipient of the Star of Ra. By the end of the First Psychic War, Brakis Tarn had tallied four hundred and three registered kills in his Koroba RA-84 Raider and was awarded the Distinguished Service Order. Though he was born a Shudyar, he had been trained by his father in the Art of Kon Jou since an early age, and due to his singular commitment and natural aptitude, attained the level of master before his thirtieth birthday becoming the youngest recorded master of the art.

In the years of peace, Brakis Tarn was awarded the rank of Sentinel of the Cosmic Sea and assigned to the Imperial Court of His Majesty The Emperor Sakara Rey I. After the Siege of Avaris, Brakis Tarn operated as a Karellan spy within the Imperial Court before failing in an attempt to assassinate the Imperial family.

During the Second Psychic War, Brakis Tarn became a Karellan operative with no official rank. He led an attack on the neutral colony of Cyclo. In direct violation of the Krivas Convention, he employed nanoviral weapons thereby killing three million colonists. It is estimated that Brakis Tarn is responsible, either directly or indirectly, for over five million civilian deaths during the Second Psychic War.

Margrave Rin Mur-Rain
Firstborn of Margrave Mur-Rain Ras Fari of Taria and the Princess Nailah, daughter of Emperor Rey Enki I and the Empress Consort, The Illustrious Lady Parvana of Tye. Margrave Rin Mur-Rain carries the rank of Space Marshal and commands the undefeated 9th Wave. He was awarded the Star of Ra, Order of the Tordon Raptor, Order of the Eternal Warrior, Star of Conspicuous Valour, Verlaine Star, Sentinel of the Cosmic Sea and Star of the Legion of Blood. He is noted for his refusal to have his left eye, which he lost in the Battle of Karony, replaced with either a cloned or artificial implant. A flamboyant individual, he is known to have always addressed his troops with a fully charged Daxia AR-6-06 assault rifle slung around his shoulder.

Commander Goren Rag
The third son of renowned artist Rag Shabaka and the Lady Khepri of Sym, Goren Rag distinguished himself in the Second Psychic War's Battle of Kish and was awarded the rank of Commander of the Order of the Eternal Warrior.

Zac Aree
The only son of antiques merchant Aree Dor and his consort Marika. Zac Aree was inducted into the Order of the Tordon Raptor for his distinguished service in the Battle of Miru.

A SELECTIVE GLOSSARY OF HISTORICAL TERMS

Compiled by Imperial Scribe, The Lady Enya Fadah

A

ANU SEA: *Milky Way Galaxy.* The mythical galaxy, from which devotees of the Mysterium believe the Karellan race originated.

APERA VERITARA: *Truth Revealed.* The Revelation of Truth. The collection of sacred writings of the Sacred Talisian Order of the Mara Kai.

ASING: *Strange.* Cult of the Asing, formed by an excommunicated master monk of the Mara Kai named Koylas Morda and dedicated to the worship of the Winged Serpent. Koylas Morda claimed to have found enlightenment on the forbidden planet of Drak Benegol in the Beli-Al System, after encountering what he believed to be the Supreme Spirit, in the form of a winged serpent, whose name could not be pronounced.

ARASHI PAKSA: *Storm Force.* Way of the Storm. The traditional martial art of the Talisian armed forces characterised by speed of movement and minimal dependency on physical strength.

AROSIAN TEN-SHI: *Arosian Angel.* A rare flying insect with brightly coloured orange, black and white wings. Native of the Arosian sub-continent of Karella thought to originate on the mythical planet Ki and adopted as the official symbol of The House of Enki. See MONARCH BUTTERFLY.

ASTRAL BEING: Manifestation of the total consummation of the physical body by the inner-self or soul, according to Karellan mysticism. Wraith-like, inter-dimensional form assumed during Complete Astral Projection; character-ised by speed-of-thought movement, physical regeneration, enhanced pre-science, telepathy and telekinesis. See COMPLETE ASTRAL PROJECTION.

ASTRAL PROJECTION: The act of manifesting an astral twin, separate from the physical body, according to Karellan mysticism.

ASTRAL TWIN: A wraith-like, inter-dimensional form, separate from the physical body, according to Karellan mysticism.

AVARIS: Capital city of the planet Talis.

B

BIBLICARA MYSTERIUM: The collection of sacred writings of the Holy Karellan Order of the Brotherhood of Mysteries.

C

CHAKULA: [Ancient – Talisian / Karellan]. *Food.* Derogatory reference to humans intended as a Saurian meal.

COMPLETE ASTRAL PROJECTION: The act of transforming the physical body into an astral form, according to Karellan mysticism.

COUNCIL, HIGH: Talisian High Council. The executive Supreme Chancellor and twelve elected Lord Chancellors that comprised the governing political body of the pre-war Talisian Commonwealth.

COUNCIL, OSIRIAN: Governing political body of the Osirian Colonists, believed to be the secret protectors of the mythical planet Ki, according to an obscure Karellan legend.

COSMIC SEA: Name given to The Known Galaxy after the fall of the Talisian Commonwealth.

CUSTODIAN, IMPERIAL: Most trusted servants of the Royal Houses, charged with the protection, education and care of royal minors.

D

DANEKA: Capital city of the planet Karella.

E

ELIDIUM: Experimental drug, developed to match specific DNA, believed to enhance psychic awareness.

ENDAR: Enhanced Detection And Ranging system.

ESH MERNUMES TOOFTA: [Vulgar – Talisian]. *You will perish from stupidity, idiot.*

F

FOLLOWERS OF SETH: Setians. Legendary progeny of members of the Talisian Long Range Scientific Expedition who rejected the humanitarian philosophies of Osiris Geb, in favour of the dominion of Ki, proposed by Seti Geb. Smaller in numbers than their rivals the Osirians, the Followers of Seth are thought to employ Neph Alim technology, and are also believed to be affiliated with a clandestine and extremely powerful organisation known as the Luminata Prefectara.

FACK: [Vulgar – Talisian / Karellan]. *Copulate with.*

FTL: *Faster Than Light.*

G

GREAT SPIRIT: Sole deity in the ancient, monotheistic religion of The Sacred Order of the Mara Kai.

GREAT CLEANSING: Military codename given for the unsuccessful Talisian High Council plan to eradicate Karellan humanity through genocide. Cause of the First Psychic War.

H

HADES: *Hell.*

HATARI IKOU: *Dangerous Power.* The Way of Matchless Power is an extremely ancient martial art developed by Mara Kai fighting monks. Members of the Royal Houses and the Talisian Military Elite, with the required aptitude, are the only secular individuals instructed in the art. Instruction normally commences before an initiate's third birthday. Eighteenth-level masters not residing in Mara Kai monasteries can conduct instruction, but all final assessments are carried out by the Grandmaster of the Sacred Order, in the Wu-Zan Mara Kai Temple on Talis.

HOLY ORDER OF THE BROTHERHOOD OF MYSTERIES: The Order of Mysteries. The Mysterium. The Brotherhood. A powerful, ancient, patriarchal religion of Karellan origin that seeks salvation through astral enlightenment, gained from knowledge, meditation and the application of psychic discipline. Martial monks of the Mysterium developed the Kon Jou way of the spirit warrior. Followers of the religion believe that Karellans are the direct descendants of astral beings from a distant world called Ki. The religion is also characterised by legends of a Kian soter possessing supernatural abilities, who will deliver Karellans from Talisian domination and establish a utopian age of peace, righteousness, and prosperity.

HYPERSPATIAL JUMP: An interdimensional journey through hyperspace, which results in faster-than-light travel to a distant point in normal space.

HYSKOTH: [Standard – Osirian]. *Karellan.* A hybrid race of fierce giants engineered, by rogue Talisian scientists, from the genetic manipulation of Kian humans.

I

ILIAC: *Snow.* Prohibited bio-synthesised narcotic stimulant, associated with significant physiological tolerance, moderate physical and severe psychological dependence from frequent and regular administration. Widely used by members of the lower military ranks during the last six decades of the Psychic Wars. In extreme cases, addicted soldiers were known to have introduced minute quantities of iliac crystals into the air-filtration apparatus of their battlesuits.

J

JINZOU NINGEN: *Artificial Human.*
JINZOU NINGEN – MARK SIX: A pre-apocalyptic race of super-intelligent artificial humans, secretly developed by enslaved Jinzou Ningen on the planet Hori Kawa. The physically and mentally superior Mark Six models systematically replaced their Mark Five creators and revolted against their natural human masters. It is believed this began a series of wars between natural humans and artificial humans, known collectively as the GREAT NINGEN WARS, which brought all humanity to the brink of extinction.

K

KAIRI: [Standard – Osirian]. *Hummingbird.* Land of the Hummingbird. Trinidad. The larger of the two islands, comprising the mythical, Kian archipelagic state of The Republic of Trinidad and Tobago.
KAK: [Vulgar – Talisian / Karellan]. *Excrement.*
KI: *Earth.* A mythical planet thought to be the birthplace of the Karellan race, by devotees of the Mysterium.

KON JOU: *Spirit.* Way of the Spirit Warrior developed by martial monks of the Holy Order of the Brotherhood of Mysteries. Arguably the highest form of combat in the Cosmic Sea, requiring a minimum of fifty years to master because of its aspiration towards astral purity. According to legend, Brakis Tarn's complete mastery of Kon Jou directly led to his unique astral abilities.

KURAI: *Social Rank.* A strict pre-war system of social ranking, imposed on Karellan society by the Talisian High Council, consisting of four levels: The Brahmyars (teachers, scholars and monks), the Khatras (royalty and warriors), the Vyshars (landowners and traders), and Shudyars (peasants, service providers and artisans).

KUROTAY: *Black Hand.* See MARA KAI.

L

LAPYS FUSCIAN: *Brown Stone.* A naturally occurring brown metacrystal, commonly used as a thermo-conductor in engineering and a constituent of various metallic alloys.

LAPYS NERIAN: *Black Stone.* The hardest substance in the Cosmic Sea. Exists as an extremely rare, black, single crystal alloy, believed to have been the product of lost Niburian superscience; and as an equally rare naturally occurring crystal from classified Imperial mines. Several eminent scientists have theorised that lapys nerian could be used to harness immeasurable energy from dark matter; but admit that such an application is far beyond the science of the Cosmic Sea.

LAPYS RUBERIAN: *Red Stone.* A red crystal of immense power according to Karellan legend. Less than one talent (thirty kilograms) is known to exist.

LAPYS VIRIDIAN: *Green Stone.* A priceless substance that exists as an extremely rare, green, single crystal alloy, believed to have been the product of lost Niburian superscience, and as an equally rare naturally occurring crystal from the distant moon of Spiro Majur. At least one pistol of unknown origin and advanced design, employing a lapys viridian crystal power source was discovered during the Second Psychic War.

LUMINATA PREFECTARA: *Prefects of Enlightenment.* An extremely powerful, clandestine organisation believed to be indirectly controlled by the Neph Alim Principality.

M

MA ISHA: *Life.* Way of Life. Ancient Osirian martial art.

MAKRA-GAK: A mythical beast; which, according to Talisian legend, roams the forests of the planet Alpha Tameri.

MARA KAI: *Face of Truth.* The Sacred Order of the Mara Kai is the oldest religious order in the Cosmic Sea.

MEDOVINA: A rare and exotic, alcoholic beverage made of honey. Medovina is one of the few remaining, naturally produced alcoholic beverages in the Cosmic Sea. Because of the extremely reclusive nature of its Siouxbatai producers, and the remoteness and harsh conditions of the planet Miru, Miruvian Medovina is the most expensive beverage in the Cosmic Sea.

MIRCON: A semi-precious metallic alloy, consisting of lapys fuscian with verlaine as the main additive.

MONARCH BUTTERFLY: A mythical flying insect from the planet Ki, mentioned in the Biblicara Mysterium books of Kasgar and Mithnos.

MYSTERIUM: See HOLY ORDER OF THE BROTHERHOOD OF MYSTERIES.

N

NAJURA: *Key.* See SWORDS OF POWER.

NEPH ALIM: *Cloud Scholars.* The Neph Alim Principality. Enlightened beings of the clouds. Mysterious, mythical race believed to have genetically engineered the Seriak.

NIBURIAN: Ancients of Niburi. Beings of the Inner Light. Guardians of Humanity. An ancient race of highly advanced alien beings that mysteriously vanished during Talisian pre-history. The Niburians are thought to be the secret mentors and protectors of humanity. According to Karellan folklore, the Niburians were shape-shifters who had the power to give humans of their choice the gifts of wisdom, prescience and astral projection.

NYOKA SENTOU: *Snake Punch.* Way of the Serpent. A deceptive martial art developed by Koylas Morda and his disciples to counter the speed of Arashi Paksa and the power of Hatari Ikou. Before his death, Koylas Morda claimed to have received instruction in the form through visions given to him by a herald of the Winged Serpent named Behryt.

O

OSIRIAN: Osirian Colonists. Legendary progeny of members of the Talisian Long Range Scientific Expedition, led by Osiris Geb. According to Karellan folklore, the expedition became marooned on the mythical planet Ki, where Osiris Geb authorised forbidden genetic experiments on the indigenous humans. The Talisian/Kian hybrids produced by these experiments were the original Hyskoths, banished to the planet Karella by the Talisian Commonwealth.

P

PIROS KREEGAN: *Red Kreegan.* The Kreegans were a notorious terrorist group that developed on pre-war Karella, known for their effective use of guerrilla tactics against Talisian targets. The group was formed by Havek Izom a Vyshar peasant from the southern plains of the Mevaal valley, in a region of Karella known as Navora Karavak. Havek Izom was the grandfather of Brakis Tarn.

PLEASURE SKIN: [Colloquial – Talisian / Karellan]. Artificial human prostitute, expert in the art of lovemaking.

PSYCHIC PROJECTION: Telepathic Communication.

PSYCHIC STORM: A massive psychic attack, usually created by the combined, artificially amplified minds of several stormbringers - individuals, possessing advanced telepathic abilities. Psychic Storms have been effectively used against enemy forces to inhibit their psychic and telepathic abilities, as well as to spread propaganda and counter-intelligence, diminish morale, impair judgement and disrupt mind-controlled systems. Psychic storms have also been used to help bolster declining morale and enhance the fighting spirit in friendly forces.

PSYCHOSIS VIRUS: Computer virus causing paranoia, hallucination, delusional beliefs and disorganised thought in Jinzou Ningen and systems incorporating artificial intelligence.

R

REE-SOK-BOU: Ancient, traditional plasma-tipped three-sectional-staff weapon used by Kon Jou masters.

ROYAL HOUSES: Royal Dynasties. The seven dominant royal families of the Cosmic Sea: *Enki (Arosian Ten-Shi)* – Black & Gold. *Seti (Beast of Typhon)* –

Red, White & Black. *Ebla (Tamerian Lion)* - Red, Gold & Brown. *Wotan (Snow Wolf of Utak)* – Black, Grey & Silver. *Xaan (Eno Fire Wasp)* – Purple, Yellow & Bronze. *Kaito (Orinx Dragon)* – Green & Bronze. *Arat (Varian Silver Hawk)* – Dark Blue & Silver.

S

SERIAK: *Lizard.* Saurian. Mythical race of evil reptilian, humanoid aliens often depicted in both Talisian and Karellan folklores and ancient myth.

SERIVELEN 5-1-2: A nanoviral, pathogenic agent that specifically targets Saurian DNA, first introduced in the Battle of Miru.

SHAMASH: A distant star mentioned in the Sacred Scrolls of the Holy Order of the Brotherhood of Mysteries; believed to be the nearest star to the mythical planet Ki.

SHAMIRA: *Protector.*

SHON-GHŪL: Large, malevolent, highly intelligent serpents from the Beli-Al System, which possess hypnotic abilities - deified by members of the Asing cult and the primitive inhabitants of the planet Koraskou.

SKIN: [Colloquial – Talisian / Karellan]. See JINZOU NINGEN.

SNOW: [Colloquial – Talisian / Karellan]. See ILIAC.

SOK-BOU: Traditional, collapsible, plasma-tipped staff weapon of the Talisian military.

SOTER: *Messiah.*

STEALTHSUIT: Shield-protected Osirian environmental battlesuit, outwardly identical to Talisian Shadow Warrior battlesuits, but employing advanced Niburian technology and capable of virtual invisibility.

STL: *Slower Than Light.*

STORMBRINGER: Individual possessing advanced telepathic ability, employed in the creation of psychic storms.

SWORDS OF POWER: Three ancient Niburian swords possessing unbelievably great power, when wielded by astral beings. *Najura* the nerian key, *Salya* the viridian timepiece and *Anikou* the ruberian scythe.

T

TALISIAN COMMONWEALTH: Official name of the pre-war republic that governed the known galaxy. Led by an executive, Supreme Chancellor who was constitutionally answerable to a High Council, comprising twelve elected Lord Chancellors.

TALISIAN EMPIRE: Established by First Consul Rey Enki who crowned himself Rey Enki I, Lord of the Imperial Host, Emperor of the Cosmic Sea, after leading a combined force of Karellans and Talisians to an overwhelming victory against the superior forces of the Talisian Commonwealth in the battle of Rak No-Var.

TAN-KYU: *Inquiry.* IMPERIAL ORDER TAN-KYU. Imperial Intelligence inquiry into the possible survival of The Prince Armon Sakara believed killed in the Siege of Avaris by Seti Aljyk. Tan-Kyu was also used to refer directly to The Prince Armon before his appearance in the Fields of Aaru.

TEROSERIAK: Ferocious, dinosaur-like predators, up to two metres tall and six metres long at full maturity, armed with curved eight-centimetre-long septic teeth, and very powerful jaws. Indigenous of the planet Miru.

T'HARIAN GATE: Mouth of a mythical traversable wormhole that allows swift intergalactic travel between the Cosmic Sea and the Anu Sea - a distance believed to be beyond the range of hyperspatial jump technology, by devotees of the Mysterium.

TINKI WINKI: Call sign assigned to Zac Aree, a hero of the Second Psychic War. The name has no meaning in the languages of Talis or Karella. According to devotees of the Tinki Winkian cult, who worship Zac Aree, the name means great warrior in a language of the mythical planet Ki. But, thirteen days before his mysterious death, eminent linguist Aram Brenlint maintained that the name Tinki Winki was closely related to the archaic Talisian words tikiari wikiari literally meaning small organ.

TINKI WINKIANS: Winkis. A small but increasingly influential, monotheistic religious cult, centred on the life and philosophical teachings ascribed to Zac Aree. The enigmatic son of a wealthy but extremely reclusive Talisian merchant, Zac Aree's military call sign during the battle of Miru was Tinki Winki. Adherents of the Tinki Winkian faith, known colloquially as Winkis, believe that Zac Aree is the soter prophesied in the Biblicara Mysterium books of Kasgar, Leemar and Mithnos. Controversy still surrounds the Imperial government's decision to reject, as false, over a hundred eyewitness accounts of Zac Aree assuming astral form, aboard the starcarrier Kach, during the Battle of Miru. The Imperial government maintains that eyewitnesses were victims of an extremely potent psychic storm, generated by monks of the Mysterium. The scribes recorded that Zac Aree has consistently denied having astral abilities or soterial status.

TRANSPONDER, PERSONAL: An ENDAR transmitter-receiver activated for transmission by reception of a predetermined signal. Used extensively in the form of cranial implants by members of the Royal Houses, as a deterrent against abduction by enemy forces. Transponders establish the exact location of an individual and confirm whether that individual is alive or dead.

TRANSPONDER, VESSEL: An ENDAR transmitter-receiver on a vessel, which broadcast a signal identifying that vessel by name, design, and political allegiance.

TYE-SOK-BOU: *Two-piece rod.* Archaic martial arts weapon developed during the AGE OF DARKNESS.

U

UNITED EMPIRES OF TALIS: Also known as the UNITED EMPIRES or EMPIRES OF OLD, was the post-apocalyptic phase of the ancient Talisian civilization characterised by an autocratic form of government. It was led by a member of the original Royal Houses holding the title of Supreme Emperor of the United Empires. This period of Talisian history came to an end with the GREAT NINGEN WARS that almost destroyed all natural and artificial human life in the known universe. The apocalypse led to the AGE OF DARKNESS, which lasted approximately three thousand years.

V

VERLAINE: Rare precious metal with a brilliant, bluish-white metallic lustre that can be polished to a very high degree.

VIMANA: *Raptor.* Raptor-class warship operated by martial monks of the Cult of the Asing.

W

WAVE: *Fleet.*

WINGED SERPENT: Main deity of the Cult of the Asing, considered by Asing adherents to be the Supreme Being. In other religions and folklore, the Winged Serpent is considered a powerful entity of immense supernatural ability and the personification of evil; and is commonly associated with enemies of humanity.

WINKIS: [Colloquial – Talisian]. See TINKI WINKIANS.

About the Author

Wayne Gerard Lionel Trotman is a British writer, filmmaker, artist, photographer, composer and producer of electronic music.

Born in the Republic of Trinidad and Tobago, Trotman studied history and art at Presentation College, San Fernando, where he won the Presentation College Art Prize twice - 1979 and 1982. During the early 1980s, Trotman won several national art prizes in Trinidad and Tobago. His artwork during this period consisted largely of comic book illustrations and acrylic or oil paintings.

In August 1984, Trotman moved to England to study art and design at the Heatherley School of Fine Art in Chelsea, London. In 1985, his work was chosen for the London Youth Festival Exhibition.

Between the late 1980s and mid 1990s, Trotman produced compositions for television; as well as independent film productions. He completed his second feature film script entitled 'Ashes to Ashes' in 1994; and in 1995, his short film – 'London: Metropolis of the Future' premiered at the British Short Film Festival.

Trotman, who is trained in several martial arts disciplines, directed, co-produced, scored and edited the British independent film 'Ashes to Ashes' in 1998 - arguably the world's first digital feature film and Britain's first martial arts movie. He also played the film's lead role of Gabriel Darbeaux and used real martial arts weapons including the nunchaku or two-piece rod.

In 2006, Trotman co-produced a training DVD, which tackles the cause of anxiety and panic attacks: The Fight or Flight Response.

Between 2006 and 2009, Trotman wrote part one of his epic 'Psychic Wars' sci-fi saga: 'Veterans of the Psychic Wars'.

Lightning Source UK Ltd.
Milton Keynes UK
10 March 2011

169014UK00001B/63/P